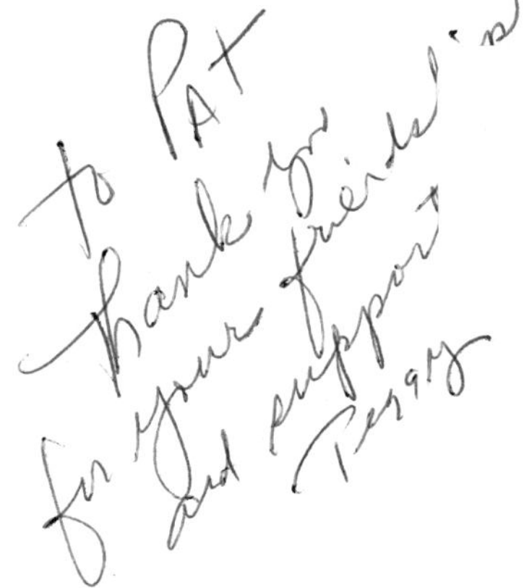

The Lies That He Told

Marguerite Mooers

Books by Marguerite Mooers

Take My Hand (2014)

The Shelter of Darkness (2015)

A Casualty of Hope (2016)

The Girl in the Woods (2017)

The Life That He Lived (2018)

The Lies That He Told (2019)

Praise for Marguerite Mooers' novels

*"**Take My Hand** is a very good read--a well constructed mystery with an appealing detective reconstructing the scene and possible suspects of a 'cold case' child abduction. Mooers constructs the pieces of her puzzle nicely with an ultimately persuasive but not immediately obvious solution." Amazon review.*

*"The tension of '**Take My Hand**' really builds from the moment the detectives start investigating and does not let up---no easy feat for a procedural like this. Lorna is a great secondary character, with a well-developed emotional arc and compelling relationships that make her involvement in the case even more tense and dangerous." Writers Digest 23rd Self-Published Book Awards*

For **The Shelter of Darkness** *"The character of Al brought great tension to the story and when they found his body, well, it only got better until ending on a wonderful, heartwarming note. A wonderful book. I thoroughly enjoyed it." Goodreads Review*

*"Marguerite Mooers is a talented writer whose characters will send your heart pounding with fear and your palms sweating with suspense. Overall I loved this novel. **A Casualty of Hope** is everything readers will want and ask for in a fictional piece. Brilliantly well written and told for readers worldwide to enjoy. I highly recommend this book to all" Universal Creativity Inc14 review*

"A deftly crafted and riveting novel. **A Casualty of Hope** *is a compelling page-turner from beginning to end. Very highly recommended." Midwest Book Review*

For **The Girl in the Woods**. *"I loved this book right from the beginning, it grabs at you, making you keep turning the pages. I would highly recommend this book!" Amazon review*

For **The Girl in the Woods** *"Being a northern New Yorker myself, I plucked this murder mystery off my to-read pile, figuring to spend a few spare minutes looking into it, only to find that I couldn't* *put it down, ending up reading it in one setting, something I almost never do. Ms. Mooers, an Adirondack '46'r' is a marvelous storyteller, a crafter of mystery plotting whose intricacies will keep you guessing right up to the jaw-dropping ending. If you're ever camping in the Adirondacks, Ms. Mooers is just the yarn-spinner you'll want around the midnight campfire." Amazon review*

For **The Life That He Lived**: " (I) *Would like to say I loved this book and would refer it to everyone that reads. The book only took me 3 days to read. I couldn't put down." Amazon review.*

 This is a work of fiction. Names, characters, places and incidents are either the product of the author's imagination or are used fictitiously, and any resemblance to actual persons, living or dead, business establishments, events or locals is entirely coincidental.

ISBN: 978-09904448-5-5

Library of Congress Control Number:

LCCN Imprint Name: Potsdam, New York

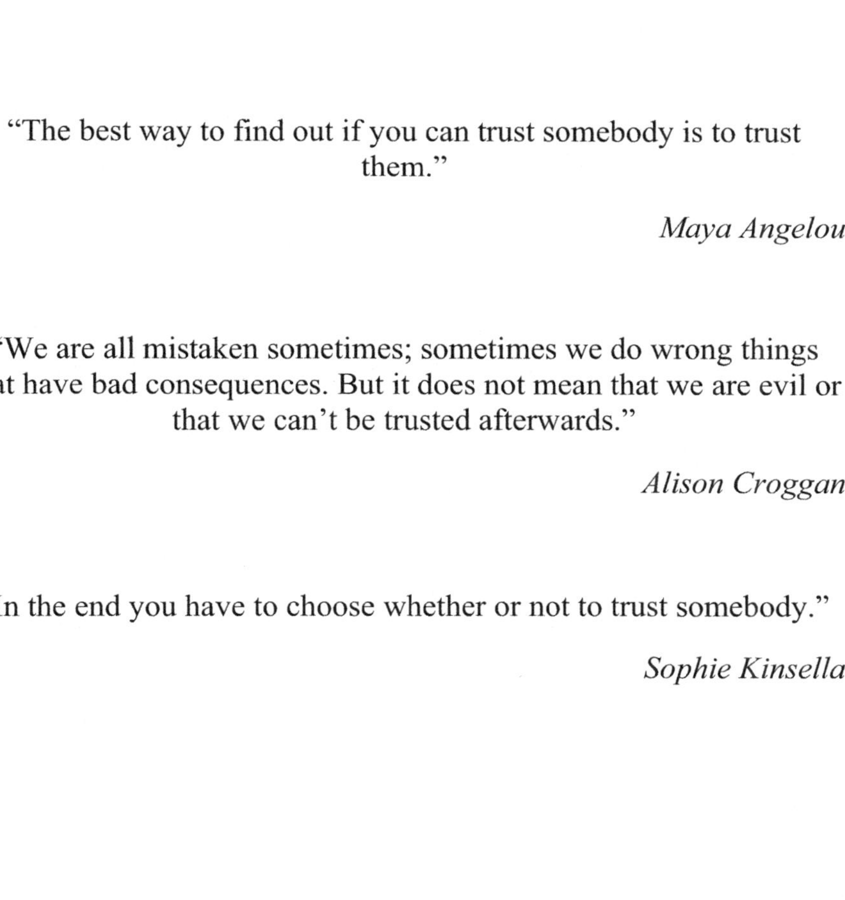

"The best way to find out if you can trust somebody is to trust them."

Maya Angelou

"We are all mistaken sometimes; sometimes we do wrong things that have bad consequences. But it does not mean that we are evil or that we can't be trusted afterwards."

Alison Croggan

"In the end you have to choose whether or not to trust somebody."

Sophie Kinsella

Table of Contents

Chapter One

April 1, 2016

Kiki

I shouldn't fight with my mom, I thought. I always regretted what I said, even though Mom had the ability to find my weak spot and drill in, leaving me frustrated, jumped up and unable to sleep. Water had always been my solace, and so I tried to calm my breathing as I walked downstairs from my mother's bedroom where the fight was, through the kitchen, pausing at the door to flip off the yard lights, and moving out into the darkened night toward the pool.

I crossed the grass to the pool, grabbing a towel from the basket as I went. At the lip of the pool, I took off my shoes, socks, jeans, shirt, panties and bra and slipped quietly into the warm water. Lifting my feet to the inside edge, I pushed off, gliding across the water with my face to the sky, imagining myself a dot in the universe, traveling ten thousand miles an hour through space. I was a grain of sand, moving faster than a jetliner, and though this was happening, there was not a ripple on the water. Above me Jupiter,

Orion and Mercury were way points in the vast universe, lighting my way in the darkness as I hurtled past, snug on my round blue rocket ship.

"Hello."

I froze. A man was standing in the yard watching me.

"How the hell did you get in?" I asked trying to keep the fear from my voice. "That's a locked gate."

"Your mother gave me the code last week," he said.

"Why did my mother give you the code?"

"I delivered some art here. I guess she forgot to change it."

"Stay right where you are and turn around while I get dressed," I said.

He turned and I slid out of the pool wrapping the towel around myself. Quickly I dried, and put on my clothes. Then I sprinted toward the house and flipped on the yard lights, turning the yard into an airport landing strip.

"I just need to use the phone," he said, starting toward me. I held up my hand.

"No closer." I couldn't see a weapon, but he could still be carrying. This was Texas after all.

"I'm sorry to bother you," he said. In the bright light, he seemed young and vulnerable, but then Ted Bundy had a baby face, didn't he?

"My van ran out of gas and I need to call a garage." He stepped gingerly forward and handed me a business card.

I studied the card which read, "O'Donnell Antiques and Collectibles, Trevor O'Donnell prop."

"You're Trevor O'Donnell?"

"Nate Marks. I work for Trevor."

"What are you doing out here at this time of night?" This was a gated community and every single house had a secure fence around it.

"I was delivering art to the Applegates on Dolphin Lane."

I knew the Applegates, had been to parties at their place. He was some kind of financial analyst and she ....what did it matter?

"You're delivering art at..." I looked at my watch. "ten-thirty?"

"Lots of these people work late and want to be home when the art is delivered so they can inspect it personally. " There was a note of annoyance in his voice. "I'm not a UPS man who is going to leave a package on the porch."

I could have bolted into the house and locked the door, but my mother was sleeping upstairs and Mr. ran-out-of-gas might knock on the door loud enough to wake her. She would come down, the police would be called and even though it was my mother who hadn't changed the code on the gate, I would be blamed for standing in the yard chatting with a stranger. Considering all of this, running inside seemed like too much of a hassle.

In fact, the man standing in front of me appeared to be reasonably clean and might even have been telling the truth. Additionally, my cell phone was upstairs in the bedroom, which meant that if I tried to get it, there would be a repeat of scenario A.

"OK," I said. "Let's see your vehicle."

He sighed and led me back down the path, through the gate that hadn't had the code changed, to a delivery van emblazoned with the words "O'Donnell Antiques and Collectibles" parked at the curb. "Show me what's wrong," I said.

He got into the van and turned the key. The vehicle struggled and stalled. He pointed to the gas gauge which registered empty.

"And you don't have a cell phone to call a garage?"

He held up his phone. "Battery's dead."

"Out of gas, out of juice. You are in a pickle, aren't you?"

"Look lady," he said. "Obviously you don't want to help me." He got out of the van and locked it. "I guess I will have to walk up and down the street hoping someone else's gate is miraculously open."

"Every gate will be locked," I said. "People are more careful than I am." I thought about my choices. I was taking a chance, but if I didn't help this man, he might end up spending the rest of the night looking for a house that would take him in. He could go back to the gatehouse and make the call there, but that was half a mile away.

"Follow me," I said, leading him back up the driveway through the gate and to the garage. I pushed the opener and the door slid up revealing two cars.

"Why don't you just let me call a garage," he said.

"It will take a half hour at least for a garage to get here, and in that time I will have to entertain you."

"I've already been entertained," he said with a small smile.

"You peeked."

He shrugged. "You can't flash a beautiful body in front of a man and ask him not to look," he said. "It isn’t possible."

I hadn't missed the part where he called my body beautiful, but I was trying to concentrate on the job at hand. "The gardener keeps a can of gasoline for the lawn mower somewhere around here," I said, pushing past the cars to a separate shed in the back. "He won't be happy when he finds the gas missing, but that can't be helped." I found the can, handed it to him and then we walked back to the road where he poured gas into the tank. When he put the key in the ignition, it jumped to life.

"I'm very grateful," he said. "You saved my life…Miss?"

"Caroline Coleman," I said. "Friends call me Kiki."

"Thank you, Kiki," he said and was off.

I walked back up the drive, changing the code at the gate before shutting it firmly and then went into the house.

In my bedroom, I Googled O'Donnell Antiques and Collectibles. A web page popped up with a picture of two shops, one in San Antonio and one in Corpus Christi. Nate Marks must have driven from Corpus to Port Aransas, a twenty-five mile trip to deliver a painting. It made sense. As he said, people who paid big money for art, wanted personal service.

I scanned the site. O'Donnell Antiques and Collectibles seemed to be a legitimate business with lots of laudatory comments from former customers. I scooted around the site, looking for pictures of staff. There was one shot of a middle-aged man wearing tweeds standing in front of the shop, but there was no picture of Nate Marks. He had said he was only an employee, but it seemed strange. Wouldn't a business owner who had a trusted employee delivering art to a wealthy, and maybe suspicious buyer, want the buyer to see who the delivery person was? Nate's absence on the site could be harmless and maybe I was just being paranoid. Still I wondered.

I Googled Nate Marks but there was nothing. No Facebook, Twitter, Instagram, Pinterest, or LinkedIn accounts and no personal information listing him as an employee of O'Donnell Antiques and Collectibles. What human in this day and age didn't have a digital footprint?

Trevor O'Donnell, on the other hand, had plenty of footprints. He had started selling antiques in San Antonio in the 1990's and had expanded to a second shop in Corpus in 2002.

The web site didn't say where Trevor O'Donnell had got the money to start his business, but I knew that this sort of thing wasn't always publicized. My own parents, Larry and Demeter Coleman had started their business, Demi's Velvet Skin Cream, in the kitchen of their Corpus Christi apartment. My father, an industrial chemist, had perfected the formula, and with time, and generous donations from their friends, my parents had managed to bring the company to life. That had been more than twenty years ago. In the intervening years, my father had died and my mother remarried, but the company was still going strong.

I suddenly realized that it was close to twelve and I needed some sleep. Sleep was one of my mother's remedies for good skin, that and no sunlight.

Chapter Two

Kiki

The next day was Saturday, a day when I didn't have to go into the office, though my mother and stepfather did. My stepfather Grainger Starland seemed to be the only one able to keep my mother's temper in check. I wasn't particularly fond of Grainger, but he kept my mother happy.

I put on a shirt, jeans, sneakers, and a wide- brimmed hat and with a cup of coffee in my hand, I headed for the beach, using the boardwalk over the dunes. The sun was almost up and I could smell the salty sea air as soon as I got close. I closed my eyes and breathed it in letting it fill my pores. When I opened my eyes, I could see someone walking toward me leading a small dog, and as the man got closer I realized it was Nate.

"Hello again."

Up close he was taller then I'd remembered, with dark hair and a finely sculptured nose. He was wearing khaki shorts, sandals, a blue shirt, and a billed hat with the Dallas Cowboy's logo on it. He also had just the faintest shadow of a beard which gave him the look of a GQ model. At the end of a leash was a Yorkshire Terrier, an adorable bundle of energetic fluff who rushed over and put its front paws on my leg.

"Nate," I said. "I thought you lived in Corpus?"

"Sometimes I come to the island on weekends."

"You have a place here?"

He pointed to a high rise about a mile down the beach. "Surfside Towers," he said. "But I'm just renting until I find a place of my own."

Surfside Towers rented for at least two thousand dollars a month in the winter and more in the summer when you'd pay by the day. How did a delivery person, whose name wasn't even on the web site make that kind of money?

"It's just temporary," he said.

"I've seen the units," she said. "They're nice."

The dog was dancing around, eager to get going.

"This is Mitzi," Nate said. "Her owner is a neighbor who is unable to walk her." He moved closer. "How about something at Coffee Waves?"

In bright daylight he seemed less threatening than he'd been last night, and we were only going for coffee, nothing more. Besides on Saturday, Coffee Waves was my favorite place to sit with a cuppa. "Why not," I said.

We left the beach and started up Avenue G toward Alister. Nate was walking fast.

"Wait," I said.

He turned. "I'm so sorry." he said. "Most of the time I walk alone."

"How come you're not on the Facebook page for the business?"

"You've been cyber stalking me."

"No, I'm just curious." We crossed Avenue G and threaded our way past What-A-Burger.

"I don't have any pets or kids to post pictures of. In fact, I'm too busy to put up anything."

I looked down at Mitzi who was panting with the heat and struggling to keep up. "Come here, sweetie," I said, picking her up. I looked at Nate. "You said she's not your dog?"

"Nope, just a loaner. Think I should put her picture up on Facebook?"

"If I had a dog like her, I would put up her picture." I kissed her on the head and she settled into my arms.

"You'd be great with a dog. Look how she takes to you."

I shook my head. "My mother wouldn't stand for it," I said.

He leaned closer. "Screw your mother. Get a dog if you want one."

I laughed. His words wouldn't help me get a dog, but I liked his confidence in me.

We got to Coffee Waves where, because Mitzi was a dog, we had to sit outside. We settled into two Adirondack chairs sipping our coffee while we watched the traffic on route 361.

"Where'd you go to school, Nate?" I asked.

"A & M, but I left before I graduated, so you won't find me on their website."

"Why did you leave?"

"My mother had cancer, I left school to take care of her."

"I'm sorry," I said, reaching over to take his hand, "I really am." He smiled and I breathed in his regard. I was sitting here, having coffee with a good-looking man who was showing some interest, something I hadn't had much of lately.

"What about your dad?"

"He split when I was four. I haven't really tried to find him. Who needs that shit?"

"Parents can really screw you up."

The loaner-dog Mitzi was panting with the heat. "I need to get her some water," I said. When I returned with a cup of water, I put it on the ground where Mitzi gratefully lapped it up. Nate had finished his coffee and was rising. "I've got to go," he said, taking the dog into his arms.

"Carry her," I said. "It's too hot for a little dog to walk."

"Yes, Mama," he said. I leaned toward Mitzi and patted her one more time. Would my mother really throw a fit if I got a dog?

"The Applegates are having a party next weekend," Nate said suddenly. "Want to come?"

I hesitated. I had just met Nate, and I didn't know him well. On the other hand, I had nothing on for next weekend except a movie I'd seen before and a bowl of popcorn.

"Sure," I said. "What time?"

"Eight o'clock," he said. "I'll pick you up at your place." And then he was gone.

As I was walking back to the house via the beach, I tried to get my head around the puzzle that was Nate Marks. Lots of young, well-educated, good-looking men took temporary jobs until they could find their way to more lucrative sources of income. So far, his presentation of himself as a delivery boy for an antique shop seemed legit, but where did he get the money to rent an expensive condo? Were his commissions on sales that high? He remained a puzzle.

I got to the boardwalk leading to Salt Spray Estates, our beach home. I walked through the open gate that had a warning sign that this was private property and only owners could enter. Did it make sense to have a gatehouse in the front, if anyone could come in from the beach? At least my house, and most of the houses around me had steel fences around them.

When I reached home, I retrieved my car from the garage and drove to the gatehouse. I wanted to trust Nate, I really did.

George was on duty. He looked at me strangely when I parked my car on the estate side of the gatehouse and knocked on the window.

"George," I asked. "Can you tell me if someone driving a white van with the words 'O'Donnell Antiques and Collectibles' on the side, came through last night?"

"Just a sec," George said retreating inside the gatehouse. "A man named Nate Marks, came in at 8:00 p.m., left at eleven."

Eight o'clock. How long did it take to deliver a piece of art? My mind whirred and I saw Nate and Marcia Applegate admiring the art work together, then Nate and Marcia admiring each other, then going upstairs to continue their admiration up close and personal, until they realized that Mr. Applegate would be arriving home any minute and Nate had better get going. Would that take us up to the moment when he ran out of gas at ten thirty? It might.

When I got home it was almost noon. My mother was standing in the kitchen drinking a glass of wine, while Grainger cooked chicken at the stove. That was their routine. Mom drank, Grainger cooked. Mom worked at her computer while Grainger straightened up in the living room, or washed the dishes. Mom ranted; Grainger listened.

"You're home," I said. "I thought you'd be at the office all day."

"I needed a break," my mother said. "Where have you been?"

"Walking on the beach. At Coffee Waves."

"Walking on the beach without a hat? Kiki what have I told you."

"You can always redo your hair but you can never re-do your skin," I said waving my hat in the air.

"Good girl," she said. I wasn't a girl; I was a grown woman. I pulled a glass from the cupboard and filled it with water. My stepfather was already headed toward the den to watch TV and in a few minutes, my mother would go upstairs to the computer.

"I've been invited to the Applegates on Saturday," I said.

"Marcia's throwing a party? I wonder why she didn't invite me?"

"Nate Marks invited me."

"I know who he is. How did you meet him?"

I hated lying. "He was at Coffee Waves this morning with Marcia Applegate and she introduced us and then he invited me, well they both invited me to the party. How do you know him?"

"I bought a pen and ink drawing of a bird from the store, something from the seventeenth century Dutch school. It's charming. He waited on me at the store and then delivered it here."

"What did you think of the store, Mom?"

"Everything seemed to be of good quality, though I always think that word 'collectibles' describes the cheap stuff that's sold at yard sales."

"Apparently it's owned by a man named Trevor O'Donnell, was he there?"

"Nope. I did all my business with Nate. He seems like a nice person. You could do worse, Kiki."

"I'm fine, Mom. You don't need to fixed me up."

"Caroline," my mother said, facing me. "You are twenty- eight years old and haven't had a date in six months. You need to do something with yourself." She came toward me and lifted my hair which I wore long. "Get this cut, and put some color in it. Mousy brown is not sexy. And get rid of these glasses. You look like a librarian." Her eyes traveled to the shorts and T-shirt I wore. "Cover your arms when you go out. You're going to get skin damage, and when you reach fifty you'll have wrinkles you can do nothing about."

"I'm fine," I said, pushing past her. I didn't need her to tell me what I already knew, that no one was going to take an interest in me because a) I worked all the time and b) I hated going to bars or finding dates on the internet.

In my bedroom, I went to the closet and looked at my clothing choices for the party. I needed something that would make people notice. Was I interested enough in Nate Marks to make a play for him? Tomorrow we would be in the Corpus apartment where I had a larger selection of dresses and more shopping opportunities. I stood in front of the mirror, took off my glasses, and pushed my hair up on top of my head as I considered my mother's suggestion. A little color wouldn't hurt, and unless I were asked to read the fine print on something, I could get along for one evening without my glasses.

Chapter Three

Kiki

It was a busy week, where I scarcely had time to breathe. Even so, on the rare times when I had a minute to myself I would think about Nate Marks. I even spent the better part of a lunch hour walking over to Shoreline Drive where O'Donnell's Antiques and Collectibles was tucked in between a shoe repair place and a jewelry shop. The shop was closed. I peered in the window. where a couple of painted chests were displayed, but I couldn't see much else.

I had come on a whim without a clear plan, but now that the shop was closed, I felt a deep disappointment. What was he doing this afternoon? Delivering art somewhere? Shopping at an estate sale? Walking someone's dog? Maybe he had a girlfriend here in the city and was even now enjoying a noontime quickie.

Take it easy, Kiki, I told myself. You have no relationship with this man. And yet, it was hard to convince myself that he was only a stranger.

When I got back to the office there was a package on my desk in florist's paper. It turned out to be a blue glass jar, holding a dozen tiny violets. The whole thing was so charming, so simple that I felt my heart melt. How could this stranger know that I hated the large, showy bouquets that mother put on every horizontal surface, matching the oversized portraits of herself. I liked small. I liked simple. I longed to call him, to hear his voice and thank him, but I did not have his number and when I tried the shop, it went to voice mail.

My secretary Gwen came into the office. "You got flowers," she said. "New boyfriend?"

"Nothing like that," I said. "He's just a guy I met on the island."

"That's really sweet," she said. She moved closer to the flowers. "I like the matching blues he chose for the jar and the flowers. If you put the vase near the window, the color glows." I did and it did.

On Wednesday, I had lunch with my two best friends, Wendy Gilman and Tania LaCrosse. Wendy was a lawyer, who'd recently become engaged to Rick, another lawyer. Rick and Wendy were moving to California where Rick was going to work for a big movie company and Wendy would be the trailing spouse. I'd had a long talk with her, when she'd first flashed the big square-cut diamond in my face.

"You said he comes from a big family and wants lots of kids. Are you really going to be happy, staying home with kids?"

"It will be nice to take a break, Kiki. You know what a big law office is like. They expect you to be there eight a.m. to midnight every day."

"Kids are more than eight to midnight."

We were standing in the ladies' room, putting on makeup. "You're just jealous because you don't have anyone," she said.

"I want the best for you, Wendy," I said, ignoring hurt. "You can leave a job and find something less stressful, but you can't leave kids."

"I love him, Kiki. We're going to make a go of it."

I hoped that was true.

When we got back to the table, Tania said. "You've done something to your hair, Kiki. Let's see." She moved in closer. "I like the cut and the highlights. What's going on? Someone new?"

"I met him on the beach last weekend," I said. "He works at an antiques place on Shoreline. O'Donnell Antiques and Collectibles."

"Name?"

"Nate Marks."

"Cute?"

I shrugged. Tania looked at Wendy. "We have time. Should we check him out?"

"Don't do that, please," I begged. "He's just a friend."

"A friend you cut your hair for?"

"And put in highlights?"

I felt myself coloring. "He asked me to a party on Saturday."

"Obviously you need something spectacular to wear."

"Let's see what you've got," Tania said. "Greg's going to be home with his wife tonight, so I've got time to come to your apartment. "

Tania was dating her boss who was ten years older and had a wife and two kids. I'd had 'the talk' with her too. Why should he marry her, when he could shack up with her in their little love nest whenever it was convenient? Tania argued that all Greg needed was time, but I knew his type. Tania was throwing her best dating years away on someone who would be married to the same woman for the rest of his life, while she sat alone waiting.

I looked at my watch. "Want to help me shop for a dress?"

Wendy took one last bite of her salad and chugged her water. "I'm ready," she said.

In the end we chose a deep blue crepe dress with rhinestones spangled around the plunging neckline and blue strappy heels to match. Combine that with sparkly earrings that hung below my hair line and I'd be a smash.

"You need to ditch those glasses, Kiki," Wendy said. "They spoil your look."

I put my glasses in my purse and then reached out, pretending to 'read' Wendy's face with my hands. "Blind is the way to go?"

"You have pretty eyes. You should get contacts to enhance those blues."

I couldn't get contacts before Saturday, so nearly blind would have to do. In a pinch I could stuff my glasses into my purse, just in case I needed to sign a contract or read a good book.

On Saturday, bathed, perfumed and outfitted in the new blue dress, I presented myself downstairs. I'd brought a silver lame shawl just in case it got cold. Grainger was in the living room watching a Dallas Cowboy's Game. He turned.

"Well you look smashing. When is Nate making his appearance?

"Soon."

"I should meet him. Make sure he's going to take good care of you."

I could see Nate through the glass door coming up the walkway. Grainger went to the door and threw it open, and Nate stopped. He looked at me and then took my hand. "Nice to meet you, sir," he said, and then we were down the steps and into the car.

"That was pretty rude, you know," I said as we sped away. "He only wanted to meet you. He's my stepfather but he likes to protect me."

Nate mumbled "Sorry Kiki. I didn't think we had time to get into a long discussion about whether my intentions were honorable and all that stuff."

"He wouldn't have asked you that. He knows what happens with people our age."

"Which is?"

"Well, we're just going on a date. You haven't promised me anything." This conversation was getting a little weird. "Thank you for the flowers by the way. They were very pretty."

"You are welcome. Did I get it right?"

"It was perfect. How did you know I love simple bouquets, not big showy ones."

"I pay attention," he said.

We got to the house which was lit up as if it were Christmas. The Applegate's house sits on a rise, and the second floor where the living room is, has floor to ceiling windows that when you are inside, give a breathtaking view of the Gulf with the lights of Corpus Christi in the distance. The sun was setting, leaving a vermillion and tangerine stain across the sky. A barge moved slowly across the darkening water and a group of white pelicans flew by in formation, one behind the other.

"Nate," Marcia Applegate gushed when she saw us. She was wearing a low cut white evening gown that showed off her tan, and her bleached hair had a white gardenia tucked above an ear. My mother would have whispered "too much sun," but for some women there is no point in being near the ocean unless you can have a tan.

She moved toward us in a thick fog of perfume and kissed Nate on the cheek. He smiled, but I couldn't tell if he was pleased or embarrassed. Marcia turned to me, "Caroline, how nice to see you. Let me show you where the drinks are."

She led us to the drinks table, her arm through Nate's. A lot of people, especially women seemed to know him, whereas I, who had lived on this island for the last ten years, was a stranger.

I stood before the bartender trying to decide. White wine, Merlot, or maybe a Margarita. “What are you going to have?” I asked Nate.

“A coke,” he said.

“We have lots of nice wines,” the bartender said. He held up a bottle. Nate shook his head.

“You don’t drink?” I asked when we were walking away.

“Nope,” he said. I filed that away in the data bank I was creating about a man I was just getting to know. We walked out onto the wraparound deck where we stood gazing at the sunset.

"You have a lot of customers here, in the Estates?"

He nodded. "Word of mouth is the best advertising. I give them a good deal." *And more*? I didn't want to ask. Standing here looking out at the sun just grazing the top of the ocean made it too lovely an evening to quarrel.

"You look beautiful tonight, Miss Coleman," Nate said, moving closer.

"Thank you. You clean up pretty well yourself." We were silent for a moment. "How's Mitzi?"

"She's fine. The poor thing never gets to go anywhere because her owner is a little old lady who can hardly walk. She lives about two doors down from me, so whenever I have free time, I give her an outing."

"I've been actually thinking of getting my own place," I said. "I am the Publicity Director of the company; actually I am the Publicity Department but my mother doesn't pay me diddly so my job is a sort of involuntary servitude. What she does do is house and feed me, but sometimes, well---I think it's time to grow up and move out."

He was listening carefully. "You should do it," he said.

"Have you always lived alone?" I asked. Was I fishing? Waiting for confessions about former girlfriends or current wives?

"Not always, but for the last few years."

"Nathaniel." Our conversation was pierced by Nate's name being screeched by a middle aged woman, squeezed into a bright pink dress, wearing too much makeup and too many large clunky jewels. "I heard you were here, sweetie. Why are you hiding from me?"

He blushed and turned to me. "Geneva Sanders," he said, "this is Caroline Coleman."

"I'm a neighbor of Marcia's," Geneva said, dismissing me. She turned to Nate. "Honey, I absolutely adore that little chest you sold me. I have had sooo many compliments on it. Now let me introduce you to some of my friends. Good for business you know." With that she whisked him off to the land of lonely ladies dying to buy art.

I finished my 'rita and wandered back into the house. Marcia was standing by the bar downing a glass of champagne.

"He's yummy, isn't he?" she said when I grew closer. "If I were twenty years younger, I could show that boy a thing or two."

I pushed away the image and changed the subject. "Nate said that you bought a painting from him last Friday? Would you be willing to show it to me?"

"Of course. It's up here on the landing and it's just exquisite. He, or the owner, has very good taste."

We walked up the stairs to a hallway and she pointed to a painting measuring about six by ten inches. I fished my glasses from my purse and perused the scene which was windmills in front of a sky of puffy clouds and a foreground of lime-green grass. "Sixteenth century," Marcia said.

"It's beautiful."

"And a steal for something that old. You should visit his shop."

"I tried to, last week, but it was closed."

"Well, I expect he's very busy, He scours the papers every day for estate sales. He's got a wonderful eye for things, don't you agree?"

I knew nothing about Nate's eye. I knew hardly anything about Nate. What I could see was that many people in this little community thought he was God's gift to the art world.

"We'd better get downstairs, I can't just leave my guests to fend for themselves," Before she could start down, I said. "Do you know that Nate turned up at my house last Friday? He said his van had run out of gas. It was ten-thirty at night."

"Ten-thirty? He left here at eight-thirty."

I looked at Marcia. This was a small community, and if Nate was doing something other than delivering art, everyone would soon know it.

I walked down the stairs, seeing Nate in a corner, surrounded by ladies who were leaning toward him as he talked. Should I rescue him? In spite of my living in this community I knew almost no-one, and was starting to think that being here was a mistake. Then Nate caught my eye, waved and rose, giving his apologies to the women.

"Let's get out of here," he said as soon as we were within whispering distance.

"My thoughts exactly." I grabbed my shawl and before anyone could haul us back. We booked it out the door and down the walkway to Nate's car.

"Where to?" he asked.

"The beach?"

"I don't think that dress is made for the beach," he said. "Let's go somewhere for a drink."

We got in the car, but before he put his key in the ignition, I put my hand on his arm. "What were you doing between eight o'clock and ten-thirty last Friday night?"

"What are you, C.I.A.?"

"I talked to Marcia Applebaum and she said you left there at eight-thirty. If you were at my place at ten-thirty, that's two hours unaccounted for."

He said nothing.

"It doesn't matter what you did in the meantime. I'm just curious."

"What do you mean, it doesn't matter? If it didn't matter, you wouldn't be asking me these questions." He was looking at me sharply. "You don't trust me, do you?"

"I want to. I really do." I was messing this up badly, possibly pushing away a man who'd been my first chance at romance in a dog's age.

"Why is that? Why don't you trust me?"

"OK, I'll tell you. Five years ago, I had a relationship with a guy named Matt who was a website developer. He was great and I fell for him hard. Our company was going through reorganization and thinking about merging with a cosmetics company. It turned out that Matt was a spy for the other company. He never learned anything from me, but I was devastated when I found out what he was doing.

The worst part was that he had a wife and two children in Dallas. So, I am sorry I seem suspicious. I want to get to know you, but I don't want to be hurt."

"After your mother bought the picture, she said she wanted me to deliver it. I stopped by the office with it, but then she said she wanted it sent to your house in Port A. When I was leaving her office, I saw you and thought it would be fun to meet."

"Why didn't you just stop by and say hello."

"I should have. It would have been easier. I decided that on a night when I was delivering art, that I would conveniently run out of gas in front of your place and ask for your help. I had gone into the gated community with not much gas, but it took longer than I thought to drive around burning up the stuff. It would have been embarrassing to say I'd run low and then have the van start with no problem."

"How did you know you could get through the gate?'

"I didn't. Luckily for me, your mother forgot to change the code."

"Do you come into Salt Spray Estates often?"

"Often enough."

"I have to tell you, I find this a little weird," I said. "No one in my entire life has ever gone to this kind of trouble to meet me."

He moved toward me and took my face in his hands and kissed me. "I did, and I'd do it again," he said.

We drove to a small empty restaurant and ordered two glasses of wine. When the wine was delivered, he looked at me. "Where did you go to school?"

"Believe it or not I was going to be a teacher," I said. "But my mother had other ideas. She'd decided that I would join the company when I finished, so I took business classes which I hated. Sometimes

I feel totally trapped in that place." Suddenly I felt wiped out. I yawned.

"I should get you home," Nate said, looking for our waiter. There was no one else in the place and our waiter was standing at the bar, yakking with the bartender, totally ignoring us.

Nate got up and went to the bar, and it was then that I noticed his wallet on the table. He was standing at the bar talking so I eased the wallet open and looked inside. There was his driver's license with his picture and name Nathaniel J. Marks, with an address in New York City.

He rushed back to the table and scooped up the wallet. "I thought I'd lost it," he said.

Later as we were driving home, I asked, "You lived in New York city?"

"I'll have to remember to lock up my things away when I'm around you."

"Sorry, I shouldn't pry. It's just that when you like someone, you're curious about them. Your car has Texas plates."

"Yup."

"Don't you worry about getting stopped with Texas plates and a New York city license?"

"It hasn't happened yet. I'm a careful driver."

We had reached my house. Nate stopped the car, got out, came over to my side of the car, opened the door and helped me out.

And then I was in his arms. We kissed. I savored the smell of him, the taste of him, the feel of him in my arms. "There all asleep," I said. "Want to come in?"

He shook his head. "I'm bushed," he said.

I kissed him again. I was falling for this guy, secrets or no secrets. I watched him detach himself and turn toward the car. He got in, started the engine and drove away.

Chapter Four

The next day was Sunday. I woke late thinking about Nate. I looked in my closet, choosing a blue shirt that brought out the color of my eyes, tan shorts and sparkly sandals and went downstairs.

While I'd been sleeping, my mother and step-father had gone back to Corpus because there was a note on the table. I grabbed a cup of juice, pushed a wide brimmed hat on my head and headed out to the beach. If I knew what apartment Nate was renting in Surfside Towers I would have gone and knocked on his door. I tried to imagine the scene. Nate in his pajamas, his hair mussed from sleep, or Nate in a robe with nothing underneath, or Nate with someone else in his bed. No, this would not be a good idea. Even though I was definitely attracted to the man, he had to make the first move.

I headed down the beach looking for a man with a small white dog. There were plenty of single men with dogs and couples with dogs. Some of those dogs were on leashes, with owners carrying plastic bags ready to pick up the pet's excrement. But there were other dogs, running loose in the surf, or pooping on the beach, while their owners looked on unwilling to pick it up. I resisted the urge to go up to them and say that this was a public beach and that I didn't want to walk in their dog's shit. What had happened to me that I'd become such a Grinch?

What had happened to me was Nate. He wasn't here, and he hadn't called, and I didn't know if I'd just been a casual date or if there was something more going on. I headed over to Coffee Waves but Nate wasn't there either. I glanced at my phone. No message. Damn.

While I was still sitting, finishing my coffee an elderly woman, dressed impeccably came into the place with a little dog. I probably wouldn't have noticed her, except that the owner said, very loudly, that dogs weren't allowed in the place. It was then that I noticed that dog was Mitzi.

The woman ordered coffee and went outside. I followed.

"Excuse me," I said. "My name is Kiki Coleman. I live here on the island. I've met your dog before. Mitzi isn't it?"

The woman nodded. Just at that moment her coffee was delivered. I sat down beside her.

"You must know a man named Nate Marks. He's a neighbor of yours in Surfside Towers."

"He's not a neighbor," the woman said.

"He's not?"

"Sometimes he comes and stays in Trevor's apartment. He's a nice enough young man. I've even bought art from him."

"But you let him walk your dog."

"He promised on his solemn oath that he would bring her back. I had an eye doctor visit, which meant I couldn't go out in the sun and he offered to take her. I didn't think he was going to abuse her." She leaned in conversationally. "He said dogs are a chick magnet."

I nodded. I looked down at Mitzi, who came over and nosed my bare toes. Had Nate set this whole thing up? Planning to meet me again and needing a ‘chick magnet’ to bring us together?

“Thank you,” I said. I headed back to the house which was empty because my mother and Grainger were at the office. I fished a pint of ice cream from the freezer and wandered into the living room where I flipped on the TV. There was nothing.

Pulling out my phone I dialed Tania.

"Kiki," she said in a half-whisper. "What 'cha doing?"

"I'm home alone," I said. "Is Greg there?"

"Yup. He's asleep though. We had the most awful fight last night and then we made love. How can I leave him, Kik? I love him."

I put her on speaker phone, so I could pour myself more coffee. This drama would go on forever. Tania should leave the shmuck, but she never would as long as they could make glorious love, and she could think he would marry her.

"Got to go, Kik He's getting up. I'll call you later."

I dialed Wendy who was walking along the waterfront in Corpus. "We're talking about our wedding in California," she said. "Did you know that for only five hundred dollars a day you can get married in the house where Joan Crawford lived? We could have the bridesmaids in thirties dresses, maybe even a speakeasy serving drinks." She went on and on, but I was only half listening. I was imagining myself living alone except for a cat, and the week after I died they would find my desiccated body in the house with a half-starved animal. It was not a cheerful prospect.

When Wendy had wound down, I hung up and flipped on the TV, where a Robin Williams retrospective was showing. Nate wasn't around, and I'd probably never have the life Tania or Wendy had, but I could have Robin and he would make me laugh.

On Monday I went into my mother's office with the layout for the new ads. Our target audience was now forty to fifty year olds and we'd found some beautiful women, who though not actually in their fifties, had convincingly grey hair and pale skin.

"It's good," my mother said, giving the layout barely a glance.

"What's wrong. Isn't this what you want? Older women? We can use some younger models if you think..."

"No, no. It's fine." She picked up a pen from the desk and twirled it in her fingers. My mother is rail thin mostly because she lives on carrots and air and has the nervous energy of a rabbit.

"Do you think I look old, Kiki?"

"Old? No, you're beautiful," I lied. My mother is fifty-five with flawless skin, thanks to religiously avoiding the sun. She dyes her hair, has her nails done every week, and from a distance she could be thirty. But age is relentless and in spite of all her work, the years are catching up with her.

"Grainger says I'm looking old," she said picking at the skin around her nails. "I saw him yesterday with that new secretary in accounting. They were head to head laughing at something. I almost fired her on the spot. And the other night at the Weiss' party he spent the whole evening in the corner with Eleanor's daughter. The girl is younger than you are."

She looked at me. "I could get some work done, but what if something goes wrong? My face is *the* image for Dodi's Skin Cream. If that gets messed up, people won't buy our product anymore."

"It's probably just a phase, Mom. Lots of men go through this. How old is Grainger? Sixty? He'll come to his senses and realize what a treasure you are."

"I can't lose him, Kiki. He makes me feel like I'm young and desirable and I don't want to give that up. Do you know what it's really like to be alone? Well, of course you do. But I don't want to be that woman."

My mother moved closer. "You know Kiki, if you'd wear something other than those awful dark colors, you might be able to get a man. Show a little cleavage. You have lovely breasts. Hike those skirts up. You have pretty legs." She pulled my glasses off my face and ruffled her hand through my hair. "If you'd take more pride in your appearance, you could do very well for yourself."

"I like how I look," I said. And at least I didn't have a husband who was flirting with younger women.

My mother had returned to her chair behind the desk. "I've given Grainger twenty five percent of my shares of the company," she said. "Don't look at me like that. He's my husband. He makes me very happy and I want to keep him."

"But twenty-five percent of your shares gives him majority control. What if something happens to you? He could take Dodi's Skin Cream in directions that would be disastrous. He has the power to gut the company completely."

"He's not going to do that. I am still in charge. He's the CFO, but I still oversee everything he does and everything anyone else does. There's nothing to worry about." She was toying with the papers on her desk, moving things around without looking at them. “Kiki, I want to tell you that Grainger and I are going on a little trip next month. Just the two of us. Sort of a second honeymoon. You'll be in charge until we get back."

"Where will you be?"

"There's a conference in Paris. I love Paris; it's so romantic. The lights along the Seine, the Champs Elysee, the Eiffel Tower. I haven't been there in years, but it will be perfect for us, don't you think?"

I didn't know what to say. Should I lie and say that giving Grainger control of the company and taking him to Paris was a good idea, or should I tell her the truth, that in my limited experience once a man started looking elsewhere, nothing would make him look back. I simply nodded numbly.

"Good," my mother said. "It's all settled then." She raised her arms in the athlete's salute. "Paris here we come."

I had turned toward the door when my mother said, "Kiki, think about what I said. You're not getting any younger and soon all the eligible men will be gone. Put on some bright colors, show a little skin. Remember we're selling cosmetics and you're an advertisement for the company."

I held on to my tears long enough to get to a stall in the bathroom where I let them fall. I didn't need my mother to tell me I was over the hill. Why wasn't I strong enough to find another job, to move out of the house, to make my own life as an independent woman? I had let myself become trapped in the net of a spider.

"Kiki?"

I dried my eyes and opened the door, to see Gwen, my secretary, standing there. Gwen was a fifty something matron who was not only my right hand woman but my substitute mom.

"Your mother?"

I nodded, then went to the basin and washed my face, hoping to hide the blotchiness. "I don't know why that woman ever had me," I said. "If a woman carries a baby in her body for nine months you'd think she'd have just the smallest amount of affection for that child. I've seen her be nicer to a stray dog than she is to me."

Gwen put her arm around my shoulder and I leaned into her. "She told me if I didn't start wearing more revealing clothing I'd never meet a man. I don't want to meet a man that way. I'm not ashamed of my body but I'd like to attract someone who is interested in me as a person, not just how I look in a low-cut dress."

Gwen nodded. "You are a talented, beautiful woman," she said.

"You're not just saying that because you work for me."

"Well bonus time *is* coming up soon, but I mean it. You are going to meet someone who realizes what an amazing person you are."

"How much do you want for that bonus?"

"That one was free."

"You are the best, Gwen," I said giving her a hug. "Do you know that my mother is giving my step-father twenty-five percent of her shares in the company which will make him the majority shareholder. She did it because she thinks he's flirting with other women."

"He *is* flirting with other women."

"You know this for sure?"

"Yup. The secretaries are complaining about it. He runs his hands over their rear ends when he's supposedly helping them read a document. He puts a hand on their shoulder and it accidentally ends up on their breast. He asks about their underwear. I've heard stories."

"Why didn't you say something?"

"I thought you'd side with him. He is your stepfather."

"I would never condone what he's doing. Does my mother know this?"

"No one dares tell her. Last week he caught Angie Wright in the elevator and tried to kiss her. She came to me in tears, threatening to quit."

"I am so sorry. I'm going to talk to Angie myself."

"You're not going to fire her, are you? She's a single mom with two small children."

"Of course not. I only want to talk with her. Will you promise me something, Gwen?"

"This might cost you at Christmas."

"Tell me what you hear about Grainger. I don't care what it is. If he's the majority shareholder and he's doing this kind of thing, it could be bad for the company."

"There have been some talk about irregularities with the books."

"What kind of irregularities?"

"Missing money."

"Can we get in and look at the accounts?"

"I don't think so. He's got the password and he protects it very well."

If Grainger and my mother were going to Paris next month and if I were acting CEO of the company, I would find a way to get to those books and see what the problem was. In the mean time I would have a little chat with my stepfather.

Chapter Five

I headed down the hall to Grainger's office. I could see him through the glass door sitting at his computer. I was glad he was alone. I didn't want anyone else overhearing our conversation. I knocked quickly and then stepped in.

"I'm busy, Kiki," he said. "Can it wait?"

"Sorry, it can't," I said. I pulled up a chair, so I was facing him across the desk.

"What can I do for you?" he asked pushing the cover of his computer down.

"I've heard a complaint," I said, trying to gauge what his reaction would be. "About you."

"Me? Really?" I didn't believe him, but I moved on. "Gwen told me that you tried to kiss Angie Wright in the elevator the other day. Angie went to Gwen in tears."

"Honestly, Kiki, do you believe that stuff? Angie is a drama queen who's just looking for anything to get her noticed."

"I believe Angie was telling the truth, Grainger. Did you try to kiss her in the elevator?"

He pushed up the cover of his computer and started typing. My blood was boiling.

"Grainger," I said. "This is a small company. We sell cosmetics to women. You can't be hitting on the women who work here."

"I was just fooling around," he said. "Having a little fun."

I moved around the desk and slammed the cover of his computer down. "You will not 'have a little fun' with any of the women who work for this company."

He stood up so we were face to face. He was taller than I was and towered over me. "You forget who you're talking to, Kiki," he said. "I am now the majority shareholder, and can control what happens here. If Angie doesn't like how we do business, she can find a job elsewhere."

"You would fire her because she complained about sexual harassment?"

"If you have a problem with me, talk to your mother."

I stormed out of his office and marched to my mother's corner office. As soon as I got close, I could hear the two of them, my mother and Angie Wright. Angie was sobbing and my mother was standing behind her desk, her face stony.

"What's going on?" I asked pushing open the door.

"She's firing me, because I complained about Grainger," Angie said between tears. " I can't lose this job. How will I feed my kids? I told her that I was sorry, and I'll never complain again. Please talk to her."

"This isn't Angie's fault, Mother," I said. "It's Grainger. He was the one who made the advances, not Angie. You are punishing her because she tried to complain? I can't believe it."

My mother wasn't budging. I put my arm around Angie. "We're going to solve this," I said softly.

"You will get two weeks' severance pay," my mother was saying.

"If she leaves, I'm leaving too," I said.

My mother looked at me. "You're not serious, Kiki. What about the new ad campaign?"

"The hell with the campaign. I have worked my butt off for this company, and if this is how you treat your female employees, I don't want to be part of this place anymore."

"Kiki," my mother said, and then was silent.

I turned to Angie. "Come with me, we're going to Human Resources"

"That was pretty brave of you," Angie said as we walked toward the elevator.

"I'm giving you two more weeks of salary in addition to your severance pay," I said.

"Your mother won't like it."

"She's not going to know. This is coming from my own savings."

She started to cry then. We stopped and I held her while she sobbed in my arms. When she was quiet, we started walking again. Reaching the elevator, I pushed the button. "I'm going to sort all of this out," I said. "My mother just gave Grainger enough of her shares to make him the majority stockholder. Now he thinks he can do anything he wants. I'm going to try and stop him from hitting on the female employees, even if I have to bring this whole thing to the police."

"You would do that?"

"I'd rather not, but I would do it." We had reached Human Resources, and Jane Arnold, perhaps alerted by my mother had the paperwork spread out in front of her.

"Can she keep her health insurance?" I asked Jane. "She has small children at home."

Jane looked at the paperwork and then at Angie. "We usually don't do that," she said.

"I'm authorizing it," I said. I took out my checkbook, wrote a check to Angie and handed it to her. "Take a vacation with your kids and try not to worry."

She wiped at her eyes. "I know, it is easy for me to say," I said. "I don't have little ones depending on me." I gave her a sideways hug. "I will try to get them to change their minds. You've been a good worker, Angie. I'm sorry to lose you."

Leaving Angie at Human Resources, I went back upstairs to my own office and got my coat. It was eleven thirty, but I was so angry about the whole affair with Grainger that I needed a way to cool off. Grabbing my purse, I headed toward the front of the office. The receptionist's desk was still empty. If I hired Angie for that spot, would it keep her away from Grainger? I just needed to clear my brain.

I found myself walking toward Shoreline Drive where O'Donnell Antiques and Collectibles were. I wasn't worried about the time away from the office. Hadn't I just effectively fired myself from the job? When I reached the corner where the store was, the door was standing open, which meant that Nate was in.

I stepped into the store, which smelled faintly of a chemical. Paint? Varnish? I couldn't tell. Then my nose picked up beeswax and just the faintest hint of damp.

"Hello," It was Nate, coming into the store from the back, carrying a small painted chest. "What's up?" He was wearing a white shirt, chino pants, a tie with colorful chairs imprinted on it, and his hair was slicked back.

"I've come to invite you to lunch," I said. "Can you get away?"

He looked at his watch. "It's eleven-thirty, but I guess I can close up for a bit."

"Good," I said. "I need to talk to someone."

He grabbed his coat, turned off the lights, changed the 'open' sign to 'closed', locked the door and we were off.

"Where to?" I asked. "You know this neighborhood better than I do."

"There's a What-A-Burger just down the street or the Union Street Oyster House."

"I am treating," I said. "So I vote for the Oyster House."

We walked arm in arm to the Oyster House, and on the way I told him about my encounter with Grainger.

"He honestly didn't see anything wrong with what he was doing," I said. "It makes me want to scream."

"So what did you do?"

"I told my mother if she fired Angie, I would quit."

"Did you?"

"What?"

"Did you quit?"

"I didn't do it exactly. I just left." I looked at him. "You think I'm a coward, Nate?"

"Nobody is going to take you seriously, Kiki, if you make idle threats."

I felt a sinking in the pit of my stomach. If I were serious about making changes in the company, he was right. I needed to stand by my principles.

"Be careful of him, he can be dangerous," Nate said.

"Grainger? He's not going to physically hurt anyone. He's just a man with a lot of power that no one can say no to."

Nate stopped and took my arm so we were facing each other. "It's more than that, Kiki. I know men like him. He'll go right on ahead and do what he's doing, and now that you're not there to protect the women, he'll be even more blatant."

"So you think I should stay?"

"Did your threatening to quit help Angie?"

"No. I'm just the lowly Publicity Director. I gave her two weeks' extra salary out of my own savings, but I couldn't make my mother keep her."

He turned and we started walking. "I would go back to the job," he said.

"Go back? Didn't you just tell me not to make idle threats?"

"I did, but if you are out of the office, you can't help protect the girls that are still there. Do you have anything you can use against your step-father? Something you can threaten him with the next time he tries one of his tricks?"

"I think he's stealing from the company," I said. "My secretary said there are irregularities with the books."

"Do you know this for sure?"

"I haven't been able to get into his computer?"

"Want some help with that?"

I looked at him. "A partner in crime? I would love it."

"How about tonight."

Chapter Six

I told my mother and step-father that I wouldn't be coming home for supper. I hadn't made up my mind about whether I was going to quit, and I was still angry at Grainger over what he was doing, and at my mother for firing Angie. Nate pleaded that he needed to go back to the store, so I took my car over to the mall and shopped for a while, and then because it was only two o'clock in the afternoon, I went to the cinema and watched a strange, silly movie.

I got out of the movie at six-thirty and called Nate. Grainger sometimes worked late, but tonight was his poker night, which meant he would leave the office at five sharp, grab a bite at McDonald's and then drive to the house where he always played. The problem was my mother, who would sometimes stay late and work, but when we got to the office building, I saw no sign of her car.

"This doesn't mean she might not come in later," I said as we got out of my car. "But on Monday night, she watches 'Game of Thrones" on TV. I went in the front door of the building, said hello to George the night-watchman. It was possible that George would tell Grainger that he'd seen me here tonight, and Grainger would figure out what we'd been doing, but I could always lie and say I'd had some extra work to pick up. It wasn't perfect, but it would have to do.

We took the elevator to the floor where the business was. I opened the front door with my key and flipped on the lights. Then we walked down the hall to Grainger's office. Thank goodness, none of the offices had locked doors, so we went in and I turned on the lights.

"This is nice," Nate said, looking at the cherry paneling that housed the file drawers and bookcases. A lighted bar stood against one wall and below that, a refrigerator with a cherry panel front that housed Grainger's drinks.

"Would you like something to drink?" I asked.

Nate shook his head. He looked at the refrigerator. "Does he keep his chocolates in there?"

"How did you know about his chocolates? " I asked, opening the door to reveal a couple of ice trays, a few cokes and a dark box labelled Michelangelo's Finest.

"I saw the chocolates on the kitchen counter when I delivered the drawing to your Port A house. Your mother said they were Grainger's."

Grainger's chocolates were never on the kitchen counter unless he was at the counter eating them. Grainger's chocolates, at twenty-five dollars for a tiny box were for him alone, and were kept in the refrigerator. The one time I tried to grab a taste, I was severely chastised.

"We'd better do this, before someone comes in," I said, sitting at the desk and opening the computer. Nate pulled up a chair beside me. A password request flashed on the screen.

I tried Demeter (my mother's real name) Grainger, GStar (my step-father's last name was Starland), but none of those seemed to work. We spent another fifteen minutes thinking about possible names.

"How about Michelangelo?" Nate asked.

"The name of the chocolates?"

We tried Michelchoc. No luck. Mich123Fin45. No luck. MichelChoc123. Bingo

I typed it in and the screen snapped to life showing a dozen or so files on the screen. There was a noise that seemed to be coming from the entrance. "Did you hear something?" I asked.

"It sounded like the elevator."

"Damn." I glanced at the screen where I could see the word, 'finances' on a file. I stuck the zip drive into the computer and began downloading the contents onto the drive. I could hear footsteps in the hallway.

When the zip drive had finished downloading, I grabbed it and turned off the computer. Nate punched off the lights. We ducked down beside the desk and I watched as my mother moved past us in the hallway.

"I thought she was home watching *Game of Thrones*," Nate said.

"Shhh." My heart was beating and my palms were wet. Nate and I were crouched inches from each other. I could smell his aftershave, feel his thigh pressed against mine. He put his arm around me, then I turned my face toward his. His lips were inches from my own. I had the strongest urge to move forward and kiss him. I moved toward him.

"We should get out of here," he said, pulling back. "This isn't the best place for a romantic rendezvous."

I got up slowly, my body cramping. "Let me go first," I said, walking to the door and poking my head out into the corridor. I could see light in my mother's office. Slowly I eased myself out, pulling Nate by the hand. "I'll meet you downstairs," I said and pushed him toward the entrance. Then I walked toward my mother's office.

"Kiki," my mother said as I went in. She was sitting at her computer typing, but she looked up. "Are you still angry at me?"

"I am," I said. "I came up to my office, thinking I would clean out my desk. I don't like what Grainger is doing, Mom."

"I talked to him. I'm not going to bring Angie back to work, but he's agreed to behave himself around the staff. I hope you've decided to stay."

"I will, but I'm keeping an eye on him, and you need to do that too."

She nodded. "Is Nate with you? Security said the two of you came in half an hour ago."

"How did he know it was Nate?"

"I assumed it was Nate. You have someone else you are seeing?"

"No. It was Nate. I got him to come along for moral support and to carry boxes and then when I got here, I changed my mind."

She stood up and walked toward me. "Honey," she said. "Grainger is just going through some male menopause thing. We're going to be in Paris on May 14, and then I will have a serious talk with him. We'll straighten this all out."

I doubted that that would happen. In the meantime, I would be watching him all the time.

Chapter Seven

When I got downstairs to the street Nate was standing on the corner. "What next?" he asked.

"I want to see what's on that zip drive."

"If he's got porn on his computer you could talk to the cops." Nate said.

I shook my head. As much as I wanted to see Grainger busted, I didn't want a scandal to hurt the company. We needed to keep our dirty linen private.

I looked around me. We weren't far from the apartment I shared with Grainger and my mother, but one of them would be there, or be coming home soon. I wondered if Nate had a place here in Corpus, or if he just lived in Port A. I waited for him to offer something. He said nothing.

“There’s a What-A-Burger down the street,” he said finally. “You have your computer with you. We could look at the zip drive there.”

At What-A-Burger we pushed the zip drive into my computer but when we tried to open the file the word ‘password’ flashed on the screen.

"Damn," I said. "He's encrypted the file."

"He's smart." Nate said.

"You approve of what he's doing? Hitting on girls at the office and maybe stealing from the company?"

"Of course not, but if I wanted to keep something secret, especially in a busy office where anyone can walk in and use the computer, I would encrypt the files."

I leaned back in the chair, looking at the screen. Nate was right. It would be silly to think that Grainger would just let anyone see his files. I wonder if my mother even knew what he was doing.

"Are there people here in Corpus who might be able to open this file?"

Nate shrugged. "I don't know. Are you thinking of going to the police with this?"

"Police? No. I'm not even sure anything is going on. My secretary said there were irregularities with the accounting and Grainger is the CFO. It could be that she is just trying to get something on him, because she's angry."

"Let's call this a day," Nate said. “We're not experts in encryption. Well, maybe you are, but I'm not."

"Thanks for your help," I said. He nodded. "If I can figure out his encryption, I'll let you know."

He got up from the chair and walked slowly to the door. God, he was a good-looking man.

“Wait, Nate,” I said. It was now evening and we had driven to the office in my car. He was striding away from me. I ran to catch up with him. “Do you need a ride back to your store?”

“Nope,” he said. “I’m good.”

He turned and began walking away. I wondered why he hadn’t asked me to come to his place. It was possible that he didn’t live here in Corpus, and I knew the apartment in Port A wasn’t his. Was he homeless? He didn’t seem to be. Was it possible he was living with a woman? That might be true. Maybe he liked men rather than girls, but I wasn’t getting that vibe from him either. I watched as he faded into the distance, wondering what I could do, if anything, to bring him back.

When I got back to the apartment, Grainger and my mother were already in bed. I slipped the zip drive into my computer but the encryption held just as securely at home as it had held in the restaurant. I needed more professional help.

The next morning a call came in at work. It was Nate. "Have you ever been kayaking in the gulf?" he asked.

"Kayaking? You mean paddling one of those narrow little boats in the ocean? The ones that look like they'd tip over if a wave even breathed on you?"

"I just started doing it myself," Nate said. "Two weeks ago there were a bunch of kayakers on the beach and they loaned me a boat and took me out. You'll have a good time, I promise."

"How many times have you been kayaking, Nate?"

"Twice. Actually the first time was just going out into the waves and letting myself surf back in, but the second time we kayaked for an hour. The Gulf is beautiful and except for the occasional power boater, it's very quiet. You might even see dolphins."

I'd only ever seen dolphins as they were leaping through the bow waves of ships going through the channel. What was a little sun-damage against the chance to see dolphins up close?

"What do you say?"

If I agreed to this, it was possible that my boat could be overturned by the wake of a power boater and I was paddling with a man who'd only done it twice. How risky was that? Pretty risky. "When do you want to do this?"

"How about Saturday?" He read off a list of things I needed: a good hat, sun screen, water bottle, flip flops and snacks. "We'll just go out for an hour and then have lunch. Meet me at the fishing launch called Dirty John's in Aransas Pass."

When I pulled into the fishing launch, Nate was already there and beside him were two kayaks, one red and one yellow. I pushed my sun hat down on my head.

"Does your hat have a chin strap?"

"Why?"

"The wind can come up." I looked out at the water which had a few wavelets rippling the water. Without even registering my nervousness he had me sit in the kayak to adjust the foot pegs, then I got out, put on the spray skirt, and life jacket, tucked my water bottle in under the bungees and we pulled the boat forward so it sat in the water. When I got in, he adjusted the spray skirt, handed me the paddle and then lifted the back of the boat and pushed it forward so I was floating. I watched as he got into his own boat.

When we were side by side, he said. "Draw the paddle along your side with the blade at right angles to the boat so you are scooping the water. Are you ready?"

I nodded and we paddled under the bridge and along the shoreline, past fishermen in power boats rushing to their fishing spots. It was a bright, clear day, the sun sparkling on the water. A heron flew by and landed on a farther shore near a group of sanderlings. We left the open waterway and moved into a small channel where Herring Gulls, Laughing Gulls and Oyster Catchers crowded the shore. When we came out into open water again, I saw the first dolphin, it's humped back just visible as it moved through the water. We stopped paddling and watched. We were close enough so I could almost hear its breath.

"Wow," I said.

"Great, isn't it?"

We paddled for half an hour then drew our boats up on a muddy sandbar. I took out my water bottle and Nate grabbed peanuts from a back pack.

"Thank you for asking me to come," I said when we were sitting.

"I thought you'd like it," he said.

"I've lived near the ocean most of my life, but.." I waved toward the scene in front of me. "I’ve never spent time on the water. I need to get more adventurous."

"Sky diving next week?"

"I'm not sure about that," I said. "Do we hold hands as we go down?"

"You don't need me to hold your hand, Kiki. You can do anything you decide to do."

Did he mean it?

Out of the blue he said, "I'm sorry about the other night. When I picked you up, I should have stayed and talked to Grainger."

"It's OK." I leaned toward him. "Do you know he dyes his hair. He thinks I don't notice but when he comes back from the barber it's always a slightly different color. He's sixty but he wants to look forty."

Nate nodded.

"He wears Hawaiian shirts that are way too bright and orange shorts."

"And buys expensive watches."

"He does," I said. I looked at Nate. "How did you know about the watches?"

"The other day I was in the Texas Mutual bank and he was bragging to some teller about his watch."

"Texas Mutual? We don't bank at Texas Mutual."

"He was there. I saw him."

We sat for a minute in silence. I was thinking about Grainger's account at a different bank and wondered whether he was hiding money there.

"How did Grainger meet your mother? Nate asked.

"My mom was at this business conference and Grainger struck up a conversation with her. He'd been the owner of a small cosmetics company, like hers, that had been bought out by someone else and he'd lost his job. He seemed to know a lot about her business. He moved to Corpus Christi and pretty soon they were dating. My mother was lonely, and Grainger seemed perfect. He took her to nightclubs, sent her flowers and small gifts and within a year they were married."

"Did you ever research the place Grainger worked for before he met your mother?"

I shook my head. "Do you think I should have?"

"He's hitting on women in the office and you think he's stealing from the company. I would be careful of him, Kiki. Now," he said standing up, "let's go get some lunch."

Later we were sitting in the small restaurant eating when two guys came in, obviously athletes. One was wearing a sweatshirt that featured the A & M Logo.

"They're from your college," I said. "You might have even taken classes together?"

He glanced at the men but didn't seem interested.

"You could ask them about Miss Rev?"

"Who?"

"The mascot. Miss Reveille. I read that the dog gets her own bed and her handler has to sleep on the floor."

"I only went there for a little while, Kiki."

"I'm going to talk with them," I said getting up.

"Don't do this, Kiki," Nate said, but I was already walking toward the table. The young men were willing to chat, though when I pointed to Nate, they admitted they'd never known him. When I got back to the table, he was signaling the waitress for our check and boxing up our lunches.

"Wait," I said, "I'm not done."

He didn't respond, just put his credit card on the folder.

"Nate," I repeated, a little annoyed. "I wasn't finished eating."

"I need to go, Kiki," he said. "I'll drop you at home." He gestured toward my box. "Come on."

I followed him reluctantly out the door. "What's wrong with you?" I asked when we had reached the car.

"Why did you go talk to those guys? You just make a decision without asking what someone else wants."

"I thought they could be friends of yours. You went to the same school, didn't you? They said they'd never met you, but you might have had a different major. What was your major anyway?"

He said nothing.

"You must have majored in something. Everyone does."

He opened the driver's door and got in. I slid in on the other side.

"I changed my major three times when I was at A & M." He started the car as I struggled to fasten my seat belt.

"How long have you been in Texas?" I asked.

"A few months."

"But you went to school here?"

He shrugged. Sometimes Nate could freeze me out.

"Nate," I said. "Where did you grow up?"

"Oklahoma."

"How did you happen to go to Texas to college?"

"I had an uncle who was an alumnus who offered to pay my tuition if I went to his school. I took math, psychology, art history, drawing. I was a liberal arts major."

"You were partying, weren't you?

"That's it. Every night a kegger with girls and lots of strong drugs. If my mother hadn't gotten sick, I would have flunked out."

I glanced over at him wondering if he was playing with me. I had made my own share of mistakes in college, but I'd managed to graduate, even with a major that I hated.

For the rest of the ride back to the house he said nothing. He dropped me at the house without opening the door on my side, and without a word about when we would meet again. As soon as I was out of the car he sped off. I'd really blown it this time. I needed to learn to keep my curiosity to myself. Damn.

Chapter Eight

On Monday I went into my mother's office. I needed to talk to her about Grainger's being seen at Texas Mutual, a bank we had no relationship with. When I got to her office she was on a long conference call with one of our suppliers who was complaining that he hadn't been paid in over two months and unless he could see some payment he would not supply her again.

She hung up the phone and slumped into the seat with her head in her hands. I sat facing her. "I know you trust him, Mom. But I think you should look into this."

"You, too, Kiki?"

"Nate said he saw Grainger in Texas Mutual, bragging about a new watch he was wearing."

"He does have a new watch. I gave it to him."

"Why was he in Texas Mutual? We don't do business with them."

"Who knows why he was there? Can't a man go into a different bank if he wants to?"

"Mom, do you have access to his files?"

"If I ask, of course."

"Do you know there are rumors that he's stealing from the company."

"Why would he do that? I give him everything he wants. He has complete control of the finances."

"Is that smart? What if something happened and you couldn't get into his computer to see the accounts? "

"Kiki," she said with a huge sigh. "I married the man. I love him and trust him. Don't come in here complaining about him."

I stood up. I know love can blind you to a lot of things, but my mother was not only blind but deaf and dumb. She needed Annie Sullivan to wake her up.

Two days later I left the office at lunch time and made my way down to the antiques shop. I needed to apologize to Nate, and to try and make things right between us. In my hands, I carried a peace offering, chocolate chip cookies I'd baked myself. Cookies hadn't been my first choice. I'd scoured the stores for something he'd like, a new hat? A watch? He needed a hat for the sun, but the ones I'd seen didn't seem to be his taste. Ditto with a watch. And I'd never seen him drink alcohol, so Scotch wouldn't work. Finally, in desperation I resorted to what I could reasonably accomplish, bake cookies.

When I got close to the store I noticed that the door was closed. He might have the AC running or he might be out. I hoped it was the former situation. I turned the knob and it opened.

"Hello?" I called. There was silence.

"Nate?" I called again.

There was a noise at the far end of the room and then Nate came through the door wearing a dark apron covered with paint stains.

"Touching up some things," he said, pulling off the apron. What can I do for you?"

"I want to tell you..." I hesitated. He was watching me coldly. "I am sorry. I should have asked whether you wanted to meet those guys. I just blundered around." I wound down. He was still looking at me not giving me an inch. "I guess I tend to do that a lot."

He nodded.

"I brought you some cookies," I said, holding out the plate. "If you don't like them, you can give them to your customers."

"You mean the crowds in here buying things?"

"Or just put them in the trash," I said, turning to go.

"Kiki, wait," Nate said. "Listen, I'm sorry too. I over-reacted. Stay here for a minute and I'll get us some coffee." He disappeared through the door and I sat for a while waiting. Then, bored, I got up and began circling the place, my attention grazing over pictures, small painted chests, glassware, chairs and tables, mirrors, and rugs. Everything was clean and in good shape. I paused by a hat stand with several hats displayed. On the top was a bright red cowboy hat. I reached toward it and put it on my head.

"Looks good on you," Nate said. He was standing behind me, a tray in his hand.

I snatched the hat off my head and plunked it back on the stand.

Nate pulled up two chairs around a tiny tea table, set down a tray with sugar, cream and two cups of coffee. I opened the container of cookies.

"So what's with the cowboy hat?"

"It's not much, really," I said.

"So if it's not much, why did you try it on?"

"OK," I said. "When I was seven I was in love with the gals in TV westerns. Not the saloon gal who dresses in low cut gowns and flirts with the cowboys, but the smart, tough cowgirls who were terrific riders and crack shots. I wanted to be one of those gals."

"Annie Oakley?"

"Yeah, kinda."

"So?"

"I asked my mother for a cowboy hat, boots and fake guns for Christmas. My father supported me, but my mother was definitely against it, and whatever my mother was against, didn't get done."

"You didn't get the outfit for Christmas."

"For Christmas I got a red velvet dress with black patent-leather shoes and a little purse to match."

"If you'd got that cowgirl outfit, you might even now be riding the rodeo circuit."

"Probably not, but I did get to ride a horse. When my dad saw my disappointment at Christmas, he insisted on it."

"How was it?"

"Scary, but I did OK."

We had finished our coffee and cookies, at least Nate had finished his. I'd been talking the whole time.

"Let's spend the day together next Saturday," Nate said, leaning toward me.

"Sure," I said. "Doing what?"

"Not saying. This will be a surprise. Dress in casual clothes and I'll pick you up at your house on the island at ten o'clock."

"You're not telling me?"

"Nope. It will be fun, I promise."

The following Saturday Nate picked me up at the Port A house. I was wearing a long sleeved shirt, jeans and sneakers. We drove toward the causeway, but before we reached the end of the island, he pulled off onto a narrow rutted road.

"Where are we going?" I could smell the ocean ahead. Was this another kayak ride? The road began to widen and ahead of me I could see horse trailers, lined up along one side of a parking lot.

"Before we go in, I need to give you something," Nate said, walking around to my side of the car and opening the door. He reached into the back seat and pulled out a large white box. When I was outside the car he handed it to me. "You'll need this," he said.

I opened the box. Inside was the red Stetson that I'd admired in Nate's shop.

"Put it on," he said.

I leaned down to see myself in the side mirror of the car. The hat fit perfectly. "I love it," I said, leaning forward and kissing him.

"I thought of getting you boots to go along with it, but I didn't know your size," he said. He looked down at my sneakers. "But those will do."

Then he locked the car and led me down a path leading toward makeshift stables. Two large dark-red horses were standing inside a rough corral, partly shaded by an old green tarp. A woman was standing beside them, stroking the nose of one of the beasts.

My heart started to hammer in my chest. The horses seemed so big, and now I was going to be asked to get on top of one. These animals seemed gentle, and obedient but still, they were horses.

"Nate," the woman said. "And you are Kiki," she said looking at me. "I'm Mary Downing. Are you ready to begin?"

"Begin what?"

"Riding on the beach." She gestured upward toward the blue sky. "It's a perfect day for it. " At my look of apprehension, she said. "You've ridden before, haven't you?"

"Not for a long time," I said. My palms were sweating, and I was dizzy with fear.

"Nate said you loved doing this," Mary said, looking at him.

I should have told him, I thought. Was it too late to back out? What would Nate have said if I'd told him, sorry, I will do anything else, but don't make me get on a horse.

Mary had gone to the corral and was leading one of the horses out. She tied the reins to a post and did the same with the other horse. Then she went into the makeshift barn and led out a very large snow-white male and tied him up so three horses were standing placidly side by side.

"This is Whisper," she said pointing to the white horse, “and Betty and Red. These horses are retired police horses that have been trained to be very gentle. During the week we have children with handicaps and mental health issues riding on the beach and not one child has ever been scared or hurt.”

I was, I almost said.

"Kiki we'll start with you," Mary said. She pushed a small step-stool up to the horse and gestured me to step up onto it. My knees were shaking.

"You'll be fine," she said. "Once you get on a horse, it's a different world. Grab hold of that bump on the saddle and haul your leg up over the horse. Don't worry. He's not going anywhere."

I did as she said. My head was spinning, my heart was racing. I didn't know if I could sit upright I was so scared. Mary tucked my feet into the stirrups, and I felt the horse shift under me. The tears had started behind my sunglasses, and I wondered if anyone would see, but Mary was busy getting Nate settled on his own horse. She untied the two horses from the rail and while I half expected them to bolt, they stood there patiently. Then she untied her own horse and mounted him. Moving her horse in front of the two of us, she clicked softly and the three of us were off at a slow trot.

I can do this, I said to myself. I can do this. I thought of my favorite cowgirl action hero, woman and horse moving as one across the desert. What would it be like to try and shoot a gun from atop a moving horse?

"How we doing?" Mary called.

"We're great," Nate said. He looked at me. "Aren't we?"

I nodded. I didn't trust my voice. We had walked up a sandy path between the dunes and now we were on the beach. Few people visited this part of the beach, so it was less manicured, but that seemed to suit the horses fine. My horse lifted his head, smelling the salt breeze and whinnied softly.

"You like the ocean, don't you Red," Mary said. "I think these guys get bored when they're just standing around waiting for customers."

"Does he ever…gallop?" I asked.

"Gallop? Sure. He can run, but he knows he's not supposed to when he's carrying a client."

"What if something spooked him like a coyote? Has that ever happened?"

"You don't need to be nervous, Kiki. Red is the most cautious gentleman you'll ever meet. Once in a while we do have coyotes out here, but he doesn't try to chase them. He knows better, don't you baby."

She had brought her horse next to mine and reached over to pat him gently. "Sit up, Kiki," she said. "Relax. Enjoy the breeze." The horses were splashing in the surf at the edge of the ocean now. They seemed to be having fun, and slowly I found that my heart rate had slowed and I was able to turn away from what the horse was doing to the view of the ocean. It was a gorgeous day, with white clouds scuttling across the face of an impossibly blue sky. I just needed to face my fear and move on. Sometimes when something scares you, there is no other way that to just get back on the horse and ride again.

We rode for a mile up the beach and then turned and rode back again. At the end of our trip I found myself sitting erect and relaxed, trusting my perfect gentleman to carry me safely.

When the horses were back in the corral, Mary handed each of us a peeled carrot. She pointed to the horses. "Give this to them to say them thank you."

Red gratefully gobbled his down and I put my hand on his velvet nose and stroked it. He didn't bite, he didn't curse me out, just chewed as I patted his nose. When he had finished, I leaned forward and kissed him.

When we were back in the car, Nate said. "Well how was the surprise?"

"Definitely surprising," I said. "Let's go somewhere for coffee, I have a story to tell you."

"A good story or a bad story."

"It's a surprise."

When we were sitting in Coffee Waves, I said. "I appreciate what you did today, Nate. I never in a million years would have gone horseback riding if you hadn't taken me."

He looked startled. "I thought you loved horseback riding. Didn't you always want to be Annie Oakley?"

"I did."

"So what happened? I can't believe you hated what we did this morning. You seemed in control of the horse, like you'd done this a million times."

I took a sip of my coffee and cleared my throat. "I didn't tell you the whole story about my parents taking me horseback riding when I was seven."

He was watching me sharply.

"The horse I was riding was young, probably not fully broken, and I think the folks who ran the riding stables were new at the business."

"This doesn't sound good," Nate said.

"My father and I got on the horses with the owner leading. My mother absolutely refused to do anything but stand and watch. It was a beautiful day, but instead of going to the beach we headed out through a patch of woods to pasture. I felt tall in the saddle, and brave like a cowgirl and we were riding along quietly when all of a sudden my horse spooked."

"My God."

"I don't know what did it, but the horse stopped, gave a little hop sideways and then he took off at full gallop across the pasture with me hanging on for dear life and screaming for help at the top of my lungs. I could hear the owner and my father behind me, yelling at the horse to stop. Suddenly without warning, he did."

"He stopped?"

"Yup. When he did, I fell off his back and landed on the ground, breaking my arm."

"Kiki," Nate said, leaning forward in his chair. "If I had known, I never would have set this up."

"My mother wanted to sue the business, but my father talked her out of it. He thought the owner would be a lot more careful with children in the future, and he said my arm would heal."

"He didn't care about your feelings? About how scared you were?"

"You know it sounds callous, but he really did love me. He came into my room when I was in the hospital and we talked for a long time about being brave. He'd once fallen from a tree trying to rescue a cat and had broken his arm too, but he told me that even if he'd known ahead of time what would happen, he would do it again. You have to be willing to take chances, he said, even if you are scared to death."

"I'm sorry," Nate said. “I owe you,” Nate said.

"No you don't. Once I stopped being scared I had a great time."

Nate leaned forward and kissed me. I put my arms around him and returned his kisses. I knew people must be watching us, but I didn’t care.

When we came up for air, Nate said. “Want to go back to my place? It’s not far.”

“Sure,” I said. I ditched my coffee and we headed away from the coffee place. The sun was shining; I could smell the ocean. It was a perfect day and I was walking on the beach with a man I loved, ready to give myself to him.

My phone rang. It was my mother. Damn. I answered it.

“Kiki,” she said. “I can’t find my passport. We’re leaving for Paris in a week and I can’t find it. I’m at the house. Can you come help me find it?”

“Mom, I’m really busy right now.”

“Please. I can’t depend on anyone else but you.”

“I’ll be there in a few minutes.”

When I hung up I turned toward Nate. “I am sorry,” I said. “My mother is at home and needs my help finding something.” He leaned toward him and kissed him. “Please ask me again.”

Chapter Nine

A couple of days later I got a call from Nate. "The Corpus Christi Symphony Orchestra is having a concert on Saturday night. Would you like to come?"

"You're spending all this money on me. We'll go Dutch this time."

He nodded. "I'll pick you up at six thirty."

We got to a hall crowded with people, all dressed in their finest clothes. I had booked our tickets on line so all we had to do was pick them up. We were on the second balcony, where outside the seating area a bartender was serving wine.

"I've never been here before," I said.

"Two firsts in one week," Nate said.

"The horseback ride wasn't a first, but it was certainly better than my first."

I ordered a glasses of wine and Nate got a lemon soda and we stood by the windows avoiding most of the crowd. Nate's gaze was focused on a woman in a lovely red dress with a matching scarf wrapped around her head. Many African American women wear scarves in this way, but this woman was white, and I could see a little bit of bare skin peeking out from under her scarf.

"I'll be back in a minute," Nate said. I thought he might be headed for the men's room but instead, he walked toward the woman in the head scarf and engaged her in conversation. I don't know what they talked about. She seemed reluctant to talk at first, and then I saw her lean toward him, wiping her eyes, and at last she gave him a warm hug.

When he returned, I said. "That was pretty unusual. Going to talk to a complete stranger."

"I know what she's going through," Nate said.

Of course. His mother. I reached over and squeezed his hand.

Just at that moment, the bell rang to let us into our seats. The concert was glorious and I sat there thinking how limited my life had been. With Nate I'd paddled a kayak into the gulf, rode horseback on the beach and now I was sitting at the Symphony.

As we were walking back to the car, Nate said. “Would you like to come back to the apartment for coffee?”

"Sure," I said. I leaned forward and kissed him, wrapping my arms around him and feeling the softness of his lips responding to mine. When we came up for air, he said. "I've got to tell you something, Kiki. Something important."

"Not now." I said. "Let's just have fun."

Chapter Ten

When we got inside the apartment Nate went to the kitchen and started brewing coffee. I'd been sitting in one of his modern chairs which seem to be more for looks than for comfort.

"This is a nice place," I said. "Have you had it long?"

"For a while. I sublet it from a friend."

I was walking around the place looking at Nate's stuff. On the bookshelf was a collection of books, mostly early American and European history. Beside it was the delicate terracotta head of a child and a Tang horse. A photograph of four people: man, woman and two children stood in a silver frame beside the horse. The man was not Nate.

"My brother," Nate said.

"Where does he live?"

"Oklahoma. Runs a Feed and Grain store there."

“He’s nice looking. You never mentioned that you had a brother. He doesn’t look much like you. What’s his name?”

“Tom.”

“And what are his kids called?”

Nate hesitated. He studied the picture as though he’d never really seen it before. “Sally and Ben,” he said.

“They look like they’re still in elementary school.”

Nate had walked away. Maybe he didn’t spend that much time with his niece and nephew and really didn’t know much about them.

“I’ve got coffee made,” he said. “Or Sprite if you want. Sorry, I don’t have anything stronger.”

Without waiting for my response, he went to a sound system on a shelf and put a CD in the player. The music of a tango filled the room. “Come on,” he said. “Let’s dance.”

“The tango,” he said, taking my right hand and holding it out as he moved in close, “is a dance of flirtation and seduction.”

I was ready to be seduced and Nate looked like he was the man who could do the job. He pushed his right foot forward and I moved my left foot back as we stepped quickly across the floor. "Now," he said. "Shuffle your foot sideways. Left and then right." I was becoming intoxicated by his closeness, the smell of his aftershave and the male scent of him underneath. As the music played we stepped across the floor. I was getting the hang of it, feeling the rhythm as we moved together.

"You dance well."

"My wife and I took lessons."

"You were married?"

"Uh huh."

The music stopped and Patsy Cline singing *Crazy* started. I could do a waltz much better than a tango. I moved in, so his head was close to mine, his chin near my cheek.

"Were you married for a long time?"

"Five weeks."

Five weeks, I thought. I would never have guessed that Nate was once married. He seemed to be so independent, so content within himself. He'd never mentioned a single friend or relative and it was hard to imagine him with a family, even the ones in the picture on the shelf.

The music changed and we continued dancing, and I realized that I didn't care what his former life had been. He was a man I was falling in love with, someone I wanted to be with.

"Do you know how beautiful you are?" he said. He had reached down and kissed the top of my breasts, just peeking out from my dress. "When I first saw you, standing naked by that pool…"

"Don't talk," I said. I reached forward and unhooked my bra, and then I began to unbutton his shirt. He was breathing heavily.

"I was speechless. Your beautiful body was all I could think of." I was reaching for the zip to my dress, stepping out of it, and he had shucked off his shirt and was going for his trousers.

"Should we go to the bedroom?" he asked. I didn't care where we went, at that moment I wanted him fiercely and wantonly.

We walked to the bedroom. By now, I was naked and he was pulling off his clothes. He pressed his lips to mine, running his tongue along the seam of my lips. "Do you know how long I've wanted to do this?" he asked.

"Don't say anything," I said. "Just show me."

He wrapped his arms around me and together we sank into the bliss of making love. For me it was the joy of being with a man that I hadn't felt for a long time.

I woke to morning light streaming through the window. It was quiet in the bedroom although I knew that far below me, outside, traffic was moving. I looked at my watch. Nate opened one eye beside me. "Morning beautiful."

"I've got to get going," I said. "My stepfather and my mother are flying to Paris this morning."

"This morning?" Nate asked. He jumped out of bed and put on a robe. "Shit," he said.

It was then that we heard it. Someone was moving around in the kitchen. I put on my underwear and shoved myself into the dress I'd worn the night before. Nate opened the door and called "Hello."

"Nate," a man said coming toward us.

"Trevor," Nate said. "You're back early."

"If I'd known you were entertaining, I'd have called." Trevor said. He turned toward me and held out his hand. "Trevor O'Donnell."

"Kiki Coleman," I said. "What are you doing here?"

"Doing here? I live here."

I looked at Nate. "Trevor is the guy you're subletting from?"

"Subletting?" Trevor asked. "No. I own the place. I let Nate stay here sometimes, but we don't live here together." He looked at Nate. "Sorry, sport. I'm taking possession again."

Nate shrugged and then turned toward the bedroom. "I'll get my things," he said.

I followed him into the bedroom. As I was putting on my clothes, I said. "Why did you tell me you were subletting here? You lied to me, Nate." I could feel my anger rising. "What else have you lied to me about?"

He said nothing. He was taking things from the bathroom and shoving them into a plastic bag. "I'll talk to you later, Kiki," he said. "Trevor wants his place back; we need to leave."

I looked at him, feeling the small doubts that I'd brushed aside came roaring back. Had any of the things he'd told me been true? I didn't know. I put on my clothes, grabbed my jacket and purse from the living room chair and then we were out the door. We rode down in the elevator in silence. When we got to the street, I headed toward the parking garage and then realized that Nate had driven us there, and I was without transportation.

"Kiki," Nate said, following me toward my car. “We have to talk. I’ve got to tell you something.”

"Don't speak to me," I said, turning to face him. " Don't call me, don't text me, don't e-mail me. Don't try to contact me ever again." Then I took out my cell phone and called a taxi.

I needed to go to the office. Grainger and my mother were leaving for Paris today and this would be my only chance to say good-bye before they left. It was eight-thirty, so not everyone would be in. I had the taxi drop me at the building where Demi’s Velvet Skin Cream rented space, took the elevator up to our suite, and walked into my office. I put down my jacket and purse, thinking that I really should go home and take a shower and change, but I wanted to say good-bye.

My mother was in her office working at her computer.

"Where's Grainger?" I asked when I was inside.

"He's gone to the Port A house. I’m going to meet him there. I asked him to pick up my favorite jacket from the dry cleaners.” She smiled. “He says he has a last minute surprise.”

"You're leaving from Houston?"

"Our plane leaves at eleven, so we have time. There." she said. "I think things are in good shape for you."

She looked at me. "You shouldn't have any problems. I've left clear directions on the computer and we will be back in two weeks."

She picked up her purse. "We'll call you from the airport, and when we're in Paris, I will text you. I don't trust the international phone system."

She leaned in and gave me a kiss. "Be a good girl."

I bristled at her words. I wasn't her little girl, why was she treating me like one.

"Every day you'll hear from me," she said, and waltzed out the door.

I stood outside her office watching her march toward the elevator, hoping that her vacation in Paris was everything she wanted. When she stepped into the elevator, I went back to her office and opened her computer.

The list of do's and don'ts was long and detailed. It's like she doesn't really trust me, I thought. But I had never been CEO of this company, and maybe some of this could be valuable.

I sat looking out at the view from my mother's office, the ocean sparkled in the sun and a few boats were moving lazily across the water. A couple of joggers worked their way along the sidewalk that ringed the bay. No doubt Nate was in Port Aransas at the condo he rented. If I walked the beach in the morning, would I meet him strolling along the sand with Mitzi the loaner-dog? Grainger and my mother would be leaving from Port Aransas house, so if I went to the Corpus apartment, I would not meet them. I needed a shower and something to eat before I began a full day at the office. Closing the door to my mother's office, I went down to the street and called a taxi to take me to my Corpus apartment.

I was in the middle of breakfast when the phone rang. I'd had a shower, changed my clothes, gone through my mail and cooked myself a scrambled egg, which I was washing down with coffee. It was my mother's number.

"Hi Mom."

"It's Grainger, Kiki. Just wanted to tell you that we're on our way and we'll try to contact you when we get to Paris."

"Is my mom there?"

"She's driving. Can't talk now, but she sends her love. We'll see you in two weeks, bye."

I put the dishes in the sink, grabbed my purse and headed down to the parking garage. When I got to the office, things seemed the same as usual even without my mother. I drew in a deep breath. I was now the CEO. I could do this.

In my mother's office, I studied the list on my mother's computer, starting with instructions on how to unlock the front door. Did she think I was an idiot? I had been unlocking the front door ever since I'd come to work for the company. It was so like her to think that I couldn't do anything without her direct supervision.

I remember a conversation we'd had when I was five. We'd gone to the ice cream store, which, because my mother was resistant to fat, was unusual. I had been in a play in school and this was going to be a special treat. We stood before the counter and I gazed at the flavors spread out before me: raspberry swirl, death by chocolate, peanut butter cup, moose tracks (peanuts and chocolate chips), peach dream (bits of real peach). It was hard to choose.

After I'd dallied for a few minutes my mother said, "Oh come on Kiki. Make up your mind."

Sometimes half the pleasure in a thing is the anticipation of it, or in this case, imagining what each of those flavors would taste like.

My mother turned to the man behind the counter. "My daughter will have vanilla," she told him.

"I don't want vanilla."

"Sorry, you waited too long."

We walked out the door, down the front steps and past some tables and chairs. A potted plant stood beside the sidewalk. I took my ice cream and shoved it face-down into the dirt. My mother glared at me. "I'm never going to buy you another ice cream."

"I don't want another."

She stood glaring at me. "I don't know why you insist on being so difficult. Don't ever ask me for a treat like this again."

We marched home in silence. Out of the blue my mother said. "The next time you're in a play, lift your head up when you speak. No one can hear you when you're talking to the floor."

It had taken every bit of courage for me to try out for that play and I'd only done it because my best friend, Wendy, was in it. "I'm never going to be in another play," I said.

"Caroline," my mother said. "You can do better. You are my daughter and I've always done whatever I set my mind to. You just have to have a little confidence in yourself."

I hate you, I thought. But I didn't say it. Did that mean that I had no confidence?

Shortly after college, I joined the business and my mother made me head of the advertising department. I had lots of good ideas--we would appeal to younger users, we would advertise on Facebook and Twitter, we would engage young women who were trying to be attractive for their husbands as they wrangled young children and held down full time jobs. I developed an ad campaign, found models and put together mock-up ads. I had called my small staff into the conference room to talk about the campaign, and because my mother was CEO, she was there.

About half way through the description, she stood up. "This isn't going to work, Kiki," she said. "Younger users are not our traditional customers. We tried to market to those groups in the past and the campaigns never took."

"Because you've always marketed to middle-aged women. With a different approach we can expand our customer base."

"Kiki," she said. "I am the CEO of this company and I will decide who our customers are."

My staff looked at my mother and then at me. Who was in charge here? If I were the head of the department, didn't I have the right to decide a campaign. Clearly I did not.

"Why don't you finish the meeting, Mother," I said, and taking my notebook I left the room.

I spent a long time in the ladies' room, and then I went out for a cup of coffee. I was newly graduated from college. I had never worked anywhere else but my mother's company, and clearly I didn't have the confidence to speak up for myself. If I had been smarter I would have quit right there. But, I reasoned, if I got another job, I would start at the bottom and have to work my way up. When I got back to my office in mid-afternoon there was a knock on my door. It was my mother.

She came into the office and plunked herself down in a chair, saying nothing. I sat behind my desk, my power position.

"I'm sorry," she said finally. "I shouldn't have done that. I am used to being the one in charge."

"The worst part was being corrected in front of my staff," I said. "How can I be the boss, if you over-ride me?"

"I wished you'd showed me your plan in private," she said.

"I don't think I can work here."

"Don't say that, please. I need you."

"If you need me, you have to give me some space to make my own decisions," I said. "I can't run a department when you come into a meeting and eviscerate my ideas."

"Will you talk with me about your ideas?"

"Sure, but you don't have the right to veto them just because you're the CEO."

"I thought that's what a CEO's job was."

"Not if you want me to stay."

"OK," she said.

We reached a sort of détente. It was hard for my mother not to be in charge, both at the office and at home and I struggled to find a way of doing things that didn't involve her approval. And now here I was, looking at my mother's list of things I should do. I glanced down through the words. My mother knew the company. She'd run it for far longer than I'd been an employee, and it had been a success. But pushing me to do things her way made me grind my teeth in fury. I could do this. I might make mistakes, and I would certainly be reprimanded for those when my mother returned, but I needed to fly on my own.

I picked up the phone and called Gwen in. When she came there, I was still standing at my mother's computer.

"I guess they got off all right,"

"Yup. My mother's going to text me every day. How does it feel not having Grainger here?"

"Nice. But it won't last. He'll be back in two weeks, and then it will start all over again."

I nodded. "Have you been into his office? I would like to see if we can get a peek at the financial records."

"I've got work to do," she said. "I don't want to do anything that will get me in trouble."

"If I go with you, there won't be any trouble."

She looked at me. I was now the chief officer of the company, but even my own secretary didn't think I had the balls to run things. "Maybe later," I said.

Chapter Eleven

Three days after my mother left, I hadn't heard a word. I kept looking at my phone expecting a text, telling me what a great time they were having, or giving me some advice. Maybe no call was better. It meant that they were having fun and it kept her off my back for a while.

On Thursday of the week after my mother left I got a call from Morris White, the Vice President of the Lone Star Bank where we did business.

"Miss Coleman," a voice said. "Is your mother there?"

"Sorry, she isn't. Can I help you?"

"I really wanted to speak to her, or to your stepfather. We have some irregularities we need to discuss."

"My mother left me in charge. Is there something I can do?"

"You sure I can't speak to your mother?"

"She's in Paris. Unless you have the number of her hotel, she's unavailable."

There was a long silence. "How long will it take you to get here?" he asked.

"Ten minutes," I said.

When I reached the bank, I was shown into a small office where a portly man with white hair and horn-rimmed glasses sat behind a large desk. I felt like a child who had misbehaved being called into the principal.

"Miss Coleman," Morris White said. "I'm sorry that neither of your parents is here." He shifted uncomfortably in his seat and reached forward to move a piece of paper to one side. "I'm afraid that our business won't wait another week."

"You said there are irregularities? What kind of irregularities?"

"Your stepfather has been withdrawing money in large amounts. I thought it was for some project the company was doing." He looked at me questioningly. "Have you decided to open up a new product line or are you doing renovations? It's not my place to ask, you know, it's just that..."

"We aren't doing anything like that," I said.

"I tried to tell him that he was leaving the company without resources."

"Did you tell my mother? She's the director."

"I tried, but she wanted me to work it out with your stepfather, and he kept telling me there was nothing wrong."

"What *is* wrong, Mr. White?"

"You have barely two hundred dollars in your account."

"Two hundred? There should be a lot more money. What happened to it?"

"Grainger withdrew it."

"And put it in a different account?"

"Not in this bank."

I took a deep breath. The loss of the money meant that we could not pay our suppliers, could not pay our rent on the office space, could not pay our taxes and most importantly could not pay our employees.

"I'm sorry," Mr. White said.

"What do you suggest?"

"File for bankruptcy. Decide if you want to try and keep the company running with a minimum staff. End your lease on the space as soon as possible. You will probably have to pay a fee."

"Fire people?"

"I'm afraid so. Unless they are willing to work for free, which I doubt is the case."

"I need to call my mother," I said. "It is her company."

I dialed her number, but it went to voicemail.

"Dammit, Mom. Pick up." I yelled. Mr. White flinched. "I'm sorry," I said. "I've never had to handle anything like this."

"Few people do, Miss Coleman. Does your company have a lawyer?"

"We do."

"I would talk to him as soon as possible to see what your options are."

"Could I prosecute Grainger for embezzlement?"

"I assume you can. First, you need proof that he stole the money for his own gain, and not for some project that he and your mother have chosen. And..."

"And what?"

"To bring him to court, you need to find him"

"He's in Paris with my mother. They're supposed to be back soon."

"You're certain of this?"

"He called when they were on their way to the airport."

"And how long have they been away?"

"About a week."

"I'm not a detective, mind you. But I would double check everything connected with the trip. Everything."

I closed my eyes, trying to sort through the mountain of things that were now facing me. I needed to meet with the company lawyer and talk about closing the business. I needed to sit down with the staff and tell them they no longer had jobs. I needed to talk with the landlord and get out of the lease, and then decide whether I had the energy to keep the company going.

And after all that, what if my mother came back, and saw that I'd gutted the business she'd worked her life to build up?

I thanked Mr. White and in a daze walked out the door and out onto the street. I needed to learn what had happened to my mother. The travel agency that my mother used was about two blocks away and when I got close to the building, I saw that it was open. Inside, Helen Ayers the owner, was sitting at her desk near a back wall. The rest of the place was empty. She was the sole owner of the business and I wondered how she managed to survive when things were this slow.

"Caroline," she said. "How are you?"

"Not so good," I said, sitting in a chair opposite the desk. "Can I talk to you about the arrangements you made for Grainger and my mother's trip to Paris?"

"Sure. But I only booked the hotel, not the flight."

"So you made the deposit for the room. Did you hear from the hotel when they arrived?"

"They don't normally call unless the client doesn't arrive. Your folks must have changed their minds because the hotel called and said they never showed, and the deposit meant that they had to hold the room. You've never had a bad day unless you've spent an hour long distance with a pissed-off Frenchman."

"As far as you know they never booked another hotel?"

"That was the only one Grainger asked for."

“I know they’re in Paris,” I said. “She sent me a text.”

I handed my phone to Helen and she read the texts aloud.

"Arrived today. Long flight. Tired, but Paris is just breathtaking. Checked into the hotel and had a hot bath, and a nap. Going out tonight. M."

And the day after that.

"Walked through the Louvre today and saw the Winged Victory. Things are so much more brilliant in real life than in pictures aren't they?"

"The Eifel tower is spectacular. Saw the city from the top, then ate in the restaurant."

There were two more entries and then they stopped.

“It sure looks like they’re there,” Helen said.

“But my mother doesn’t answer my calls, or my texts. Where are they?”

Helen shook her head.

"Do you know what airline they used?"

"United."

"You don't happen to have a number for the airline do you?"

She reached for a rolodex, flipped through it and read off a number. "Be ready to wait a while," she said.

I stood up, reached forward and shook her hand. "Thanks," I said.

"You're welcome. I hope you find out where they are. And if they want to travel again, tell them to give me a call."

When I got back to the office, I asked Gwen to come in. "Shut the door please," I said

When she appeared.

"What's the matter? You look awful."

I took a deep breath. I wanted someone to tell me I was doing the right thing, but I was on my own. "Grainger has been stealing from the company," I said. "I was just at the bank."

"I thought something like that was going on," Gwen said. She studied my face. "It's bad, isn't it?"

"There's about two hundred dollars left in the account. That's all." I tried to keep my voice from breaking. "I have to make a decision about the company but..." I choked up. "Gwen, even if I can save the business, I have to let most of the employees go."

She looked down at the steno pad on her lap. Gwen's husband was already retired and she was staying on so they could pay up some bills and then she was going to do the same. Now there was nothing.

"Oh Gwen, I am so sorry," I said.

"It's not your fault. Grainger did it."

"But I'm the one they will blame, because I'm the one bringing the bad news."

"Tom will be happy," Gwen said. "He's been pushing me to quit. I was hoping to retire with a little more money but we will be OK."

I stood up and went over to her. She stood and we hugged. "Will you stay for a few weeks more and help me sort this out. I promise I will find your salary somewhere."

She nodded. "When are you going to tell people?"

I shrugged. "I need to learn what our options are. I'm sure none of them are good. Don't tell anyone yet, please."

"'Loose Lips Sink Ships.'"

"I'm afraid this ship has already sunk."

"But you don't want folks knowing it's underwater."

"At least not until I have a plan."

I took out the piece of paper that Helen had given me and dialed the number for United Airlines. True to Helen's word I went almost immediately to some cheezy music. I put the phone on speaker and sat in front of my computer working out a list of people I needed to contact: lawyer, landlord, real estate agent (I would need to sell the condo in Corpus and possibly the house in Port Aransas.) I would need an auctioneer to take the surplus equipment off my hands, and someone to help me offload excess product. I was a half hour into my list, when a woman, introducing herself as Melissa came on the phone.

"United Airlines, how can I help you?"

"Hi, yes. I'm calling for a man named Grainger Starland who bought two tickets to Paris leaving on May 14. He left from Houston, Texas and would have landed in Charles de Gaulle. Is there any way you can confirm whether he and his wife were on that flight?"

"What time did his flight leave?"

"Eleven, I think."

"That would have been the 340 with a layover in Newark. Let me take a look."

There was another long wait and then a man came on the line. "Hi, my name is Chris Durand. May I ask who you are and why you are asking about passengers?"

"Sorry, I should have told you. Grainger Starland is my stepfather and he was traveling with my mother Demeter Coleman Starland. The thing is, I'm trying to reach them."

"You are positive that they were on flight 340?"

"Pretty sure. But they never checked into their hotel."

"That doesn't mean anything. There are lots of hotels in Paris. Maybe they changed their mind."

"My mother hasn't called me back, and now I can't reach her. Please," I said. "I'm really worried."

"I'll see what I can do."

This time the wait was shorter. "I did find something, but it may not be the answer you want," Chris said. "On April 12, Grainger Starland purchased two tickets for trip to Paris leaving on May 14: Houston to Charles de Gaulle. However, his credit card was invalid, so the tickets were cancelled."

"They never flew to Paris? How can that be? I have text messages describing their trip."

"They may have flown on another day, with another airline. What I am saying is that they were never on flight 340."

I couldn't think of any other questions, so I thanked Chris and hung up.

I took out my phone and dialed Grainger's cell number. It rang and rang, but didn't go to voicemail. As I was about to hang up, a man answered.

"Lo?"

"I'm looking for Grainger Starland. Is he there?"

"Ain't no one here, lady. Just a phone ringing in the dumpster."

"In the dumpster? Where is this?"

"Route forty west rest area."

"And who are you?"

He'd hung up. Granger had ditched his phone somewhere along route forty west, wherever that was. I called my mother's cell phone, but got a message that the voicemail was full. Damn it. Where the heck were they?

Chapter Twelve

After the phone call I stood up and stretched, trying to let the stress dissipate. I wasn't my mother's minder, so I'd never looked very closely into this trip. And since she was the head of the company, I'd never thought to ask her about company finances. Now, if I were going to do anything, I needed some answers.

Leaving my office, I strolled down the hallway toward Grainger's office. It was neat and tidy. Grainger was almost compulsive in that regard. Everything seemed unchanged, except for the fact that Grainger's computer was gone. It was possible that my mother had tipped him off about my being in his office, and now he was putting the machine safely out of my reach. I opened a file drawer in his desk and found the files neatly labeled. But when I pulled out a file folder, it was empty. I pulled out every file folder in his desk. There was nothing in them. I went to the other desk drawers, and they'd been cleaned out, too. There was nothing in the refrigerator, except a single bottle of water. The closet where he sometimes kept his suits had been emptied of everything. Grainger had removed every trace of himself from his office. He'd been planning this for a while.

I sat in a chair thinking. My first priority was to find where Grainger had put the money he'd stolen. I still had the zip drive with the encrypted folder labelled 'finances.' If I could get into the folder I might get some answers, but all of this was a long shot at best, and I felt wholly inadequate to the task.

I pulled out my phone and scrolled through the messages my mother had sent. Each time I tried to call, it went to voice mail, and there was no direct reply to my texts. What had happened to her? Had she made a decision to move to France, leaving a thriving business behind? It was possible Grainger had talked her into it and she, worried about keeping him, had agreed. But my mother was too practical for such a solution, and even though she might be worried about keeping her man, I expected she would show up in the next few months, repentant and ready to carry on as usual.

I looked through my other calls. There was nothing from Nate. Had I expected there to be? I was so angry at him I could claw his eyes out, and yet I missed him. How could you hate someone and want them at the same time? I thought about the flowers, the dancing, sitting in the concert enjoying the music. All those thoughtful gestures that he'd extended to me over the past few weeks. Had it all been a sham? Did I even know this man?

My phone rang. It was Wendy, sobbing on the other end of the line.

"We had this huge fight, Kiki. He doesn't want the Joan Crawford house for our wedding, thinks it's too expensive, but I want this wedding to be special. It's the only one I'll ever have. Rick says for what we're spending, we can get furniture for our new house. But my parents are paying for some of this, so shouldn't they have a say? How can he push away my dreams like this?"

I had my own problems to cry about, and I wiped away tears. Grainger's office was a public space and sobbing there, especially if I were now in charge, was not good for morale. Wendy was still yammering on about the house and I just wanted to slam the phone down and tell her to shut up. Finally, she wound down. "How're you doing?"

"Not good. My stepfather has been withdrawing money from the company, and we are completely broke."

"Broke? Really? Oh God, Kiki."

I tried to control the tears. "I'm going to have to fire people, Wendy. I have no money to pay them. The rent and utilities are due; we have to pay our suppliers; I have fees for the condo and taxes on the beach house and I have no money for any of those. The other thing is that my mother is missing."

"I thought she was in Paris."

"According to the airline, Grainger never actually bought the tickets. I have no idea where they are."

"Oh, Kik. I am so sorry. What are you going to do?"

"Do what the Brits say, 'Keep Calm and Carry On.'"

"They also tell you to 'Mind the Gap.'"

"I never saw this gap coming, but I do mind it a lot."

"Want to go out tonight, just the two of us?"

"A ladies' pity party?"

"Why not, we both need it."

"Thanks Wendy, but I think I'm going to the island. I need to walk on the beach where I can pick up trash and listen to the seagulls."

"Have you talked to Nate about any of this?"

"We had a fight. He told me he was subletting the Corpus apartment, but it belongs to Trevor, his boss. What else has he lied about?"

She was silent for a moment. "I could go over there and talk to him."

"Do NOT do that, Wendy. I don't want to see him for a while. I just need to let this whole thing settle."

Instead of going back to the office, I drove to Port Aransas, a place I hadn't seen since Grainger and my mother had left for Paris. In the two-car garage, I parked beside the empty stall where Grainger's car normally sat. As I got out of the car, I could see something glittery at the edge of the door that led to the kitchen. It was an earring, one of a pair of real diamonds that were my mother's favorites. In her hurry to leave the house and get to the airport, my mother had probably lost it. I'd done the same thing, pulling off a sweater or slinging my purse over my shoulder. I wonder why she hadn't texted me about it. I carried the earring into the house and set it on the counter. The house was quiet and there was a strange odor as though something had gone bad in the trash. I opened a cabinet and looked down, but the trash was can was empty. Even the bag was gone.

In the refrigerator a bottle of white wine stood unopened. Pulling open the cupboard I looked for a glass. My mother had a set of four Waterford cut-glass champagne flutes which she treasured, but only two were in the cupboard. I checked the dishwasher. Not there either. I had no idea where they'd gone and their loss was yet one more thing that I would have to atone for when the two returned.

I took down a glass, poured myself some wine, then I dialed up a pizza delivery place and ordered a pizza. I needed to gird myself to face the staff tomorrow and tell them that all of us no longer had jobs.

Chapter Thirteen

I woke the next morning to a terrible headache. I'd drunk too much wine the night before, and the thought of going into the office filled me with dread. Instead of getting into my work clothes, I put on a pair of sweatpants, a t-shirt, sandals and with my hat headed for the beach. It was early morning, and except for a few hardy seagulls huddled together, it was deserted.

I walked briskly, trying to talk myself into doing what I needed to do. I stopped, faced the ocean and closed my eyes, breathing in the salty sea smell and attempting to calm my jittery nerves. A trick of yoga is to breathe out stress, and breathe in peace and I tried it. You can do this, I told myself. It will be hard, but you can do it.

I opened my eyes and saw, striding toward me a lone man. For a moment, I thought it was Nate. Would I run to him, throw my arms around him, ask where he'd been? No, I couldn't. I watched as he drew closer, and realized that it wasn't Nate. The man approaching me as though we were old friends was Trevor O'Donnell.

"You're an early riser too," he said.

I nodded. I wasn't about to unload everything on this stranger, but I was curious. "Does Nate stay with you when you're here on the island?"

Trevor shook his head. "Nate has his own place."

"But he was here when you were gone. He was walking your neighbor's dog. She told me that he was staying in your apartment here on the island."

Trevor nodded. "I told him he could do that. Sometimes he was delivering art for me and if I'm not using the apartment, I don't mind if he uses it."

"So where does he actually live?"

"Above the store." Trevor looked at me. "I was wondering if he was with you."

"With me? No. After the way he lied to me, I don't want anything to do with him."

Trevor's face grew pale. "Nate's gone," he said. "I thought he might be with you, but he's not at his own place and he's not here."

"You're better off without him," I said sourly.

Trevor gave me a sharp look and then shook his head. "Nate was the one bringing in money. He was a natural salesman and the ladies loved him."

"When did he leave?"

"Right after you did. The last time I saw him was when you two were in my apartment. When I went to his place the next day, he had vanished."

"You sure he's gone."

"His Honda Civic is gone. The one with the Florida plates. It's a piece of junk, but he's driven it away. I wish he'd told me he was leaving."

“So the Prius with the Texas plates is yours? The one he used when he was with me?”

Trevor nodded. We stood there together silently. Then Trevor said. "Why don't you come by the shop today and I'll tell you what I know about Nate. Maybe together we can figure out where he's gone."

I nodded. One small angry part of me didn't care a rat's patoot where Nate had gone, and the other part was curious. Nate apparently lived over the store, not in the fancy apartment owned by Trevor, or the place on the Island that he said he was renting. He didn't own a Prius. That belonged to Trevor. Instead his real car was a Piece of Crap. All of my previous hesitancy about him came roaring back to the surface. Who needed him anyway?

Sherman Bergstrum , the lawyer for Demi's Velvet Skin cream, had an office housed in a large glass fronted building right downtown with a fabulous view of the waterfront. I knew our business had been a large part of the money that paid for his office, and I was only a little bit sorry that the money pot would dry up soon. I'd called him as soon as I knew the particulars and I could hear the shock in his voice.

"How much money do you have?" he asked as soon as I was shown into his office.

"Only what the bank has given me," I said, handing over several sheets of paper. "I can't get into Grainger's computer."

"Why not?"

"He's taken it with him. We did get one file, but it is encrypted. He and my mother were scheduled to be in Paris last week, but they never arrived. The airline said he made the reservations but the credit card was bogus."

"So you're not sure they went."

"They never arrived at the hotel."

He picked up a pencil and tapped it against the surface of the desk. "What's your most immediate financial need? "

"Meeting payroll this week. I've been trying to reach my mother, but with no luck."

"We might be premature in this. If your mother returns after her trip, it could be that nothing's wrong.

"I can't wait for her to return. The account in the bank has been drained." I was close to tears and struggling not to break down in front of the lawyer.

"Kiki," he said. "I have been the lawyer for this business almost since it began twenty years ago. Frankly, I have done very well by your mother's inventiveness and hard work. Why don't I lend you the money to pay your staff? At least for this week."

I could feel the tears starting. I almost stood up and ran over to give him a hug, a gesture which he would reject. "Thank you," I said.

"Mr. Bergstrom, if my step-father has embezzled all the money in the firm what are my options?"

He drew his breath sharply in. "You have two choices, both of them involving bankruptcy. If your company is making a profit, or if you feel you can get yourself out of debt by continuing to run the company, you can file Chapter 7 bankruptcy, which will wipe out personal and business debt. Do you want to keep running the company on your own?"

"I'm not sure."

"You can do a Chapter 7 bankruptcy and shut down the business, sell the assets, dismiss the staff. You will then be responsible for paying off the outstanding taxes and whatever creditors you can."

"It sounds like a lot of work," I said.

"It is. I can help you with some of this, but of course I would charge you for my time."

"Of course," I said. "I will get some money from selling the apartment here in Corpus and the house on the island."

He nodded. "Where will you live?"

I might be able to get a small rental on the island, but I would have to rent storage space for whatever furniture I couldn't sell. The thought of doing all of that made me incredible sad.

I stood up, leaned forward and shook the lawyer's hand. "Call me and tell me how much you need," he said. "And I'll cut you a check."

"You've been a good friend," I said.

"Give it another week, Kiki. Maybe they will still show up."

"I can't." I said.

On the way back to my car I stopped at a coffee shop. I couldn't bear to go back to the office and face all the people I'd worked with, seeing the shock in their faces when I told them they'd lost their jobs. When I'd got my coffee I took out my phone and scrolled down through the texts from my mother. None of them was a reply to my messages. Had she ever received them?

At eleven o'clock, I was in my mother's office looking through her computer. How could she have ignored what Grainger was doing, and let all of this happen? In the meantime, I had to make a decision because we had no money. I walked from my mother's office to the conference room. I'd only been in charge for a while, and I'm sure there were folks crowding into the room who thought I had simply got this job because my mother was the founder, and I had no skills at all.

When we had gathered, I cleared my throat. "I have an important announcement to make," I said. I glanced around at the faces. I'd worked with some of these people my whole career, they'd been mentors and friends, or like my secretary Gwen, substitute parents. Others were new employees with families, mortgages, children in private schools or college. How would they deal with what I was about to tell them?

"I have learned from the bank, that almost all of the money in our company's account has been embezzled by my stepfather." There were looks of disbelief. Someone giggled.

"I wish this were a joke, but it isn't. Apparently Grainger has been stealing money from the company for years. There is not enough left in the account to pay the current rent on this space, to pay our suppliers, and I'm sorry to say, to continue paying all of you."

There was shocked silence and then the room erupted. Most of the questions were directed at me. Why didn't I know what was going on? Why hadn't my mother known what was going on? When was the business closing? Would they get paid through today? Rather than blaming Grainger who had brought this all upon us when he embezzled the money, the employees blamed me, the author of the bad news.

I held back tears as I told them that the business was closed as of today, but I could pay them through the rest of the week. I gave my apologies again, but no one was listening. I had no idea if we would ever be able to find our way back to solvency, but the files, computers, e-mail lists, were all company property and would be boxed up and stored. Employees should start cleaning out their desks now.

By three o'clock most people had packed up and left. There didn't seem to be any point in continuing. I had called the rental agent cancelling our lease. We would pay a fine for cancelling before the end of the month, but we didn't have the funds to continue. At three-fifteen, I locked the door to the business. I would come in tomorrow and sort things out, but for now, I needed a break.

I walked over to Shoreline Drive where Trevor O'Donnell's shop was. The door was open and Trevor was inside, dusting furniture. The place seemed quieter than it had been when Nate was here.

Trevor smiled. "You look beat," he said.

"I had to fire everyone today," I said. "Grainger gutted the company and there's nothing left for salaries. I had to borrow money to pay everyone for this week."

"Tough," Trevor said. He led the way to the back of the store and opened a door that led directly to a set of stairs. "Let me introduce you to Nate Marks," he said. We went up the stairs, Trevor unlocked a door and we were in a single room. Along one wall was a narrow bed, and at the other end was a very small kitchenette with a sink, stove, refrigerator and, above the sink, a cabinet. A couch stood along one wall, facing a television set, and there was a table and two chairs against another wall. One wall held a partial bookcase and above the bookcase, tacked into the wall were a number of paintings and drawings. I moved to look at the art, which was exquisitely done and reminiscent of something I'd seen before.

"He was good," Trevor said.

"It looks like something I've seen before."

"Sure," Trevor said. He went to one end of the room and opened a door. Immediately the smell of paint assaulted me. Tacked up on the walls were prints of Dutch paintings and on easels around the room were the same pictures in various stages of completion.

"Nate did this?"

"It was his idea. He said we could make more money selling reproduction Dutch paintings, than we could selling original art. I wasn't so sure at first. I mean we were cheating people, but his paintings were so good that people believed what he told them. And of course he was a wonderful salesman."

We left the workroom and Trevor closed the door. I stood for a moment in the room that had been Nate's home, thinking how small it all was. Everything was neat and tidy, dishes in the sink washed, the bed made, and a narrow closet now empty of clothing. Would I have gone out with him if I'd known what his life was really like? If he'd not dressed well, sent me flowers, driven a good car, lived in an expensive apartment, would I have even talked to him? I'd fallen for the lie he had crafted, caught in an alluring invention that I wanted to believe. Nate was a con man. He'd conned women into believing that what he sold them was genuine, and he'd conned me into believing that he was just a salesman for the antiques store. I couldn't blame anyone but myself.

A black and white drawing tacked up on the wall caught my eye. It was the same hand that had painted the fake Dutch masters I'd seen. A woman looked out from the frame, her eyes bright, her mouth curved in a half smile, a cloud of curly hair framing her face.

"I think that was his wife," Trevor said.

"The one he was married to for five weeks," I said. "Did he tell you why they got divorced?"

Trevor shook his head. "People keep looking for him," he said. "They don't want to buy from me. They want Nate."

I didn't want Nate. At least not the Nate who had lied to me. I wanted the Nate of my fantasies, the one who danced with me, who made love to me, who sent me flowers, but that Nate didn't exist.

I walked downstairs to the shop and then went out the door. It was a hot day and all I wanted to do was go home, lie down in bed and wait for the day or the month or the year to end. On a whim, I took out my cell and tried my mother's number. Maybe she would tell me that all this was a mistake and she was on her way home. Don't do anything, she would say, we'll fix this. But this time there wasn't even a dial tone.

Chapter Fourteen

A month after my mother left for Europe, I was sitting in my living room on the island. I had done what I could to contain the mess Grainger had created, but I felt like the executioner at the Guillotine, with bloody corpses strewn all around.

Our account at the bank had been frozen and I had only my small personal account to draw on. I had gone through Grainger's desk in the Corpus apartment, looking for any clue to where he'd put the money, but he had cleaned that out as thoroughly as he'd cleaned out his desk at the company. He'd emptied his files in the Port A house, too. It must have taken him weeks, to dispose of everything, and I wondered how my mother hadn't noticed. But then, of course, she trusted him.

I was rummaging through my purse, looking for a pen when I found the zip drive. In all the excitement of closing the company I'd forgotten about it. If I could get the file decrypted, I might find money that Grainger had hidden. What was the bank where Nate said he'd seen him? Texas Mutual?

I put on my best business outfit, got in the car and drove to Corpus, where twenty minutes later I was sitting with an officer of the bank.

"I'd like to open an account," I said. "I believe my step-father Grainger Starland has account here and I'd like to link my account to his."

The banker had booted up his computer and was studying it. “Mr. Starland doesn’t have an account with us. He does have a safe deposit box? Do you have the key?”

“He’s on vacation with my mother. I need access to the box now.”

“You’ll need a letter of authorization. And of course the key.”

A key which I did not have.

I went back to the apartment in Corpus and strode past the boxes of stuff ready for the Goodwill into the bedroom shared by Grainger and my mother. Most of Grainger’s clothing was already on the bed, waiting for me to pack things up and put them in plastic bags. Grainger had been very careful, very careful. But even careful criminals make mistakes. He had taken his computer, trashed everything in his file drawers and his desks (all three of them), but there still might be something.

I reached for a jacket that lay on the bed. It was in a loud plaid, something that was not flattering to Grainger, but which he’d worn a few times to parties. I reached into the outside pocket and fished around, and came up with an empty candy wrapper from Michelangelo chocolate. I took the second jacket and did the same, and then I went through every pair of pants and every jacket on the bed. Sometimes I came up with a cloth handkerchief, but there was nothing else.

There must be something? And then I noticed the outside pocket, which if the wearer is especially fussy, carries a handkerchief that matches his tie. I reached inside. Nothing. But some jackets also had an inside pocket, a twin to the outside one. I reached inside and felt something. When I pulled it out, it was a key.

I looked at the key. It was small and gold colored, not a house key or a car key or the key to a padlock which all have their own distinctive shapes. Something was written in tiny print on the key, and under a magnifying glass the letters were UPS. I knew there was a store downtown that mailed packages and printed flyers and had, along one wall, a row of postal boxes.

The young man who waited on me at the UPS store seemed to be new at the job. I gave him the key and he spent a few minutes looking at it. I thought he was going to say that it was from a different UPS store, but finally he took the key and went into the back of the store. When he returned he said,

"Sorry, the previous renter stopped paying and we've re-rented the box."

"Do you ever save the material that was in the box---the stuff the previous renter left?" I asked.

"We're not supposed to. I mean we're a small store and don't got a lot of extra space. But let me see."

He returned with the contents of the box wrapped in plastic. "I have to charge you for the unpaid month," he said.

I handed over my credit card and he gave me the packet. When I got home I laid the material out on the kitchen table. There were a number of sale flyers from grocery stores, an advertising flyer from a company called Rx by Mail which thanked Grainger for his recent purchase and a postcard with a picture of the St. Louis arch on one side and the words "See you soon. M." on the back.

I looked more closely at the St. Louis picture. Had my mother and Grainger gone to St. Louis instead of Paris? It didn't seem possible. I'm sure the people who live in the city think it is the cat's meow, but honestly compared to Paris, there is no comparison. But if I could get someone to look for them there, I might hit pay dirt.

I tossed the local advertising into the trash, and put the flyer from Rx by Mail and the St. Louis postcard back into the plastic bag.

I shuffled through the pile again and something hit the floor. Another key. This one was a slim rectangle with cut outs on one side and red tag with the number twenty-four on it. This was the key to the bank safe deposit box I'd been looking for.

The banker at Texas Mutual looked at the safe deposit key and said yes it was one of theirs. I handed him the letter of authorization, giving me permission to open the box. I was getting good at forging Grainger's signature, and because the rent on the box was overdue the bank was happy, even eager to find someone who acknowledged it

The banker who'd led me to the room took my key and his own key and using them, pulled out a narrow safe deposit box. "Do you want me to return after you've seen the material?" he asked.

I pulled out my own bag. "I'm taking everything with me," I said.

He blanched, but I pulled out the letter, showing him the paragraph that gave me permission to take the contents of the box.

"You'll have to pay the balance on the rental," the man said. I nodded. It would be worth the cost, to find what Grainger had hidden. I opened the box. Inside was an enormous wad of bills in a baggie and a zip drive. I shoved the two items into my bag and went out to the lobby, where I handed in the key and paid the overdue rental.

When I got home, I laid the money on the kitchen counter. There was more than ten thousand dollars, most of it in twenties.

I went to the cupboard and found a bottle of wine and poured myself a glass, trying to wrap my head around the person Grainger had been. I had lived in the same house with him. My mother had married him, and we had no idea who he really was.

It was time for me to find a professional.

Chapter Fifteen

I took the zip drive to my computer and booted it up. This time there was no encryption, just a list of banks where he had money, with account numbers and passwords. Grainger had an account in Synchronicity Bank, that contained more than two hundred thousand dollars. In an Oklahoma City bank, he had seventy thousand, and there was one hundred-twenty-five thousand in a bank in St. Louis. I am sure there were offshore accounts somewhere, but he hadn't included the information for those

The next morning, with the letter from Grainger, I presented myself at Synchronicity Bank telling the officer that I wanted to open an account and link Grainger's to mine and showing them the letter with Grainger's signature, allowing me to do it. When it was done I said, "I want to transfer the money from his account into mine." The officer looked startled. "And I'll need a bank check for the amount."

"You're closing his account?" His voice was a squeak? "Are you sure."

"We're doing some renovations on the office," I said.

"You'll need to keep some money in the account in order to keep it active," he said.

"Of course." In cleaning out Grainger's account, I'd probably created a very bad day for this man. He left his office and in a few minutes came back with a check. I shook his hand, the last time we would meet and left the bank.

I walked down the street to American Bank, a place that neither I nor Grainger had ever used and opened an account. Then I deposited the check and the cash I'd gleaned from the safe deposit box. This was a holding pen for the money, nothing more.

That afternoon I called the bank in St. Louis and said I wanted to open an account and link it to that of an existing customer, for whom I had a letter of permission. I had to fill out a form for my own account, and then fax the phony letter from Grainger. I was told I would have to wait a day for things to happen. I wondered if in the meantime, they would try to contact Grainger. If so, I would not only lose the money, but I might now be in sights.

I thought about Grainger's money sitting in its holding pen at the new bank. If I could get some more of the money he'd stolen, I would be able to repay the lawyer for his loan, and get caught up on the taxes. I had started looking through the want ads for a job, and though there were a few positions for secretary there were no advertisements for 'former advertising director with cosmetics company.' I needed to clean up the mess Grainger had created before I could start thinking about the next part of my life.

The next morning, bright and early I called the St. Louis bank and was told that my account had been opened and the two accounts linked. With my own ID and password I could now see Grainger's account and I transferred the one hundred twenty-five thousand dollars from his account into mine and requested a check for that amount sent to my home. I expected the phone call which arrived within a few minutes. I gave them the same reason for closing the account that I'd given Texas Mutual. They would send the check.

I took out my phone and called Gwen, my former secretary. We hadn't spoken in two weeks, not since the disastrous day I'd had to fire everyone.

"Hello?"

"Gwen, it's me, Kiki. I've got some great news. I got back some of the money Grainger stole."

"You're not going to re-open the company."

"Nothing like that. Can I come over for a minute?"

"We're just about to sit down to lunch," she said. I looked at my watch. It was eleven-thirty. "But sure. Come on over. You know where we live."

The house Gwen and her husband shared was a modest three bedroom bungalow on a quiet street. The lawn was mowed and it looked like they were re-painting, but it was essentially a house that had not seen any major renovation in ten years. Gwen was at the door when I pulled up, her husband standing behind her.

I followed her down a narrow hallway to a tiny kitchen. Two filled plates sat on the table.

"I'm sorry to interrupt your meal," I said, but I wanted to give you this." I held out an envelope. "Think of this as your Christmas bonus."

"You didn't need to do this, Kiki."

"I hope you guys can go on a nice vacation somewhere."

She had opened the envelope. “Kiki, this is two thousand dollars. Can you afford this? You must have other bills to pay."

I could have said "take a number and line up for your money," but this was Gwen, my former secretary and more importantly a friend.

"You deserve something nice," I said, leaning forward to hug her, then I headed toward the door.

Did giving away money make me feel better about myself? It was a nice blip, but I was still the same Scrooge underneath. I hadn't killed the company, but I'd been the surgeon that made the final cut and now it lay inert on the table.

I went back to my favorite coffee shop and opened my cell phone to read my messages. I was surprised to see the first one from Grainger. "Stay away from my money," the subject line read.

"Your money?" I texted him. "This was not your money, it was money my mother earned and you stole it. You are a liar and a thief."

I sent the message but almost immediately it was returned as undeliverable. Where was he? Somewhere he couldn't be reached. And what was he using to communicate? A public computer, like one in a library. The bastard.

My phone rang. It was Tania. She told me, between sobs that she'd made the decision to break up with Greg but she missed him like crazy and was it really right to leave a man that she loved so much, even though he probably never would leave his wife and children, and now when she looked at the other guys she knew, the ones she worked with, or the ones she hung out with after work, she saw that some of these guys had potential, but it was clear there was only one guy for her, but she had just dumped him.

I let all this drama float by me. Tania would always have the same issues. She liked men who were unavailable, rich and egotistical, and even if she never saw Greg again she would soon be with someone just like him.

"Where are you?" she asked.

"Coffee shop. Here in Corpus".

"I'm at Benny's Pub getting drunk. Want to join me?"

I could sleep in the Corpus apartment, but that didn't feel like it was mine anymore. "I'll pass," I said.

"Kiki, you need to get out. Have some fun. Put your name in on one of the dating sites. We can do it together."

"You'll be back with him in two days," I said.

"No. I. Won't."

"Ten bucks says you will."

"All right," I said. She was right. I needed to do something other than try and find Grainger and my mother. I needed to have a little fun.

When I got to Benny's, Tania was sitting in a corner with three empty glasses in front of her. "What time did you start?"

"Three thirty." It was now almost five.

"Have you had anything to eat?" I asked. She leaned into me drunkenly. "Oh, Kiki what am I going to do?"

"First we're going to eat," I said. I looked at the glasses on the table. "What are you drinking?"

"Daiquiri. But I don't want to eat. Eating spoils the fun." I wasn't listening. I'd already started for the bar where I ordered two hamburgers with fries, a glass of wine for myself and a Daiquiri, with lots of ice for Tania. When I got back with the drinks and the food, Tania was sitting, strangely quiet.

"What's going on with you?" she asked.

"I thought you were going to tell me why you broke up with Greg," I said.

"Nah. It's an old story. He's never going to leave his wife and I'm going to spend the next ten years wishing he would and then I'll be too old for anyone else to want me."

I wondered if Tania really meant what she said, which would have been the first time she'd been able to see her situation honestly. She took a sip of her drink, pushing the hamburger away.

"Eat," I said. "And I'll tell you my story."

She pulled the hamburger toward her and took a delicate bite. I told her about finding the zip drive and taking money from Grainger's account.

"He sent me an e-mail telling me to stay away from his money. But my message back to him bounced."

"You can't call him?"

"His phone is in a dumpster on a rest area off highway 64 somewhere."

"God."

I opened my phone and pulled up my messages. There was a new one. It was from Grainger. The subject line said "Miss her?" but there was nothing in the text. Then I noticed an attachment. I opened it up and watched in shock as the picture opened up on my screen. It was a picture of my mother. There, in color and bigger than life was my mother, stark naked and draped on a sofa like *The Naked Maja*. My mother is too old for this sort of thing. Too much adipose in the wrong places, too many wrinkles. But she was smiling as though she were the Playboy bunny of the month on a cover shoot.

Had Grainger talked her into this? Probably. And why did she agree? Did she really believe that this display would make him love her more, or lure him back from wherever he was straying?

"Oh Mom," I said aloud. Wherever they were, whatever she was doing, it wasn't dignified. Instead of looking plump and luscious as I'm sure she hoped to be, she looked thin and tired, and slightly embarrassed. When I tried to respond, the message bounced.

Tania and I looked at each other in shock. "Why would your mother do something like that?"

"He told her she wasn't pretty any more, that she was getting old. It's the reason they went to Paris."

"Can you find out where it was taken? Maybe that's where they are?"

I sat back against the seat and closed my eyes. "I never wanted any of this, Tania," I said. "He's got the money. He's got my mother. How can I find out where he is?"

"You can do this, Kiki. You're strong, heck, you've bucked me up plenty of times. I'll bet a photographer can tell you where he took that picture."

"I expect you're right," I said suddenly very tired. "I'm going to the Corpus apartment to sleep. Where are you going tonight?"

"I do have a place, and a room-mate though I hardly spend any time there." She stood up and we hugged."

"Call me," she said.

A week later a check came from the St. Louis bank but when I logged onto the other three banks a message came up. "Account Closed."

I printed the picture, even though I couldn't bear to look at it. I needed to take Tania's advice and find where it had been taken.

The photography studio was small and from the toys scattered around in a corner, seemed to do most of its work with children. There was no one at the front desk and when I rang the bell, no one came. I was just about to leave when a thin woman with white hair emerged from the back room, wiping her hands on a canvas apron.

"Sorry," she said. "Didn't hear ya. You here to have your picture took."

"No." I put the picture of my mother face up between us. "I wanted to ask you something about this."

"You want it reprinted? Did you get this off the internet?"

"It came in with an e-mail," I said.

"Someone you know?"

"My mother."

She gave a low whistle and took up the picture, studying it. "This is the sort of selfie that teenagers send to their friends. I've never seen it done by someone her age."

"What I'd like to know is when and where this was taken. My mother disappeared more than a month ago and I've no idea where she went. Are there any clues in the picture that tell where she is?"

"Can you get me the original?"

"Sure," I said. I put my computer on the counter and booted it up, pulling up the e-mail with the photo. The woman looked at it.

"Every modern digital photo has a ton of metadata attached and there are computer experts who can tease out information from a picture, but…" She shrugged her shoulders. "I'm a pretty good photographer, but I'm not a computer expert."

I found a man named Sam Marcusi on the internet who claimed to be a photography expert. I hoped so, because his office on the second floor in a seedy building didn't promise much. He was sitting behind a desk, cluttered with papers, a computer within easy reach.

I put the picture down between us.

"A little old for this sort of thing, isn't she?"

"It's my mother. I got this as an e-mail attachment. Can you tell me when it was taken?"

He nodded. "You got it on your computer?"

I got the e-mail with the picture. Sam saved the picture to his own computer and then did something. In a few minutes a page of letters and numbers filled the screen. "The metadata," he said. He scrolled down through a bunch of numbers that meant nothing.

"This was taken with a cell phone on January 12, 2012 in Corpus Christi, Texas. The photographer was Granger Starland. "

"He took it two years ago? Not recently?"

"The metadata doesn't lie." He looked up. "Anything else?"

I took out my credit card and put it on the desk. He picked up the card and ran it through the machine. “Only fifty bucks?” I asked when I signed the chit. I had seen his sign listing prices for his work.

“Half price sale today,” Sam said. As I was putting my card back into my wallet, he said. "My mom was a hooker. It's not something I tell everyone. She did drugs too, so I grew up fending for myself most of the time."

"Thank you, Sam," I said.

"You can survive, even with a mother like that," he said. "I did. You will too."

I took my computer and went out. When I got to my favorite coffee shop I opened my computer and pulled up the picture of my mother again. The fact that my mother had posed naked for him made me sick, but I had retrieved some of the money he’d stolen. That had to be enough. I needed to get on with my life.

Chapter Sixteen

May, 2017

A year later I was sitting in a bar called The Surfer with Wendy and her husband, Rick. They'd come back from California for a visit. Wendy was tanned and fit, but she looked unhappy

"We've been trying for a baby for six months," she said, when we were in the ladies' room, "but nothing is working. And then last week Rick said he was rethinking the whole kid thing. 'What do you mean you're re-thinking this?' I asked. 'We talked about it.' I was actually yelling at him. We hadn't gotten to talking about in vitro or anything but that was going to be my next step."

"You could adopt." I said.

"Rick's very last choice. He wants his own kids. At least he *wanted* his own kids. Now, he says he's not sure he wants kids at all."

"Did he say why?"

"Too expensive, too much responsibility. He's too young to be a parent. What he means is that he'll have to give up his sports car, and going out with the boys on Tuesday night, or the occasional football game. There's a guy in his office that just had a new baby and I think he and Rick have been talking." She was wiping the mascara streaks from her cheeks with the rough brown paper provided by the bathroom. She looked at it. "God, this stuff is awful. You'd think they could give you real paper towels, or tissues."

"How's the job?"

"It's OK. It's a big firm and even though my title is lawyer, they give me the shit work. To tell you the truth I'm bored. Rick works all hours and I sit at home, wondering what I'm doing with my life."

She had finished wiping her face and was applying lip gloss and eye liner. "Come on, Kiki. We're here to have a good time. There's someone I want you to meet."

"Wendy, tell me you are not setting me up."

I could see the color rise in her face. "He's nice, Kiki. And you need someone."

"I haven't been sitting at home waiting for Mr. Right to ride up on his white horse. I've joined this dating site called Let's Meet. I *have* actually been dating."

"Really. How's that working out?"

I sighed. "Jeff Myers spent the whole evening trashing his ex-wife whom he called the 'B' word. I ended up paying the bartender for my drink and sneaking out the back. When he kept calling, I never picked up his calls."

"Tom Waters was sixty five and confessed that he'd posted his son's picture on the site. He was so nice I didn't have the heart to tell him I didn't date guys old enough to be my father. He spent a long time talking about his dead wife, whom he missed terribly."

"And then there was Billy Thompson who wanted to sit next to me and feel up my leg. When I moved across from him, all he did was brag about all the women he'd 'bagged'."

"You'll like this guy. He is a lawyer in Rick's office. He and Rick are very close."

"What's his story?"

"His story?"

"Why's he single?" I looked at her closely. "He is single, isn't he?"

"I swear he is. He was dating this secretary in the office, but they broke up two months ago because she wanted to get married."

"How long had they been going together?"

"Four years."

"She might have had a point."

"Kiki, he's a nice guy. He's clean. He's good looking. He has a respectable job and he doesn't drink to excess. But mostly, he's available."

I nodded. "OK," I said.

When we went back to the table, Rick was sitting beside a rugged looking guy with blonde hair and the high color of a man who spends a lot of time in the sun.

Rick rose, and the fellow I'd been studying stood up. "Kiki this is Jeff Lamont, an old buddy of mine." Jeff reached forward and shook my hand. His was warm and very strong. I could see the bulging muscles under his jacket. "So, what do you think of these two," Jeff said gesturing toward Wendy and Rick, "The newly marrieds."

"I think it's great," I said, looking at Wendy. "They seem to be very happy."

It didn't seem to be the answer he was expecting because his smile faded just a bit.

"I just wish you guys hadn't moved to California," Jeff said.

"That's where the job was," Rick said.

Jeff turned to me. "So what do you do, Kiki?"

"I used to be the advertising director in a cosmetics company," I said. "But now I'm in personal service." Personal service covered a variety of jobs from wiping butts in a nursing home to being an Uber driver. Some 'personal service' jobs could even be done from home in your jammies. I expected Jeff to ask further questions, but his attention was drawn to the TV above my head where The Aggies were playing LSU. I am not a fan of football, but clearly Jeff was. It seemed to me that if you've just met a girl you're trying to impress, you would pull yourself away from the TV, but that didn't seem to have occurred to him.

Rick nudged Jeff and then leaned over and whispered in his ear.

Jeff turned back to me.

"You live here in Corpus?"

"I did," I said. "But I had to sell the apartment when the business went bankrupt. I live in Port Aransas now. How about you?"

He described an apartment in one of those high-rises that line Shoreline drive. If he could afford a place there, he wasn't doing bad financially, but financial security wasn't the only reason to consider a man.

"I moved here to be close to my Mom who is in her eighties. When Dad died she was all alone and needed a lot of help, but she wasn't willing to go into assisted living. My sister lives here in the city, so between the two of us, we convinced her to get an apartment. My sister is basically next door and I live down the street, so we can look in on her every day."

"That's nice," I said. Maybe he had potential.

"The firm wants to promote me, but I keep resisting, because it might mean a relocation and I can't move away from the city as long as my Mom is here."

"I understand," I said. My glass was empty, and Jeff said. "I'm going to the bar for a refill." He looked at me. "Kiki?"

"Sure," I said. As soon as he'd left Wendy turned to me. "So what do you think?"

"He's all right."

"Isn't that sweet about his helping his mother out?"

I turned toward Rick. "Does he really have a mother living here in the city?"

Rick shrugged. "I've never heard him talk about it, but then why would he lie?"

At that moment Jeff returned with the drinks and the conversation turned to life in California and the movie industry. I watched Jeff. He seemed to be making an effort to include me in the conversation. He'd not reached under the table to pat my leg, nor had his eyes strayed to the TV above my head. Maybe I would give him a chance.

At the end of the evening I gave Wendy a warm hug. They were flying back to California tomorrow and unless I could afford the air fare I wouldn't see them for a while.

"Can I drop you somewhere?" Jeff asked when they left.

"No thanks. I'm driving back to the island tonight." I pointed to my car. "My chariot is right there."

"I'd like to see you again," he said.

I nodded, but said nothing.

"I hope I didn't make too much of an ass of myself. I love football; it was something that Elaine hated."

I nodded again. I didn't want to know the details of his breakup."

"Give me your number and I'll call you."

I took out a piece of paper and scribbled my number on it. He would know eventually that even though I lived on the island, I was working as a waitress and had no viable prospects for anything better. Then again, he might never call.

I handed him the paper. He took out his wallet and tucked it into the bill compartment. We parted ways, I to my car, he to his.

My job as a waitress was in a restaurant called 'A Touch of Italy." Joe Carlotti, the owner/manager was a large man who was given to rages which sent the staff scurrying. He probably wouldn't have hired me, except that two of his waitresses abruptly quit after one of his temper tantrums. But then I was left trying to do the work of two.

I'd been going for interviews for people looking for publicity directors. I certainly thought I had the experience they needed. But when I mentioned bankruptcy in my interview, I became Typhoid Mary, a woman who could single-handedly kill a company.

Before working as a waitress, I never considered how hard a job it is. A waitress is the dog that everybody beats. If the order is late being picked up, the cook complains to the waitress. If the food is too hot or too cold, the customer complains to the waitress. In addition to taking the orders and serving food, my job was to clean the booth and because Mr. Carlotti thought vacuums were too noisy, at that moment I was on my hands and knees, cleaning up spilled food left by a family with three children. Adding insult to the extra work the kids had made, the dad had left me a dollar and twenty five cent tip on a forty dollar charge. Sometimes I think tippers just reach into their pockets and pull out whatever spare change they have. I once had two quarters, three pennies and a dusty lifesaver as a tip.

That was my life. Five days a week, seven to three, I waited table and in my leisure time I was trying to sort out the remains of the business. In the year since my step-father and mother had left, I had sold both the condo in Corpus and the house in Port A. I was living in a tiny one bedroom rental in Port A, part of the living room filled floor to ceiling with boxes of things that I couldn't part with.

I'd been ruthless with most of the stuff in the two places we had lived, selling the apartment and condo as furnished and putting the rest up for auction. Someday, in the far, fairy-tale future I might have a home of my own, but that future was too far away and unreachable for me to spend a couple of hundred dollars a month storing things that I would never use, like a walnut desk, or cherry bookcase. Whatever I earned went to reduce the overwhelming tide of money I owed.

"Kiki?"

I looked up to see Jeff standing over me. We hadn't seen each other for six months.

"Oh hi," I said lamely.

"What are you doing?"

I straightened up so he could see my uniform with the thirties-era cuffed sleeves, tiny collar and scalloped apron.

"You work here?"

I nodded. Wasn't it obvious?

"This is what you meant when you said you worked in 'personal service'?'

I had nowhere to hide. I nodded again.

"I thought you were an organizer, or a special events coordinator."

"Nope," I said. "Just this."

"Waitress," one of the customers called. "Could we have a menu?"

"Are you here to eat?" I asked.

"No, I'm picking up take-out for the office."

I gestured toward the cashier. "She'll take your money."

"Kiki," he said. "I was going to call you, but things got busy."

"I was busy too, Jeff. It's no big deal."

"Waitress," the customer called again. "We need some menus."

"Wanna go to a baseball game on Saturday? The Hooks are playing Midland at Whataburger Field."

"Waitress," the customer called again. I walked over to the table and slammed down the menus. The other diners were watching Jeff and me as though this were a reality show and they would be asked to vote on whether I went out with this loser.

"No thanks," I said.

"We could do something else instead." The cashier was motioning that his order was ready and I had customers waiting. Jeff picked up his bag, nodded at me and headed toward the door.

"I'll call you," he said.

"Look," I said, pushing him toward the front door and then outside so we had some privacy. "This is not the place to ask me for a date. If you want to call me, call. If you don't, don't. You don't need to go on and on about it." Then I turned and marched toward the kitchen, spending enough time in there so that I hoped he would be gone when I returned to the restaurant.

He called three days later. He must have got my number from Wendy. I honestly didn't see her enthusiasm for the man, and I'm not a huge sports fan, but I figured because she was my friend, I would give the guy a try.

We had agreed to meet at the ball park which was OK with me because it saved Jeff a trip to Port A, and let me hide my tiny overcrowded apartment. When I got to the stands, he was already there, waiting by the gate, waving two tickets, like they were the keys to something wonderful. In fact, the tickets were for seats in the grandstand, so high that most people needed binoculars to see the play. A food seller walked by, and Jeff bought us both a beer and a hot dog.

It was hot and noisy. I would much rather have been walking the beach in Port A feeling the breeze on my face, or sitting in my bathtub with the AC on and a Linda Ronstadt CD playing, but I was here. I was going to give this thing a shot.

Jeff was riveted on the game. I resisted the urge to pull out my cell phone and check my e-mails, though it appeared to be what some other women were doing. I had let my eyes scan over the crowd, trying to guess who was here as a fan, and who, like me, had been dragged along because they were polite. That's when I saw him. He was standing up, tall and slender with dark hair. I could only see his back, but I was sure it was Nate. So, he had been here all this time and I'd just missed him. He started to move from his seat to the aisle.

"I'm going to the ladies," I said. Jeff barely looked at me. I squeezed past the folks to the aisle, keeping my eye on the tall man who was six rows ahead. He bounded down the steps and I bounded after him. I had no idea what I would say. Where have you been? Where did you go? Did you miss me?

I followed him to the refreshment stand where he took his place in line. Cautiously I moved up beside him. I looked at him and at that moment he turned toward me. It wasn't Nate.

"Can I help you?"

"Sorry, no. I thought you were someone else."

"Who do you want me to be?"

"Sorry," I said again. I moved away from the line, trying not to let my disappointment show. I needed to suck it up, get on with my life, be content with the guy who was taking me to the baseball game, and not the one who had disappeared. Slowly I walked back up the steps and squeezed in beside Jeff.

"You missed a fabulous play," he said. He looked at me. "Everything OK?"

"Fine," I said. "It's fine."

Chapter Seventeen

May 2017

After that first date Jeff and I settled into a routine. On Friday, we'd go to a bar and have drinks with his friends from work. Most of the women looked hyper-vigilant and over-stressed as though even with friends, they couldn't completely relax. I was the outsider, someone who didn't know a *torte* from *amicus curiae* and so the foreign words whizzed by me. I tried to look interested. I tried to appreciate that I was with a man who seemed to like me, but sometimes I had to admit that I'd rather be home. On Saturday we often went to a baseball or basketball game, or once in a while the rodeo, which Jeff loved passionately. On Sunday we spent the morning in bed, reading the paper and then we'd visit his mother in the afternoon. Sometimes during the week we'd go to the movies.

It was a routine that suited Jeff, but sometimes I wanted more. I wanted to be surprised, to dress up and feel beautiful, to participate in a world which was out there but away from the life I lived. One evening after Jeff had left, I was going through my closet looking for something when I found the blue dress I'd worn to the Applegate's party more than a year ago, I took the dress out and held it up against my body, remembering the glittery evening and regretting that I might never wear it again. I needed a place where I could wear something feminine, not the jeans and t-shirts that were my usual garb. The next time I saw Jeff, I said. "Let's go to the symphony."

"Really, Kiki? You like that stuff?"

"I do." I faced him, we rarely argued, but I was ready to stand my ground. "Ever since we've been going out we've gone to baseball games, or basketball games or the bar with your friends. I want a chance to wear something pretty for a change."

"You can wear a dress to the bar on Friday night. No one is stopping you."

"It's not the same. I want to go somewhere glamorous. The Corpus Christi Symphony is doing Prokofiev's Romeo and Juliet this Saturday. Let me buy the tickets."

He nodded. "We'll go out to supper beforehand. Somewhere special."

I didn't wear the blue dress to the symphony. People didn't usually dress that fancy, but I did wear a short sleeved print dress with the gold shawl and my favorite earrings. Jeff's eyes lit up when she saw me. "If I'd known how gorgeous you look, I would have suggested this earlier."

We'd eaten at the Thai restaurant and then made our way to the hall, where a group of bell-ringers were playing a pre-concert medley of tunes. After the bell ringers finished, we made our way up the stairs to the second tier and were shown to our seats, which looked down at the orchestra and up at the vast space. We settled into our seats, the lights dimmed and the music began.

I was instantly transported. I knew the story, of course everyone knows it, but the loveliness of the music made its tragedy immediate.

I looked over at Jeff to see if he was enjoying it as much as I was. He had his head to one side, and as I leaned in closer, I could see his eyes were closed and he was breathing deeply.

Damn, I wanted to punch him hard. For Jeff, anything he paid to watch, needed to be active and loud enough to keep him awake. When the intermission came, I poked him.

"Have a nice nap?"

"Sorry, Kiki. I've been working late for the last three nights. I guess it just caught up with me."

"Come on," I said. "Let's walk around. You don't have to go back if you don't want to."

"We came because this was something you wanted to do. Are you sure you want to leave?"

I didn't want to leave, but I wanted to enjoy the music with someone who was enjoying it too. "What do you want to do? I asked.

"Let's go to Shorty's"

So we went to the bar. The same bar we frequented every Friday night, and where most of Jeff's friends spent their time. There were a few comments about my outfit, but after a while the boys went back to their usual gossip and it was as if we'd never spent our evening anywhere else.

The next day was Saturday, a day when Jeff and I often stayed at my place on the island and would walk on the beach. In the spring and summer, life on the beach had a predictable rhythm. On Thursday evening or Friday evening, the native Texans would pile in, crowding the hotels, motels and rentals and on Saturday, if the weather was nice, they would set up their umbrellas, haul their giant coolers to the spot, spread out a blanket or lawn chairs and sit. This Saturday there were the usual quota of dogs. Dogs being walked, dogs without leashes, dogs chasing balls or Frisbees in the surf. I loved the joy of it.

"Do you think you'd ever want a dog, Jeff?" I asked.

"Nope. Why would I?"

"A dog is someone to welcome you home. Someone who's happy to see you."

"A dog is something you have to feed and take for walks. I've got no time."

I watched a man across the way holding the hands of his toddler son, as the baby took its first tentative steps. Standing nearby was a woman with an infant in a Snuglee, watching the scene. I thought of my friends Wendy and Rick who were now pregnant and were delighted with the prospect. Tania had broken up with Greg and was with a guy who was not only single, but treated her like a princess.

Where was I in this equation?

"You never wanted to get married?" I asked. I knew the answer to this question. Wendy had said as much the first time I met Jeff, but I wanted to hear it from his own lips.

"Nope," he said. "Marriage is for suckers."

Had he actually said that? "In what way?"

"The girl gets you to settle down, buy a house, trade your little sport car for a van to carry the kids, and pretty soon, the life you knew before that---the parties and games with your friends are gone."

"But in exchange you have someone who loves you, who has your back. What if something happened to you right now, and you had to be in the hospital for six months or longer. Who would you count on to visit you, to bring you stuff, to remember who you were?"

"You would be that person I hope."

"But I might find someone else."

"You wouldn't do that."

I didn't know what I would do. I was starting to realize the shallowness of our relationship, and I wondered if I were going to stick forever with a man, I only liked, but didn't love.

And then I had another thought. What if Jeff had said, that yes, he was re-thinking the whole marriage question and was wondering if I would consider being his wife. What would I say? Would I be delighted or would I start to see the walls closing in?

It was Wednesday evening and I was walking the beach when I saw the horses trotting toward me. I waved, but the woman, Mary, didn't wave back. It had been more than a year since we'd seen each other. I watched as the horses walked slowly down the beach, splashing in the surf. I needed to talk with Mary.

The next day I called to make an appointment. Mary's ranch was in Aransas Pass. During the fall and winter when things were cooler she would stay with her horses in Port A, sleeping in a little travel trailer, but in the summer it was too hot to leave the horses in the corral so she took them back to the ranch. I was welcome to come and talk with her.

Mary's house was small but with air conditioning. When I'd shown up at her door, she recognized me and graciously offered me cool sweetened ice tea.

"Do you remember Nate Marks, the guy who made the arrangements for our ride on the beach?" I asked.

She nodded. "Nice guy. He came out the day before to check out the horses. Said he wanted to be sure that his girl had a good time."

"His girl? That's what he said?"

She nodded. "I asked him if he'd had any experience riding and he said he grew up on a farm and he used to ride as a kid, before his mother left."

"His mother left? He told me she died when he was in college. How old did he say he was when his mother left?"

"Nine. I'm sure he said she left. I remember because my own mother did the same thing. Went off with a man she met in a bar."

"I'm sorry," I said. Mary nodded. "He prepaid you for the rides?"

"Of course. In cash. I always ask for cash. I been burned too many times before."

“Did he tell you anything about his life before he came to Texas?”

Mary shrugged. “I don’t spend a lot of time talking to customers,” she said. “But I remember we talked a little about New York City because I was thinking of going there for Christmas. Nate said, he’d spent some time in New York, even went to school there.”

“He told me he went to Texas A.& M.”

Mary shrugged and took a sip of her drink. “I do remember there was something. It was the car, I think. A Honda Civic with Florida plates. No, it wasn’t the car, it was his driver’s license. The license was from New York state and had expired more than ten years before. I told him that he’d better be careful. Texas justice can be pretty harsh. If you’re driving with an expired license, they’re just as likely to throw you in jail as to look at you.”

I had finished my drink and thanked Mary. "Say hi to Nate," she said, as I was going out the door. "And if you decide to come ride again, I'll give you a discount."

I went back to my apartment, poured myself a glass of wine and sat thinking. Jeff wasn't a bad man and I'd had a good time with him, but I would never feel about him the way I'd felt about a man who had left with no forwarding address. Nate had never contacted me again which meant that he had no wish to see me. He’d cheated others and left without a word, but still I kept thinking about him. It was hard to figure out my own heart, which was stubbornly stuck on something it couldn't have.

An hour later, the phone rang. It was Tania. Since her new relationship she was much more upbeat, even giddy.

"Kiki," she said. "I found Nate Marks on the internet."

"He's here in Texas?"

"No, nothing like that. He's having a one-man show at the Trillium Gallery on Fifth Avenue, New York City."

"Just a minute, let me pull it up on my computer." There were no pictures of Nate only photos of his art, which seemed to be on huge canvasses.

"He's changed his style. When he was faking 16th century Dutch paintings, his things were small, but these paintings are huge."

"Well, he's had time to change his style." I said.

"Are you going to go see him?"

"Tania, he lied to me about a bunch of things, and he's never, in the time he's been away tried to contact me. Why should I go see him?"

"I thought you liked him, that's all."

"I have Jeff. He's a good man, he treats me well. He has never ever lied to me."

"You're right, Kiki. Jeff's a good man."

There was silence on the line. "There's something you're not saying, Tania."

"It's none of my business, but I'm your friend, Kiki. I want you to be happy."

"You think I'm not happy?"

"Actually, no. I think you like Jeff, but there's no spark between you."

"You're going to rub it in, aren't you, telling me that Jeff and I don't have what you and Gene have."

"Oh sweetie. I wouldn't do that. I want you to find someone that makes you feel alive, someone you look forward to seeing every morning when you wake up. Someone who makes you feel loved. I think that's what you felt with Nate."

"So your advice is that I go all the way to New York City to meet a guy who is going to break my heart again."

"At least you'll know if you still feel the way you used to feel. If it's not the same with him then you can get it out of your system and move on with Jeff."

She was right. I needed to figure out what I wanted, and if Nate were the one standing in the way, I needed to get him out of the path. I made my plane reservations and booked a room in a moderately priced hotel, not far from The Trillium Gallery. Think of this as a mini-vacation, I said to myself. A weekend away.

On the Thursday before I was to fly out to New York, Jeff called. When he told me he had tickets for the San Antonio Stock Show and Rodeo, I said. "I'll be away this weekend, Jeff. We can do something next week when I get back."

"Where you off to?"

"New York city. I'm going to see an old friend there."

"I didn't know you had any girlfriends who lived in New York."

"I do," I said. "We're going to an art show."

"I can come with you, Kiki. I've never been east of Louisiana. It will be fun."

"Thanks, Jeff. She's putting me up in her apartment and she's only got room for one."

"We can rent a hotel, see the Statue of Liberty, Rockefeller Center, the MOMA."

"The MOMA? You don't even like art."

"That's true. We could take in a Mets game. I've never seen them in person."

"I'll be back on Sunday night late, and I'll tell you all about my trip then."

"So you don't want me with you?"

"Jeff, I'm sorry. This is a girl's only weekend."

It was a good thing I wouldn't see him until after I'd returned from New York because I knew he would press me for details and I'd probably screw the whole story up."

On Friday morning, I stood with the almost-packed bags on the bed, debating what to wear. How dressy was an art opening? In Corpus Christi folks would arrive in their best Stetsons and hand-tooled cowboy boots, but I wouldn't see many of those people in New York. I wanted to wear the blue dress that I'd worn to the Applegate's party and have Nate see me and remember what had attracted him. I packed the dress. If I decided at the last minute, not to attend the show, I'd find somewhere else to wear it.

At four o'clock that afternoon, I had reached the city. The hotel I'd booked was tiny and inexpensive, which meant it probably had poor food and bedbugs and I would spend the few days I was here scratching. But I was in New York and, if all else failed, and I sincerely expected it to fail, I could still have a good time seeing the city.

I registered and then went up to my room, which was a miniscule cell with a bed that seemed to take up all the available space and a tiny bathroom that if I were twenty pounds heavier, I would not be able to turn around in. There was a closet, but no dresser and a single chair. I expected that the people who used these rooms rented them by the hour, and I wondered if I would spend the night listening to wild sex. Oh well, this was going to be my vacation, and hopefully after seeing the town, I would be too tired to listen to amour going on next door.

I changed my clothes, washed my face and hands and headed out to the city, ready for any adventure that would await. I was looking for MacDougal Street, a street that had been on Nate's driver's license, but I had no idea what the street number was. I studied the subway map and found the right train.

Corpus Christi, Texas does not have a subway system, nor does Port Aransas, but I'm not a total dolt. I paid my money for a token, dropped it into the appropriate slot and got onto the platform with no trouble. It was late in the afternoon, and at that hour, I seemed to be shoulder and hip beside the finest citizens of the city. Some were reading, some were dozing standing up, and all ignored me. After a few stops a seat became available and I sat, but I needed to stay alert because my stop could easily slide by me. I could hear the stops announced but they could have been in Chinese for all the sense they made. My stop came and I got off the train.

Greenwich Village was probably at one time just that--- a village within the city. Some of that is still visible in the brownstones with their steep stone steps that sit primly side by side, like stuffy relatives in all the best chairs. In Corpus Christi as in many western towns, there is room to spread out, so buildings go up and out, taking up air. In the east, houses have to fight for room to breathe.

I started down the street, past the brownstones, wondering if Nate had once lived here, or still lived nearby. Would he come rushing out just as I was passing? Maybe talking or laughing with a woman? And what would I say if he saw me?

Yes, it's me, Kiki. Just visiting from Texas. I'm only here to see your show. Would this half-truth be convincing enough that it didn't sound like I was stalking the man? I continued walking but with my eye on the doorways beside me. What had possessed me to come all this way? I needed a more convincing story to spin when I saw him tonight. Eventually, I turned back, found the subway station and took the train back to the hotel, where I lay on the bed trying to decide what to do. Tonight, I would find Nate in the crowd of people at the gallery, congratulate him on his one-man show and if he didn't remember me, or if he did remember me and it didn't make any difference, tomorrow I would take the first plane back to Texas.

At eight o'clock I put on the blue dress and took a cab over to the Trillium Gallery. From the crowd filling the space, I guessed that Nate must be doing pretty well. In spite of my pounding heart, I was proud of him. He'd found a way to use his skills honestly. I pushed past the people, accepted a glass of wine and some small appetizers and stepped up to a painting which seemed to fill one whole wall. It was of a red adobe house, with pink flowers climbing up the wall and a distant view of mountains. The style was very different from the delicate watercolors of Dutch landscapes that he'd created in Trevor's studio, but I could see why he was popular.

"It was a hell of a hot day," a man said, coming to stand beside me. "Do you know what it's like to paint watercolor in the heat?"

"It's beautiful," I said. "And so different from the other things he did."

"The other things who did?"

I looked at the man who was tall with reddish curls and bright blue eyes. "Nate Marks," I said. I looked around. "He's here, isn't he? I wanted to talk to him."

"He is here," the man said. "What did you want to tell him?"

"Just that I'm an old friend from Texas." I held out my hand and he shook it. "I'm Kiki Coleman, and you are?"

"Nate Marks."

I looked at the man standing facing me. Indeed a name tag on his jacket identified him as Nate. "But you're not Nate," I said. "Nate is about your height, but he has dark hair and eyes and he's very slender."

"I assure you, I am Nate Marks," the man said.

"What did you do with Nate?"

"I didn't do anything with him. I don't know anyone else by that na…" He looked at me again. "You met Jim, didn't you? I wondered what happened to him."

"Jim? No. I met Nate Marks, two years ago in Corpus Christi, Texas. He was copying pictures which he was selling as originals. When my friend saw your name and the ad for this show…" I was starting to hyperventilate and blather. Everything I had planned was crumbling like old plaster, lying in shards around my feet.

"You met a fellow named Jim. At least that's what he told me his name was." Nate looked around. "I can tell you his story, but I don't have time now. Can you meet me at Tavern on the Green tomorrow for lunch?"

"Sure," I said.

He held out his hand again. It was large and strong, not at all like Nate's slender one. Was it possible for me to stop thinking of the man I'd met as Jim and not Nate?

I took a cab back to the hotel and changed into my jeans and sweat shirt. In the dining room I ordered an overpriced hamburger with fries, and though I was hungry, I scarcely noticed what I ate. My phone rang. It was Wendy calling from California.

"Wendy," I said. "Just the person I want to talk to. I'm in New York City."

"Jeff told me," she said. "Actually Jeff told Rick and Rick told me. What are you doing there?"

"Tania told me that Nate Marks was having an art show here, and I came to see him."

"Kiki, I have to tell you that Jeff is very upset. He thinks that you want to ditch him and go back with an old boyfriend."

"It's nothing like that, Wendy. I just wanted to talk to Nate, that's all."

"Rick tried to convince Jeff not to break up with you. I'm not sure he was successful."

"Over a little thing like going to New York? "

"It's not a little thing, you know that. Rick told Jeff how close you were with Nate and now Jeff is very jealous."

"I don't want to hurt Jeff," I said slowly. "I didn't come to New York to go back with Nate Marks, just to see him. And as it turns out, Nate isn't even his real name."

"What do you mean? "

"The guy I met in Corpus Christi is named Jim. I'm going to meet the real Nate Marks for lunch tomorrow, and he's going to tell me about Jim, so if Jeff is still jealous, he's jealous of a phantom."

"I'll talk to Rick. I'm sorry about this mess."

"I am too. Thanks for the call."

The next morning I met with Nate Marks at Tavern on the Green. The Tavern was in Central Park, surrounded by beautiful flowers. It was like stepping into a garden to eat there.

Nate told me about meeting a young man named Jim in Washington Square Park, Greenwich Village when they were both in their twenties.

“I wanted to become an artist, so I convinced Jim to take my place in class.”

“And he did this?”

“With some reluctance. I think he thought it was a scam. I gave him my student I.D. and took off for Europe to paint. I owe him my career. If you ever see him again, tell him thank you from the bottom of my heart." Nate took a sip of his orange juice. "So why are you looking for this guy?"

"I don't know really. I was attracted to him. But then he disappeared from Corpus."

"Without a forwarding address." Nate said.

"Don't say anything. I know what you're thinking. Loser girl goes chasing after a guy who wants nothing to do with her."

"Actually that wasn't what I was thinking. I was remembering that about twelve years ago I got this envelope from New York University. It was a paycheck for Nate Marks. Apparently the college had tried to pay Nate for a job he was doing, but he left town before they could do it. They forwarded the pay check to Florida, and then somehow it came back to me. The address was in care of a guy named Ernest Horner."

"Do you still have the envelope?"

"I think so. Give me your address and I'll mail it to you."

I gave him my Port A address. My plane was leaving in a few hours and I had to get to the airport.

"Good luck," Nate Marks said as I hurried out.

I got back from New York City the next day and there was an e-mail from Jeff. He wanted to meet for coffee so I could tell him all about my trip. I didn't know if I wanted to tell Jeff the details of the disaster. Nate Marks was a nice man, and his story about Jim allowing him to become an artist, was moving, but it didn't bring me any closer to the man I was looking for.

I put on a T-shirt and shorts and presented myself at the cafe. Jeff was sitting at a table on the sidewalk with a cup of coffee in front of him. I sat down and without looking at him, ordered a drink of my own.

"How was the trip?"

"Nice," I said. "New York city is noisy and crowded, but full of energy. I had time to see Rockefeller Center and I walked through the Museum of Modern Art but didn't go in."

"Kiki," he began.

"Jeff," I interrupted. If we were going to do this, I would make the pre-emptive strike.

"I think we should see other people. I've been thinking about us, and even though you're a great guy, we both need a break."

He looked stunned. Had that been what he'd expected? I watched as a slow smile spread across his face, replaced almost instantly by a serious expression as he remembered what we were doing.

"I've enjoyed going out with you" he said, standing up. "If you ever want someone to talk to or to go to a game with, give me a call. Just as friends." He reached down, chugged his coffee, turned and walked away.

That wasn’t so hard, I thought, as I rummaged through my feelings looking for regret. There wasn't any. Instead there was a sense that I had recovered something essential that had been lost. I looked around the café. Most of the folks were single, sitting with newspapers or cell phones, and drinking coffee. How many of these men and women had just broken up with a guy they'd been seeing for months? How many were happy about it, or maybe more specifically, not unhappy? I would certainly miss walking the beach with Jeff on Saturday morning, or tucked into bed beside him, reading the Sunday papers. But I was not going to lie awake at night longing to see his face again. But now that I'd tossed away the only eligible man I'd been with in a year, I was back to square one, watching Netflix by myself on Friday night or going to a bar on Saturday and watching the couples snuggling in the corner. I was facing a future where I had to listen to Tania talk about how much in love she was and wishing it could be me. I should have thought this thing through before I tossed Jeff away. My phone rang. It was Wendy calling from California.

"How are you?" she asked.

"Not so good. I just broke up with Jeff."

"Broke up with him? But why, Kiki. He's a nice guy."

"I know he is. He just didn't seem right for me."

"He's smart, he makes good money, he doesn't cheat on you. Kiki are you nuts?"

"Probably. Wendy when you were first going out with Rick how did you know he was the one the one you wanted to be with?"

"Oh gosh, let me think. He wasn't the best looking guy I'd ever seen, but he was funny. He made me laugh. And he seemed to be really interested in who I was as a person, not just in how I looked. He made me feel good about myself."

I thought back to my time with Jeff. We'd had fun together, but most of the activities we'd done were things that were Jeff's pleasures, not mine. He was, in Wendy's words a good catch, but he wasn't the catch I was fishing for.

"This is about that guy Nate, isn't it?" Wendy said. "No wait, what did you say his real name was?"

"Jim. I don't know his last name."

"So you've thrown over a perfectly good man, for someone whose real name you don't know, a man who has lied to you, who cheated people and then ran away. Is there anything just a little bit absurd about this picture?"

"When you put it that way, I guess I should check myself into the funny farm right now."

"It's not too late to call Jeff and tell him you're sorry."

"I know," I said. But I knew I wouldn't do it.

Part II
Jim

Chapter Eighteen

New York City, 2000

I met Little Jack when I was thirteen. Little Jack's real name was Earnest but because his last name was Horner, everyone thought it fun to rename him.

For reasons I won't mention here, I had run away from home at twelve, making my way to New York City where for the past year, I'd been living on the street. Sleeping out in the open and eating from dumpsters is a dangerous way of life, but it was the only way I could stay alive. At some point in my time on the street, I'd acquired two things, the first was a sharp knife which helped me keep away predators who wanted me, my squatting spot or my personal possessions. The second acquisition was the ability to lift money from pocketbooks left ajar by unsuspecting women.

On the evening that I met Little Jack, I had just lifted the purse from a drunken woman in a bar on MacDougal Street. I dashed into the men's room, and after taking out the money, I threw the purse in the trash can. I was standing outside the door, wondering whether I could get away with buying a drink, when a man came out of the men's room behind me. I moved out of his way, but instead of pushing past me, he grabbed me by the arm and muscled me to a table in the corner.

"How old are you kid?" he asked, keeping a firm hand on my shirt.

"Sixteen," I said. I always lied about my age.

"And where are you living?"

"Spencer Street." I had once lived on Spencer Street, just not here.

"Bullshit," he said. "You're a ten-year-old pickpocket who's homeless. Your shopping cart is parked in the alley behind this bar."

I could have protested, but he had me. The most galling thing about being found out was he'd got my age wrong. "I'm not ten," I said. "I'm thirteen."

He nodded, looking me over. "I need a boy," he said.

Kids on the street are used for all kinds of reasons, most of them sexual. I shook my head and struggled to get away, but the man had me firmly.

"It's not what you're thinking," he said. "You're not pretty enough for that."

He loosened his hold on my shirt, but when I started to move away he put his hand on my arm.

"Let me buy you a drink."

I watched as he went to the bar and came back with two beers. While he was doing that, I took out my knife and laid it beside me on the table. I didn't care if this guy saw it. It was fine if he bought me a drink, not so fine if I were going to be kidnapped.

The guy returned to the table with two beers, setting one in front of me. He held out his hand to shake mine. "Ernest Horner, " he said. "Folks call me 'Little Jack'. What do they call you?"

"Jim," I said.

"Well, Jim. Here's the story. I need an accomplice for my work. My last partner had an unfortunate accident with a couple of bullets and I find myself shorthanded." He moved closer so we were nose to nose. "How much did you get from the wallet?"

"What wallet?"

"Come on, boy. Don't lie to me. I saw you snatch it."

"Eighty dollars," I said.

"Is eighty dollars worth juvvie? That is if you're lucky enough to be sent to juvvie and not to an adult prison?"

I didn't want to have this conversation. All I wanted to do was go to the Y and have a shower and buy supper somewhere. But Little Jack had his hand firmly on my arm.

At that moment, our attention was diverted by the owner of the stolen wallet who was at the bar arguing loudly with the owner over the bill. She was still drunk and starting to weep, but the owner wasn't buying her sob story, and was threatening to call her husband, which caused her to cry harder, wailing that it was his credit card she'd lost.

"Watch and learn," Little Jack said, pulling from his pocket the wallet I'd ditched in the trash can fifteen minutes earlier. He got up from the table and went over to the bar. I ducked under the table. If he were going to turn me in, I would try and get a head start out of the place.

"Madam," he said approaching the woman. "I think this happens to be yours. I discovered it just now at the entrance to the ladies' washroom."

She turned and threw her arms around him, bursting into a fresh round of tears. "Let me reward you," she said opening the wallet. When she discovered that the cash was missing, she pulled out a credit card and handed it to the bartender. "This is for the bill, and give me an extra hundred." Little Jack retreated to the table and pulled me up beside him. "Pay attention," he said. In a few minutes the woman came over and handed Jack two twenties and a ten. "I can't thank you enough," she said. "You not only saved my cards, but you saved me from having to explain to my husband why I lost everything." She moved forward to kiss him again, but Jack ducked out of the way.

When she was gone, I whispered, "How do you know she won't turn us both in once she sobers up?"

"Did I tell her my name?" Jack asked. "Did she threaten me? I was her knight in shining armor. At some point she will realize that she lost a lot of money tonight, but right now, she is happy. By the time she is unhappy, we will be long gone. Now, is there anything in that sorry kit parked in the alley that you want to keep? If so, get it now."

I hesitated.

"I'm offering you a job," Jack said. "You got anything better lined up?"

I did not. And I still had my knife just in case Jack tried to pull something. I went to my shopping cart and got some clothing. Everything important, the plastic bag with my mother's photo and some cash was securely on my person. I followed Jack down the street, keeping my knife at the ready, and trying to memorize where we were going in case I needed to hoof it back to my cart. Jack and I walked for a few blocks until we were in a neighborhood of modest brownstones interspersed with small grocery stores, laundromats, and pawn shops. We paused before one building that had once been a fine home, and went up the steps to the grubby entrance. I followed him up the stairs and down the hallway until we arrived at two doors, situated like the point of a V. Jack unlocked the left hand door.

"Home sweet home," he said, waving me toward the inside of the apartment. I still wasn't sure what was going on. He could get me inside, lock the door and do what he wanted.

"You first," I said. Jack led the way into the apartment and we were in a modest kitchen, with a sink (covered with a piece of plywood to create a counter), a refrigerator, and a table with chairs on either end. To my left was a small living room with a desk holding a computer and a strange machine, a small TV on a table and two overstuffed chairs. To the right, on the other side of the kitchen was a bedroom with an enormous double bed, a plywood wardrobe and a two-drawer dresser. Beyond the bedroom was a bathroom. The whole apartment consisted of four rooms, laid end to end so that you had to pass through one room to get to another.

"This is what they call a railroad apartment," Jack said. "Not many of these rent controlled places left in Manhattan, and a lot of them still have the toilets outside in the hall. Want something to eat?"

Without waiting for my answer, he opened the refrigerator door and pulled out a packet of hamburger and a plastic tub which he opened, sniffed at and threw into the garbage."

"A hamburger OK?" I nodded.

He went to the cupboard and took out two glasses and a bottle of Jack Daniels. "Whiskey?"

"No thanks," I was only thirteen, but I didn't feel thirteen, I felt forty or fifty. What the heck. "A small shot," I said.

When the hamburgers had cooked, we sat at the table eating.

"Why are you doing this, Jack?" I asked. He hadn't made a move on me and though I still had my knife, I was starting to think that maybe he was legit when he said he needed someone to work for him. "You don't know me. I could be dangerous."

He snatched the knife from the table. "You gonna stab me in my sleep, kid? I've dealt with worse than you."

I took a sip of my drink and felt it burn its way down my throat. "I'm pretty good with that knife, " I said.

"I'll bet you are. How long you been on the street?"

"A year."

"A tough guy, are you?"

I could feel my heart beating fast, and I was starting to sweat. Jack still had my knife and was twirling it around in his hand. He sunk it into the hamburger and blood spurted out.

"I guess you deserve an explanation. I need a kid to work for me. I've been looking for a month or so, but haven't seen anyone that fits the bill."

“You don't have to put me up here," I said. "In your own house."

"I’m supposed to house you in the Marriott downtown? Nope. I need to keep an eye on you. Make sure you don't bolt back to the street."

"That's it? I'm your prisoner?"

"Not my prisoner. If you’re gonna work for me, you need to be clean and on time I can only make sure that's the case if I have you where I can see you."

"What if I decide I don't like the job?"

He sighed. "I hope you won't do that, but I'm not holding you to anything. Hell, you are free to walk out right this minute." He pulled the knife from the hamburger, wiped it off and handed it back to me. "Your cart might still be in the alley."

I knew there was something that Jack wasn't talking about. Something he had seen in me that made him want to give me the job. He was offering me secure shelter and regular meals, something I'd not had before.

"OK," I said. "I'll take the job."

"Let me tell you my rules," Jack said. "The first rule of business is to have confidence. Walk into a room like you are the equal of anyone there. People can read fear, they can read insecurity, so don't ever project that. Second rule of business is to be polite. Say 'please' and 'thank you'. Look people in the eye when you talk to them. Let the other person do the talking, especially if that person is a woman. If you're with a woman, open doors for her, carry her bundles, give her compliments. Those things cost you nothing, but they reap huge benefits. You want people to trust you. They won't trust you if you're not a nice person, or if you don't trust yourself. Third rule of business is to look nice. We're not all born beautiful, but being clean and dressing snappy can go a long way. Looking like a bum and smelling like a bum will not get you into the world I'm gonna introduce you to. So tonight, you're going into that bathroom and take a long shower with lots of soap and tomorrow we'll go shopping."

My head was reeling from all these rules. I still had no idea what my job was going to be but so far I'd been given food and had been offered a bath. I looked toward the bed that dominated the bedroom. "Is that where I sleep?"

"No sirree," Jack said. He went to one of the overstuffed chairs and pulled off the seat cushion. Then he unfolded the chair so it became a single bed, already made up with sheets and a blanket.

"That's your bed," he said. "Now take a bath. And one more thing. You have to walk through the bedroom to pee, but iffen I'm entertaining in there, you are not to enter that bedroom under any circumstances." He pointed to the sink. "In that case, your toilet is there."

I nodded. I was grateful for a bed, a meal and a chance at a profession. My new life had begun.

Chapter Nineteen

New York City, 2000

I woke to the smell of coffee and the sizzle of bacon. For a moment I luxuriated in the feeling of being indoors, in a real bed, with a good breakfast waiting. I would do whatever Little Jack asked, just to stay here. With any luck this could be a permanent gig.

"Rise and shine, boy," Jack said. "Rise and shine." I got up from the bed and looked around. On the desk beside me were half a dozen credit cards: Diner's club, American Express, Master Card. I picked one up. It looked real.

"Courtesy of our lady friend last night," Jack said. "Now make the bed and go take a shower."

"You stole her credit cards?'

"Never do that, boy. Get the numbers and make your own. The mark will notice a missing card right away, but it takes them a while to notice that you've stolen the numbers and are spending their money."

I was returning the bed it to its former purpose as a chair. Jack put a shirt, pants, undershirt, shorts, socks and shoes on the chair. "I threw away that crap you were wearing," he said. "Until we get you kitted out, these will have to do."

After I'd had a bath, and changed into the clothes I sat down to breakfast, with Jack rattling on about what we were going to do. He'd taken out a pad of paper.

"What's your name, boy?"

"Jim. Jim Slocum." James was actually my middle name, and Slocum the name of my stepfather, but names are personal items, and I wasn't ready to share.

"Birth date?"

"January 10, 1987."

"Birthplace?"

"Oklahoma." All of that was true.

"Social Security number?"

"I never had one."

"Not to worry. In this line of work, you'll never collect social security anyway. Which brings me to another point. Where's the money you made last night?"

"It's mine, I earned it."

"So you did, my boy. And I promise you that I'll never take anything from you that you have earned. Do you believe me?"

I wasn't sure I did. But so far, Jack had been fair. He'd given me a place to sleep, fed me and he'd promised me a job. I went to the plastic bag that was my wallet and laid it on the table.

Little Jack opened the bag and took out the picture? "Your Ma?"

I nodded. "She's a good looking woman," he said. "You look like her. We'll buy you a

wallet today. Every man needs a wallet to carry his money."

He counted out the eighty dollars, returned it to the plastic bag and handed the bag back to me, and I tucked it gratefully into my pocket. Picking up the empty plates he went to the sink and began washing up the dishes. "Today we'll get you an identity. If you want to look legit, you need a card. You're too young to drive, so we'll have to figure something besides a driver's license. After we get you ID's, we'll go to the bank and open an account for you. It will be your money, Jim, not mine, and whatever you earn, you keep. You don't get a retirement income in this line of work, in fact, you'll be lucky not to spend your twilight years in a cell, but you've got to have a bank account. It will tide you over in the lean times."

Our first stop that morning was to a man identified only as Bennie who ran a little print shop off James street. He took my picture and said he would make up a realistic looking identity card, and a social security card with numbers that would never be questioned. Then we went to a barber, who cut my hair and polished my nails. Our last stop was a men's shop on Fifth Avenue. I hesitated at the door.

"Confidence, Jim," Jack said. "Confidence and charm."

We entered. It was one of those swank shops where fellows in expensive suits are hanging around waiting to suck up to any customer with money. Little Jack had on a nice suit, but he didn't look rich. But these guys had learned that even an ordinary Joe could have some dough, so they were polite.

"May I help you, sir?"

"You certainly may," Jack said. "I'm here to outfit my boy with some togs. My son has just returned from Thailand, where he was living with my ex-wife and has come woefully unprepared for New York weather. What have you got that will fit him?"

They fussed around me while I tried on a variety of clothing from casual to Saville Row and in the end we walked away with about twelve hundred dollars worth of clothing, all courtesy of Mr. Roger Wing, the husband of the lady whose wallet I'd lifted.

"You hungry?" Jack asked as we left the shop.

I'd had a good breakfast, and I wasn't used to eating three squares, but if this gig ended soon, at least I would have something in my belly.

We ducked into Herman's Deli, which according to Jack made the best corned-beef sandwiches in New York City. We took a seat in the back. It was one o'clock and the place had recently emptied of diners.

"Who's the squirt?" a man asked almost as soon as we sat down.

"This here is Jim Slocum, my new assistant."

"What happened to Slick Charlie?"

"The owner caught him robbing a Mom and Pop. Thought he wasn't making enough with me. I expect you read about him in the papers."

The man nodded, sitting down beside me and looking me over. "He looks awful young, Jack." he said.

"He's smart, and I need someone young and believable. The marks don't buy you old guys anymore."

The man nodded and held out his hand to me. "Squeaky Al," he said. He turned to Jack. "You gonna show him Monte?"

"Sure," Jack said. "Where's your deck?"

Al pulled out a deck of cards. Jack took the cards and riffed them. "It's not a bad job, Al. If I didn't know they were there, I'd miss them." He took a card and put it face down beside me, so I was looking at the pattern on the back. "Look at the lines surrounding the blue diamonds. Right there is an inked spot, which marks it as a queen." I looked closely. I could barely see it and if I weren't studying the card, I wouldn't have noticed it at all. He turned the card over. It was the queen of hearts.

"It's not hard to spot a marking job." He took the cards and riffled them in front of me and the tiny marks on the back of the cards danced. "You know those toys where you riffle through a bunch of drawings and the mouse dances. We call this 'Going to the Movies.'

I had finished my lunch, and Jack pushed the plates to another table. "Now," he said. "The oldest con in the world. Three Card Monte."

Jack shuffled the cards and then laid three cards side by side on the table. He turned them over. On the left side was the five of clubs, in the center was the queen of spades and on the right the seven of spades. "Your job is to find the queen," he said, turning the cards over, flipping them back and forth, and switching the ones on the left to the right, until I was dizzy. He stopped to show me the queen. "Find the queen" he bellowed.

A couple of people had come over to watch, and a girl said. "I know where it is." She threw down a five dollar bill and pointed. Jack picked up the bill and then lifted up the card. It was the five of clubs. "It's there," another fellow said. He pointed. Jack lifted up the card. It was the queen. "But you didn't bet," Jack said. "So you lose."

"Ten will get you thirty," Jack said and the fellow who'd picked the right card without betting threw down ten dollars. *This is easy*, I thought. *Anyone can make money at it.* Jack threw down the three cards, and I watched as he moved them around. Finally, he stopped. The man pointed to a card. It was a Queen. Jack handed him thirty dollars.

"Ready to try?" Jack asked me. "Let's see your money." I dug out my plastic bag and pulled out a ten-dollar bill. "Ten will get you thirty," Jack said. "Twenty will get you fifty." I had a twenty-dollar bill, but I wasn't sure. I went with the ten. Jack started flipping cards. At one point he stopped and turned them over to show me the queen, and then he started moving them around again. I was sure I knew where the queen was. He stopped, put the three cards on the table. I pointed. "You sure?" I nodded. He turned it over; it was the five of clubs.

"Anyone else?" Jack asked. A man stepped up. "Let's see your money," Jack said and the man put a twenty on the table.

"Twenty will get you fifty," Jack said. "Let's see how good you are." He flipped the cards around on the table, once stopping to show the man the queen and then starting again. The man chose the wrong card and lost his twenty. We'd been playing the game for twenty minutes, and Jack had accumulated close to a hundred dollars, less the thirty dollars he'd paid out in winnings. Jack looked at me. "It gets more complicated, but that's the basics of it."

By now the crowd had disbursed. The man who'd won the thirty, came and sat down beside Jack.

"Meet Peewee," Jack said. "He's my shill, the man who makes the game look winnable. Sometimes I use him as a roper." He reached into his pocket and returned the ten to me. "No one ever wins at Monte, kid. I hope this is the only time you'll ever play it."

We sat at the table for a while longer, Jack and Pewee apparently went back a long way.

"Remember the big con we ran in Pittsburgh in 1980?" Peewee said. "We set up a shop on one hundred-twenty-second street; George was the inside man and I was the roper. We had this Australian businessman who we took for five hundred thousand."

Jack was nodding. "He caught up with you in the city three years later."

"I almost pissed myself," Peewee said. "I thought for sure, he would turn me into the screws, but all he wanted was to play again. It had taken him three years to save the money and he was ready to lose it all again."

"I haven't got the energy for the big con," Jack said. "Besides, you know what they say."

"If you're looking to make easy money …" Peewee said.

"Go into politics," they said in unison.

"What happened to Moira? Is she playing the badger game?"

Jack shook his head. "Haven't seen her," he said. He looked down at his coffee. "She was a nice kid, but you know this life can be hard on a woman."

"I hope she's not hooking."

"She's too smart for that."

Jack paid for our food and we went out into the sunlit afternoon on our way to the bank and to home.

"Don't just think of Monte as gambling," Jack said. "It's theatre. It’s a slight of hand. People lose a little but they get a lot of fun for their dough. How many times has someone invested in a stock that went belly-up, or bought an appliance only to have it crap out when it's too late to take it back? Every one of us wastes money and what do we get for that wasted cash? Nothing. The people who played today got their money's worth."

"What's my part in all of this?"

"I might use you as a roper, the one who brings people in, or the shill. I'm going to see how it goes. You're a smart kid and I think you can win folks over." We had reached the bank. "Come on, we're going to open up an account."

Chapter Twenty

New York City, 2002

On Friday evening, Jack and I headed downtown to the Ambassador Hotel, one of those aging queens that hang on near Times Square, a place where most businessmen stay. Businessmen were easy marks, Jack explained They are mostly male, away from their families, but on vacation. They're bored because they've been sitting in a room all day, being yammered at and are looking for some fun.

"We are that fun," Jack said.

We entered by the lobby and went into the bar where four men were sitting. I could see Peewee sitting at the bar, a few stools away.

"Evening fellows," Jack said, standing behind the men. "How's it going?"

The men nodded but said nothing. One of them had his arms crossed in front of his chest, and another was sitting back in the chair, his hands behind his head. Guy number one didn't trust us and number two wanted to be in charge.

"Mind if I join you?" Jack asked. No one said a word. "Bring me a whiskey and soda," Jack said to the bartender, "and a coke for the kid." He pulled out his pack of cards and began riffling them on the bar.

"What do you call a man who never farts in public?" he asked. The men shook their heads. "A private tooter. Two bananas were sitting on the river bank when a turd floats by. The turd says 'Come on in fellows, the water's great.' One banana turns to the other and says, 'Do you believe that shit?'"

All the while he was talking, Jack was shuffling, I watched a guy whose nametag identified him as Glen, the one who'd been sitting with his hands behind his head. He was leaning toward Jack, watching the cards.

"Where you from?" Jack asked.

"Oklahoma City," one man said. Another man said "Actually the company is in Oklahoma City; I'm from Antelope." I looked at him, startled. Did this guy know about my grandfather's feed and grain store, and would he recognize me? I'd left home two years ago and I'd grown some since then. I waited but he seemed more intent on the cards than on me.

"So how is Oklahoma City?"

"Crappy," crossed-arms, whose name was Pete, said. He looked over at the boss, as though gauging permission and said, "I thought New York would be fun."

"We got the same winter you have," Jack said. He laid down three cards and turned them over so we could see the queen of hearts between the five of clubs and the seven of diamonds. "I'm gonna shuffle the cards, turn them over and then you guess where the queen is. Ten will get you twenty."

He started flipping cards. "Two muffins were sitting in an oven," he began. "The first muffin says to the second, 'Is it hot in here or is it just me?' The second muffin says, 'Oh my God, a talking muffin.' He stopped moving the cards. "I know where it is," Pete said.

"Let's see your money," said Jack.

Pete pulled a ten from his wallet and laid it down. Jack picked it up and turned over the card. It was the seven of diamonds. He looked at the men. "Anyone else?"

By this time Peewee had moved over to join the group. "Let's play over there," he said pointing to a table in the corner.

"Who's buying the rounds?" Jack said. A fat guy with white hair named Arnold pulled out a credit card. "You don't have to leave the table," Jack said. "We'll send the kid."

They moved to a table in the corner. "You know what the Mexican fireman named his two kids?" Jack asked beginning to flip the cards. "Jose and Hose B."

I walked toward the bar. My job was to copy down the numbers from the card and then buy the drinks. The bartender would deliver the drinks, return the card and get the signature. All legit looking. I ducked into the bathroom to copy the numbers, but like a slow motion movie, my mind went back to Oklahoma.

"You're a lazy shit, you know that?" My grandfather was yelling. He and I were in the back of the store. I was nine and my afternoon job was to haul fifty pound sacks of bird seed, soil, grain and cement to the customer's trucks.

He cuffed me hard on the back of the head. "If it weren't for your grandmother, I'd have let you rot in an orphanage." He cuffed me again. I tried to move away from the blows, but he was taller and stronger and he had me cornered.

"I'm doing you a favor boy, don't you forget it. I'm the one that feeds you, buys your clothes and let you sleep in a bed. I'm the one that gives you a job." He turned and walked toward the front of the store. I picked up the sack of bird seed, thinking that if I had a knife I would shove it into his back. But I had nothing. My mother had left and never returned and the only relatives I had were my father's parents. Sometimes, at night, I'd sit in bed and look at her picture and wonder how could she have loved me and still left me in this hell.

I came out of my reverie, realizing that Jack and the guys would be waiting for their drinks and the longer I took, the more suspicious they would become. I went to the bar and gave the barkeep the card. He hardly looked up. In a few minutes, he followed me to the table with the drinks.

"A Polish man went to have his eyes checked," Jack was saying as we got close. "The eye doctor asked him to read the bottom line of the chart. 'Read it?' the Polish man said, 'I think I know the guy."

By the end of the evening we'd taken the four men for close to six hundred dollars, of which Peewee got a quarter. We began what would be a routine. On Monday and Thursday we would be at the Ambassador, on Wednesday we were at the Hilton and on Saturday, we went to a small, exclusive club, The Lion, close to Fifth Avenue, where we would play in a pricey little bar off the main lounge. On Sunday, like God, we rested. From September through November we worked the game in New York City and then we went to Florida for the winter, carrying the game with us on the train. We'd stay in Florida until April then we returned to New York where we worked businessmen for two months. In June we took the train north to the Catskills to a string of hotels that catered to New Yorkers anxious to get away from the city. There we fleeced sunburned Dads up from the city for the weekend, or anyone eager to have a little fun.

At the end of the first year I'd saved enough to rent the little apartment opposite Jack's. I was sick of being exiled from the bathroom when Jack was entertaining and at fourteen, I was beginning to contemplate some entertaining of my own. Another year went by. At fifteen I was tall enough to be taken for an adult and that was the year I met Moira.

Chapter Twenty One

Miami, Florida, 2002

The first time we went to Florida from New York City I was struck by how artificial the whole thing seemed. Even traveling by train, where we went gradually from the unrelenting grey of early winter through the greenness of the Southern states, the brilliant, synthetic ambiance of Florida hit me between the eyes. It wasn't just the girls, parading around the pool in the smallest bits they could find to cover their essentials, it was the surf on the beach, the fresh fruit and flowering plants everywhere. All of this lucent resplendence, meant that for the first few days, I peered at the world through glare-impaired sight.

But I got used to it. I got used to the elderly men in their Hawaiian shirts, with their skinny legs sticking out from under their shorts, and brimmed hats hiding their baldness. They would hang around the hotel pool, ogling the girls, or crowding the bar at night, hoping to pick up someone. Old men are good for business. They're rich. They're bored. They think they can beat the odds and once they're snared, they hang on long after a smarter fellow quits. I actually got to like some of these guys who were marooned in a half-life where they'd lost a spouse and were a long way from a job that gave them stature and respect. Too old to find someone new, too young to die.

We had only been in Florida for a few weeks and were about an hour into a Monte game at the Sunshine Hotel, when I looked up to see a stunning redhead walk into the room. She was wearing a green silk shirt, buttoned low to reveal a lot of her luscious breasts, palazzo pants and strappy heels. Her bright red curly hair floated like a cloud around her pale face and when I got closer I could see her green eyes. Stunning redheads did not frequent the sleazy bars in cheap hotels, where we did business. She came up to our group and put her arm on Jack's. He looked up.

"Moira, as I live and breathe. How are you?"

"Great," she said, sitting down beside him. She looked at me, "Who's the new guy?"

"Jim, my associate," Jack said. Moira held out her hand to mine. It was small and cool. "Glad to meet you, Jim." She looked at Jack. "Can I sit in?"

"Of course," Jack said. "We need some class in this joint."

Two of the men moved to give her room and she squeezed in between them. Already the atmosphere of the game had migrated up. Jack started up again.

"A pair of jumper cables walked into a bar. The bartender said, 'I'll serve you, but don't start anything.' A Mexican magician tells the audience he will disappear on the count of three. He says 'uno, dos' and then poof, he disappears without a tres. Ok, fellows, twenty will get you fifty. How bout you Ed, gotta get something out of this evening right? Twenty will get you fifty. Not bad for a single bid. Ok, you're in." I looked at Moira who had leaned into Ed, her right breast brushing his arm. Ed had turned a bright red and I was wondering if we'd have to do cardiac resuscitation before the night was over. She whispered something in his ear and he smiled. Even when he lost the bid, he seemed so dazed by her presence, that he hardly noticed.

I kept wondering why Moira was with schmucks like us, when she could have been fleecing high rollers in a better part of town. When we'd finished for the night, we sat in a corner with our drinks, Jack said. "Want to come back into the game, Moira?"

"I don't do Monte anymore Jack," she said.

He picked up the cards and started to shuffle them. "Let's see what you remember," he said.

He danced the cards from one hand to another, stopping once in a while to show the queen. Then he stopped and laid down the cards. Moira pointed. Jack picked up the card. It was the queen.

"You're reading the backs of the cards," he said.

"Of course. You taught me that yourself."

"Think about coming in," Jack said. She shook her head. Jack got out the cards and we played a few hands of poker for pennies, all of us too smart to trust real cash to the other.

The next night Moira showed up again at the bar. She was wearing a red dress that echoed the color of her hair. In her ears were pendant earrings and she wore a glittery bracelet. She was a classy dame and I was smitten.

Half way into the game I began to realize that Moira could be as much a distraction as she was an asset. Men fought to sit next to her, to have her whisper in their ear, or urge them to bet more. What these guys didn't realize was that Moira's affection wasn't personal; it was just part of the razzle-dazzle.

She'd been with us for about three weeks when she chose to sit next to a beefy guy named George. George was flashing cash like he was Santa Claus, buying rounds and betting high, unconcerned when he lost. He must have been trying to feel her up under the table, because once she slapped his hand, and later when his hands were under the table, she hit him again. "Do it again and you're on your own buddy," she said.

I wanted to step in and deck him. I'd become as protective of Moira, as if she were my own personal property, which she wasn't. But if we have one rule of the game, it is no violence at the table. We didn't want to draw attention to ourselves.

Eventually we cleaned George out. He wasn't very happy and as he walked away, I had the feeling he could be trouble. Moira excused herself to go the ladies room, and when she hadn't returned in twenty minutes I began to worry. Usually after we'd finished for the night, we'd gather in a corner, have another drink and divide up the winnings. Moira had certainly earned her share. Where was she?

I waited a few more minutes and went toward the lobby to look around. I asked a woman to check the ladies room, but Moira wasn't there. I walked outside the hotel and looked around. She wasn't there. I poked my head into the parking garage, saw a flash of red and remembered the dress Moira had been wearing.

Running toward the spot, I saw George's back hunched over someone who was struggling against him. Then I saw that he had Moira shoved up against the cement wall, his face pushed into hers.

"Get away from her," I yelled.

George turned and started to laugh. "You gonna rescue your mama, little boy."

I moved in and swung hard. Even though I was young, I was tall and strong, and he was soft and drunk. My fist connected with his nose and blood spurted.

He swung and missed. I swung again and got him square in his paunchy belly. He doubled over and I chopped the back of his neck so he was face down on the ground. Then I kicked him hard in the ribs.

He groaned and was quiet.

I turned to Moira. Her dress was torn, her hair tousled, and mascara was running down her cheeks where she'd been crying. I took off my jacket and wrapped it around her.

"I can't go back in there, Jim," she said. "I don't want them to see me like this. He was going to show me his new car and what I did was really dumb." She burst into another round of tears.

I led her from the parking garage to the lighted back entrance of the hotel and set her gently down on a seat. "Wait right there," I said. Then I went to the registration desk and got a room for the night. When I got back to the seat, she was still there. She'd cleaned herself up a little bit, but her lip was bleeding, and her nose running.

"Come on," I said. leading her to the elevator and walking her down the hallway to the room. I unlocked the door for her and held it as she went in.

"Thanks Jim," she said as we were standing in the doorway. "I'm not sure I'm in any shape to repay you tonight."

"I'm not looking for a reward," I said. "I just want you to be safe. I'll see you tomorrow."

She leaned toward me and kissed me on the cheek. Then she shut the door.

The next morning at ten, I knocked on the door. Moira answered it, wearing a terrycloth robe provided by the hotel. When I went inside, I saw that the bed was still unmade, the TV was on and a breakfast of eggs, bacon, hash browns, coffee and juice sat on the table.

"I ordered room service," she said. "I hope you don't mind."

I shook my head. All that mattered was that she was safe. She would have a nasty bruise on her neck where he'd tried to choke her, and a cut on her lip, but it looked like she would recover.

As if reading my mind, she said. "It could have been a lot worse. He was stronger than me. But you pack a mean punch. Been working out?"

"Some," I said. What else did I have to do with my days?

"I have a little problem," she said. She slipped the corner of her robe down to reveal a bare shoulder and an enticing sliver of breast. "Other than what I was wearing last night, I have nothing. Could you get me some clothes?" She pointed to a bra and panties thrown carelessly over a chair, and on the floor were the red dress and pumps she'd worn the night before. "You see the issue."

"I'm staying in a hotel downtown." She looked at me. "I would send you there to get clothes, but it's too far. Could you just go out and buy me a few things?"

I'd never ever shopped for a woman before, but for Moira, I would have walked naked down the middle of the street.

"Write down your sizes for me, and give me an hour."

I got a lot of strange looks at the stores, but once I explained that my sister was in the hospital having surgery and she'd not brought clothes to be released in, people were helpful. I purchased a red silk blouse, a pair of jeans, a couple of pairs of panties, socks and shoes. Since it was a bright, sunny day, I added some sunglasses and a straw hat. When I got back to the hotel, Moira was sitting on the bed watching TV, the breakfast things having been cleared away. Without her makeup she looked younger, and even with the cut lip and the bruised neck, she was still the most beautiful woman I'd ever seen.

"You did great, Jim," she said, when I laid out the clothes on the bed. "Let me go change."

When she emerged from the bathroom, she looked like a different person than the girl George had roughed up the night before. The shirt set off the color of her hair, and with the hat and the sunglasses, she looked like a young Rita Hayworth.

"Where should we spend the day Mr. Slocum, she said. "Can we go to the zoo, and then have lunch at Angelo's Italian Restaurant on the waterfront?"

I hadn't expected that we'd spend the day together, but it was wonderful. At the zoo, we laughed at the antics of the monkeys, studied the gorillas and watched the tiger pace back and forth in his cage.

"Tiger, tiger burning bright. In the forest of the night," she quoted.

"What immortal hand or eye, could frame thy fearful symmetry." I added

"Do you think William Blake ever saw a real tiger?" Moira asked. "Other than one in a zoo?"

"I don't know. But he caught the tiger's greatness and the fact that that greatness was being confined."

"Little Jack was right," she said. "You are pretty smart. Where did you go to school?"

"Nowhere really. I left home when I was twelve, and Little Jack rescued me when I was thirteen."

"How long ago was that?"

"Two years," I said.

She turned to look at me. "You're fifteen?"

I nodded. We'd been walking hand in hand, and she pulled away. "I am twenty seven, and I'm on a date with a fifteen year old. Don't get me wrong, you're smart, polite, and you clean up very well, but …"

"I'm fifteen," I finished.

We walked in silence for a moment more. "I can't do anything about my age," I said. "Just as you can't do anything about yours, but I'd like to be your friend, Moira."

She threw back her head and laughed. "Why not," she said. "I've done weirder things. I owe you a lot, Jim. You saved my ass last night, and I can't forget that. What the hell, let's just have a good time today and forget ages."

It sounded like a plan to me.

When we were sitting across from each other in the Italian restaurant, she said. "Where'd you grow up, Jim?"

"A little town in Oklahoma."

"And what did your folks do? I assume you had folks?"

"I did. At one time I had both, but my dad died when I was four, so it was basically my mother who raised me."

"And she's back in Oklahoma?"

"It's a long story."

She leaned forward. "I have time," she said.

"When I was seven my mother started a company that made jams and jellies which she sold to local restaurants. The company did pretty well and by the time I was nine she'd opened up a little shop where she sold her own stuff, and things like pickles, bread mixes and home-made candy. It was enough to keep us going, and she was looking to expand to a second shop."

"And…"

This part was hard, I hadn't said it often. "My mother met this guy, Gus Slocum and married him. At first he was nice to me, took me places, bought me stuff, you know the way you suck up to a kid, so you can get on the mother's good side. I didn't like him much and pretty soon, he and I were enemies, and he was turning my mom against me."

"So what happened?"

"They went away and never came back."

"They just disappeared?"

"I moved in with my grandparents. It was OK for a while, but my grandpop was a drinker, and he didn't like me. After my grandmother died, he started beating me up. When I was eleven, I took off and never looked back."

"So you lived on the street for a while?"

"Yup."

"Wow," she said. "I can't believe how…well…you turned out."

"Little Jack was good to me. I think of him like the dad I never had. He helped me grow up. What about you?"

She leaned back in her chair, toying with the straw from her drink. "I had a pretty normal childhood compared to yours. I grew up in a small town, Green Springs, in Florida. My dad was an auto mechanic and my mom waited tables. I had two siblings, both entirely normal, unlike me. My older sister Patsy, married an airline mechanic and they have two kids, my brother Randy is in the Navy. When I was growing up, I wanted something different than waiting tables, or popping out kids, but then I got married to this guy who had big dreams, but that's all they were. Just dreams. He talked good, but he didn't do squat to get ahead. I got married when I was eighteen, and we divorced when I was twenty-one."

"How did you meet Little Jack?"

"Let's see. I was working as a waitress in this bar in Hialeah. Yeah, that shows you how far I'd gotten away from my dreams. I was bored, looking for something to do, and Little Jack was doing his Three Card Monte shtick at a table in the corner. He'd drawn a small crowd and money was flying around. I watched him for a while, and I realized that he had some kind of secret, where he could win all the time. The next night when he was there again, I was off duty, but I snuggled up next to this big guy and urged him on getting him to put more money down. After the game was over, I went back to Little Jack and asked for my cut."

"You know what he said?"

I shook my head.

"You're too much of a distraction."

"I argued my case. I told him how much money he'd made that night, because I'd been keeping track, and I told him how much he would have made if I hadn't got the guy to bet everything. In the end he gave me fifty bucks and said he would hire me on. 'You know this is illegal?' he said, as he was leaving. I didn't care. I'd been working as a waitress, had done some time selling food at the dog tracks, and I figured maybe illegal would be more profitable than legal. We moved around the state, always working at night. Sometimes, if the players were big spenders and wanted something more serious, we'd play poker instead of Monte. I didn't make much that first year, but it was a living, and I was having fun."

We finished our meal and I paid. Then we walked two blocks to the Cinema where Alfred Hitchcock's *Strangers on a Train* was playing. Halfway through the movie we started kissing, and I had just gotten to unfastening her bra when she pulled away.

"Jesus, Jim," she said. "We can't do this."

It seemed we were already doing it. "Why not." I had a terrific hard on and I didn't want to stop.

"You're too young for me, or I'm too old for you." She straightened out her clothing and stood up. "I'm going home."

She strode out of the theatre and hailed a cab. I was trying desperately to get myself together. "Can I drop you somewhere?" she asked, when the cab pulled up.

I shook my head. Walking the three blocks to the subway, would give me the time I desperately needed to clear my head.

The next evening Moira didn't show up. She'd said her hotel was downtown, but I didn't know where. When the Monte game was done for the night, I asked Jack if he had an address for the hotel, and he pulled something out of his book. The following day I went there.

Moira had left no forwarding address. She had blown away like dandelion fluff that moves effortlessly on the air. My heart was broken, and I couldn't believe that I would never see her again. I was so down in the dumps, that even Jack noticed.

"She'll be back, kid. Moira is like that. One day she's gone and the next she's sitting there, acting like she's never been away. Go to a rock concert, spend some time on the beach. Find a girl your own age and get laid."

He was being kind, but meeting a girl my own age wasn't what I wanted. I wanted Moira, a woman twelve years older than I was. I wanted to hear her laugh; I wanted to put my arm around her waist as we walked down the street or watch her eyes light up. When your heart is caught on someone, there isn't a single other person that will unhook you. Only time can do that.

Chapter Twenty Two

New York City, 2006

It was late August, and we'd just returned to the city from the Pocanos. I was trying to get used to the heat, the crowding, the dirt and the boredom of the game. When you are in this profession, boredom is a dangerous trait. You might have played this game a thousand times and you know just what the marks are gonna do, but you gotta make it fresh and fun. And the other thing is, that as drunk and doozy as these shmucks are, there could be, among them a cop waiting to nab you. So, you stay awake, keep your wits about you, make it look like a fun game and in spite of your boredom, push through.

It was afternoon and I was sitting on a bench in front of a duck pond. A couple of kids were throwing bread at the ducks, bonking the ducks on the heads as soon as the birds came within eating distance while a pregnant woman who looked terminally bored herself, watched them with a lazy maternal fondness.

Someone sat down beside me on the bench, a tall kid, about my age with a head of bright, curly red hair.

"Hell of a day, isn't it?"

I nodded.

He took something that looked like a credit card and tossed it casually toward the water. It landed just inches from the pond.

I stood up and went to the verge and picked it up. It was a student ID from New York University.

"Aren't you going to need this?" I asked. "It's for the current semester."

"You take it, " he said. "I'm not going back."

I turned the ID over in my hand. "What are you doing here in the middle of the day?" he asked. "You look like you should be in college yourself?"

People in New York City barely look at each other when they pass on the street. They certainly do not ask personal questions.

"Sorry," he said. "That was uncalled for." He held out his hand. "Nate Marks," he said.

"I know," I said. "It's on your ID."

"Today is my first day of college and I'm not going back" Nate said. "You're the first person I've said that to. I'm trying to get up the courage to tell my father." He looked at me. "Are you in school?"

"Nope. I work nights."

"I knew it. You're one of those dot-com millionaires who invented something in his father's basement when he was sixteen and now runs a company in Manhattan. What's your name?"

"Jim Slocum," I said. I didn't try to disabuse him about the dot-com millionaire thing which sounded kind of cool to me.

"Let me ask you something, Jim. Can I call you Jim? If your dad forced you to go to college to become a lawyer, when what you really wanted was to become an artist would you leave school and follow your dream?"

"Following your dream is over-rated," I said. "You need to earn a living."

"But you had a dream, didn't you? When you were down there in the basement, fiddling with whatever it was. Didn't you think school was a waste of time? And aren't there enough lawyers in the world?"

"The world always needs more lawsuits," I said. I looked at him. "You're giving up the chance for a college education to become an artist?"

"You got it," Nate said. "I withdrew the funds my father sent me and I'm flying to Rome tonight. I'm going to spend the semester studying the old masters in the great museums and painting."

"What will you do when your father finds out?"

"That's a bitch, isn't it? He's in Japan with his job, so it might be a few weeks before he checks in with me. And then he will be very, very angry. He'll probably hire some toughs to find me in Rome and haul me back to college." He looked at me. "Unless…"

"Unless what?"

"Unless you take my place. Have you ever been to college?"

I shook my head.

"There you go." He pointed at the ID card in my hand. "Wear a hat so they won't see your hair, and you'll need this." He rummaged in his backpack and pulled out a couple of sheets of paper. "This is your class schedule. The profs take attendance, so only go to the classes on that sheet. What else?" He took back the sheet and scribbled something on the corner. This is the website and passwords for the college internet system. You'll sometimes get readings and assignments that way."

"You never asked if I wanted to go to college," I said.

"Of course you do. I'm giving you a chance to do it for free."

"What about my job?"

"You said you work nights. Go to school in the daytime and work at night."

"Listen, Nate," I said. "I think you're making a big mistake, giving up college and all. And what if you change your mind? If I take a class as Nate Marks and you come waltzing into the classroom what will I say to the teacher?"

"I'm not going to do that," he said. He leaned toward me. "Jim. You are saving my ass. You're giving me a semester to find out if I can follow my bliss. If you're taking classes, the college won't be sending messages back to my father asking why I'm not in school. Hell, you don't even have to get descent grades. Just be there."

"I'm not sure," I said, even as the idea of taking college classes was worming its way under my skin.

"Here," he said, pulling a hundred dollars from his wallet and handing it to me.

"You're not going to change your mind?"

"No sir. You've given me a new life. I'm not backing out now."

He stood up. I expected that he would sit down, tell me this was all a joke and demand everything back. But he turned and began walking away. Was I crazy to do this, pretending to be another student, so I could take college classes? I watched Nate's retreating figure. He never turned around or looked back. Maybe he was really on his way to being an artist.

The next day I took Nate's student ID to Bennie, the man who had made my original identity cards.

"You gonna be college student, Jim?" He looked at the student ID. "Is this legit?"

I nodded. "I'll need a driver's license too. Just for extra identification."

"We'll need a current picture," he said. "And we should probably update your other cards. Are you old enough to drive yet?"

"I'm nineteen."

"OK, we'll make you a student ID for Nate Marks and a driver's license in the same name, so you can drink at the bar."

I was already drinking at the bars where Little Jack and I worked, but I didn't tell Bennie that.

"I'll need a driver's license for Jim Slocum, too," I said.

"You want two driver's licenses? "

"Yeah."

"Don't get 'em mixed up now. Better get two wallets, one for Jim, one for Nate." He went over to a table and started fiddling with a calculator. "Cost 'ya fifty bucks."

"Fifty bucks? Are you kidding?"

"You think I do this for free? I'm making up a new student ID with your picture and two driver's licenses. Where else can you get quality work like I do?" Reluctantly I pulled the money from my wallet and handed it to him.

"You a good boy, Jim," he said. "You gonna be a smart fella, going to college."

"I was hoping to pick up girls," I said.

"That too," Bennie said.

Bennie pushed me over to one side of the room and snapped a couple of pictures. "Be ready in three days," he said.

We shook hands and I went out the door. In a week I would officially be, not the rich city kid who had carelessly thrown his college ID onto the grass but a young man who'd always wanted an education and now was going to get one for free.

Four days later I headed over to the campus of New York University which was just off Washington Square Park. It was late August and I had no idea if school would even be in session. When I got to the front door there were lots of people milling about and I followed a group of them down the hallway.

A girl right in front of me was wearing a tight blue sweater, blue jeans that molded her rear end nicely and when she turned, I saw her light blonde hair and blue eyes. Maybe this wasn't such a crazy idea after all. I studied the list Nate had given me, and then catching up with the girl, got directions to my first class. The classroom was small, smaller that I wanted. I'd been hoping for a big classroom where I could hide in the crowd, but here I was exposed. Grabbing a seat beside a boy with blonde hair and zits, I tried to still my heart.

Most people seemed to know each other and were deep in conversation. The blonde guy to my left was talking with the person to his left and there was an empty seat to my right. The door opened and closed and a middle aged woman with grey hair walked in and took her place at the front of the room.

"Good morning," she said. "I'm Dr. Angela Weitz. Welcome to Psych 101." She took out a clipboard and scanned it. "Abrams," she read. A kid raised his hand. "Betterman?" Someone answered. "Marks?" She read a few more names. “Marks,” she read. I looked around. Would this be the time where the police would come and drag me out? I looked toward the door, wondering whether it was too late to duck out. "Marks," she said again. "Nate Marks."

"Here," I said.

When she'd finished taking attendance Dr. Weitz leaned back against the desk and scanned the classroom.

"I know all of you are new to college, so I'm going to remind you of a few rules. Don't worry about writing these down. They're on the website for this class. Number One: I am the one in charge, not you. Don't come to me asking me to change your grade or give you an extension on a paper. Those things are your responsibility, not mine."

"Number two: Learn to use a computer. If you don't know how to open a document or attach a file, or if you're confused about the university's internet system, ask a friend or hire someone to help you."

"Number three: Don't tell me how busy you are, as an excuse for why something is late. I'm not your mother, figure out how to manage your time."

"Number four: I see that most of you are taking notes on your computers. If I catch any of you texting your girlfriends or searching for porn on your device, that device will be taken away and you can get it at the end of class. Questions?" She looked around at the stunned freshmen. "Good."

She had reached toward a pile of papers on her desk.

"I've decided to do away with the textbook this semester, so if you've bought one, go back to the bookstore and get your money back. Instead," she began passing out Xeroxed sheets. "We're going to work from articles."

I looked at the Xeroxed article entitled *Perception and the Human Mind*. "By our next meeting I expect you will have read this thoroughly and we will discuss it."

I took out the notebook and pen I'd purchased that morning, and wrote Psych 101 at the top of the page. Writing in a notebook when half the class was putting their notes in some sort of electronic device marked me as a hopeless dweeb, but I didn't care.

"Human beings often perceive things differently than they actually are," Dr. Weitz was saying, "and the difference between actuality and perception is the subject of numerous studies. Take for instance confronting someone who is lying."

The kid to my left looked at me. "You're Nate Marks?" he whispered.

I nodded.

"Where'd you go to school?"

If I'd stayed in school at home I would have gone to Central High, but that seemed dorky. "Phillips Exeter," I said.

"With Farney the Faggot? "

I nodded.

"Mr. Henderson," Dr. Weitz said. She looked at me "Mr. Marks."

Beckoning to me, she said. "Come up here, young man."

My legs were shaking. "Since you obviously know more than I do about this subject, let's talk about perception. You're sitting in front of man and you need to make a judgment about him." She sat so she was facing me. "Sit down, Mr. Marks."

I sat.

"You suspect that the person sitting in front of you is lying, but you aren't sure. Tell me some of the things you would look for?"

I felt my confidence returning. Little Jack and I talked a lot about body language and we both used that knowledge to put up the mark when we played Monte.

Dr. Weitz was sitting with her arms crossed in front of her. "A person crossing her arms in front is protecting herself," I said. "She's got something to hide." I remembered my stepfather's statements that he loved me. "If a person is lying, he can be smiling with his mouth, but his eyes are telling a different story. And," I continued. "He protests that he's innocent (or in the case of my step-father, that he loved me). The person who's lying might fidget or talk about himself in the third person, or seem to have answers to your questions that he's memorized, instead of thinking about them. You got to soften him up, get him to relax, work your way under his defenses."

Dr. Weitz stood up from her chair. "Thank you, Mr. Marks."

I nodded and went back to my seat.

"Sometimes when a person is lying, not only do they try to protect themselves, crossed arms, crossed legs, but they will manifest their discomfort in other ways. They will lean back in a chair and put their hands behind their head, a 'power' move or they will spread their legs, taking up more space in the chair, daring you to mess with them."

"What about a lie detector?" a student asked.

"What a lie detector measures isn't necessarily lying. It measures fear. What you need to learn as a psychologist is whether that fear is there because the person is lying or because he's sitting in front of an authority figure who's asking questions. Understanding whether a person is lying is all about paying attention to human nature."

She talked for forty minutes more about human behavior, especially as it pertained to lying. When the clock reached the hour, she said. "That's it for today. See you next week."

There was movement in the classroom. Students were glancing at the clock, putting notebooks in backpacks, grabbing sweaters and drink cups. "Read the article," Dr. Weitz said, "We'll talk about it next time."

I was the first one out the door. I hadn't planned to be the star pupil the first day, and I wondered if I really wanted to go to college at all. Suddenly I felt someone grabbing the straps of my backpack.

"Marks, we need to talk."

It was the blonde guy who'd been sitting beside me. Henderson. "I've got another class," I said, pulling away.

"You don't have another class," the guy said. He had spun me around so we were facing each other. "I know because you're not Nate Marks."

My heart dropped to my stomach. I waved my ID in his face. "Look at this. It says 'Nate Marks.'

"You can fool Dr. Weitz, but you can't fool me. I knew Nate Marks, and you're not him."

I was screwed. The guy held out his hand. "Ziggy Henderson. Come on, let's get a coffee."

When we were sitting with our coffee Ziggy said. "You've got incredible balls, Marks. I've never known anyone who's taken a stolen ID and busted into college."

I took a sip of my coffee not knowing where this was going. Was he going to march me down to the registrar?

"I admire you, man," Ziggy said. "You were pretty smooth up there. If it were me, I'd be shitting myself for sure."

"How did you know?"

"There's no Farney the Faggot at Phillips Exeter," he said. "I know 'cause I went there. And you're not Nate because Nate was at Exeter with me. If you're going to lie for a living, get your story straight. Where *did* you go to school?"

"Central High in Oklahoma City," which was in itself a lie.

"A grunt? You're not living in the dorm?"

I shook my head.

He was smiling broadly. "Man," he said. "I've never met anyone like you, but I want to help you if only to see how this is gonna play out." He reached into his backpack and pulled out a piece of paper. "Here's a map of the school so you can get around." He pulled out another sheet. "There are lots of things going on: parties, movies, clubs. This map tells where they're meeting."

"Are these a good place to meet girls?"

"Someone having a kegger is a good place, but you'll learn."

I took the pages from him and put them in my backpack.

Ziggy stood up. "I've got Calculus," he said. He reached over and shook my hand. "Nice meeting you, Nate."

When he'd left I glanced at the map he'd given me. The campus wasn't large and it wouldn't take me long to learn everything. If the teachers took attendance, I'd be limited to what was on my sheet. It didn't matter. As long as I kept my cool, I was in.

It turned out that I enjoyed Psych 101. I suppose part of it was because I worked with the public (so to speak) and knew how to persuade people to part with their money, but the other part was living with a stepfather who saw me as an impediment to his romance and a grandfather, who hated me. In Psych 101, I could ponder the reasons why, with those two men, I'd always been the enemy,

At the end of the third week of classes, Dr. Weitz caught me at the end of a session. "Nate," she said. "Can you come to my office this afternoon?"

She knows, I thought. She's talked to the registrar and has seen the picture that was sent with the admissions material, and she knows I'm not Nate. But when I presented myself at the tiny, crowded cubicle that was her office, she asked me to sit. She didn't seem angry, so I waited.

"I've been looking for an assistant," she said finally. "It's not a big job, mostly making copies of the articles I'm handing out. I have to say I've been impressed by you, Nate. You come to class with your homework done. You ask good questions. You have a notebook." At this she smiled. "In fact, I think you're probably the only student in that class who writes things in a notebook."

"At any rate the job pays minimum wage, and you will be working about twenty hours a week. Would you like to work for me?"

I was stunned. "Sure," I said.

"Good," she said. "You need to go to the office and fill out a form so you can get paid and when you've done that, come back here and we'll talk about what I need you to do."

From then on I spent every Tuesday and Thursday afternoon (a time when I had no classes) Xeroxing articles and delivering them to Dr. Weitz' office. Sometimes when I'd go back, she'd still be there working on her computer, and once in a while she'd talk. She told me that her husband was a detective with the NYPD and they often had conversations about criminals. When she retired from teaching in five or six years, he would retire too and they would move to Georgia where her grown daughter lived. "And what about you?" she asked. "Where did you grow up?"

"Oklahoma," I said. “My father died when I was small. My mother raised me.”

Dr. Weitz was nodding. "She must be very proud of you," she said.

"She is," I lied.

"Well then, Nate," Dr. Weitz said, glancing at the clock. "I need to be getting home. I'll see you next week."

Chapter Twenty Three

New York City 2006

October drifted toward November when the semester would end. One day Dr. Weitz announced that there would be mid-year exam in two weeks encompassing everything we'd learned since the beginning of the semester, and that this exam was listed on the syllabus. "If you've kept up with the work," she said. "This test will not be a problem. But remember your score on this exam, along with the score on your final exam, makes up half of your grade." More groans.

I was sitting in the cafeteria having a late lunch when Ziggy plopped into the seat opposite me. "You worried about the test?" he asked.

I shrugged. I'd always been pretty cool under pressure and I'd been keeping up with the homework.

"If you need help, see me," he said.

"You have a study group going?"

"Something like that."

A day later, I saw Ziggy in the cafeteria surrounded by students. They were laughing and talking. When I got closer, I saw a student hand Ziggy some money. Ziggy handed him something in return. Was Ziggy dealing drugs here in the cafeteria? I moved closer and pulled up an empty chair.

"This is the study circle, right?" I asked.

One of the students guffawed and the others looked at me strangely. "Something like that," Ziggy said.

"Dr. Weitz is a royal bitch," a girl named Heather said loudly. "Isn't she *paid* to help us? My parents paid a ton of money for me to be here, and when I asked her to help me with the internet system, she said she could give me only twenty minutes. Twenty minutes. She's got her nerve. I told my parents and they wrote a nasty letter to the Dean about her."

"You could do better in class if you partied less." This comment was from a pale, bespeckled girl.

"Or she could be a suck up like you," another girl said to the speaker. She looked at me. "Or like Marks."

"Come on guys," Ziggy said. "This is the half-way mark. A few more weeks and you'll never see Psych 101 again."

"I hear her husband's a cop," Heather said sourly. "I'll bet she holds the victims down while the cops waterboard them."

"They only do that in Gitmo," another student said. "Not here."

I was sitting next to Ziggy and glanced down to see, at his feet, an open backpack filled with small white boxes. I reached down and palmed one of the boxes. Ziggy had been a friend, but I didn't like the idea of drugs being sold in the school.

When I got back to my apartment, I opened the box. Instead of drugs, there was a zip drive. I pushed the zip drive into my computer and what popped up on the screen was a test. The Psych test.

Somehow Ziggy had got hold of the mid-term exam and was selling copies to the students.

Now I had a problem. Was I willing to go to Dr. Weitz and tell her about the copies of the test? If I did, Ziggy could reveal my secret to the administration. It was possible that Dr. Weitz would figure out, when most of her students got high marks, that someone had given out copies, but she needed to know now. She had given me a job, and treated me fairly and I owed her the truth. One day, when I knew she would not be in her office I let myself in, putting on her desk the pile of articles I'd copied for her. Then to one side, I placed the zip drive. The mid-term was only three days away. Hopefully she would see it there, look at it, and have enough time to re-write the test.

On the day of the test, Dr. Weitz passed out blue books and a question sheet. On the sheet were four essay questions, not the twenty-five page multiple choice questionnaire that Ziggy had provided. There were gasps and groans. Clearly people thought they had aced this and hadn't studied. There were a few nasty looks directed at Ziggy. When Ziggy looked at me asking if I knew anything about the changes, I just shrugged.

I was walking out of the room later when Ziggy grabbed me by the shirt. "We need to talk, Marks," he said.

I couldn't plead another class because Ziggy knew my schedule. We walked to the cafeteria together.

"How did she know?" he asked when I'd sat down opposite him.

"Know what?"

"Come on, don't play butter-won't-melt-in-my-mouth with me. You took one of those zip drives and gave it to her."

"What you did was wrong,"

"Unlike sneaking into college under someone else's name? You're not one to talk about what's wrong, Marks."

"You gonna turn me in?"

"No," he said finishing his coffee with a gulp. "But let me tell you this." His face was inches from mine and I could smell sweat and under that anxiety. "As long as you are here in this college, I am gonna make your life a living hell."

That night we were into a game of Monte at The Ambassador when two people walked in and sat at the bar. I recognized Dr. Weitz immediately. She was dressed in a pink pantsuit and her gray hair was pulled back with a jeweled comb. Beside her was a tall, grey-haired man whom I could have spotted from five miles away as a cop. I thought about the stolen credit card numbers on slips of paper in my pocket, the cash in Jack's wallet and the marked cards spread out on the table.

I turned to Jack. "We've got to shut down the game," I whispered.

He shook his head. "The place is safe," he said. "The barkeep's been taken care of and the local cops are bought."

I pointed to Dr. Weitz and her husband at the bar. "He's a cop," I said.

"How do you know?"

"She's my college teacher. She told me. Doesn't he look like one? "

"You'd better be right on this," Jack said and reaching forward, he scooped the cards from the table. "Game's over fellows. Things just got a little hot and we're closing down."

There were moans and groans, especially since most of the men had lost a good deal of money that, as drunk as they were, they were hoping to win back.

"Come back another night and we'll do this again."

At that moment, I could see Dr. Weitz turning toward the table where we sat.

"Get out of here, Jack," I said. "I'll take care of this." He grabbed his coat and walked quickly toward the door. I crossed the room to the bar.

"Dr. Weitz," I said. I turned toward the cop. "Mr. Weitz."

"Detective Weitz, " the man said.

"What are you doing here, Nate?" Dr. Weitz asked.

"I work here, waiting tables," I said.

"You are a hard working young man. College during the day, waiting tables at night."

"You're not dressed like a waiter," Detective Weitz said.

"An accident with a spilled drink," I said. "They wanted me to stay and work rather than go home and change." I gestured toward the room. "Weeknights, this place is pretty quiet."

"Except when there's a convention," Detective Weitz said. He pointed to the fellows sitting together at the table. "The card game looked like fun. Do you know what they were playing?"

"I just wait tables, sir. I don't control what people do."

"But you said something to the guy who left."

This man was way too observant. "The man who left couldn't cover his bar bill, so he went to his room for his wallet," I said.

"What is this, Henry, an interrogation?" Dr. Weitz said to her husband. "Leave the kid alone. He's working here. What does it matter what he's wearing and what those other men were doing? We came to have a good time."

He gave her a sour look and went back to his drink.

I moved to the bartender and spoke to him softly. I needed to get away from here, but if I were pretending to be a waiter, I required the bartender's permission to leave.

"What?" the bartender said loudly. "You're going now? First you spill a drink on a shirt, and now you're leaving early. Don't do this too often Marks or you'll find yourself out of a job."

I ducked my head as if embarrassed, and nodding toward Dr. Weitz, I went out the door. I took a cab to the Wellington where Jack was in the back room deep in a Monte game. Sitting beside him was a woman I hadn't seen in four years, but whom I'd often dreamed about. Moira.

I sat down beside her. "How've you been?"

"You're not driving us out of here too, are you?" Jack asked.

"No sir." I looked at Moira and winked. Suddenly the evening had taken on a lightness that had been missing from my life. When the players wanted drinks, I did my job copying down the numbers from their cards, but I was so excited to see Moira, I almost got them wrong. When I got back to the table, followed by the waiter with the drinks I sat opposite Moira. so I could look at her. She looked tired and her hair was duller, not the lush mane of reddish curls it had once been. She was thinner too. The dress she wore, one I'd seen on her before, bagged at the hips. But none of that mattered. I'd been thinking about her, looking for her, and wanting her since she'd left. Now she was back and I wasn't going to deal with the 'you're-only- fifteen' foolishness. I was nineteen and considered myself grown up.

Two days later I was back in Psych. The grades had been given out and I was very proud to get an A. Not bad for a kid who'd only ever gone as far as seventh grade. As I was leaving, Dr. Weitz called me over.

"I'd like to talk with you Nate," she said. "Can you be in my office in a few minutes."

When I got to the office she was sitting behind her desk, the zip drive in her hand.

"Did you do this?" she asked

I shook my head.

"One of the students came to me the day after the test and told me you were the one selling the zip drives. You were charging students twenty dollars for the answers to the test."

"It wasn't me," I said.

"Who was it Nate?"

I said nothing.

"I've been trying to think who, of my students, has access to my office and you are the only one."

"I didn't steal the answers," I said.

"But you won't tell me who did."

I shook my head.

"The other night, at the hotel …" she began.

I waited.

"My husband said those men were playing a gambling game called Three Card Monte. He got in a conversation with one of them, and the man admitted it."

"I don't control what people do in the bar," I said.

"Of course you don't, but you seemed to know the man who was running the game."

My legs had started to shake, and my palms were sweaty.

"My husband is a good detective. I trust what he tells me. He talked to the bartender, but the man wasn't really sure what days you worked. Henry is convinced that you weren't working as a waiter at all, but that you were involved with the illegal game. Is that true, Nate?"

I was silent. I liked Dr. Weitz but to tell her the truth would open up a tub of snakes that would come back to bite not only me, but Jack and Moira.

"Do you know there have been complaints about that bar? Something about their stealing people's credit card numbers. I would be careful if I were you."

She leaned back in her seat. "Well obviously this is not the police station, and you haven't been accused of any crime." She picked up the zip drive and turned it over in her hands. "I like you Nate. You have a good mind and you work hard to boot. I don't often get students like you. But I can't keep you working for me with all these unanswered questions. I hope you understand."

I nodded.

I turned to go. "I'm sorry," she said as I left.

It was eleven o'clock in the morning but I needed a drink. I needed several drinks. I could drink as Jim Slocum or as Nate Marks. It didn't matter. Both ID's said I was old enough.

There's a bar not far from the college which now, in the early part of the day was inhabited by the kind of droopy drunks who spend their lives in bars, with the addition of a couple of professor types winding down after a hard morning, and one or two girls who looked barely old enough to be there.

I liked the place. I'd only been here once before. OK, it smelled of stale beer and the men's room was not very clean, but there were little hidden pockets of dark where a man could hide and get comfortably soused. I had three quick whiskey and sodas, enough to dull the ache. From my hidden spot, I watched the place fill up, but except for the waiter no one came near me. I considered my job with Jack. Did it really matter if I missed an evening? Jack had been good to me, taken me in when I needed a place, but what did I really owe him?

By three in the afternoon, I was regally if not legally drunk. I got myself out to the sidewalk, hailed a cab to my apartment and

God knows how, got myself upstairs and into bed. It seemed I had just closed my eyes when there was a pounding on the door.

"Jim, are you there? Rise and shine, boy."

"Go to hell."

A key turned in the lock. I'd forgotten Jack had a key. He was standing over me. "What's going on? Are you shit faced boy?"

"I wish the hell you would stop calling me boy. I'm nineteen."

"So you're a grown up, are you now? Well let me tell you something, my friend. Grown men show up for work on time. They do not whine or whimper and they don't get drunk."

"I need the night off, Jack. I don't feel well."

"I can see that," he said. His image was swimming back and forth and I suddenly felt the need to heave. I sat up in bed and vomited on the floor."

"Jesus, Jim," Jack said. "All right. You get the night off. I guess you deserve it. But tomorrow, as sober as a judge, spiffed and ready, you are coming to work."

"Aye, aye, Captain."

"Don't give me that shit. Get some sleep."

That night I dreamed of my mother. We'd just come out onto the street from a Batman movie and were standing in front of an ice cream stand. I was getting to choose the biggest ice cream I could eat. I was probably four or five and it was during that time between my father and Gus.

"Have you decided?" my mother asked. I tried to make up my mind, but when I turned to tell her my choice, she had changed. She was an old lady with white hair and thin arms. I put my arms around her, but even as I did she began to dissolve under me. I started to cry. "Don't go," I said.

"I have to," she said. "But I'll come back. I'll see you again."

I woke to find myself sobbing. For a long time I'd held onto the dream that I would see my mother again, but now I had to admit that she was gone for good. I stood up and then saw the vomit on the floor. I stank and I needed to pull myself together, get on with my life and figure out where I was going. Right at the moment, nothing seemed like a good choice.

Chapter Twenty Four

Two nights later we were at the Morrison on Sixth Avenue. Moira had joined us wearing a bright turquoise silk blouse, buttoned low to reveal just a tiny sliver of lacy bra and black Palazzo pants. In spite of Jack's earlier complaint that she was a distraction, he was allowing her to sit in with us and it was fun having her.

We finished the night up at about eleven. The bar was due to close in half an hour and we were having a few drinks and divvying up the take.

"We're off to Florida in a few weeks," Jack said, looking at Moira. "You coming with us?"

She shook her head.

I looked at her. Jack and I always went to Florida when December rolled around, but if Moira weren't there, how would I see her?

"How can you resist Florida," Jack said. "The sun, the surf, Mai Tai's and Jazz clubs. Who would want grubby Manhattan in the winter when you can have all that?"

"I'll pass this year," she said quietly.

"We leave here December first if you change your mind," Jack said.

"I'll remember that," she said. She stood up. "Excuse me, I'm gonna find the ladies."

The bartender was closing up. It was time for us to leave too.

"What's wrong with that woman?" Jack asked. "She always loved Florida."

I watched her walk away. Moira had always been an enigma, but a bright, enthusiastic enigma. Something had changed in her. She was quieter, more thoughtful, but something else---I might have said sad.

I went out to the lobby to look for her and caught her just as she was leaving the ladies room. "Can I offer you a ride home?"

"Sure," she said. She was wiping at her eyes.

"What's wrong?"

"Nothing."

"I know it's none of my business, but you seem kind of down."

She looked at me with a bright fake smile. "Nothing's wrong, Jim. You worry too much. " We walked out of the hotel and hailed a cab.

"The Manhattan Hilton," she said, as we got in the cab. The Hilton was a pricey place.

She looked at me. "It's just until I can find something cheaper," she said.

When we pulled up to the entrance, a woman who'd been standing in the lobby rushed toward us. "Moira," she said. "Where've you been? I've worried about you."

"I'm fine," Moira said. She turned to me. "This is my mother Elise Hannigan. This is Jim Slocum."

"You should be in bed," her mother scolded. "I thought you were going to be home hours ago."

"I'm not a baby," Moira protested. She turned to me and smiled. "Good night, Jim." As the two women were walking up the steps to the hotel, I heard Moira's mother say.

"I know you're not a baby. I'm just trying to keep you well, honey. You've got to remember…" They were too far away to hear the rest.

I got into the waiting cab and returned to my own apartment. I flicked on the TV, but there was nothing that held my interest. Jack and I still had a few weeks here in Manhattan before we went to Florida and maybe in that time Moira would tell me what was bothering her.

My chance to talk with Moira occurred two nights later. It had been a slow night, so we retired early and since we still had part of the evening, we went to one of my favorite clubs, The Brown Goose, for drinks and Jazz. Jack bowed out early. Jazz wasn't really his thing, but I was grateful that Moira was there. We each ordered a cocktail and when the combo lit into a soft, lilting version of "You Do Something to Me," I stood up.

"Would you like to dance, Miss Hannigan?"

"Don't mind if I do, Mr. Slocum."

She moved into my arms and pressed her head against my chest. I was a head taller than she was, and though I wasn't a great dancer, I was OK. Mostly we stood there holding each other.

"Have you ever thought of dance lessons?" she asked.

"You're hinting that I've stepped on your feet too many times?" I said.

She smiled. "No, you're fine. It's just that, I've always wanted to be a real dancer. If we took lessons, would you be my dance partner?"

"I'd like to be more than that," I said. "But for now this will have to do."

"How old are you, Jim?"

"Nineteen. I'll be twenty in January," I said.

"And some lucky girl will snatch you up soon."

"I was hoping you would be that lucky girl."

"You were, were you?" She had cocked her head to one side in that old, flirty, Moira way, with a smile on her face.

"I'm serious, Moira," I said. "Are you still going to say I'm too young for you?"

"Jim, Jim. You don't want me. I'm damaged goods."

She was suddenly serious, the flirting laughter gone.

"What's wrong?" I asked.

Instead of answering she led me back to the table where our drinks sat, untouched.

She sat. I sat.

"I have cancer," she said. "I was diagnosed about a year ago with breast cancer and they did a lumpectomy and said things were fine. I was in remission until September, but…"

"But?"

"It's come back. That's why I'm here in New York. They've got specialists here who know all about this disease." She reached forward and took my hand. "I think I can beat this thing, Jim, but if you want to be with me, you should know what you're getting into."

I sat stunned. Moira, my beautiful Moira had cancer. I didn't know what that meant exactly. My grandmother had died of cancer but her death had been in a hospital and I'd been eleven when it happened, unable to see her.

"When is your next doctor's appointment?" I asked.

"A week from today."

"I want to come with you." I said.

"You don't need to. My mother will be there."

"I want to be there, too. Moira. I want to help you."

She leaned forward and kissed me lightly on the lips. "You are the sweetest guy, Jim Slocum. Who else would want to come to the hospital with a tired, sick old broad like me."

My anger rose. She didn't understand how I felt about her, how I had dreamed about the day she would be back in my life. Did she still see me as the kid who was too young for her, and what would she say if I told her how I really felt?

"I want to come with you," I said again.

"All right. You won't like it. I hate hospitals but I have to be there. The appointment is for eleven thirty on Thursday at Memorial Sloan Kettering. I'll meet you on the Oncology floor.

She was right about the hospital. The minute I walked into the main lobby and found my way to the Oncology floor, I hated it. I might have been in a hospital once when I broke my wrist, but the antiseptic smell still lingered in my mind. I kept telling myself that I was here for Moira and when I rounded the corner to the waiting room she was sitting there, with the woman I'd met on the steps of the Manhattan Hilton, her mother.

"You've met my Mom, Elise," Moira said.

"Mrs. Hannigan," I said, reaching to shake her hand. She gave me a look that said I didn't need to be there, that she could take care of her daughter. Just at that moment, a nurse came and stood in front of us. "The doctor will see you all now," she said.

"All of us?" I said.

"This is my brother, Jim," Moira said. "Can he come in too?"

"Well not for the examination, but later when the doctor talks to you, it's OK. Sometimes it helps to have other people there to remember what's been said. " She put her hand on Moira's shoulder and Moira rose and followed her.

"How long have you known my daughter," Mrs. Hannigan asked.

"I met her four years ago. Some guy pretended to show her his car and when I went to look for her, he was trying to…" I looked at Mrs. Hannigan. How much had Moira told her mother about the incident? But she was smiling at me like I was the son she'd never had.

"He tried to rape her and when she resisted, he choked her. She told me. You're the boy who saved her."

I nodded, happy that she had a good opinion of me.

"I'm glad you're in her life, Jim. She's been awfully blue lately. Even though I've given her all the support I can, it's hard to fight cancer."

We were quiet for a moment, then Mrs. Hannigan said. "Do you like her, Jim?"

I nodded.

"Enough to see her through this terrible disease? A lot of men are attracted to women when they are healthy and good looking. But if this goes the wrong way, she could lose her hair, and her good looks. It could be a terrible battle. Are you ready for that?"

"I think I am," I said.

"Well, at least you're honest," she said.

At that moment the nurse appeared and we were ushered into the doctor's office. Moira was already there, sitting in a leather chair. Her mother squeezed in beside her and I sat on a folding chair just inches from the door.

"It's nice to see that Moira has a good support system," the doctor said. He looked at me. "Welcome Mr. Hannigan." It took me a moment to realize that since I was now Moira's 'brother' I had a new name.

He pushed an x-ray into a holder in the wall behind him. "I'm afraid to say that the cancer has spread." He pointed to a small white spot on the x-ray, somewhere below the navel. "It's in the liver. This doesn't mean that we're ready to give up. What I proposed to Moira is that we try a regimen of radiation and chemotherapy that is tailored specifically to this disease. The radiation will be given once every two weeks for three months in an attempt to reduce the tumor. Then if that doesn't work, we'll try something stronger.

He looked at Moira. "What we have working for us right now is that Moira is strong and relatively healthy. She doesn't smoke. She says she's given up drinking and I think she can fight this disease."

He was saying some other things but I wasn't listening. I looked at Moira who had bowed her head and was picking at the skin around her nails Maybe it wasn't that bad. Hadn't the doctor said that even though the cancer had spread, there was still a chance? I never pray, have never even gone to a church, but at that moment I closed my eyes and thought, please let this be OK.

"I will see you in two weeks, when we'll start the treatment," the doctor said. We stood up, Moira shook his hand and we filed out.

We were standing outside the hospital waiting for a cab, when Moira said. "I need to walk just to get some air." She looked at her mother.

"I'm going back to the hotel," Mrs. Hannigan said.

"I'll walk with you," I said to Moira.

"Fine," she said and started off at a fast clip. If she was ill with cancer you wouldn't have known it by the pace she was keeping.

"Slow down, please," I said catching up with her and threading my arm through hers. "Where's the horse race?"

"I just want to be my old self again," she said. "Not a woman with cancer. Women with cancer have people looking at them, feeling sorry for them." She stopped and looked at me.

"Do you feel sorry for me, Jim?"

"Not on your life. You're tough. You can beat this thing."

"What if I lose my hair?"

"I know lots of great wig shops."

"What if I get sick from the chemo, throw up on the rug or on you."

"I got drunk two weeks ago and threw up on my own rug. It happens."

"Let's get a Latte at Starbucks, and then go to see one of those silent flicks at the Rialto. I think Charlie Chaplin is playing there."

"You didn't want to make out the last time we were at the Rialto."

"I was pretty mean, wasn't I?"

"Starbucks, the Rialto. Is there anything else you'd like my dear?"

She leaned over and kissed me on the cheek. "Just you, Jim."

Chapter Twenty Five

Rather than coffee we went to see Charlie Chaplin's *The Gold Rush*, where the indomitable prospector dangled from a house that was perched perilously over a cliff, ate his own shoes because he was starving, danced with a dog attached by rope holding up his pants, and fell in love with a girl making fun of him. I could commiserate with that last role. Moira was no longer making fun of me, but she would do nothing more than hold my hand. As we were walking back toward her hotel we passed a large brick building with a sign out front advertising dance lessons.

Moira looked toward a lighted window, in which we could see the shapes of people moving. "Want to try it?" she asked.

"Are you sure? I've never danced in my life, you know."

"Neither have I, but I'm game if you are."

We walked up a set of old wooden steps, smelling faintly of mildew and disappointment and went into a large room. A small man in an old-fashioned checked suit was sitting behind a counter and as soon as he saw us he hurried over.

"I'm Mr. Johnson, the instructor. Are you here to dance?"

"We'd like to," Moira said. "Is it too late to sign up?"

He shook his head. "We're just about to start. The cost is forty dollars per person for six weeks. We start with the waltz and then we move on to the Rumba, the Tango, the Foxtrot and some other Latin dances.

Moira looked at me. Clearly this was something she wanted to try. I fished out my wallet and withdrew four twenties.

"Good, good," Mr. Johnson said. He hurried to the counter and returned with a piece of paper. "This is the schedule. We meet every Tuesday and Thursday from three until four-thirty. We're ready to start now, if you will take your place with the others."

Standing to one side of the room were four couples. One couple were teens, maybe thirteen or fourteen. One couple consisted of two women. One couple featured a very tall man and his tiny wife, and the last couple must have weighed five hundred pounds between them. Then there were Moira and me.

"Stand facing your partner," the little man began. "The man puts his left hand in hers and the right hand on her back. No, not her rear end," he said to the teens. "Her back." He went over and rearranged the hands of the tall man and his short wife. They seemed to be so mismatched, but she was gazing up at him as though he were the Eiffel Tower. "Now," said Mr. Johnson, "The man will walk forward. Slow, slow, quick, quick, slow. Whatever the man does the woman does backwards."

"And in high heels." This was from one of the pair of women. There were murmured assents from the other women.

"Don't forget your count. Slow, slow, quick, quick, slow" the teacher said. "Mrs. Burnbalm, the man is supposed to lead. Give him a chance to do that. Mr. Morrison, you are not putting a cow into the barn, you are guiding a woman into the dance. Remember folks, dancing is a gentle seduction. Men, you are not going to step on her feet, or pinch her bottom. You are in charge, so take control, but gently. " He stopped to wipe sweat from his forehead. "All right, let's put some music on and see how it goes."

The music was something I'd never heard before but with a rhythm that was easy to follow. We set off around the floor, keeping to the outside of the room. The chubby Morrisons were having a hard time with the count. The teenagers, Trudi and Jeff wanted to boogy instead of waltz, but the two women who were called Ruth and Amy seemed to have it mastered. Our teacher was moving among the dancers, helping people find the rhythm, and rearranging hands. Moira and I had already found our stride. I could smell the perfume in her hair, feel her slender back under my hand and her breasts pressed against my chest. The intimacy of the dance was having its effect on other parts of my anatomy, and I worked hard to try and concentrate.

"Good, good." Mr. Johnson was saying. "Let's try something with a little different tempo. Trudi and Jeff, this is not the jitterbug so no twirling. We're just going to waltz."

We waltzed again, around and around in a big circle. By this time, most of the people seem to have caught the hang of the thing and no one was bumping elbows or rear ends. We waltzed for another hour and then called it a day.

"That was great," Moira said as we were walking toward the subway. She twirled around and caught me by the hand, so we were waltzing down the sidewalk. It was fun to see her laughing and fun to be holding her as we danced. It was almost five o'clock. I needed to go back and get dressed so I could work with Jack tonight.

"Are you coming to work?"

She shook her head. "You're not going to tell Jack about me, are you?"

"I won't if you don't want me to."

"You're a prince," she said, and reached forward and kissed me on the cheek. I didn't want the we're-just-friends kisses. I kissed her back on the mouth, and we stood there, on the sidewalk, lost in the kiss. Moira drew back. "You've grown up a lot, Jim," she said. Then she turned and walked toward the subway I had only a short walk to my apartment. "Call me," she called.

I spent a lot of time that evening thinking about Moira. In two weeks she would begin her treatment. Would that put an end to our dancing? In three weeks, Jack would head south to Florida and I had to decide whether to go with him or stay in New York with Moira. And, if I stayed in New York, I needed a way to earn money.

Later, as Jack and I were sitting together over drinks, Jack asked. "I missed Moira tonight. Do you know why she's not here?"

I shook my head.

"She doesn't seem herself," Jack said. "I think something is wrong." Jack had been in the people-reading business for a long time and was pretty good at it.

"She seems thinner," he continued. "She's still a beautiful woman, but something's going on with her."

I nodded. I wasn't going to give away Moira's secret. It was now quarter to twelve and they were closing the place. "I'm going home," Jack said. "Go home yourself, Jim. You look beat."

I nodded and waved him away. I was still wide awake, but it was too late to call Moira and ask if she wanted to go dancing. I could go to one of several bars I knew and if Moira hadn't been in town, I would have gone there and tried to find a woman to spend the night with, but the thought that she was here and I might have a chance with her, kept me away. Other women were just a temporary diversion. She was the one I wanted, and until that happened, I could wait.

Two days later we were back in dance class. It was the end of our first week and most of us had mastered the waltz. For some couples like the Morrisons, the rhythm would always be a challenge, and Trudi and Jeff, the teens, were itching to be more adventurous. I was good enough so I didn't even think about the slow, slow, quick,

quick, slow glide forward. I was just enjoying holding Moira in my arms.

On week two we started the Tango. "The Tango starts like the waltz ," Mr. Johnson said. "Men you are stepping forward but with bigger steps, and ladies you know what to do."

"Dance backward in high heels," one woman said.

"Exactly," said Mr. Johnson. "OK, we'll start with the men, because you are the leaders in this dance." We lined up on one side with Mr. Johnson in front. He turned his back to us and strode forward, his short legs stretched out as far as they could go. "You start with the left, then the right, then left, but instead of bringing the right foot forward you move it to the right, and then drag the left toward it, not completely closing the gap. Let's practice that." We practiced, one long step left, one long step right, one long step left and then the slide to the right. "Now let me show you how to hold your partner." He gestured toward Moira. "Some dancers hold the woman's right hand straight out, but I like taking her hand and putting it like this." He took Moira's hand in his, tucked her hand under his chin, and began moving her forward. It looked so graceful and effortless. "We'll practice this part first," Mr. Johnson said.

After a half hour of the Tango we were all tired so we took a break. Mr. Johnson was telling us the history of the dance. "It has become much more sensual than it was originally," he said. "And of course more athletic. Different Tango dancers have their own styles and if you want to see Tango done beautifully, you need to go to the Centurian ballroom on Seventh Street. They have demonstrations on Friday and Saturday night." Moira looked at me, and I nodded. Moira had another week before her chemo began, so if I could get off work for an evening, we would go.

"Moira," I said, as were outside the building heading away from each other. "You need to tell Jack what's going on. I'm not going to Florida with him this winter and he will need to know why."

"You're not going to Florida?"

"I'm going to stay and help you through this."

"I've got my mother, Jim. You don't have to."

"I'm not doing this because I have to; I'm doing it because I want to."

She was subdued for a moment and then she half turned. "I'll tell Jack," she said.

That evening Jack and I were sitting at the bar waiting for customers. It was Friday night, a night when people usually thronged the hotels, but tonight seemed unusually quiet.

"Moira told me what's going on," Jack said. "What a shame about her illness." He looked at me. "You're stuck her, aren't you."

"Like glue. I've decided to stay in New York instead of coming to Florida. I'm sorry if this leaves you short-handed, but I want to help her."

He nodded quietly. "You're old enough to make your own decisions, my friend. But you should think about finding someone your own age."

"Someone who doesn't have cancer?"

"I wasn't going to say that, but yeah."

"I've tried that," I said. " I've been with a lot of girls. In Florida they flaunt their bodies right in front of me, but all I can think about is her."

"It's going to be a long game Jim. You'll need patience and what poker players call a leather ass. You know what I mean? You have to see this through to the end, not bolt when things get tough."

He took a sip of his drink. "Look Jim, if you're not working for me, you'll need a job and maybe a little nest egg. Why don't you come with me to my poker game on Tuesday. We play Texas Hold 'em. Watch the game for one hand and then if you're good enough, you can sit in. Heck, you're smart enough to make some money."

Tuesday was the night Moira and I went dancing, but Jack was right. If I were staying in New York I needed an income.

The following Tuesday, dressed in my best suit, I presented myself at the lobby of the Marriott. Jack was waiting and as we rode up in the elevator, he said. "A word about these guys. Ernie Wilson's a stockbroker who thinks with his cojones not his brain, he raises when he should fold and calls when he should raise. Hank Arnold's a good player and Bill Peters always loses. We let Bill stay on because he pays the tab for the rest of us." He turned to face me. "The best poker players play the other men not the cards. Watch their body language and you'll know whether they have a good or bad hand. Don't spend time thinking about the money. There's a reason that poker cash comes as little plastic discs; it's so you don't think about how much you're winning or losing. If you're going to play well, always think about the 60/40 proposition. You're gonna win sometimes and you're gonna lose sometimes. If there's no loss in losing, there's no high in winning."

We had reached the elevator, but Jack wasn't finished. "One last thing. Don't gripe when you're losing and don't gloat when you're winning." I could hear men talking as we moved toward the open doorway and when we went into the room, three men were clustered around a table set up as a bar. The room was part of a suite with a large table set up in the middle and a stunning view of the Manhattan skyline along one wall.

"Jack," one man said, as we came into the room. "And who's this?"

"Jim Slocum," Jack said. "A friend of mine. I thought you guys might let him observe for one hand and then let him sit in."

"No problem for me," the man said. He held out his hand. "Ernie Wilson," He pointed to the other men at the bar. "Hank Arnold." Hank held out his hand and shook mine. “Bill Peters.”

Bill just took a sip of his drink and glared at me. Clearly not everyone was happy to have me there.

The men moved to the table which was covered with a green cloth. In the middle were a pile of chips, and cards.

"We're playing fixed limit hold'em," Ernie said to me. "Five/ten. I'll be the dealer, " Ernie sat with the dealer's marker in front of him. The others sat left to right, Bill, Jack, Hank.

"We don't do Big or Little Blinds," Ernie said. "Not with this small a table." The players were busy exchanging money for one and two dollar chips. "Come on Jim, you can sit," Ernie said. I pulled up a chair behind the players which meant that I wasn't actually at the table but could see the faces of the players.

"Ante up," Ernie said, and they went around each player putting a five dollar chip in the middle. Ernie shuffled the cards and dealt one to each man face down. Then he dealt another card face down. Some of the players left the cards flat on the table and lifted the corner so they could see what they were. Others picked them up, holding them close to their chest. At this point I could get a good guess what the cards were. Jack had a gleeful look on his face that he was trying to control. Bill's shoulders had slumped. Hank looked slightly bemused and Ernie was shifting in his chair, and grabbing at his drink, gulping it down. "OK, Ernie said to Bill, "Give us your opening bid." Bill pushed a ten dollar chip in front of him. "Raise," Jack said, with twenty. "Check," Hank said, looking at Jack's stack. Ernie looked at Jack's stack too. "Re-raise," he said and put down thirty dollars worth of chips. He swept the chips into a pile in the middle of the table. Everyone took a deep breath. I looked at the flop. The queen of diamonds, the seven of spades and the six of diamonds. Someone would have to have at least one or two diamonds to make a flush. It was possible that Ernie had two diamonds, but he could be just bluffing. Hank had something, but it wasn't anything he believed in. Sometimes to be a good player, you had to believe even in the little things and hope you could smoke out your opponent. Bill was looking more hopeful and Jack was having a hard time hiding his excitement.

"Ready boys?" Ernie said and laid out the Turn. It was the ten of diamonds. Jack's eyes lit up just for a second, but I caught it. Hank sighed and I saw Bill's eyes widen. Ernie was practically dancing in his seat. Things had just gotten better for three out of four. Ernie looked at Bill. "Raise," Bill said and pushed forty dollars in chips forward. "Re-raise," Jack said and pushed fifty dollars in chips forward. "Check," Hank said, the men glared at him. "OK, Call," he said and reluctantly put fifty dollars into the pot. Ernie was last. "Re-raise, re-raise, re-raise," he chortled gleefully. He pushed sixty dollars into the pot. He could hardly sit still.

Theatrically Ernie picked up the deck, burned the first card and laid down the second on the river. It was the eight of clubs. Hank said, "I'm out."

"What about you?" Ernie said looking at Bill. "Two pair," Bill said, laying out the six of hearts and ten of hearts from his hole and pulling down the six of diamonds and ten of diamonds from the river.

"You?" he asked looking at Jack. Jack laid out his hole cards, the king of diamonds and two of diamonds, then he pulled down the six, queen and ten of diamonds from the River. I could see Ernie's whole body slump. He turned toward Hank who had a pair, the five of hearts and five of spades. With a little less flourish he laid out his own cards, the eight of diamonds and the queen, six and ten of diamonds from the river.

Hank had already folded. He had only a pair of fives. Ernie looked subdued. He put down his hole card, the eight of diamonds and added to it, the queen, six and ten from the river. Jack had beat him.

Jack swept the chips into a bag and we broke for some liquid refreshment.

"When did you know you had him?" I asked when we were standing apart from the others.

"When he started preening," Jack said. "It was possible, but not probable that we could both have got diamonds as hole cards. I could have bet more, but Ernie always bets high even when he's got nothing." Hank came over to the two of us. "Want to sit in on the game?" he asked.

"Sure," I said.

I made two hundred dollars that night. Jack was probably the best player in the room, and what I was learning from him was that in poker, as in life, you play the hand that you are dealt, doing the best you can with what you've been given.

Chapter Twenty Six

The next week, which was the first of December, everything happened at once. Moira started her chemo treatment, which knocked her for a loop right from the beginning. Jack went to Florida and offered his apartment to Elise Hannigan, Moira's mother so she could help Moira when I was working.

I had applied for a job working as a janitor under the name of James Slocum in the same college, NYU, where I'd been a student. Since the job required a high school diploma and I had none, I asked my friend Benny to make me up one. I was also asked about my criminal history, and since I had *no* history, I was clean on that score. I peed into a cup and was declared free of drugs. On my first day on the job, I was given a locker and paired with a tall, overweight man named Sandy who was going to show me the ropes. My job started at four in the afternoon when most of the college staff had gone home and ended sometime around ten. And we were in Tunney Hall which houses the faculty in Arts and Sciences.

"This is a pretty easy job," Sandy was saying as we were loading up the janitor's cart with cleaning supplies. People mess up their offices but they expect the places to be clean when they return to them in the a.m. You wouldn't believe the stuff I've seen." He looked at me. "Ready?"

I nodded and followed him down the hall to the first office. "One time," Sandy said, reaching to dump a full wastebasket into the cart, "I come into the Dean's office and there on the floor are a pair of women's panties. Wha hoo, was I surprised. Now what do I do? The Dean was this middle-aged guy and the panties didn't look like they belonged to his wife, who from her picture wears a size ninety-seven large."

"Finally, I just picked them up and tucked them into the top drawer of his desk. The next time I cleaned the room and peeked into the desk, they were gone."

He was moving around the room, dusting things with a spray and a rag. "Here," he said, handing me a different spray bottle and a clean rag. "Do the glass in the windows and the door."

When we'd finished that chore, Sandy took out the vacuum and hoovered up the rug.

"This will be all yours in two days," he said. "It's a lot of physical work, but you look up to it."

"You retiring?"

"Yup. My ticker's not working right, and my wife convinced me to quit. She wants us to have a little fun before I kick the bucket."

"Florida is nice," I said. "Lots of good looking girls on the beach."

"Good looking girls? That will give my ticker a workout." He looked at me "How come a kid like you is doing something like this?"

"My girl is sick," I said. "I'm staying here in New York for her."

"I'll bet a good looking fellow like you could do anything, be a stockbroker, or a college teacher. Hell, you could sell stuff on TV."

"You need an education for those things," I said.

"You're young. Why don't you take classes here?"

I didn't tell him that I'd already done that. I moved to the desk to straighten some papers and Sandy said, "not that, Jim. Don't ever touch personal stuff, especially books that are open or spread around. They don't mind you emptying their trash but don't mess with the other things."

I nodded. We flipped off the lights and went on to the next office. We worked steadily for three hours and headed down to the janitorial break room for coffee. The break room was in the basement of the building. To get to it, you moved past the heating system and a storage room to a tiny space with cement walls and a single table surrounded by four folding metal chairs. A coffee pot stood on a counter and beside it an open box of doughnuts. Two men were sitting at the table playing cards.

"Maurice, Leroy, this here is Jim. He'll be the new Sandy."

Maurice looked up but gave me hardly a glance. To Sandy he said, "We'll think of you, buddy, lying on the beach looking at the waves, drinking them Pina Colas."

"Coladas, Maurice. But it's Rum and Coke for me."

"Come on Mo, will you play for God sake." Leroy said, "We've only got twenty minutes."

Maurice turned back to the table and spread his cards. "I got nineteen," he said.

"Twenty one on the money," Leroy cackled. He reached to the center of the table and scooped up a pile of coins. "Better luck tomorrow, buddy."

The two men rose and took their dirty cups to the sink but didn't wash them. I suppose when you spend your evenings cleaning up other people's messes, you don't want to deal with your own.

"See ya, Sandy," Leroy said. "You know they're having a party for you next week, over at the Blue Dog A chance to give you a good sendoff." He looked at me. "You can come too, Jerry."

"Jim," I said.

"Whatever," Leroy said. "We'll miss you, Sandy." And then they were gone.

"It's not a bad place," Sandy said. "Once the guys get to know you, they're all right."

"What was the hardest thing to get used to about this job?"

"The bending and stooping, but it's kind of lonely. Except for those guys you just met, you don't meet anyone else."

He took a sip of coffee. "The first couple of years I did this, I hated it. I hated cleaning up other people's shit, and being seen as 'just a janitor.' But then I thought I'm seeing the underside of a college. All the professors leave secrets behind, like the panties on the floor. Once someone left a dog. I guess she'd come to work with it and just forgot it. Turned out she was divorcing her husband and she thought he was going to pick it up. The poor thing was just sitting in the corner whining. He needed to pee. I took him out, gave him some water, let him ride around with me on the cart and when I left him he was asleep in the corner of the office."

"A janitor is like a bartender or a psychiatrist. You learn people's secrets by looking at what's on their desks. You learn who's going to get canned, who's being sued for divorce. I've seen letters from a married man to the woman he's fooling around with. I mean if you wanted to blackmail someone you could make a ton of money just by being the janitor."

"Do you play Blackjack?" I asked.

"With Mo and Leroy? I don't do cards. My wife and I play dominoes." He leaned forward. "I'm a demon player."

I laughed and finished my coffee. We had another few hours before my shift would be over.

When I got back to my apartment, Moira was awake and sitting up in bed. Her first chemo treatment had been the day before and she'd felt fine until she began to vomit steadily in the toilet. Now, she looked pale and tired.

"How did your first day at work go?" she asked.

"Good," I said. "Do you know that this is the first legitimate job I have ever held? I lied to them about having a high school diploma, and if they wanted to check my credentials they could fire me."

"They're not going to fire you, Jim. They're lucky to have you."

I sat down on the bed beside and her, put my arm around her shoulder and kissed her.

"I stink," she said.

"Mmmm, you do," I said nuzzling her neck.

"Jim," she said pulling back. "Do you know that are very strange?"

"But you love me, don't you?"

"God help me, I do," she said.

I got a coke from the refrigerator, sat down beside her and began telling her about my job as a janitor. About half way through my tale, I could see her eyes starting to close. She lay back on the bed and I covered her with the blanket. It was midnight. I felt tired too. My job as janitor was physically busy but there was nothing for my mind to do and if I were going to make a better living, I needed to study poker.

The next day at work, I timed my break to match that of Maurice and Leroy. They had already pulled out the cards when Sandy and I got our coffee and sat down.

Leroy looked at me. "You play twenty-one?"

"A little," I said.

Maurice looked at Leroy as if asking permission and Leroy nodded very slightly.

"Sit in if you want," he said.

I watched them play a single hand. Leroy was a better player than Maurice, who could have had a neon sign over his head broadcasting his cards. Part of playing twenty-one is luck as it is with any card game. Part of it is judgment. If you've got two cards, say a nine and an eight, should you draw a third card, which would have to be a three or a four to keep you under or at 21. Or do you stick with your two cards and hope someone else doesn't have the magic numbers? They were playing for nickels and dimes so the pot probably held two dollars at most. I was not going to increase my wages with this game, but it was a chance to practice my skills.

"Do you guys ever play Hold 'em?" I asked.

"Sometimes," Leroy said, eyeing me warily. "Look Jerry we just play for fun here, we're not into making money."

"It's Jim," I said. I looked at Maurice who'd said nothing. "What about you?" I asked.

"Don't matter what we play. I stink at everything."

I still had about ten minutes left in my break. "Can we play a round?" I asked.

Leroy nodded, shuffled and dealt the cards. As it turned out I had two magic numbers, eight and nine which are always a good place to start. I declined to get a third card, and it was possible that one of the other guys was holding a face card and an ace. But then both fellows called for a third card. Maurice had two kings and a queen, and Leroy had three fives, so I was the winner.

Chapter Twenty Seven

It was late February The weather had deteriorated from the bright blue skies of October to the lifeless gloom that the city settles into in the winter. We'd already had snow which clogged the streets and made an unholy mess with traffic. I had no car, which was probably a good thing because I'd have had no place to park it, so I was getting lots of exercise walking the five blocks to the university and my job. Hanging over all of the gloomy weather was Moira health. She'd had a round of chemo, where she'd lost her hair and spent most of the time vomiting in the bathroom, but now things seemed to be stabilized, and she seemed to feel better. So much so, that she sometimes took over the cooking from her mother.

Since Moira and I were right next door to Elise Hannigan, we often ate supper with her after my shift. That evening at the end of the meal, I helped Moira to bed and then did the dishes with her mother.

"I've got to go out," I said.

"Poker?" Elise Hannigan asked.

"Yup." I'd been playing a weekly game with the same guys Jack had introduced me to.

"I know you don't approve of this," I said, "but it's the only way I can make any money."

She leaned over and kissed me on the cheek. "You're a good man, Jim. You aren't doing anything illegal, and I know you love my daughter." There were tears in her eyes as she pushed me away. "Go. And I hope you win."

I took a cab, something I usually didn't do because of the expense, but the apartment was not familiar and it was bad form to arrive late. When I got to the apartment, Hank and Bill were there, standing near the drinks table talking. There was a knock on the door.

Bill went to answer it and when he came back into the room he was followed by a large man whose bulk seemed to take over the room and a person I recognized. Ziggy Henderson.

"This is a Jonas Henderson," Bill said waving toward the big man. And his son Siegfried."

"Ziggy," he corrected, walking toward me. "How you doing Nate."

"Jim," I corrected.

"Get a drink," Bill said, and pointed to a pile of poker chips. "I'll be the banker."

There was some bantering as Jonas and Ziggy got their drinks and then we sat at the table. Bill, as the host would take the first turn as dealer.

After playing with Bill and Hank for a month I knew how to read them, but Jonas and Ziggy were ciphers. Still, as I glanced across at Ziggy I thought it might be fun to clean him out.

We ante'd up and Bill dealt two cards to each player. I watched Ziggy. He lifted his cards up by the corner, glanced at them. His eyes widened and a tiny smile spread across his face. He glanced around hugging the cards to his chest.

I looked at my cards. Two aces. I put my hand on my forehead, trying to look like I'd already been beaten.

Ziggy liked to bet high, which suited me fine. I had a good hand, and when the river came up with two more aces, I was the winner.

We played until ten o'clock at which point I'd taken Ziggy for about three hundred dollars. His father, more wisely, had folded early, as had Hank, so it was just Bill, Ziggy and me.

"Better luck next week," I said, scooping the chips toward me.

"You son of a bitch," Ziggy said. His father gave him a sharp look but said nothing.

As I was cashing out, Ziggy came and stood beside me.

"Remember Heather? Complained the teacher never helped her?"

I nodded.

"She dropped out mid semester."

I nodded, unsure where this was going.

"Before she left, she told Professor Weitz that I was the one who stole the test. She did it just to fuck me up, I know."

I was putting money into my wallet.

"They called me into the Dean's office and gave me a warning," he said. "Good thing my dad is a big donor or I'd have been kicked out."

"I've got to go, Ziggy."

He put his hand on my arm. "Heather didn't tell Weitz who put the zip drive on her desk because she didn't know." I took a deep breath and nodded. What did it matter now? Heather was gone. I was gone. The whole problem had been taken care of.

"This isn't over, Nate," Ziggy said. "Not by a long shot."

Chapter Twenty Eight

It was April. My new helper in the janitor job was a scrawny kid named Lyle who joined me the next afternoon in the locker room. I showed him his locker and where he could change and then we set about on our rounds. Like my mentor had done with me, I trailed behind him as he did the various parts of the job, reminding him that everything he saw on desks, in cabinets, on the floor was confidential. We might be the lowest paid employees in the place, but we would keep the secrets.

When we stopped for lunch, I was surprised when Lyle pulled out a paperbound book the size of the Manhattan phone directory.

"I'm studying for my GED," he said, seeing my look.

"GED? Some kind of college course?"

"Ain't you never heard of the GED? You take a test and they give you your high school diploma."

I'd gone directly from elementary school to college, but the thought that I could get my diploma and then go legitimately to college enticed me.

I moved beside him and he pushed the open book toward me. On it were algebraic equations. "I suck at math," he said.

I studied the equation. 5(4b+5b) = 405 In my brief foray into college, we'd done some of these. I walked him briefly through the rules for parenthesis and equal signs. After I'd told him how to solve the equation, I left him to do it. He did it with a lot of erasing and re-writing. When he came up with the answer, I made him prove it.

"Always prove your equation," I said. I looked at my watch. It was time to get back to work.

Working as a janitor gave me lots of time to think, and working in an institution of higher learning is like being a midget in a candy store. Lots of delicious things that were just out of reach. At the end of the day, I went to the college bookstore and bought a GED book of my own. When I got back to the apartment, I put it on the table. Moira was up and around, her mother having gone back to Jack's apartment to sleep. I leaned forward and kissed her.

"What's that? she asked pointing to the book.

"I'm going to study for my GED." At her puzzled look, I said. "I'm going to get my high school diploma and then I'm going to try college again---this time under my own name."

"What is your own name?"

"Arthur James Martin, Jr." I came up behind her, put my arms around her waist and kissed her on the cheek. "Would you like to be Mrs. Arthur James Martin?"

"Do I have to call you Arthur?"

"Nope. I was only ever Jim. Arthur was my father."

She turned in my arms and kissed me. "Jim," she said. "If I do marry you, you're not going to turn all head-of-the-family on me, are you?"

"What do you mean?"

"Some men, when they marry, think of their wives as property. They start telling the woman how they want things done, when to put supper on the table and all that stuff."

I looked at the empty table behind me. "You can see how well having supper on the table when I get home, has worked for me. I don't expect that will change."

She punched me playfully. "I do love you, you know."

"I'm glad to hear it. And since you are in such a good mood, why don't we go out."

"I'm going to wear that red dress I bought before I got sick, and strappy heels and maybe my new wig." she was already moving toward the bedroom. I needed to shower and change into something less grungy.

When we were ready, we caught a cab and went downtown to our favorite place. A blues band was playing in the corner and the place was jumping. I ordered two glasses of wine and we found a seat. Moira looked stunning. In spite of the fact that she'd lost a lot of weight and her natural hair was replaced by an auburn wig, her eyes sparkled and her smile was bright. I knew other men couldn't take their eyes off her.

She got up to use the bathroom and I went to the bar to order drinks. A man sidled up to me.

"How much does she charge?" he asked.

I looked at him. "Who?"

"The girl. I'd like to get a piece of that ass. Can I get her number?"

My anger rose. I knocked the drink from his hand and pushing one arm behind him, I marched him out of the bar into the alley behind.

"Listen, jerk. That woman is my girl. She's not for sale."

"Hey man, I was just making a joke."

I released his arm so I could both hands to squeeze the air and the words out of him. "You owe me an apology."

He squeaked something and I released my hands. He rubbed at his neck and said. "Listen man, I didn't know you were so sensitive."

"I'm waiting," I said.

"I'm sorry. OK? Listen, I didn't know you'd get so uptight about it."

I wanted to punch him, kick him in the ribs, but he had given me an apology. "If I see you look at her, even glance her way, I will come back and the next time I will gut you with my knife."

"Jesus man." he said.

"Understand?"

He nodded. He turned and went back into the bar and I followed. Moira was sitting at the table when I got there.

"You were gone a long time," she said.

"I had some business to take care of."

"That guy that came in before you?"

"Uh huh."

"I saw him looking at me. He made some kind of remark, like 'how much?' but I just ignored him. I hope you ignored him too, Jim."

I said nothing.

"Jim," she said leaning toward me. "People are always going to say something. If it's not remarking about how I dress, it's how I wear my makeup or do my hair. I'm not a hooker, but for some men, that's what they see."

"I like how you look."

"Thanks sweetie," she said reaching across the table to hold my hand. I was looking toward Mr. Macho to make sure his eyes were elsewhere.

"You want me to wear something less revealing, don't you?"

"No, it's fine," I said.

"I want to go out with you without having a problem. If it's not fine with you, maybe I can wear something else."

I turned to look at her. "You would?"

"No," she said. "I can't be someone else, not even for you, Jim. I want to be with you. Hell, I'm even thinking about marrying you, but once that happens I don't want you restricting what I wear, who I see, what I say."

"Our earlier conversation?"

"Yup."

The band had segued into a dance tune, "Someone to Watch Over Me," and I reached for Moira's hand.

"Let's dance," I said. "I didn't come out with you to argue. I just want to hold you in my arms."

She smiled and stood and together we began the dance.

The next evening when I came home from work Moira was in bed. She seemed to be taking a long time to get over the chemo treatment, some days feeling tired and listless, and others days, she would be well enough so we could go out to the movies or dancing, like a normal couple.

I went to the bed and sat down beside her, taking her hand in mine. I could see the surface of her pale skin already wrinkled as though she were an old lady. She was thirty-two and I was twenty.

"You know," she said, "I used to have a beautiful ass. Now it's nothing."

"I still think it's beautiful."

"You're not a very good liar."

"Have you thought about my question?" I asked.

"Are you out of your mind? You know there's never going to be a little house in the suburbs for us, kids running around in the yard. These are the things people get married for."

"Sometimes people marry because they love each other, Moira. Will you marry me?"

She was silent for a long time and then she began weeping without any sound, the tears running down her cheek. I took her carefully in my arms.

"I love you, Moira," I said.

"How can you? I'm hideous. Jim, why don't you go find someone you can have kids with, have a future with."

"So is that a no?"

She pulled back and looked at me. "You are serious, aren't you?"

I nodded and moved to the chair beside her bed but kept my hand in hers. "When you left I kept looking for you. Every time I saw a redhead on the street I would hurry after her thinking it was you. Once I chased a woman for a full city block. After six months I realized that you weren't coming back and I'd never see you again, so I started picking up girls in the bars and on the beach. We'd go to her place or mine, have sex and sometimes I'd call her again, but mostly I didn't. My love for you was a stone that had settled itself in the middle of my heart and no amount of liquor or sex could move it. I could never find a way to put my longing for you aside. So now you are here and I am here and I want to be with you. I want to marry you."

"OK," she said.

"You will?"

"I will. I probably won't be able to walk down the aisle but…"

I reached forward and hugged her. "I don't care if we have to carry you on a gurney down the aisle, we will get married."

"How do you see this wedding," she asked. "Lots of guests, big church? I don't even know anyone who would marry us, do you?"

"We could do it at City Hall. I'll find someone."

"You're not going to turn me into a little housewife, are you?"

"I promise."

Chapter Twenty Nine

On a Saturday afternoon we went down to City Hall and got married. I'm sure Moira would have liked a big church wedding, but we knew very few people and would never have filled such a space. Jack had flown in from Florida with two of his friends from the game and Elise, Moira's mother was there. Other than that it was just the judge. For such a momentous occasion, the actual wedding seemed to take seconds to complete.

After the wedding we went to the Café d'Oro for a fancy French meal. Jack's treat. We laughed and joked. I watched Moira's face--her color was high and her eyes sparkled. In the old days, I would just have enjoyed watching her, now I worried about fever.

Later, back in our apartment as we were lying in bed, naked I asked.

"How does it feel to be married?"

"You forget I've done this before?"

I *had* forgotten. I wanted to ask whether this marriage felt better than her earlier one, but I was afraid she might find this one lacking.

"This is a good marriage," she said. "I'm lucky to have met you."

"I was worried you'd change your mind."

"Me? No, why would I?" She had propped herself up on one elbow, her lovely naked breast within easy kissing distance. I reached over and did that. "Aren't you worried about being called a cougar?" I asked.

"Oh please," she said, laughing. "I think you are capable of holding your own against me." She bared her teeth and then said, "Come here, husband. I'll show you what a cougar can do."

Two weeks later the doctor told us that Moira's cancer, which had been in remission, had returned. She had gone through weeks of treatment, and we thought she was getting better.

“I’m not going to do chemo again, Jim,” she said. “I don’t think I’ll survive.”

I went to her and put my arms around her. Her chemo had been brutal. I’d been there for all of it, and as much as I wanted her to stay with me, I understood how she felt.

“Let’s go on vacation,” I said. “Just the two of us.”

At the time, Moira was at the stove, burning steaks for our evening meal. I moved behind her and turned off the heat under the meat.

"Hey," she said. "They were cooking."

"I think they're charred enough." I turned off the heat under the beans which were already mushy. The potatoes would be undercooked, but I was getting used to eating them that way. I kissed her on the neck and asked. "If you had your choice of any vacation spot at all, where would you go?"

"Really?"

"Really. I have a little money saved from playing poker. I think we deserve a honeymoon, don't you?"

"Let me think. Woods, water, quiet. I'm tired of the city. I want to go somewhere where I can breathe without smelling auto exhaust."

"The Adirondacks aren't far. It's May, a little early in the season, but maybe we can rent a camp."

As it turned out, because it was early a cabin was available on a place called Little Pine Lake, a place that allowed rowboats, kayaks and canoes but no powerboats. We would have to bring our own groceries, but bed linen and towels were provided. I sent the owner a deposit. The rest would be collected by him the day we arrived.

Going on vacation seemed to energize Moira. While I was at work, she was packing and re-packing and making endless lists. On the appointed day we rented a car, and stuffed it with our suitcases and a big cooler of food. Elise stood outside the apartment, and waved us off.

I had a driver's license, but I'd actually driven very little, so I was nervous as we headed out of the city, north to the Adirondacks. Soon the city traffic gave way to lush farm fields with cows grazing, to farmsteads and small towns, and then we were in the Adirondacks with the mountains rising all around us. We passed a boy of about nine, dressed in dark Amish clothing , walking alone behind a horse-driven plow.

"How can they let kids that age work by themselves?" Moira asked.

"I worked for my grandfather when I was about his age. I helped him in the hardware store that he owned.

"Was it fun?"

"We didn't get along very well," I said. "He blamed me for my father's death. When I wasn't working for him, I used to hide in the barn."

We got to the house which was small and had tiny porch, but which looked directly out on a lovely lake, but when we opened the door smelled strongly of mildew. mildew. An ancient wood stove, that looked like someone had poured rust over it, stood in one corner, and the kitchen cupboards screeched when opened. It was not palatial but it was ours for a week.

Moira was walking around the house. There were three bedrooms, two upstairs and one down. The downstairs bedroom had a back-wrenching mattress, but the upstairs bedroom had a breathtaking view of the lake. While I put food away in the cupboards, Moira made beds upstairs and hung up toiletries in the bathroom. When I hadn't heard from her in a while, I went quietly upstairs. She was stretched out on the bed asleep.

I went downstairs and let myself out onto the open porch. It was now late afternoon and though it was sharply cold, a soft light was spread across the lake A kayak was moving across the water and in the distance, a chickadee called. I could smell pine needles and when I walked down to the water, I could see tiny fish moving in the shallows. I dipped a bare foot in the water which was much too cold to swim. In a corner of the yard sat a kayak and a canoe and on the porch were life jackets and paddles. Quietly, so as not to wake Moira, I took a paddle and a life jacket from the porch and dragged the kayak down to the water. Like my driving, I'd never actually done any kayaking. But the lake, ringed with mountains and lit by the soft afternoon light, beckoned. Putting on a life jacket, I stepped into the kayak and with the paddle in one hand I pushed myself off.

The kayak thrust itself forward, like a bird taking flight. Dipping my paddle in the water I learned the rhythm between water and boat and soon I was a considerable distance from shore. A couple of ducks flew by, I could see fish swimming below me, and my paddles made almost no sound. I was a creature of the water, unbound by flesh, moving across a radiant surface, while the light settled itself on the mountains, dyeing them rose and purple. Moira had been right in wanting a place like this. We needed time to be a couple, to talk, to make love, to enjoy something that would renew us both.

I paddled for half an hour around the lake, which was not very big, and when I got back to the house, Moira was up, sitting in a lawn chair, drinking wine.

"I thought you'd decided to go back to the city."

"You didn't see me?"

"I saw someone out there. I didn't realize it was you."

"How do you feel?" I asked.

"Great, but it's quiet. At home there is always noise on the street, in the hallway, from other apartments. I don't know if I can get used to the quiet."

Just then a frog croaked, and a cardinal landed on the picnic table. We watched as the bird walked around, unconcerned that we were so close.

"I could get used to this," I said, leaning over to kiss her. "I'm glad you suggested it."

"Are you hungry?" she asked.

"I'll cook," I said. "Hot dogs and salad. Is that all right?"

Over the next four days we paddled around the lake (there was a canoe in addition to the kayak), read books, slept, made love and watched the birds. It seemed to me that Moira looked better, and I could almost forget that she had cancer. One night, we were sitting out on the lawn chairs looking up at the sky. It was a glorious night, the stars miniature dots of fire against black velvet. There was a full moon, its light spread in a wide swath across the lake before us.

"Jim," Moira said. "When I'm gone, I want you to re-marry."

I drew in breath, realizing that this marriage and the honeymoon was a way to grasp something that was ungraspable. I loved a woman who was dying, and I could only watch helplessly as her life trickled away.

She leaned toward me and I could smell the lingering scent of her perfume. "You won't forget me, will you Jim?"

It was good that it was dark and she couldn't see my tears. "I won't forget you," I said.

On our last full day at the camp, we decided to take some snacks and go for a walk. There was a hiking trail nearby that led to a very nice restaurant. I had a good pair of sturdy walking shoes, and a hat and Moira had the same. We set out on the trail.

About half way around the walk, we heard thunder. I hadn't been paying attention to the forecast and we had no raincoats or umbrellas. "We should turn back," I said.

"Let's go on," Moira said. She walked to a place where she could see up to the sky. "It doesn't look bad. If rain comes we'll duck under a tree to stay dry." Just at that moment, I felt the first drop. I took off my jacket and wrapped it around her. We moved into a grove of trees, but the rain was coming down so hard that the trees couldn't do much to protect us.

"I think we should go back," I said.

Moira nodded. We left the grove and went back onto the trail, working our way back. The rain was cold and in addition to the rain, there was now wind, gusting fiercely. Moira gestured. "I see an old barn across the field," she said. "We could make a run for it."

"We'll get soaked," I said.

"We're going to get soaked anyway. With the barn we can be temporarily dry."

I looked at her. In spite of the small warmth my jacket gave her, her shoes and pants were soaked through. And the rain continued to come down hard. We would be wet not only from the rain, but from the grass that covered the field. "OK," I said.

We held hands and headed across the field, plowing through the wet grass and trying to avoid the unexpected dips in the terrain.

When we got to the barn, a door was partially open and we ducked inside. There was a strong smell of horse manure and old hay and though rain was still coming through the pierced roof of the cathedral ceiling, it was warmer than outside. We settled ourselves onto a couple of piles of hay. Moira was shivering. I put my arms around her and started rubbing her back to warm her.

I could feel her shivers subside and she leaned against me. "When I was little, my mother would tell me stories she made up herself," I began. "We didn't have many books, so she created these tales that were sort of a mishmash of all the fairy tales she could remember. My favorite was about a rabbit who fell through a hole in the ground and met a girl who was in trouble with a wolf. The rabbit was very brave, even though he was small and he killed the wolf with his sword, and then the girl went back to live with her grandmother."

"Sounds like little Red Riding Hood meets Alice in Wonderland."

"When I finally did read Alice in Wonderland, I kept looking for the place where the rabbit kills the wolf. That was always my favorite part."

"Were you close to your mother? "

"I was. After my father died, it was just her and me. We would stay up late on Friday night, eating popcorn and drinking root beer floats and watching corny old movies. When she married my stepfather, he put a stop to that nonsense right away. He didn't want a kid hanging around in competition for his wife's attention."

"So you didn't get along with your stepfather?" Moira was yawning now, leaning back on the bales of hay.

"Why don't you take a nap." I said. "At least until it stops raining."

"Tell me about your stepfather," she said.

I stood up. It was always difficult talking about Gus. "He was OK at first, but then he was courting my mother and she wanted me to like him. Later, after they were married, he pushed my mother to send me to a private school, which she resisted. He would catch me in the garage when my mother was in the house and lecture me about my manners, telling me that now that he was my father, he needed to treat me with more respect. I hated him."

"Were you happy when he left?"

"I didn't care about him, but I was devastated that my mother was gone. And then I went to live with my grandparents. My grandmother died when I was ten and it was just my grandfather and me, and he really hated me."

"Really? Why Jim?"

"My father died in a car accident when I was four. From what my mother told me, he'd gone out to get medicine for me, because I had a bad cold. He was hit by a drunk driver coming home. My grandfather blamed me for that accident. And he blamed my mother for forcing his son into an awful marriage. Maybe my parents had to get married, but I think they really loved each other. My grandfather always thought that his son could have done better than my mother."

"He was the one who gave you that scar on your shoulder?"

"He hit me with a shovel and then told people I ran into a tractor."

I had returned to sit by Moira who was gazing up into the ruined ceiling through which we could now see blue sky. "We should walk back," I said.

When we got back to the camp, Moira went immediately to bed, pleading that she was tired. I made a cup of cocoa and took it up to her, but by then she was snoring. I took the hot cocoa outside and, sitting in an Adirondack chair, I looked out at the lake. Whatever joy the two of us had felt here wasn't going to last. The light was fading and in the growing dark a loon called, the sound like someone crying for help.

"Give me more time," I said to the dark.

Chapter Thirty

We got back to New York City the next day.

On the drive back, Moira slept most of the way and as soon as we got to the apartment, she went to bed. I was a day early in returning from vacation, a day I could have used to spend with Moira, but I went to the college. When I got to my locker, there was a note, "See Baker," taped to the door.

"What's this about?" I asked Bree, my seventy-two year old co-worker. Bree was pot-bellied, grey haired, smoked like a chimney, and had continued working long after he should have retired because his wife had COPD and needed home health care.

"He come looking for you, last Friday," Bree said. "Something about a theft."

"A theft?"

"Said you stole something. I tried to stick up for you, but you wasn't here."

"He thought I stole something?"

Bree looked at me, considering the question. "He seemed to think you done took something, but I don't know what evidence he got."

With a sigh, I unlocked the locker and put my lunch bucket inside and went to see the supervisor.

"Jim," Baker said. "Glad you could make it."

"I'm back a day early from vacation," I said. "You authorized it for me, remember?"

"I want you to clean out your locker today, Slocum." He leaned forward in the chair. "You know that the professors trust us to go into their offices and respect the objects there. That is an important rule in this job"

I nodded. Don't touch anything had been drilled into me from the first day I'd been working.

"I respect the privacy of the offices we clean," I said.

"Apparently you don't. Last Wednesday, an envelope with one hundred dollars went missing from Professor Dana Bartold's desk. We brought in every single cleaner and questioned each one for a half hour. To a man, they insisted that they hadn't touched anything in the desk. That leaves only you."

"Did Bartold leave his door unlocked?"

"Never, why would he do that?"

"I don't know, carelessness. Maybe he left the office, thinking about something else, and forgot to lock it."

"Are you saying that you never went into his office?"

"He was one of my regulars. Number 234 in Harrison Hall. I cleaned that office every night. But I did not take any money. In fact, I wasn't even in the office last week. I was away on vacation." I could have added that Bartold was such a slob, it would take him years to recognize that something was missing, even an envelope full of money.

"You're telling me that you never touched the envelope with the money in it?"

"I wasn't even there. Someone did my job while I was away. Did you ask them about the missing money?"

Baker shrugged.

"Look, Mr. Baker, I have done a good job for you. Have you heard anything about my slacking on the job, moving or touching things? How could I have done this kind of thing when I was on vacation?"

Baker sat back in the chair and studied me. "I've been hearing things about you, Slocum," he said. "After the money went missing, I talked to the professors, to see if this was a regular problem. One of them, Dr. Weitz, told me she thought you had stolen a copy of a test and sold answers to other students. A classmate of yours, Ziggy Henderson, swore that you were the one who did it."

"Ziggy lied," I said.

"Are you aware that Ziggy Henderson's father is a big donor to this school. If Mr. Henderson knew that we had kept an employee who helped students cheat on a test, AND who stole money from a professor, he would not be happy."

"I didn't steal the answers, and I didn't steal the money. I wasn't even here when the money disappeared."

"You could have taken it before you left. The professor didn't realize it was missing until last week."

I didn't know what to say. It looked as though whatever I said in my own defense was not going to be accepted.

"Leave your keys, and employee ID card with personnel. We will mail you your last check," Baker said.

I did as he said. It wasn't as though I loved the job, but I needed it to support Moira and me. I got my jacket and on my way home I stopped at a local Deli to buy food for supper. Moira was at the moment ,too sick to cook and I didn't care what I ate.

When I got to the apartment and let myself in, it was empty. I walked through all the rooms. Moira's mother should have been there, watching over my wife while I worked. The bed where Moira slept was rumpled, and there were clothes spread out across the top, as though someone had packed quickly. My heart started racing. Where were Moira and her mother? Then I saw it, a note on the kitchen table.

"Gone to St. Elizabeth's hospital. Meet us there."

It took me a minute to remember where St. Elizabeth's was. I locked the apartment door, rushed down to the street, and got a cab. At the hospital, I was told that Moira Martin was on the second floor and I raced toward the room. Moira was lying in bed, her eyes closed, an oxygen mask strapped to her face. Her mother, Elise, was sitting beside the bed holding Moira's hand and leaped up when she saw me, giving me a hug.

"Oh Jim," Elise said. "When I went to check on her this morning, she was struggling for breath, and I was lucky to get an ambulance to come right over. They think it's pneumonia."

"I got fired," I said. I took the seat where Moira's mother had been sitting and reached out for my wife's hand. "We should never have gone on vacation," I said. "It rained and she got wet and cold. It's all my fault."

"She loved you Jim," Elise said. "And she loved being on vacation."

"She might have lived for a while longer, if we hadn't gone."

Elise leaned forward and hugged me. "You can't prevent something that is going to happen," she said. "She will be one of God's angels."

I started to cry. Everything in my life was collapsing without my power to stop it. For the next three days Elise and I took turns, sitting with Moira as she labored to breathe clutching her hand and telling her that we loved her as she lost the fight to live. Toward the end, she suddenly opened her eyes and looked at me. It took her a minute to catch her breath. "Jim," she said. "I don't want a memorial in a church. That's not me. Have a party. Let the world know I was somebody."

The tears were starting and I was trying to control them. I took her hand, which was growing cold and held it to my cheek. "I love you, my dear wife," I began. "How can I live without you in my life?"

She had closed her eyes and her breath was slower now, a breath in, a long hesitation, a tiny rattle, then an outward breath, a longer hesitation. I put my head down on the bed, wetting the sheets with my tears. I am not a praying man, but I prayed. I waited for the next inhale but it never came.

I reached toward her and touched her face. She no longer belonged to me. She was probably already on her way to paradise where she would make the angels laugh. I stood up and went to the window, where I could look out at the parking lot and the distant lighted towers of the city, gazing out at a world that seemed to have lost all color and life. Behind me, Elise was sitting beside Moira's bed, stroking her face.

The funeral was a small, quiet affair. Moira's mother and Little Jack arranged for a local Unitarian minister to officiate in his church, though there were a bare handful of us attending. Besides Elise, and Jack, and some of Jack's friends, a few buddies from the dance class came. We had got to know the other people over the few weeks we took lessons, and they were sympathetic about Moira's illness. Afterwards, went to an Italian restaurant where we had a subdued meal, and then we repaired to our favorite bar, where I got seriously drunk. The world had torn itself into two halves: the world with Moira in it, and the one without.

A week after Moira's death, I was lying asleep in my apartment. I didn't have the energy to get rid of Moira's hospital bed, her medications, her special toilet seat or the other signs of her illness. I heard a noise and looked up to see Jack, walking around the apartment cleaning up the empties and dirty clothes.

"Get the hell out of here, Jack. Just leave me alone."

"You coming with me to the Catskills?" he asked. "You've done pretty well with the poker games; you could make some good money there."

"I don't think so," I said.

He sat down on a chair facing me. "Jim," he said. "I know this has been a blow, but you will get your life back. You just have to give it time."

I had lots of time. I was twenty, but I didn't want time, I wanted Moira. She wasn't going to return, and nothing I could do would bring her back.

"Jim," he said. "This isn't going to work."

"It works for me," I said.

"Look son," he said. "Why don't you come back to the game. The Catskills are nice in the summer. Better than being here in New York."

"Go away," I said.

"Whatever you need, I will be there for you," he said. "Elise has gone back to Florida but if you want me to stay here, I will."

"Go away and leave me alone," I said.

"As you wish." He went out the door, leaving two hundred dollars in cash on the kitchen table. I kept drinking for the next week and then, because I wanted to see where Moira had grown up, I went to Florida. For two years, I drank, did drugs, pan-handled on the street, and tried hard to die.

Chapter Thirty One

It's not easy being homeless. You have to be determined to live without a job, forgo human interaction and do without good nutrition and hygiene. You have to want to be lost. With alcohol and some serious drugs, my conversion from college janitor and con man to homeless bum took about six months. It was warm in Florida, and in a beach town I could bunk on the sand in a cheap tent. Most of the time I did as little as possible to stay alive. I begged on the street corner, carving out a place where I could get enough to live. I slept on the beach or in parks, or under bridges and ate at what I called Dumpster Diners.

People in America throw away an amazing amount of stuff, food being the most plentiful. I settled in Punta Gorda, and found Mickey's Deli where the owner was more careful than most and threw away food that was edible but past it's sell-by date. And that was where I met Buddy.

Mickey's didn't do suppers, so at about quarter to four, the doors were locked and the staff cleaned up the place, moving through the refrigerated section to clear out old food. That's where I came in. I had learned not to get there too early, because the owner saw feeding a homeless man as something that might give them a bad name. And since I was the only one who knew about this free food, I could arrive promptly at quarter to the hour and not have to worry about competition.

But that evening I did have competition. I watched as the food was delivered to the dumpster and when the kid left to lock up the restaurant, I moved in to see what the offerings were. That was when I saw it, a small, skinny yellow dog, crouched near the base of the dumpster. Sometimes these dogs can be mean, so as I approached the animal I began to talk.

"How you doing pal? You living on the street like me?"

The dog slunk back further into the shadows. I tried to ignore him as I reached inside to find my food. There were rich pickings tonight. Lots of sandwiches in plastic containers, a piece of apple in a plastic wedge, and a banana with only a few brown spots. There was a plastic bottle of water, (probably a mistake). I loaded up my arms with food and retreated. I could still see the dog, crouched in the shadows, watching me, but making no move to approach.

I tore open the seal on one of the plastic containers. The sell-by date was a week ago, but this sandwich (baloney) had been refrigerated and looked edible. I parted the bread, took out some of the meat, tore the meat into strips and carefully put them within reach of the dog.

Cautiously, the animal moved forward, snatched the meat and retreated to the shadows. I took part of the sandwich for myself. At this time of night, things were pretty quiet around the deli. The doors were locked, and no one came near the dumpster. I debated whether I should go back and dumpster dive again, looking for more food. It would be here tomorrow morning, a little older and staler, but I was the only one who was fed here. I approached the dumpster. The dog growled timidly. I moved back to my stash of food and found some more meat and cautiously approached. Some dogs have been homeless for a while and are truly fierce. They have learned to attack first and ask questions later and will bite without provocation. But this dog was shy, and uncertain. Perhaps in the not too distant past, he was someone's pet, living in a warm house with regular food and a bed. But whoever had owned him had dumped him, like so much trash on the street.

I knelt in front of the dog and held out the meat. I could see that he was uncertain whether to approach a stranger and get something to eat, or remain safely hidden and be hungry. Hunger won out over his fear. Slowly he moved forward and took the meat gently from my hand and then retreated.

"Good boy," I said. I could hear the dog's tale thump against the ground. I took another piece of meat and held it out. This time the dog, after he ate, stayed where he was. Gently I held out my hand and touched his head. He could have taken a bite out of my hand, but he didn't.

I went back to my stash of food and gathered it up, stuffing it into my backpack. Then I stood and began walking away. I had walked for about five minutes, when I heard a noise behind me. The dog was following.

That was the beginning of our friendship. Having a dog when you are homeless is mostly a good thing. People often respond to homeless animals more generously than they respond to homeless people. I suppose they reason that a homeless person is there of his own volition, but an animal has no choice. This isn't completely true. Some folks are not homeless by choice.

The coins in my collection hat increased by a small amount when I had Buddy on my corner. Sometimes people would drop in dog treats, or packets of kibble. Once in a while they would stop and pat his head. It was always the dog that brought out their generosity, not the smelly guy who was his owner. The most important thing about Buddy though, was that I now had a friend, someone who didn't see me as a bum with no prospects. When you have someone who trusts you, even if it is a scruffy mutt, you think of yourself a little differently. I think, having Buddy started me back to sobriety.

Buddy and I were partners. At night if the weather was warm we would bunk on the beach where it was quiet. The shelters did not accept animals and I was reluctant to leave Buddy on his own, especially in the cold. One night we were camped in a city park, under a bridge. Parks are heavily patrolled, and I was more likely to be rousted out of my sleep by a cop in a park than on the beach, but this night it was down in the fifties and even the cops didn't want to be out.

I was dreaming that I was on an ocean liner in the middle of the ocean. The boat was rocking back and forth. I could hear the wind, see the waves threatening to overwhelm us. Struggling up through the nightmare, I woke and realized that Buddy was in trouble.

He was thrashing around, breathing heavily. When I turned my flashlight on him, I could see foam coming from his mouth and his eyes rolled up in his head.

"Buddy," I said. He didn't hear me, lost as he was in the chaos of his illness.

"Buddy," I said louder. I knelt beside him, trying to assess the situation. His eyes closed, his breathing slowed, his chest rose and fell and then his breathing stopped. I put my head to his chest but could hear no heartbeat.

Was it too late to rush him to a vet? Wait a minute. I was a homeless bum with fifty dollars to my name. No one would allow me into a cab and I had no idea where the nearest veterinarian was. I was sure no decent clinic would be open at this time of night, and no vet would admit me.

I looked down at my friend, a dog I had loved. I put my head to his chest and sobbed.

It wasn't until later that I learned that a well-intentioned neighbor had stashed rat-poison near a building close to where we slept. The poison was wrapped in a piece of ham, and well concealed, but Buddy was a dog who'd been starved much of his life, and would gobble down anything that looked like food. Since I was a homeless bum, I had no right to protest that rat poison had killed my dog. Nevertheless, I missed him terribly.

Six weeks after Buddy's death Little Jack found me. I was sitting in my regular corner, not feeling so good. I wasn't eating or sleeping well. The death of my friend made me feel less secure, and though I could now go to a shelter, personal hygiene wasn't a priority. I was nodding off when I felt someone shaking me.

"Jim, Jim." I looked up. It was Jack.

I struggled to rise. I didn't want him to see me like this, but I wasn't in any condition to gather my things and sprint into the distance. I got to my knees, but then fell forward onto my face.

"Where you been?" Jack asked. " I looked everywhere for you. Is this what happened?"

"Leave me alone, Jack."

He knelt down beside me so we were face to face. "Jesus you stink," he said.

"I didn't ask you to be here."

"No, you didn't, but let me tell you that Moira wouldn't want this. She believed in you. She loved you. She would be ashamed that you've let yourself go this way."

"Get the hell out of here, Jack. I don't need your sermons." I was struggling to rise, but it was hard. It was eleven in the morning, but I was already pretty looped.

"Come home with me. Let me get you fixed up."

"I don't want to be fixed up, Jack. Just leave me alone."

"Look son," he said. "I can't say I know what you are feeling, but I do know that this sort of thing isn't healthy. Come home with me. Let's talk this over."

I pushed him away. I was too wasted to get away and at the moment, I had nothing to numb the embarrassment of his seeing me.

But Jack stayed. Eventually, with a lot of talking, he got me to come back with him to the house in Florida, where he'd retired. It was a long uphill fight back to sobriety, but after a few years I was finally able to say that I was truly sober.

Part III

Trust Me

Chapter Thirty Two

Kiki

After my breakup with Jeff, life seemed to slow to a boring routine. I was still in 'personal service' at the restaurant. I still had the crappy two-bedroom apartment in Port A, with one of the bedrooms crowded with boxes of stuff. I still had my life, but it was lonely.

I had the address Nate Marks had given me for Jim, but I hadn't made the call. What would I say? Hi, I'm the girl you lied to about your name, where you lived and what you did for a living. Would he laugh at me? Of course he would. Why was I even thinking about him?

Sometimes at night I would look at the red Stetson I called my power hat. In spite of the lies he had told me, Nate had believed in me. He was a man who thought I could do anything I wanted to do.

What would he think of me now, moping around a sleazy two-room flat, with no friends, no lovers, no anything? Even if I never saw Nate Marks again, I needed to pull myself out of this slump.

Nevertheless, the questions persisted. Was it just a coincidence that Nate had disappeared the same day my mother and Grainger left for Paris? I liked Nate too much to believe he might have had anything to do with my mother's disappearance, but his leaving at the same time made it possible.

One Saturday, when it was too crappy to walk the beach, I decided to go through the boxes in the spare bedroom. It had been more than two years since my mother left and I had to face the fact that she was not coming back. The company had been dissolved, the creditors paid, the employees fired and even if she walked in the door today, she would not pick up where she'd left off. I had made that impossible.

I had stopped for a break when there was a knock on the door, and when I opened it, I faced a short, plump woman with teased white hair and a wild, zebra striped jacket in shades of pink and purple.

"Miss Coleman?"

"Yes?"

"Deloris Schmidt." She glared at me

"Can I help you?"

She started in. "A year ago we bought a condo in Corpus from you. We paid a lot of money for that place and we expected everything to work well. I have to say, I have never, ever dealt with this level of duplicity. I came here in person, to tell you." She pulled a small cloth packet from her purse. "And to give you this."

I had no idea what she was talking about. "Want to come in?" I asked. When she followed me into the apartment. "Can I offer you coffee?"

She was looking around the apartment, realizing that in spite of my selling a condo, I wasn't rich.

She sat down. "Coffee would be nice."

"So tell me what's wrong."

She took a deep breath. "We had this problem with the heating, especially in my son's bedroom. Thank goodness he's not there often, but when he was, we could never get the place warm enough. We hired a heating specialist at two hundred dollars for a couple of hours. You know what he found?"

I waited.

"That." She pointed to the bundle I held in my hand. "Someone had taken the heat register on the wall, and made a hidey-hole out of it. There was no connection to the heating system at all; that's why we never got heat."

Grainger. I don't know when he'd had the time. "I'm sorry this happened to you," I said.

"Yeah. Me too." She looked around the small, crowded apartment again. "I was gonna ask you to reimburse us the money, but I think you need it more than we do." She rose and went out the door.

When she'd left, I opened the cloth packet and spread the contents on the counter. Inside was a collection of ID's and a plastic bag with jewelry. This was something important enough that Grainger had gone to a lot of trouble to hide it. There were six driver's licenses, ranging in date from 1998 through 2014 all featuring Grainger's picture. I put the licenses in chronological order. The Grainger Starland from 1998 had dark hair and a moustache. Only the name on the license wasn't Grainger's, it was for a man named Gus Slocum and it was issued in Oklahoma. A 2000 license issued to Gary Stark in Wichita, Ks. showed Grainger with blonde hair. A 2005 license issued to Gibbs Sinclair from Dallas, Texas showed a slightly older Grainger, clean shaven and wearing glasses. A 2013 license issued to Grady Stewart in New Orleans, Louisiana showed Grainger with grey hair. There were three credit cards. One dated 2005 had been issued to Gibbs Sinclair; one dated 2013 was for Grady Stewart, and a 2010 card was for George Stern.

I looked at the bag of jewelry but didn't open it. They say that killers keep souvenirs from their victims. Was this what I was looking at?

I took a deep breath, realizing the extent of Grainger's duplicity. How could my mother have married this man? He had conned her into marriage, and embezzled money from her company. If I were going to find out what happened to my mother I needed a private detective, and now with the drivers' licenses and credit cards on the table in front of me, I might have the help I needed.

The next morning, I presented myself at the office of William Arnold Collins. The title on the door was fancy, but William Collins "Call me Billy," didn't seem to have many clients. Maybe he was doing well and his client work was temporarily over, but he seemed awfully glad to see me.

"I'm trying to find this man," I said, putting the driver's licenses on his desk.

"He moves around a lot, and changes his name. What's he done?"

"Two years ago, he left with my mother for France. Neither one has ever been heard from. And he embezzled money from the company before they both disappeared."

Billy nodded as he studied the ID's.

"There's more," I said, putting the credit cards on the desk. "I think this is important."

"Maybe you should go to the cops," Billy said, picking up the credit cards and studying them.

"I did go once. The trouble is, I have no proof that he's done anything except take money from the company."

"And you haven't heard from your mother since she left."

I shook my head. "She sent me a couple of messages, but they were actually from him, and then he ditched his phone in a roadside dumpster."

Billy sighed "OK," he said. "I'll see what I can do. Do you have a social security number for him?"

"I think I can get it. Why do you need it?"

Billy leaned back in the chair and smiled. "People think the social security system is just a way to collect money for our old age, but the system is a vast data bank on every citizen in the United States. When we file taxes, get a job, buy insurance, go to the hospital and of course die—it all goes into the system. If this man is no longer alive and someone puts him into the Death Index we can tell where and when he passed. Have you filed a death certificate for your mother?"

I was still coming to terms with the fact that my mother was probably dead. "I don't know where she is," I said. I was almost in tears. "I don't even know if she's alive."

"Bring me his social security and I'll see what I can do." He looked at the drivers' licenses. "Can I keep these?"

I nodded and watched as he reached into a drawer and pulled out a sheet. "The contract for my services," he said. He handed over another sheet listing his retainer fee, and daily rates. "The daily rates are higher if I have to travel."

I was getting used to this outlay of money. I tried to tell myself that it was actually Grainger's money, but it pinched nonetheless.

That evening, I had the late shift at the restaurant. I would much rather have gone back to my crappy apartment and gone to bed, but I needed the money. I needed to pull myself together and face the fact that my life was what it was---no parent, no boyfriend, no good job that would give me a living wage and great self esteem. I had to power through as best I could.

A week later Billy called. He'd had some luck with one of the names on the list. Could I come into the office? When I was sitting in the chair across from his desk, he set a picture of a marriage certificate in front of me.

"A man named Gibbs Sinclair married Marilyn DuMonde, in St. Mary's Catholic Church on December 25, 2004 in Dallas Texas. DuMonde ran a bunch of hairdressing salons in the area. She is listed in the death index as expiring on January 12, 2011. Apparently the woman who filed the death certificate is her daughter, Vivienne."

"Twenty eleven? So she died seven years after her marriage?"

"I think she died shortly after her marriage, and her daughter had to wait to file for a death certificate. When a person dies, and there's no body, the next of kin are allowed to submit a request for a death certificate, but they have to wait seven years. It's an old English law—apparently it gives the 'dead' person time to change their mind about running away."

"Are there lots of people who die without leaving a body?"

"Sometimes. Look at nine-eleven. Those people in the twin towers. For some of those folks there was nothing left."

If my mother were really dead, where was her body?

"How did Marilyn DuMonde die?" I asked.

"Can't say. I don't think her daughter knows either."

"Can I talk to this Vivienne DuMonde?"

"I don't have an address for her. I would Google the white pages for Dallas. Want me to continue looking for this guy?"

"Yes, please." I gave him my credit card.

When I got home, I Googled the white pages. Thank goodness for people who never move. A Vivienne DuMonde was listed on 12

Bay Street. Was this Marilyn's daughter and, more importantly, would she talk to me? I dialed the number.

"Hello?"

"Miss DuMonde, my name is Caroline Coleman. I'm wondering if we could sit down and talk about your mother, Marilyn."

"My mother's dead. Are you selling something?"

"No. Nothing. Miss DuMonde, please hear me out. I think my mother was married to the same man, Grainger Starland, that your mother married."

"I don't know any Grainger Starland. My mother was married to Gibbs Sinclair."

"Miss DuMonde, I think my stepfather and yours were the same man, and it is possible that my stepfather killed my mother. Can we talk?

"I don't have time right now."

"I live near Corpus Christi. I can get to Dallas in less than a day. Please, give me a minute."

There was a long pause. "You sure you aren't selling something?"

"Nope. In fact, if you want to Google me, my mother used to run a business called Demi's Velvet Skin Cream. The company is gone now because Grainger embezzled the money, but there might be traces on the net."

"He took every bit of my mother's money. The businesses that she worked a lifetime to build up."

"Where were they going on vacation?"

"How did you know they were going away?"

"My mother disappeared the same way."

"They were going to England. My mother wanted to see the crown jewels, and the House of Parliament. She was so excited."

"And they never got to England, did they?"

"She sent me a postcard, but it was in his handwriting, not hers."

"I can come to your house on Saturday. I need to get time off from work, but I will see you then."

"Yes," she said and gave me the address.

It took me all day to drive from Corpus to Dallas. I hoped that my conversation with Vivienne wouldn't force me to pay for a motel room, which would be a stretch on my limited income, but I would do it if I needed to, but when I got to the small, neat house on a cul-de-sac, and knocked, no one answered.

I knocked again. Nothing. I stepped up to the window and peered inside. The house looked clean, but there were no lights on and no indication that anyone was home. Damn. I pounded again. Nothing.

"She left. Early this morning." A woman was standing on the sidewalk with a baby on her hip and a toddler clutching at her leg.

"Do you know where she went?"

"Nope. Sorry. I'm not usually a nosy neighbor, but the car squealed in the driveway when she left. It was early, like seven."

"Damn," I said again, and then looked down at the toddler who was watching me with more alarm than curiosity.

"I'm probably not allowed to swear in front of the boy, am I?" I said.

"He's heard worse," the woman said, "especially when his Dad's been drinking." She held out her hand. "Kat Wilson. I live next door. I was just out picking up the paper."

"Can you tell me anything about your neighbor?"

"Not much. She keeps to herself." Kat looked around the cul-de-sac. "Most of these folks don't socialize. My husband travels a lot and I thought, since I'm home during the day, that I'd get to meet my neighbors. You know the fantasy of back-yard barbecues, a friendly face at your door when you move in, neighborhood Christmas parties, that sort of crap. Doesn't happen. Almost every one of these people work, and when they get home at night they just want to eat supper and veg out in front of the TV. This is the first conversation I've had with a human being in my front yard since we moved here six months ago."

It was getting cold and the baby was starting to fuss. I had a long drive ahead of me, so even though Kat would have liked my company, I got in my car and headed toward home.

On the trip back to Port Aransas, I thought about my mother. Had I really done all I could to find her? What if she were still alive, and just wanted to jettison her old life and be someone new? That would have been strange and cruel, especially to loved ones waiting at home, but others had done the same thing. And if Grainger had killed her, how would I know?

All killers had patterns. At least that's what I'd read. Grainger seemed to go for women who owned their own businesses and were childless or like me, whose children were grown. Maybe Vivienne DuMonde was a teen when her mother married Gibbs Sinclair. Older children were less trouble to a new relationship, especially if they were away from home. But younger children would be more traumatized by the loss of a mother.

When I got home I went immediately to the bedroom and got into my PJ's. It was seven thirty on Saturday night and possibly half the known world was shopping, dining out or partying. No one was going to call, asking me for a date. Jeff had moved on and my best friends now had lives of their own. I looked at my dirty work uniform crumpled in the corner of the bedroom. I hated the damn job—the standing all day, walking all day, the fact that the manager whom I loathed, could run his hand over my bum whenever he felt like it, or that customers to whom I had been attentive or polite thought a fifty cent tip was adequate. A fifty cent tip hadn't even been adequate in 1970 when it more reasonably represented ten percent of the cost of the meal.

In my pajamas, I padded to the refrigerator and dug out a pint of ice cream—Rocky Road, my favorite. I caught my reflection in the mirrored surface. I looked pale and puffy, no wonder I never got any second dates. It had been two years since my mother died, and though I hadn't been over the moon about living at home, I had been comfortable. And then Nate Marks had come along and made me feel---what? Desired, beautiful, important. Something I hadn't felt for a long time, and which, after his departure, I'd lost the sense of. I pulled a spoon from the drawer and dug into the ice cream.

Where was the man anyway? Maybe he'd continued crafting fake art for little old ladies, or maybe he'd found the real love of his life somewhere else. I looked down at the pint of ice cream. It had been full when I took it out of the fridge and now it was almost empty. If you were going to eat yourself to death, you might as well enjoy the suicide.

I got up and walked to the desk where I kept papers. The real Nate Marks had given me an envelope that had been mailed to Florida and back to him in New York. I rummaged through stuff until I found it. It had been mailed to Nate Marks, in care of Ernest Horner, 25 Egret Circle, DeLand, Florida. I called information and got a phone number, but it was now too late to call. Was I trying to find this man because he might know what happened to my mother, or because I just wanted to see him? I put the envelope back on the table. Tomorrow would be time enough.

Chapter Thirty Three

I waited until ten the next morning to call Florida. The woman who answered the phone told me that she was the cleaning lady and Mr. Jack, which she pronounced ' Mr. Yack' was at the pool. If I could wait a few minutes, she would run and catch him.

"No," I said. "Just give him a message.

"Si. You tell me slow. I will write it down."

"I'm looking for a man named Nate Marks, actually Jim, I think."

"And you name, Miss?"

"Caroline Coleman." I gave her my number.

I got a return call two hours later. I was eating lunch and working through the boxes that I had stored in my single spare room. Most of them should have just been carted directly to the dumpster, but I kept thinking there might be some clue in all those papers to tell me where my mother was.

"Miss Coleman" the caller said. "This is Jack Horner. You're looking for Jim?"

"I am," I said. "Do you know where he is?"

"I do. Are you the Caroline Coleman who lives in Corpus Christi?"

"I am. Granger Starland was my stepfather. He left for Paris with my mother but never came back. Did Nate… Jim tell you about me?"

"It's been two years. Why didn't you call sooner?"

"I didn't know where he was. I met the real Nate Marks a few months ago in New York City and he gave me an envelope which had been mailed to you with Jim's paycheck and then returned."

"OK," Mr. Horner said. "Let me talk to Jim. I have your phone number. If he wants to talk with you, he will call, otherwise you won't hear from us."

"Thanks," I said. I put down the phone thinking about the man I'd been trying to contact. When I'd known Nate, he'd been open and friendly. It was true that he'd been engaged in some shady dealings but he'd never been mean or cruel. What was he doing now that he needed a guard dog like Jack Horner? And what was I getting myself into?

I was in the middle of the lunchtime rush at the restaurant, the worst time to get a phone call. Normally, I turn off my cell so it doesn't disrupt anything, but I had forgotten, and now it was ringing loudly, just as I was serving a meal. I pulled it out and glanced at the number. I put the dishes down and said, "Sorry, I've got to take this."

Moving to a corner near the rest rooms I put the phone to my ear.

"Kiki?"

"Yes. Is this Jim?"

"Listen," he said. "I'm sorry about leaving you like that. I'm sure you thought the worst of me."

I glanced around. Sam, the manager was watching me, making a no-personal-calls-during-working-hours gesture.

"Jim," I said. "I'm in the middle of work. Give me your phone number and I will call you tonight."

"Sure," he said. He rattled off a number, which I probably could have retrieved from my phone. I grabbed my pad and scribbled it on the back.

"I will talk to you soon," I said.

As soon as I put the phone away, Sam was on me like a tick. "Kiki," he hissed. "You know we don't allow personal phone calls here."

"I'm sorry," I said.

"You're on thin ice, girl," he said and strode away.

I had an overwhelming urge to take off my apron and throw it down in the middle of the room. I didn't make enough to justify the crap I took, but it was a job. It was my only job. Next week, on my day off, I would seriously start looking for something else.

I was at home when the phone rang. It was Jim, apologizing for calling me at work.

"That's OK," I said. "You didn't know what time of day I worked."

"It sounded like a busy place."

"It's a restaurant."

"You're a waitress?"

"Yes," I said remembering my fancy office at Demi's Velvet Skin Cream. I'm sure Jim remembered it too. Oh, how the mighty have fallen.

"Kiki," Jim said. "We need to talk, but I don't want to do it over the phone. Can you take a few days off from work and come to Florida?"

Florida in April? Now that was an idea. It had been a difficult winter in Texas and a few days in a tropical climate would be a change.

"Sure," I said.

"If you fly into Deltona, I will meet you at the airport," he said. "Let me know when you are coming. Here's my e-mail."

I copied the address wondering if Jim were so open with me, why Jack had been so guarded. But I was going to Florida. More importantly, I was going to Florida to see Jim.

Hold on. Don't get too excited, I told myself. He might have a girlfriend, or he might have gotten married. He might be calling from his jail cell where he was incarcerated for art forgery. But he sounded upbeat, as though his life was going well.

Chapter Thirty Four

The flight from Houston to Deltona took the whole day, and as soon as I got off the plane, I noticed the difference in temperature. Texas is hot and dry, but Florida was hot and wet. Tropical.

Jim was standing off to one side in the tiny reception area. I had forgotten how tall he was, how his dark hair fell across his forehead and his dark eyes lit up when he smiled. That smile. Oh dear, I'd forgotten the charm of the man.

He walked toward me and took my bag and then leaned forward and brushed my cheek with his lips. I could smell his cologne, feel the pressure of his hand on my arm as he led me out of the airport. We walked to a small, bright-green Kia Sport in the parking lot. Jim unlocked the door and put my suitcase carefully in the back seat.

"What happened to the Honda Civic?" I asked.

"I was careful not to take you anywhere in that piece of junk," he said. "How did you find out about it?"

"I talked to Trevor."

Jim nodded. He walked around to the passenger side of the car and opened the door for me. I got in. He went to the driver's side. We buckled up and drove off.

"Have you had lunch?" he asked, as we were leaving the airport.

"Airlines don't feed you any more, unless it's a long flight. I had peanuts and a can of coke but that was it. Let me show you the town and then we'll eat."

"Sounds nice," I said. It had been two years since we'd seen each other, and it was hard getting past the awkwardness. We rode in silence for a while.

"I'm glad you came, Kiki," Jim said. "I should have called you earlier and told you where I was."

"When you disappeared at the same time as Grainger and my mother, I thought you were part of the scheme. What happened to you?"

"Can we talk about this later?" he asked.

"Sure." We were coming into a small downtown, with shops, restaurants, clothing stores, candy and ice cream stores on both sides of the street.

"Welcome to DeLand," Jim said. Instead of stopping in the downtown area, he continued driving until we were in an area where live oaks arched over the street creating a canopy of green overhead.

"This is beautiful," I said.

Jim pointed to the brick buildings on either side of the street. "Stetson college," he said.

"Stetson, like the hat?"

"Like the hat. Would you like to walk around the campus?"

My stomach was beginning to rumble, but I was game. We parked the car, and headed toward a central quad. Palm trees stretched overhead and tall plants filled the spaces around the walkways. It felt like a jungle tamed and educated. A young woman passed us and said "Hi Jim."

"Stacy," Jim said.

"See you in English," she said and moved on.

"You're dating her?"

He gave me a sharp look. "Are you kidding? She's eighteen and I'm almost thirty-two. We're in the same class that's all."

"You're taking classes here?" Why did I sound like such a doofus?

"I have been for a while now. When Jack found me here in Florida, he suggested I go to college. It was a good idea."

"So you never actually went to Texas A & M."

"Nope."

"That story was a lie?"

"Uh huh."

We walked in silence for a few minutes. I was here, in a lovely tropical part of the country with a man who was charming and attentive. But that man had lied to me. As if reading my thoughts, Jim said. "Kiki, I'm sorry I wasn't straight with you. It's a long story. I know I should blurt it all out now, but I promise I will tell you everything."

"What's your major?" I asked.

"Psychology. After I get my undergraduate degree next year, I will go to graduate school so I can be a psychologist, or maybe teach. I plan to stay here in DeLand because Jack is here, and I want to keep an eye on him."

"Jack is pretty protective of you. I had to work hard to get him to take my name and number."

"He doesn't remember you, although I told him the whole story of being in Corpus Christi."

"Where did you meet Jack?"

"New York City. I was twelve, living on the street. He took me in and has been a substitute father to me ever since. Come on, let's get lunch and then I'll introduce you."

After lunch, we drove to Azalea Gardens a group of homes, nestled under towering Oak trees. Though these were, in essence, double wide trailers, the houses were all well maintained, nestled side by side, each with its own neat yard. We passed a man walking a little white dog, who smiled and waved.

"Jack is at the pool," Jim said. "He's there every day." He parked the car beside a swimming pool enclosed in screening. Inside I could see a wiry man sitting at a table with three women. The man was wearing a Hawaiian shirt and tan shorts which revealed thin legs. On his head he had a black, ill-fitting toupee which showed a lot of his bald pate. The toupee kept slipping sideways, and one of the women would reach up and gently pat it back into place.

"Jim," the man said, seeing us.

Jim went to the man and kissed him on the forehead.

"You've met Marta, Gracie and Eileen."

"Ladies," Jim said, bowing slightly. I glanced at the women. Marta was plump with white hair and a vast area of freckled bosom which she seemed unashamed to expose. Gracie was tiny and was wearing a bathing suit, a large sun hat and enormous sun glasses. Eileen, who was also wearing a bathing suit, scowled at us.

"And who is this vision of loveliness?"

"Caroline Coleman," I said. "I called you."

"Ah yes," Jack said. "You're Kiki."

"Come on Jack," Eileen said. "Let's play."

Jack started shuffling the cards in his hands. "OK, ladies, we're gonna have a winner here. Twenty five will get you fifty. Fifty will get you a dollar. You know, I once had a dog who used to chase people on a bike. It got so bad I finally had to take his bike away."

"Whatcha got Gracie? A quarter? Twenty five will get you fifty." He continued to shuffle. "Find the queen. Find the queen. What did Snow White say when she came out of the photo booth?"

"Some day my prints will come," the ladies said in unison.

"You heard about the two satellites that got married? The wedding wasn't much but the reception was incredible. Come on Gracie. Where's the queen?"

He stopped shuffling and Gracie pointed. Jack turned up the card. It was the six of hearts.

"Sorry dear," he said. "Better luck next time."

Gracie burst into tears. "I watched you, you son of a bitch and you cheated me."

"Language. Language. There's a lady present."

"I put my money down and I know I had it right." Wiping her eyes, Gracie stood up and started marching away.

"Gracie, darling. It's only a game. Hell, I'll give you the twenty-five cents. I'll give you fifty cents." He stopped and fished a bill from his pocket, waving it in the air. "Here's a dollar."

"Does it always end like this?" Jim asked.

"Pretty much," Eileen said. She reached toward Marta and touched her hand. "Come on honey. Let's go for a swim."

Chapter Thirty Five

We drove to a small house tucked neatly between two others. "I share this place with Jack," Jim said as he opened the front door. "Although he spends most of his time with Gracie. Come on in."

The house opened to a large living room with hardwood floors and a high ceiling. I could see a bathroom and an open door to another room. Next to the bathroom was a tiny room with a desk and computer. "My office," Jim said.

On the other side of the house were two bedrooms with a large bath between them. We came back into the living room. Tucked to one side was a galley kitchen, with newish appliances. "Jack bought this place years ago," Jim said. He was reaching into the refrigerator.

"Would you like something to drink?"

"Lemonade would be nice," I said.

"I'm saving my money for a place of my own, but right now most of my funds are going toward school."

"How long have you lived in Florida, Jim?"

"Eleven years. I came here after Moira died."

"Moira?"

"My wife. I came to Florida after she died, but I was homeless for a while. I moved in with Jack eight years ago."

"And this is her?" I'd wandered over to a bookshelf where there was a photograph of a woman. She had reddish hair and green eyes and was smiling broadly into the camera. "She's pretty."

"Sometimes I can go a long time without thinking about her. Isn't that strange? In the beginning, I couldn't go for ten minutes without remembering her, now I go a day or even a week. I met her when I was fifteen and she was twenty seven. We married when I was twenty. We were married for six weeks before she died."

He'd turned away from me. I think he didn't want me to see the expression on his face.

"Let's take our drinks to the porch," he said.

I had just taken a sip of my drink when Jim said. "I meant to call you a hundred times, but when I got back here to Florida, Jack had a heart attack, and when he was better, I just kept putting it off. I guess I was embarrassed."

"Embarrassed by what?"

"By what I was doing to make a living. By the things I was telling you that I knew were lies. I had gone to Corpus intending to catch Grainger in the act and then I was too late."

"You knew what Grainger was doing? How did you know?"

Jim put down the glass he'd been started drinking from. "Grainger was my stepfather. He was married to my mother. Only when I knew him, he was called Gus Slocum."

"I need to show you something," I said. I ran to my purse where I'd stuffed the ID's and credit cards that I'd gotten back from Billy. I spread the phony ID's and credit cards on a table. "Grainger had hidden these in the Corpus apartment," I said. "And this was with it." I put out the baggie with jewelry on the table.

Jim took the plastic bag with the jewelry in it, and dumped it out on the table. Reaching toward a gold necklace with a small heart, he held it tenderly.

"This was hers," he said. "I think my father gave it to her. She never went anywhere without it." I wanted to move toward him and put my arm around him, but we were just getting to know each other and I wondered if that would be too foreword. Jim had picked up the phony ID's and was studying them.

"I hated him," Jim said. "He thought I was in the way and I kept expecting he would get rid of me somehow. What I didn't expect was that he would take my mother away."

"You should have said something," I said.

"I wanted to. I liked you, but I didn't think you would believe me. If I had come up to you and said, 'Your stepfather is going to murder your mother. They are going on a trip and neither one will ever come back,' would you have believed me?"

"I'm not sure. Probably not."

"You would wonder how I knew these things. I don't have a single picture of Gus and my mother together. I don't even have proof that she's dead."

"When your mother disappeared, did someone go looking for her?" I asked.

"I was nine, living with my grandparents. I don't know if my grandparents went to the police to try and find my mother. And I think my grandfather was glad my mother was gone."

"He was glad?"

"He didn't like her and he didn't like me."

"I'm sorry," I said.

"I did look for her later, but I had no luck." He glanced at his watch. "I have an AA meeting, Kiki. You can come with me or you can stay here and read. If you brought a bathing suit, you can swim."

"I'll come with you," I said.

"My name is Arthur James Martin and I am an alcoholic."

Jim had gotten me into the meeting under the pretense that I was an alcoholic looking for a group. I wouldn't have to get up and speak if I didn't want to. The people sitting in the hall were a fair cross section of humanity. There were women wearing a small fortune in designer clothes, men in khaki pants and work shirts, men in business suits and kids barely out of their teens wearing hoodies and jeans. If I'd met any of them on the street, I would not have guessed that they were all alcoholics.

"I started drinking heavily eleven years ago. I drank before that; in fact, I had my first whiskey when I was thirteen, but until I lost my wife, I never drank to excess. When my wife died, I wanted to end my life, and the only way I could do that was to find oblivion in the bottle. In the time I lived on the street, I panhandled, I filched food from a dumpster, I did drugs and stole money to get those drugs. I was lucky that I never had any close relatives I could steal from, because if they'd been around, I would have taken advantage of them. I would still love to have a drink, but I remind myself every day how fortunate I am to be alive and to have friends. I also never forget that moving back to the hell of the bottle is just one sip away."

He sat down to scattered applause. I reached over and touched his hand and he squeezed mine.

After everyone had spoken, we got up for cookies and coffee. A beefy guy with bad teeth named Leslie introduced himself to us and said that the group met every Tuesday afternoon if I ever wanted to join them.

"Leslie is my sponsor," Jim said. "He helped me get sober." Jim put his arm around Leslie's shoulder and gave the man a sideways hug. "I owe him a lot."

"You owe Jack a lot too," Leslie said.

Jim nodded.

With more handshakes and hugs we made our way out the door and onto the street. It was about five thirty, and there were people walking around, shopping, drinking coffee, enjoying the warm temperature.

"Let me take you to supper," Jim said. "DeLand is a nice little city and it's a lovely night."

We walked past a couple of clothing stores, an antique store, a museum, a coffee shop, a restaurant. I stopped in front of an art gallery that had two small landscapes in gold frames. The pictures looked vaguely familiar.

"Are these yours?" I asked Jim.

He nodded. "I paint under my own name," he said. "And some of them have sold."

"People will love to hang them in their homes," I said.

Jim laughed. "Well I don't know about that, but I'm proud I don't have to lie any more."

"Trevor showed me your place in Corpus."

"Painting landscapes and selling them as Dutch antiques was Trevor's idea," Jim said. "Not mine."

"Trevor said forging art was something you thought of."

"That bastard," Jim said. He stopped walking and looked at me. "Why don't we find a place to eat and I'll tell you the whole story."

We stopped at the Boston Coffee House. The restaurant was small with murals of historic Boston buildings and unrealistic Puritans on the walls.

"Do you come here a lot?"

He nodded.

We ordered a meal, I a chicken melt with mocha mint coffee and Jim a Colonial Club with black coffee. When the waitress had left, I said.

"OK, from the beginning. You were living here in Florida. Why did you come to Corpus?"

The waitress appeared with our coffees and Jim took a sip. "I saw Gus in Miami in 2014. I was sitting in at an outdoor restaurant, and he just walked by. He was with this woman, and I wanted to run up to him and confront him about my mother. I hadn't seen Gus since I was nine, and I realized that he probably wouldn't recognize me. I followed him for a while and when he and the woman went into a restaurant, I watched where they sat. Then I found a waiter and gave him some money, asking him to tell me the name of the woman or her partner. When I went back later, he gave me your mother's business card."

"So you came to Corpus to find the man you knew as Gus Slocum?"

"And confront him."

"But you didn't do that."

"I should have. I might have prevented your mother's death. I will regret that for the rest of my life."

"But you knew they were planning a trip. That should have given you a clue."

"I didn't know about the trip. The first I heard of it was that morning in Trevor's apartment when you mentioned it. That was the reason I rushed out of there. I assumed they were leaving from the

Corpus house, but they left from the Island, and then of course, they didn't go to the airport at all, because Grainger had already killed her."

I winced when he said the words 'killed her' because as much as I knew my mother would never come back, I hadn't spent much time thinking about the way she'd died.

"I remember the trip they made to Florida," I said. "They were still dating then."

"I was living here with Jack at the time, but I didn't have a lot of money to go to Texas. I dithered around for more than a year, wondering if I could afford the trip. That's when I saw the ad for a job."

"The job with Trevor?"

"Trevor needed someone to manage the antiques store while he was in Europe, but he wanted, in addition to my resume, a sample of my art. I sent him a couple of drawings, and I made up some crap about having run a small antiques store here in Florida. Two weeks later he called and offered me the job. It wasn't until I got to Texas, that he told me he wanted me to create paintings in the style of old Dutch masters. He thought this would bring in customers. And of course, if I got caught forging art, he would be away in Europe. The agreement we had was just verbal. There was nothing in writing."

We sat in silence.

"You know that Grainger embezzled money from the company," I said. "I had to fire everyone, and sell off all the assets."

"I'm sorry," Jim said.

"I was able to get some of it back. Grainger had money in a safe deposit box with Texas Mutual. Ten thousand dollars. I withdrew it all."

"Good for you."

"He had two hundred thousand in a bank in Oklahoma. I got that too. He closed the accounts in other banks before I could get to them."

Jim nodded.

"You didn't want to meet Grainger the night we went to the Applegate's party. Was it because you didn't want him to recognize you?"

Jim nodded.

"I thought you were being rude."

"I was afraid you would feel that way."

"You should have explained everything, Jim. I could have warned my mother."

He only nodded. In a short time our food was delivered and we tucked in. I had many more questions but I didn't know where to start.

"I hired a private detective," I began. "I gave him the phony driver's ID's I showed you. The detective found a woman named Marilyn DuMonde, who was married to Gibbs Sinclair, one of Grainger's aliases. Marilyn's daughter Vivienne, applied for a death certificate seven years after her mother died, which was probably shortly after she married Grainger."

Jim nodded.

"There could be others," I said. "From the phony driver's licenses, we know he moves around and changes his name. What we don't know is how many other women there were."

"How did he meet these women?" Jim asked.

"He seems to be drawn to business women. My mother was Demi's Velvet Skin Cream and Marilyn DuMonde ran a string of beauty salons."

"My mother had a small specialty shop where she sold her home-made jams and jellies," Jim said. He pulled out his wallet and extracted a badly worn photo. He passed it over to me. A woman was standing with her arm around a boy of about seven.

"She was pretty," I said. "How did she meet Grainger or Gus as he called himself ?"

"I don't know how they met. I was just a kid."

We had finished our meal. Outside it was dark and we strolled through the downtown for a while, each lost in our own thoughts. Finally, we returned to the house. Jack was in the kitchen, frying a hamburger.

"You young folks having a nice evening?" he asked, as though we were teenagers coming back from a homecoming dance.

"How's Gracie?" Jack asked, moving toward Jack and giving him a hug.

"Don't ask. You know why there are very few men in places like this? The women kill them off. We went back to her place right after we saw you at the pool and all this time, she's been working me to death—and I don't mean getting me to repair the plumbing. I came home to get a rest."

The phone rang. "Don't answer that," Jack said. "It's probably Gracie, wondering where I am."

Jim looked at me. "You are welcome to sleep here tonight if you want."

I nodded. "I could get a hotel room."

"Don't be silly. This is a three-bedroom house; there's room for all of us."

Staying with Jim and Jack would certainly save me the money for a hotel. Was I doing this only to save money or to get closer to Jim?

Jim led the way to the guest bedroom. The room was small but neatly put together. It was painted a light blue and the bed had a white spread and pillows, giving it a clean, open feel. Paintings of the ocean hung on the walls.

"It's pretty." I turned to him. "I don't want to put you out, Jim."

"It's much better than having you in a hotel and my having to drive there if we want to talk."

"I am tired," I said. "I think I might lie down for a while."

"We will be very quiet," Jim said.

I lay down on the bed and within minutes I was fast asleep.

I woke to silence and absolute darkness. Where was I? I couldn't' think. There was light from a lamp outside, a branch outside rubbing against the window pane, and I remembered that I was in Florida. I was still in the sweaty clothes that I'd put on that morning in Texas and I desperately needed a shower. What time was it? I glanced at the clock which showed eleven. Would I wake Jim and Jack if I got a brief wash? I took off my shirt, pants, panties, bra, and socks and slipped into a robe. Then I opened the door to the rest of the house. I tried to remember what Jim had said about the location of the bathroom. There was a faint light at one end of the house, just beyond the kitchen. I headed toward that. As I neared the room that I assumed was the bathroom the door opened. Jim was standing there wearing nothing but pajama bottoms.

"Hi," I said. "I think I just crashed, right after we talked. Can I use this bathroom?"

He nodded. "I'm finished in here," he said.

"I'm going to take a shower, if that's OK."

He nodded again. He moved to one side but was still standing in the doorway. I turned sideways to get by him so that we were standing face to face.

"Kiki," he said, and then reached forward and gently kissed me. I could smell the soapy clean-ness of him, feel the pressure of his lips on mine, I moved into that kiss, abandoning all pretense of propriety. I pushed myself against him, could feel his erection. I was getting hot too. He had pushed aside my robe and was working his way down my neck to my breast.

"Oh God," I said. Together we moved to his room which was just next door and I fell into his arms.

Chapter Thirty Six

I woke in Jim's empty room, but Jim himself who had been there the night before, was absent. I got up, put on my robe and peered out the door. From the room, I could look out at the living room and kitchen. The door to Jack's room was open, so he must be gone. The door to my room was closed.

I desperately needed a shower and a cup of coffee, not necessarily in that order. Grabbing my shower things, I went into the bathroom and washed under wonderfully hot water. Then I returned to my own room, dressed in T-shirt and shorts and went into the kitchen. There, on the counter, was a note. "Sorry. Class today. See you at noon. Jim"

No notes of endearment to the woman he'd made love to last night. I didn't regret for a second what we'd done. Did he?

I found the Keurig machine on the counter and made myself a cup of coffee, scrambling myself some eggs as the coffee was brewing. It was now about nine thirty. I had more than two hours to kill.

In Port Aransas, I had gotten used to walking on the beach every morning. I love watching the sea birds and seeing the waves rolling up onto the sand. Give me a walk on the beach over an exercise machine any day. Walking here would not be in a straight line, but I had seen a map of the community, which was laid out like a flower drawn by a two–year-old, a large sloppy central oval, surrounded by circular 'petals.' If I walked in the same direction each time I came to a junction, I would end up where I started.

I poked my head out the door to gauge the temperature, then I went back to grab my hat and a light sweater. Outside I could hear birds calling, and two squirrels scampered across the street in front of me. I passed a man in a golf cart with his Yorkshire Terrier riding shotgun. A woman walked toward me with two dark-colored dachshunds on leashes. She smiled and said hello. No one asked what I was doing there, whether I was visiting an owner or had come to rob and murder. People were open, friendly, curious but not rude.

After twenty minutes, I returned to the house and made myself another cup of coffee, then spent the time washing the breakfast dishes. It was getting warm outside. Maybe I could find a book and take it and the coffee to the porch, where I would amuse myself until the boys came home.

The bookcase held an eclectic sample of books. Fiction: John Grisham, Tom Wolfe, Tom Clancy, Lee Child, Sue Grafton. And non-fiction: *Birding in South Florida*, *Winning Poker Hands*, *The Art of Vermeer*, *Dutch Masters of the Rijksmuseum*, *Drawing Landscapes*, and *How to Find a Missing Person*.

I wasn't interested in the novels, but I was curious about the Dutch masters, whom I guess Jim had copied to create the paintings he'd sold in Texas. I took *Dutch Masters of the Rijksmuseum* off the shelf. It was large and heavy and when I held it in my hands, there was something wedged between the pages. Tipping the book up, I shook the book. A plastic baggie fell to the floor.

I picked up the baggie and took it to the counter where I emptied it. There in front of me were three credit cards: a Master

Card made out to Jim Slocum, dated October 2000, a Visa in the name of Nate Marks, dated January 2006 and a Master Card for Arthur J. Martin, dated 2015. In addition, there were four driver's licenses. The first was a New York state license issued to Jim Slocum on October 19, 2000, showing a picture of a very young Jim. He didn't look old enough to drive. The second was another New York state license issued to Nate Marks on January 2006. He looked like a teenager, and the third license was from Florida issued to an Arthur J. Martin on October 2014. Were any of these legitimate? And if so, why the different names?

And then it struck me. The phony identification and the phony credit cards were exactly like the ones Grainger had used. Grainger had moved around the country more than Jim did, but was Jim doing the same thing?

I could feel my heart pounding. What was I doing here? Had I come to Florida to meet a man who was doing what my stepfather had done?

Jim had been nothing but kind to me, and I was falling in love with him. I'd even SLEPT with him. I'd always wondered how women fell for con men and now it looked like I was becoming the same kind of victim. What a fool I'd been. What a damned trusting fool.

The front door opened and Jack came in. His hair was wet, so he'd either showered at Gracie's or he'd gone for a swim.

"Kiki," he said. "Did you sleep well?"

I pointed to the cards and ID's spread out on the counter. "Do you know about these?"

He glanced briefly at the collection, and nodded.

"You know what Jim is doing?"

"He's not doing it any more. I wouldn't worry about it."

"What do you mean, don't worry. Why does he have all this stuff?"

"Kiki," Jack said. "I don't know why he kept those things. It was something the two of us did many years ago. It's over." He went to the coffee machine and started to brew a cup.

"What did you do that required a phony driver's license and phony credit cards?"

"I should let Jim tell you," Jack said. He got his coffee, walked to his bedroom and slammed the door.

I looked down at the collection. What Jack had said was true. All of the ID's were old. That didn't mean Jim wasn't still using them and didn't have more. The door opened and Jim walked in. He threw a backpack on a chair and moved toward me, kissing me on the cheek.

"What's up?" he asked. "You look angry." He went to the coffee machine and made himself a cup, then he opened the refrigerator door. "God, I'm starved," he said. "Want something to eat."

"Tell me about these," I said, pointing to the collection of ID's and credit cards spread out on the table.

"Don't worry about that, Kiki. That's over," he said.

"Tell me exactly why you needed a phony ID and credit cards."

I could see a look cross his face. He was about to say something that he might regret. "How did you find these?" he asked finally.

"I didn't go through your things, if that's what you think. I wanted to read a book, *Dutch Masters of the Rijksmuseum*. When I took it off the shelf, the plastic baggie fell out." This wasn't exactly how it happened, but I hadn't rummaged through his drawers or anything.

He went back to the refrigerator and starting removing sandwich ingredients. Lettuce, mayonnaise, a package of sliced ham, a tomato. I watched as he methodically began to build his sandwich.

"Would you like one?" he asked.

I was too keyed up to eat. I shook my head.

"Jack," Jim called. "I'm making lunch. Want some?"

Jack came out of the bedroom. He had changed his clothes and combed back his hair. He walked up to Jim and the two began talking softly, one of them nodding now and then.

"Are you going to tell me what's going on?" I asked, trying to keep the anger out of my voice.

The two men sat down at a table with their sandwiches. Jack was drinking iced tea, Jim coffee. I waited.

"I was running a scam called Three Card Monte in New York City, when we met," Jack said, gesturing toward Jim. "Jim came to work for me."

"I was thirteen," Jim said.

"You said Three Card Monte was a scam. Is it illegal?"

"It's a game rigged to benefit the dealer," Jim said. "Most of the time the players lose. We moved around a bit. New York City in the fall and spring, Winter in Florida. Summer in the Poconos. Sometimes we gave ourselves different names."

"And used phony credit cards."

"So that's all it was? An illegal game you were running. How did you get the cards?"

"Sometimes we 'borrowed' the card numbers from the marks, sometimes we had them created with our new names."

"The marks?"

For the first time, Jim looked uncomfortable. "A mark is someone you set up to take their money."

"And you are proud of this?"

Jim shook his head. "I didn't have a choice. I was a kid, I'd been living on the street for a year and Jack took me in. I was grateful to have food and a bed. I would have done anything he asked."

I stood up and went back to the counter where the cards were still spread out. I was not so much a fool to believe that everyone in the world was honest, but I'd never met, talked with, and fallen in love with someone who had deliberately deceived others.

"I'm going back to Texas," I said. "I can't stay here."

Jim moved to stand beside me. "Kiki," he said. "Don't do this. I am not proud of what I did, but I have moved on. I'm a different person. I don't drink, I don't sell forgeries, and I don't play Monte, at least not for serious money."

"I play for quarters," Jack said. He had finished his sandwich. "You should listen to him, Kiki. He's a good catch."

"My stepfather was a con man," I said. "I know the damage he did to everyone's life, my own included. How can I pretend that playing a rigged game and stealing credit cards is OK? I can't. I'm going home."

Jim was standing beside me, his head down, listening. "Suit yourself," he said.

I went to my room and packed my bags. When I came out Jim was standing by the door, car keys in his hand. "I'll drive you to the airport," he said.

"I don't need you to drive me. I am perfectly capable of calling a cab."

"Listen," he said. "It might take a while for a cab to get here, and if you are in a hurry it will be better if I drive."

I hesitated. On the one hand, I wanted to spend as little time as possible with him, and on the other hand, if he drove, it would get me to the airport faster.

We went out the door and I got in the car. He started the engine and in silence we headed toward Sanford where the airport was.

"Did you check the schedule?" he asked.

Of course I hadn't. I was prepared to sit in an airport all night if I needed to. I said nothing.

"I appreciate your taking me to the airport," I said.

"Is that meant as an apology?"

I put my head down. I didn't want to apologize. Maybe I had been wrong in the way I said things, but I wasn't wrong in what I had said. Jim and Jack had cheated people and stolen their identities. They had ruined lives, just as Grainger had ruined mine.

"Are you going to look for him?" Jim asked.

"Who?"

"Grainger. I know you hired a private detective. He helped you find Marilyn DuMonde. Will he help you find others?"

"I don't know," I said. "Did you ever think of looking for your mother?"

"Every day. But I was a kid. I was living with my grandparents, and then my grandmother died and everything went to hell."

"How?"

"You don't want to hear this. I'm the guy who is a criminal, remember, the one you can't get away from fast enough?"

I looked over at him. He was staring intently at the road as if memorizing every pothole.

"You were twelve when you were living on the street in New York?"

"I was, but it was easier than living in Oklahoma with my grandfather, who put me to work in his Feed and Grain store, hauling forty pound bags of bird seed and salt, and beat me when I dropped the bags."

"I'm sorry."

"How did you get away?"

"My grandfather sprained his wrist and one of the neighbors drove him to the hospital, leaving me, at eleven, in charge of the store. I'd never worked the cash register before, but I knew how it was done. I put a closed sign on the front door, emptied the register of money and walked to the bus station. It wasn't far, but all the time I was waiting for the bus, I kept thinking that if my grandfather beat me for spilling a bag of bird seed, he was certainly going to crucify me for stealing money. Luckily for me, the bus came before he did."

"But didn't they question you—being alone and all."

"I tucked myself in behind a family of five. The bus driver thought I belonged to them."

"And you never contacted your grandfather."

"Why should I? He didn't want me. He would have missed the money a lot more than he missed me."

We were coming into the parking area for the airport. Jim pulled to a stop. "Want me to wait?" he asked. "It could be a while."

For the first time I considered what I was doing. He was right. It could be hours before a plane arrived and I would be all alone in an airport. "Would you come with me and see when the next plane leaves?"

"Sure," he said. He opened the driver's side door and then walked around to the passenger side and opened it. He grabbed my suitcase from the back and together we walked into the terminal. The attendant at the counter was very nice and told us that the next flight to Orlando, which would connect me to a Dallas flight would not be for three hours. I looked around. The place was very small, and there were only three couples currently occupying seats. A man was stretched out on a bench. Drunk? Dead?

"Change your mind?" Jim asked. "I can take you to a hotel."

"I hate to put you through all this," I said. "Especially after what I said."

"You are here because of me. I feel responsible."

"OK, a hotel please."

We drove to a motel near the airport, and Jim deposited me in the lobby and then came in to make sure that I could get a room. "Call me tomorrow when you get the time for your flight," he said. "I'll take you to the airport."

"Thank you," I said.

He turned to leave and then turned back. "Kiki," he said. "I think you should keep looking for Grainger. If nobody stops him, he is just going to keep on killing women. I believe you have the courage to find him."

I started to say that he thought I was braver than I really felt, but he'd already turned and headed out the door.

In the motel, I unpacked my suitcase, putting things into the cheap dresser and hanging my coat in the closet. At the bottom of my suitcase was the evidence I'd collected on Grainger: the bag of jewelry, the material from the UPS mail box and Grainger's collection of phony ID's and credit cards. What had Jim thought when he saw the phony ID's? Did he feel a twinge of guilt because what Grainger had been doing, was exactly his own game? I picked up the bag with the jewelry, and rummaged through it, finding the necklace that Jim had identified as his mother's. I had no evidence that this necklace was actually hers. It could be something Jim had made up on the spot to gain my sympathy. In fact, there seemed to be very little in what Jim had told me, that I could actually prove to be true. He'd said that Trevor had hired him to run an antiques store, specifically asking Jim to paint forgeries. But this was Jim's word against Trevor's. Nate Marks said that he'd given Jim an ID so that Jim could take Nate's place in school, but it could have been otherwise. How did people learn to trust each other? I had done exactly what my mother had done, fallen for a man without looking carefully. Leading with my heart and not my head.

It didn't matter now. I was free of Jim and through with this whole stupid game. I took out my computer and made reservations for a flight that would go from Sanford to Orlando to a final destination in Dallas, Texas. Jim said he would drive me tomorrow, but I could take a cab. I didn't need to see him ever again.

Now that things were set for tomorrow, I needed a walk. The motel was at the edge of town with McDonalds and Taco Bell within walking distance. It was now late afternoon, and the sticky heat that had been with me all day, was starting to fade. I stepped outside and found a patch of woods behind the motel. The path was a sandy walkway snaking past trash under towering live oaks, hung with Spanish moss. Being in the woods made things a little cooler. I heard a jay call, answered by another. What was I doing here? What was I doing with my life? I made a resolution that when I got back to Corpus, I would quit my waitressing job and find something else. If my mother were around, she would have said that I was a girl with plenty of talent that I was simply wasting.

Would my mother really have said that? I could count on the fingers of one hand the compliments my mother had paid me, and yet, she was my mother and had sometimes done her best to help me gain my own self confidence. I remember a pink billed cap with rhinestones that spelled out World's Smartest Girl that she'd given me when an eighth grade essay I'd written won a prize. She'd been proud of me then. Did I still have the cap? Somewhere.

We all have mothers, and if we are lucky, some of the love that we're given at the beginning of our lives, continues to enrich us, even when the source of that love is gone. My mother had loved me in her own way. What had I done to return that love? Had I made any real effort to find out what happened to her? Had I really tried to find the man who killed her?

I turned around and went back toward the motel where I pulled from my suitcase the plastic bag that Grainger had left in the UPS mail box. There was something here, I was sure of it. If I could just figure it out.

I laid the two items in the bag on the table. The first was the postcard from St. Louis with the words "See you soon, M." written on the back. Obviously Grainger knew someone in St. Louis. Was this person a woman with whom he'd been corresponding? Someone who was going to be his next victim? St. Louis is a big city, and if Grainger were there, he'd most likely have changed his name by now. How would I ever find him? I could call Billy Collins, my go-to detective and tell him that I thought Grainger was headed for St. Louis, but Billy would need more evidence than a postcard to find him.

Pushing aside the post card, I looked at the flyer thanking Grainger for his business. It came from a company that filled prescriptions called Rx by Mail. Why would Grainger need a prescription, and if he did need one wouldn't he have it filled locally? Whatever he'd purchased, probably had been done without a doctor's knowledge, and had been something he didn't want my mother or anyone else to know about.

I took out my computer and Googled Rx by Mail coming up with a website for a legitimate company that sold a variety of drugs. But what had Grainger bought? I looked at the flyer again. In the upper right hand corner, partly obscured by the company logo were the words Atr Sul.

I typed the abbreviation into the website for Rx by Mail and the words Atropine Sulfate popped up. Atropine was a common enough drug, used before anesthesia to decrease saliva and to keep the heart beat normal. It was also used in eye examinations. So what was Grainger's problem that he needed this drug? Then I saw it. Under 'Precautions' was the warning, "Improper use of this medicine may cause irregular heartbeat, hallucinations and loss of coordination. In large doses, Atropine can be fatal."

Grainger had used this drug to kill my mother. I thought of the champagne glasses missing from the Port Aransas house, and the fact that though the two had probably drunk champagne, there was no empty bottle in the trash, or trash of any kind. I remembered my mother's earring in the corner of the garage. She'd no doubt been wearing them when he killed her, and one of them fell off when he carried her to the car.

Had my mother taken a long time to die, struggling against her growing weakness and loss of coordination? At what point did she look over at Grainger and realized that the man she loved was the one killing her? And if she didn't die right away, as she became increasingly unable to move, did he hasten her death by strangulation? I tried not to think of it, but I had to. One way or another Grainger was a murderer. I needed to find him.

It was now close to five o'clock, and my stomach was cramping with hunger. Putting on a sweater against the evening chill, I walked out the door, heading for McDonalds. It would be enough.

I got back to the motel at seven and turned on the TV hoping to find something to keep me occupied, and found myself in the middle of *Steel Magnolias*. All through the movie, which is about a strong mother-daughter relationship, I was thinking of my own mother. I couldn't fly back to Corpus Christi without at least attempting to find her killer, and the best person to help me, the man whose mother had also been Grainger's victim, was Jim. Reluctantly I dialed his number.

"Yes?" he asked.

"I learned how Grainger killed my mother. There was a flyer addressed to him from a company called Rx by Mail. The flyer thanked him for a recent purchase. The purchase was a drug called Atropine Sulfate."

"What's Atropine Sulfate?"

"It's a drug used by doctors as pre-anesthesia and it has other uses. Atropine in large doses can kill."

"How do they administer it?"

"Either by injection or as a liquid in another liquid. The thing is, there were champagne glasses missing from the Port A house, and nothing in the trash."

"Is it undetectable?"

"If you don't have a body, it is."

"Would he incapacitate her with the drug and wait for her to die?"

"Or maybe strangle her?"

I took a deep breath. "Jim," I said. "I need help finding Grainger, or Gus or whatever the hell he is calling himself now. He killed my mother. He killed your mother. If we do nothing, he will kill other women and some of those women may have children."

There was a long silence. "This could be dangerous, Kiki. We're not police. We're not detectives. Where will we start?"

"St. Louis? Grainger got a postcard from someone in St. Louis. It said 'See you soon.' And was signed M."

"M, like a person's initial?"

"Yes."

"So someone in St. Louis is expecting Grainger to visit. I don't even know where we would start."

"I don't know either, but we have to try."

There was silence.

"Jim, I am sorry for everything I said. I need your help."

"OK, I'll come to the motel and get you."

"Come tomorrow morning. I may change my mind between now and then and if I do it will save you a trip."

"As you wish," he said.

Chapter Thirty Seven

I didn't change my mind, but I was subdued the next morning when Jim picked me up at the motel.

"So you've decided to forgive me?" he asked when we were driving back.

I looked over at him. A lot of my initial attraction to this man was still there. "I'm thinking about it," I said.

"Kiki," he said. "I need to apologize. What I have done is unforgivable and I haven't been able to think of anything else since you left." He was looking toward me, and I was worried about traffic on the road.

"Pull over, will you?" I asked.

"Sure," he said. He stopped the car and turned toward me. I could see shadows under is eyes and the pale stubble of a beard. "I didn't sleep well, thinking about this. Actually about us."

"You thought about us?"

He nodded. "I should have told you everything when we first met, but I was so attracted that I was sure you would dump me as soon as you knew what I was doing."

"You might have stopped Grainger from killing my mother," I said.

"I know. I had my chance and I blew it. And I blew my chance with you. I am sorry, Kiki. Do you think we can start from the beginning?"

I thought back to the beginning. "I don't want to start from that beginning," I said. "I want a different beginning, one where we are honest with each other."

He nodded. "I promise that from now on, I will only tell you the truth no matter what your question is."

We went into the house. I dropped my suitcase in the bedroom I'd occupied before. Jim was in the kitchen brewing coffee. "Have you had breakfast?"

I shook my head. "No classes today?"

"Nope. But I do have homework." He set a cup of coffee down on the counter. Tell me why you changed your mind."

I doctored the coffee and took a sip. "We have both been hurt by Grainger. And he's no doubt murdered other women. I think we need to protect women he hasn't killed yet."

"How do you propose we do that?"

"I honestly don't know."

He was standing at the refrigerator with the door open. "Would you like an omelet?"

I moved to stand beside him. "Thank you Jim."

He nodded, and then took eggs, milk and cheese from the refrigerator and began making the dish. “You hired a private detective, right?”

“I did. He was the one who found Marilyn Dumonde’s daughter, Vivienne.”

“And you talked to Vivienne?”

“No. She wasn’t home. It was almost like she was afraid to talk with me.”

He was scrambling the eggs as we talked. He poured himself a cup of coffee, plated the eggs and put them on the table with a jar of salsa.

“Jim,” I said as we started to eat. “Billy Collins can get information about where Grainger has been, but he can’t tell us where Grainger is now. If we’re going to protect anyone, that’s what we need to know.”

“It was just a matter of luck that I saw him in Miami,” Jim said. “If I’d missed him I would never have learned that he was in Texas. I should have confronted him then.”

“It wasn’t your fault,” I said. Did I really mean that? Was I beginning to soften toward Jim? “What do people do when they are trying to find someone?” I asked.

“Go on the internet,” Jim said. “Googling someone will cost you a small fee, but it’s fairly easy.”

“We don’t know the name he’s currently using,” I said.

“He always uses the same initials: Gibbs Sinclair, Grainger Starland, Grady Stewart, Gary Stark, Gus Slocum.”

“He doesn’t want to change the monogram on his shirts?”

“Maybe a name with the same initial is easier to remember,” Jim said. He took a mouthful of egg and ate slowly. “Do you have a current picture of him?”

"I do. Grainger didn't like having his picture taken, but I got one of him and my mother at a country club dance. It's on my computer."

"He seems to favor women in a certain states: Oklahoma, Texas, Kansas, Louisiana andMissouri."

"Let me find an atlas," Jim said getting up from the table. In a few minutes he returned and spread a map of the United States out on the table between us. He drew a circle with his finger. "This is a large area to be working in. He must have a home base."

"A home base?"

"What does he do with the bodies? Dump them in the woods when he's traveling? And he has to do something with their luggage. A suitcase left by the side of the road will give away the game that the woman isn't traveling."

I tried not to think of my mother, dressed in her best suit, decomposing in a shallow grave somewhere. If I could find where he'd put her, at least I could give her a proper burial

"NAM-US is the national missing persons system," Jim said. "They can help cops search for anyone missing in the US. Five years ago, I did try and find my mother that way, thinking somehow that she was still alive."

"No luck?"

"No luck."

I went to my computer and Googled NAM-US. The site wanted a recent photograph, nickname or alias, physical description, birthdate and social security number, places the person frequented, description of the car the person drove and the situation where the person disappeared. "I've got most of this," I said. "It will take me a little time to get it all together, but I can do it. Who gets to see this information?"

"Local police or anyone looking for a missing person. "

I was looking at the website. “There is a list of people who are missing,” I said. “I’m going to register and see who has been put on the list. Maybe a relative of one of Grainger’s victims put Grainger’s name up here, hoping to find her.”

“We only have the initials, G.S.” Jim said.

“But we know the area where he’s likely to be. I doubt if he is in Portland, Maine or Los Angeles. He seems to be in the middle part of the US.”

I was looking at the list of missing persons. I had three things to go by: Grainger’s initials, the geographical area that he worked in, and something that happened after May 14, 2016, when he and my mother vanished. I searched the list of missing persons with Jim looking over my shoulder.

“Do you see anything that might be a match?” I asked.

He shook his head and sat down in a chair nearby. “What makes a person unique? What is it about Grainger that would cause him to stand out in a crowd?”

“Grainger is pretty ordinary looking,” I said.

“Which makes it easy for him to do what he does. The NAMUS site asked if the missing person had scars or disfigurations or were taking a rare kind of medication.”

“Or prefers an expensive candy like Michelangelo’s Chocolates. He got them by mail.”

“So the company would have a mailing list of customers.” Jim said.

We looked at each other. “It’s not going to be easy,” I said, already Googling the name of the company. “Its headquarters are in Paris, France.”

“Does it have stores in the US?”

“Los Angeles, New York City, Washington, D.C.”

"How about a trip to New York City?" Jim asked.

"I think we should put his name up on the NAM-US site first," I said. "There may be someone who knows him by his picture, if not his name. It would save us a lot of work. And there might be other sites where we can put his picture up."

"Your information about him is more current than mine," Jim said. "But whatever I can do to help, I will do."

He was smiling that smile that always melted my heart. Was I falling again? "Thanks," I said.

Chapter Thirty Eight

The next morning, I got together all the information I could find and posted a missing person report for Grainger on Facebook, saying that I was looking for my dad. OK, technically he wasn't my father, just my no-good stepfather, but I didn't want to stray too far from the truth.

I put up a missing person report on my mother too, although I was pretty sure that I would never see her again. Jim was at college, and so I had most of the morning to myself.

I decided that spending the time in the house where I might find other unpleasant information on Jim wasn't a good idea. I had no vehicle so I couldn't go shopping. What I could do was walk around the small community of Azalea Gardens. I put on my wide-brimmed hat (thanks Mom for that tip) and set out. This was a community of small homes, set around a green space with a pond. Around the pond were Azalea bushes now coming into full bloom. Shades of bright pink, orange and red were dazzling in the early morning sun. A man passed me walking a small dog.

"Pretty, aren't they?" he said.

I nodded.

"Are you new here?"

"Just visiting," I said. "I'm staying with Ernest Horner and Jim Martin."

"Little Jack," the man said. "At least that's what he calls himself. And Jim, I think Jim's his son. A real friendly chap." He held out his hand. "I'm Larry Harding." He pointed to a small white dog. "Little Bit," he said. At the sound of his name, Little Bit came over and gingerly sniffed my leg. I put down my hand and he sniffed that, and then gave me a friendly lick.

"This seems like a nice community," I said.

"Oh yeah. Folks watch out for each other. We're all reaching that age, when we need a little help." He pointed to a small red house with a neat front yard. "She has Alzheimer's. He does the gardening. Someone from the neighborhood, goes over once a week to read with her and give him a break." He pointed again. "He has Parkinson's, but he still walks every day. You look around here and all of us got something: Heart disease, arthritis, cancer but we're still upright. And as I said, we look out for each other."

I thought of my apartment in Corpus Christi where I knew none of my neighbors. I could be dead and decomposing in my place and it might be days or even weeks before anyone came to find me. Little Jack and Jim had chosen a good place to live.

Larry was studying me. "I didn't catch your name," he said.

"Kiki Coleman," I said. "I live in Corpus Christi, Texas."

"And how do you know Little Jack and Jim?" It was a question that in another circumstance might be rude, but I understood. Larry was just watching out for his community, making sure that no stranger was going to hurt his neighbors. He was just protecting his friends.

Explaining how I knew Jim would take me a long time. Where could I start? If I told Larry that Little Jack was really a con man who'd run an illegal gambling game where he'd taken people's money, it would not make Jack popular and might even result in a request for him to leave. I didn't want to do that. Could I lie? But if you are going to do that, it is best to stay as close to the truth as possible.

"I met Jim in Texas," I said. "He was selling antiques out of a little store while the owner was in Europe."

"Jim's a good looking fellow," Larry said. "I'm not surprised you followed him down here. Half the unattached ladies in this place are scheming to get him."

I nodded, remembering how Jim (whom I known as Nate) had charmed his way around the Applegate's party. By now, Little Bit, clearly bored by our conversation was pulling at the leash, eager to get on with the walk.

"Nice meeting you," Larry said and headed off.

I spent the next half hour walking around. I visited the clubhouse, where a man was putting together a puzzle, while a group of women did chair yoga to a videotape. Everyone was pleasant, and guardedly friendly. In the swimming pool, a man and woman were leisurely floating around. They smiled and I smiled back, but I didn't stay long enough to get grilled about my identity.

It was a warm day. If I'd brought my bathing suit, I might have returned and joined the couple in the pool. I strolled back to the house, hoping someone would be home.

When I walked inside, Jack was sitting in front of the TV, eating a sandwich and drinking a beer.

"Wondered where you'd gone," he said.

"I went for a walk," I said. "I met Larry Harding and his dog."

"Larry Harding," Jack said. "Don't think I've met him."

"He has a white dog named Little Bit."

"Oh yeah, him," Jim said.

"Do people recognize each other because of their dogs?"

"Sometimes," Jack said. "Almost everyone has a dog, usually a small one. The dogs get to know each other and then the people interact."

"There was a couple in the swimming pool."

"Ken and Kay. They are there every day, rain or shine."

"Do you know when Jim will be back?"

Jack shook his head. "He posts his schedule on the refrigerator, but I don't pay much attention to it."

I went to the refrigerator and found the schedule. Jim's class, Introduction to Research would be done in half an hour.

"Want something to eat?" Jack asked.

"Sure," I said. I'd not eaten breakfast and my stomach was telling me that I was overdue for a meal."

Jack got up and went to the refrigerator, pulling out packages of sliced meats: chicken, ham, and salami. When you work in a restaurant, you pay attention to food, and I knew that most of these meats were full of chemicals. On the other hand, it was all I would be offered. I opted for the chicken. Jack pulled out a loaf of bread, mayonnaise, mustard, and a tomato long passed its expiration date. He laid all of this stuff on the counter and then went back to his chair and his own meal. That was all right. I knew how to fend for myself. I fixed the sandwich, put the meats back in the refrigerator, poured myself a glass of lemonade and settled into a chair beside Jack.

"How long have you lived in this community?" I asked.

"About twelve years. When Jim and I split up, I realized I was getting too old for the game. If you aren't paying attention when you play Monte, you make mistakes. If you make mistakes, you can end up in jail. This is a much better situation."

I thought about my conversation with Larry Harding. The people in this community watched out for each other, but there might be some folks living here, like Little Jack, whose previous occupations would give their neighbors goosebumps.

"When did Jim get here?"

"A while ago. He was really messed up when I found him, but he's straightened himself out. I'm proud of the kid."

At that moment 'the kid' walked in through the door. He threw his backpack on a nearby chair and moved toward the kitchen.

"I got an A on the paper I did for class," he said as he opened the refrigerator door. "The professor wants to publish in a journal."

Jack nodded. Jim looked at me and I gave him a thumb's up of approval.

"Can I get you coffee or lemonade?" I asked.

He moved closer. "Are you feeling friendlier toward me today?"

"I'm not angry at you, if that's what you mean." I had moved to the coffee machine and was putting in a K-cup. I got down a mug from the shelf. As I was reaching for the sugar I remembered the first time we'd had coffee together at Coffee Waves. I poured the coffee into a cup and passed it across the counter to where Jim was standing, eating his sandwich.

"You remembered that I took it black," he said.

I nodded. What does it mean when you remember little things about a man? The smell of his aftershave as he holds you in his arms. The fact that he sleeps naked and drinks his coffee black. His confidence. His charm.

But of course he had confidence and charm. He was a con man, depending on those things to convince unsuspecting marks that he was legit. Jim took a sip of the coffee, studying me over the rim of the cup. Could he read my thoughts? He smiled and my heart lurched. Oh God, what was I getting into?

"I Googled Michelangelo's Chocolates this morning between classes," he said, moving toward the living room and settling into a chair. "The store in New York is big and it could be the corporate headquarters for the U.S. It is possible that they have a mailing list for all their U.S. customers."

I had been so engrossed in my previous thoughts that it took me a minute to process what he was saying. "You want me to go to New York city with you and talk to people at the store?"

"I thought you were my partner in this, Kik? He killed your mother too. Don't you want to find him?"

"I do." I was pretty sure that the corporate headquarters wouldn't voluntarily release the names of their customers. On the other hand, it might be fun to go to New York city again, this time with the real Jim Martin.

"When do you want to go?"

"I have a break from classes in a week." He got up from the chair and grabbed his backpack. "The store is on Fifth Avenue and thirty-second street. We can find a cheap motel and I can book us two round-trip flights from Orlando. If you don't want to fly, we can take the train, but it will take longer to get there."

I was mentally running through the money in my account. It was just possible that I could afford a round trip plane ride and a night in a motel. I didn't want to say no, because Jim and Jack had been generous enough to feed and house me.

"We'll go Dutch," I said.

"Dutch it is," Jim said.

We called that day and made reservations for a plane ride which would be shorter and cheaper than the train, and we booked a motel on the east side of New York. I was thinking about the trip with a mixture of anticipation and dread. Anticipation because I would be in New York city with Jim, and dread because I had no idea how we would convince the people at the chocolate store to part with the names of their customers. We would be looking for a man whose initials were G.S. and who would be living somewhere between Louisiana and Oklahoma. A needle in a haystack.

But things turned out differently than we'd expected. Two days before we were due to leave for New York city, I got an e-mail. I almost trashed it before I saw the subject line: "Looking for my Father." It was a response to the post I'd put on Facebook.

"To 'Looking for my father.' I hope you find the bastard because if I could meet the man again, I would put a knife in his gut. Two months ago, I caught this bum putting the make on my nineteen-year old sister. The guy was probably sixty and he had her pushed up against the wall in the back of the church. She was crying, telling him to let her go, but he was bigger and stronger. I managed to pull him off her and punched him hard in the face. No one knew this guy's name, but he seemed to be with the wedding planners. The wedding took place on Montgomery, Alabama on March 27. Hope you find the son of a bitch."

I showed the e-mail to Jim. When we tried to e-mail the sender, we got no response.

"He said this incident happened two months ago," I said.

"Which means that Grainger could still be in the area."

"How many wedding planners can there be in Montgomery, Alabama?"

We cancelled the trip to New York city. Jim still had most of his week off, so we booked a flight to Montgomery, Alabama.

Chapter Thirty Nine

Two days later we flew into Montgomery and got a room in a cheap motel. We searched through the yellow pages for wedding planners; one was out of business, another was on vacation. The third, Your Special Day, had an ad in the local paper, but when we called the office we were told that the owner, Mary Ellen Barnes, was working a wedding and couldn't be reached. When I pressed the woman, saying that this was important, we were told that we might catch Ms. Barnes at home. As we headed out, I wondered if the employee would get in trouble later for that lapse in protocol.

We got to the house, a newish model on a cul-de-sac where every lawn was green and cleanly mowed.

"You or me," Jim asked.

"We'll do this together," I said taking his hand. We walked up to the front door and Jim rang the bell.

We waited. Would Grainger come to the door, recognize us, and pull out a gun?

We waited some more. I reached over and rang the bell again. Just as we were about to leave the door opened and a small boy stood there.

“Hi,” he said.

“Is your mom or dad at home?” Jim asked.

“She’s doing a wedding,” the boy said. “Her and Gary.”

“Gary?”

“He ain’t my real dad. My real dad died over in Af---gar—something. But when they get married, he’s gonna be my dad.”

“Jerry,” someone called from inside the house. “What did I tell you about answering the door.” A girl of about fifteen appeared behind the child. She pushed the boy behind her and said. “Can I help you?”

“We’re looking for Ms. Barnes.”

“She’s not here. She’s doing a wedding.”

“Can you tell us where she’s doing the wedding? The woman at her office wouldn’t say, and it is very important that we talk to her.” I took Jim’s hand and leaned against him. “Jim and I need to get married. He’s going overseas to Iraq within a month and…” I put my hand on my stomach, “we’d like to do it soon.”

“She’s not a minister, but she can arrange for one. Just a minute,” she said turning back into the house.

The boy looked at us. “Can I show you my truck?” he asked.

“Not now, Jerry,” the girl said coming up behind him with a piece of paper and handing it to me. “This is her office,” she said.

I took out my photograph of Grainger and held it up to the girl. “Is this Gary?” I asked.

She studied the photo and then nodded. “What’s this about?”

"Jerry said that his mother and Gary are getting married soon. Are they going away on their honeymoon?"

The girl stared at me. "How did you know?"

"I think the man you know as Gary used to be my stepfather," Jim said. "He called himself Gus Slocum then."

"And I think he was my stepfather," I said. "Only he was called Grainger Starland then."

The girl stared at us. "So you don't want to get married?"

We shook our heads. The girl stood riveted in the doorway with the little boy fidgeting beside her.

"Please, just tell us where we can find Ms. Barnes."

The young woman hesitated and then said. "They're at the Presbyterian Church on Cervantes and Elm setting up for a wedding tonight. You'll see the van that says Your Special Day on the side. That's her company."

"Thank you," Jim said, and we left.

We drove in silence toward Cervantes. The church was a large brick structure with an impressive front door and parked in the driveway was a white van. The back door of the van was open and a couple of teens were lounging near it, drinking sodas. As we walked past the van toward an open door, a small, dark-haired woman came running out.

"What are you doing?" she said to the teens. "We don't have time for this. We have a wedding in two hours and lots of things to do. Come on, get moving."

"Mary Ellen Barnes?" I asked.

"Yes?" she said, turning toward us, her look of annoyance softening.

"I'm Kiki Coleman," I said. I pointed to Jim. "Jim Martin."

“We need to talk with you,” Jim said.

“I’m sorry, I can’t take the time right now. I’m right in the middle of setting up for this wedding.”

“It’s important,” Jim said.

“What is your event?”

“It’s not about an event. It’s about Gary.”

“Gary?” She looked at Jim sharply. “He’s not in trouble is he? I know he overspends, I’ve warned him about that, and if you need to talk with him, he’s in the social hall.”

Just at that moment, Grainger appeared at the distant open door. Mary Ellen looked at us, but Jim shook his head.

“We need to talk with you,” I said.

Mary Ellen reached into her pocket and pulled out a business card. “Come by the office at nine on Monday. I’ll have some time then.” She turned toward the open door. “Gotta go.”

Today was Saturday, which gave us two days before we could warn Mary Ellen. If the babysitter didn’t tell Mary Ellen Barnes our names we might have a chance to warn her, otherwise, Grainger could have another victim.

On Monday at nine we were waiting outside the office of Your Special Day. The storefront was small, tucked in between a dress store and a coffee shop. We waited. When the clock read nine fifteen, Jim said.

“Should we go to the house? Maybe he found out about us and she’s already dead.”

“Give her five more minutes,” I said. And then we saw her, hurrying toward us. She gave us a quick nod and unlocked the front door, ushering us into a tiny front room. Colorful posters for weddings, retirement parties, Bar Mitzvah’s, family reunions, and anniversaries covered the walls. In every picture, people were smiling and laughing, enjoying a peak moment in their lives.

Mary Ellen was watching me study the pictures. "I love what I do," she said. "It's a lot of work, but I get to participate in happy events."

She looked at Jim. "I know that you aren't here about a wedding. Jenny told me that you stopped by the house."

"Mary Ellen," I began. "The man you know as Gary is very dangerous. I think he killed my mother."

"And mine," Jim said.

"I don't believe it. Gary is a good man, a loving man. OK, he sometimes overspends, but some of those expenditures are for me. There is nothing you can say that will convince me otherwise."

Jim looked around the open room. "Is there somewhere more private where we can talk? We'd like to show you something."

Mary Ellen nodded and led us back to a tiny kitchen, where she began making coffee on an apartment-sized stove. She pulled three cups from the cupboard, and put them on the counter, along with sugar and 'whitener.'

"How do you know about Gary?" she asked.

"We got a complaint on the internet that Gary tried to seduce a teenager at one of the weddings you had planned."

"Which wedding?"

"The one on March 27. Apparently it was here in Montgomery."

"Gary told me about that," she said. "You have to understand that Gary is a hugger, and some people don't like to be hugged. I know him. He would never do anything like that."

“So he told you about the incident? Did you notice any bruises or cuts on him after the wedding?”

“He gets careless, especially after he’s had a few drinks. Is this why you wanted to talk? I paid the girl, just to avoid the negative publicity. We have moved on.”

“Does Gary like a particular chocolate, Michelangelo’s Finest that he orders from the internet?”

“He does. He gets it from a store in New York City.” She looked at me. “What does this have to do with assaulting a teen at a wedding? And let me tell you, kids aren’t the innocent victims they pretend to be. They will pick out an older man, especially one who looks well-heeled and begin kissing him, just so they can cry ‘rape’ and make a few bucks.”

“I think you need to sit down Mrs. Barnes and let us show you a few things” Jim said. She sat and we sat opposite. I could feel the tension in Jim, as he laid out the driver’s licenses on the table.

“This doesn’t mean anything,” Mary Ellen said, barely glancing at the ID’s. “He told me he used to travel a lot.” I put the picture of Grainger and my mother on the table.

“The man you know as Gary was my stepfather, Grainger Starland,” I said. “He and my mother went to Paris in May of 2016, but they never returned. And after he was gone I learned that Grainger had stolen money from my mother’s company, leaving us bankrupt.”

Mary Ellen leaned forward to study the picture.

“He was married to my mother, too,” Jim said. “Only he was called Gus Slocum then.”

“I don’t want to hear any more,” Mary Ellen said, rising. She walked toward the coffee maker and poured herself another cup. I could see that her hand was shaking.

"Gus and my mother went on a honeymoon trip, and disappeared," Jim said. "This is the way he works."

She turned to face us.

"Do you know what it's like to be alone, to raise a child alone? I was always the odd woman out at parties or the object of pity from my friends who were trying to fix me up. I tried internet dating and I had a couple of short term relationship with men I met through the business, but nothing stuck, until I met Gary. Gary makes me happy. Now you're telling me that you think he's a killer. Sorry, I don't believe it."

"Look at this driver's license for Gibbs Sinclair," Jim said, handing the license to Mary Ellen. "On December 25, 2004, Gibbs, aka, Gus, aka Grainger married a woman named Marilyn DuMonde in New Orleans. We think Marilyn was killed shortly before or after her wedding, and because there was no body, her daughter had to wait seven years to file for a death certificate."

"You've only told me about three women. Anything could have happened. Maybe they just decided to split from him. You don't have any proof that he killed them," Mary Ellen said.

We were silent. There was probably nothing we could say that would convince Mary Ellen that Gary/Grainger/Gus was a threat, especially if she wasn't willing to believe it.

Suddenly she put her head in her hands and began to sob. "He made me happy. I hadn't felt like that in a long time. I knew he was making the occasional play for a younger girl, but I thought it was just a passing phase---a mid-life crisis kind of thing."

"Have you given him financial control of your company?"

She shook her head. "He wanted me to. He said he knew a lot about running a company, because he'd had an events planning business in Dallas Texas. He told me he could run Your Special Day better than I could. We had some arguments about it. I did give him money for clothes and other things but I wasn't going to give him control."

We sat in silence.

"The man you know as Gary always works in the same way," Jim said. "He will suggest a trip to some exotic location. Were you planning a trip for the two of you?"

"We were going to Scotland for our honeymoon."

"We think he gives his victims Atropine," I said. "either in a drink or as an injection. It may kill them outright, or just incapacitate them enough so he can kill them somewhere else."

"Mary Ellen," I continued. "If my mother hadn't given Grainger control of her company, she might still be alive. I think he kills for money and…"

"I'm the next victim," she said.

We nodded.

"Think about your son," Jim said. "If you are killed, what will happen to him?"

Mary Ellen was nodding numbly.

"Please be careful," Jim said.

We got up from the table and had turned toward the door when Mary Ellen said, "Jerry has his own phone. I know lots of people think it's crazy to let a young kid have a phone, but I worry about him. There is an app on his phone that traces his movements, so I know where he is at any time. If it looks like Gary is going to do something, I will try to leave you my cell so you can trace us through Jerry's phone."

I nodded, thinking of the difficulties of finding someone who was being transported alive or dead. We weren't police officers who could put a tracer on Grainger's car, and unless we knew exactly when he killed Mary Ellen and Jerry, he would have a huge lead in getting away.

"Give me your cell number and I'll give you mine," Jim said. "If things look suspicious, call or text me."

"You will come after us?"

"We will," I said. I reached forward and took Mary Ellen's hands in my own and then when she started to cry, I held her in my arms. "We will do what we can to find you. I promise."

Chapter Forty

We went back to the hotel where it was hard to wait. I kept wanting to drive over to Mary Ellen's house, park on her street and watch her place just to see what was happening. But whatever Grainger was going to do, he would do it inside the house, and unless I were there at the exact moment he was carrying the bodies to his car, we had nothing.

We could go to the police again. We had the jewelry and the phony ID's. But what did those really prove? That Grainger was a man who had a number of women. Wives? Sweethearts? Three of those women had never been seen again. We might get him arrested for embezzlement—if he confessed to the crime. The process of catching him in the act would be a long slow slog of finding evidence and connecting it to a killer who moved around a lot and left no trace—like a tortoise chasing a rabbit.

Because detective work was slow didn't mean that killers couldn't be caught, but by the time Grainger was brought to justice for his crimes, Mary Ellen and Jerry would be dead. I couldn't bear that thought. We had to try and save them.

Three days after the interview in Mary Ellen's office we got a text.

"It has started. My phone is beside the front door. Help us."

"Should we text her back?" Jim asked. "Just to let her know we got the message?"

"And tell him that we're watching him? He would ditch her phone and we'd never be able to follow her."

"You're right," he said. We had already packed our bags in the event we had to leave early. We threw them in the car and headed out.

Fifteen minutes later we were at the house. Evening was settling in and the house was completely dark. Were we already too late?

"Should we try the door? Maybe they are inside?"

"Let's look for the phone first. If the app is working, he hasn't found Jerry's phone and we can follow them."

Jim pulled out his flashlight and played it around the front of the house. There was a nearly-dead potted plant to the right of the door and when Jim reached into the dirt he found a plastic bag with a phone. The cover had Mickey Mouse logo; this was a phone owned by a kid. We turned it on and with no password required, found an app called "Map My Route." But when we turned on the app, it asked for a password.

"Damn," I said. "Did she give us this information?"

"Not in her text," Jim said. He handed me a flashlight and I trained it on the bottom of the bag where there was a piece of paper. "The user name is jerryb," Jim said. "One word, all small letters and the password. I can't really read it. The writing is all wonky. She must have been doing this in a hurry. MickandMin456. Capital M's." I held the flashlight while he typed in the information. The app opened. There was Grainger's path. He had left Montgomery, Alabama a half hour ago and was headed west.

"He's taking 65 North," Jim said. We hustled toward the car. Jim handed me the phone and the flashlight. We got out our own GPS and set it up to find route 65.

In Nashville, Grainger changed to route 40 west., which I recognized as the place where he'd dumped his cell phone. We drove for the next five hours, stopping every once in a while to change drivers. I was amazed at Grainger's ability to drive without a break. Obviously he was in a great hurry to get where he was going. We traveled across Tennessee, and into Arkansas. By then it was close to midnight, and even sharing the driving, we were both bushed.

"He's finally stopped driving," I said. "We need some rest, too." We pulled into a Motel 6, found a room with two double beds and settled in for the night.

The morning, I checked Mary Ellen's phone, which I had plugged into a charger overnight. The app for Map My Route was blinking, but when I opened it up, nothing had moved. Good, we had time for breakfast before we got on the road again.

Twenty minutes later we were moving across the rest of Arkansas. I was watching the image from Map My Route but it was getting fainter and fainter. "Jerry's phone is losing power," I said.

"Is Grainger turning north toward Missouri?"

"I can't tell. No. I don't think so. It looks like he's headed straight west. Oh come on, please," I said to the app on Jerry's phone. "Just hang in there a little longer." I was watching the movement of Grainger's car. "Why isn't he going north to Missouri? Isn't he going to St. Louis?"

"We need to look at that postcard," Jim said. He pulled over at the next gas station and I reached into my purse and handed him the card. Jim studied it carefully. "We've been fooled," he said.

"Fooled?"

"We thought because the post card had a picture of St. Louis that it was sent from St. Louis, but it wasn't." He pointed to the date stamp. "I don't know the location of the zip code, but this was sent from Oklahoma."

It was one o'clock in the afternoon. Grainger was still moving, and we were losing time, especially since Jerry's phone was running out of juice.

"We need to find a post office," Jim said. "They can tell us the location of the zip code."

When we reached the post office, we found a clerk who told us that the postal code was from a small town east of Oklahoma city called Shawnee. Jim gasped.

"What's wrong?" I asked.

"I should have recognized the zip code. I grew up near Shawnee."

"That's where he's going?"

"I think so. He has a helper who sent this postcard and expects him there."

We were taking a chance. If Grainger were going somewhere other than Shawnee and Jerry's phone died, we would have no way to find them. I hadn't wanted to think about the possibility that Mary Ellen and Jerry were already dead; I was still hoping we could rescue them.

I looked at the app which was slowly fading. Hopefully, Shawnee was small enough so we could find Grainger there. Jim started the car and we set off.

Chapter Forty One

We reached Shawnee late that evening. We'd stopped only for gas and snacks and we were tired, but anxious to push on. If Grainger had something going on in this town, and if we had any chance to stop his killing spree we had to catch him in the act.

The main street of Shawnee had two churches, four bars, a hardware store, diner and police station. There was a small park in the center, with swings for children and a tiny duck pond. In the daytime it must have been charming.

"What next?" Jim asked as we parked the car in front of the restaurant.

"Something to eat? Maybe the locals have seen a suspicious man around."

"Someone with two dead bodies in the back of his car. I don't think Grainger is that obvious. However, I am hungry and sometimes you can learn things by asking around."

We went inside. The diner had a single customer, an elderly man finishing his pie and coffee. The waitress, who was studying her watch, looked up as we came in and smiled.

"Sit anywhere," she said.

We sat. She handed us a menu. "Haven't seen you folks around here before," she said. "Just passing through?"

"We're actually looking for my uncle who used to live here," Jim said.

"What's his name?"

"Gary Stark," I said.

She shook her head. "Don't know anyone by that name. Where did he used to live?"

We were winging it. "An old house on the edge of town. He used to be a farmer, but I don't know what he does now," Jim said.

"The Thomas place. That used to be a farm. But no one has lived there for years. It's become a public nuisance and the county is going to tear it down."

"Can you give us directions to the house?" Jim asked.

"Sure. But I'm positive no one is there now."

"Could people be squatting there?" I asked.

She shrugged, and taking out a piece of paper, wrote out the directions.

When we were sitting in the car, I looked at Jim. "You think he's there?"

"If Grainger were hiding bodies in this town, he would choose somewhere that no one visits. I grew up in a town like this. An old person dies or moves away and the house they lived in sits vacant. Even the county doesn't care what happens, because it costs money to tear the thing down." He looked down at the app on Jerry's phone, but that screen was blank. We were on our own.

The house stood at the end of a long, rutted road, overgrown with oak and maple trees. As we got closer we could see a vehicle parked in the drive, a utility van with the words "Big Truck Rental," on the side.

Gingerly Jim approached the van. I followed with the flashlight. Jim opened the door and I gasped. Sitting behind the wheel was a man in a green uniform. He was slumped to one side so it was difficult to see his face.

Gently Jim touched the man. His body tilted toward us and in the light from the flashlight we saw the bullet hole in the center of his forehead and the blood.

"God," I said.

Jim moved to the passenger side of the van and opened the door. On the seat was a clipboard with a yellow form. "This guy was delivering a backhoe to someone named MacKensie Thomas."

"The Thomas farm," I said.

"I don't see any fields," Jim said looking at the trees surrounding us.

"He could be burying them in the woods," I said.

"Do you suppose he left any clues in the house?"

I looked over at the darkened building. The path to the front door was overgrown; there were broken windows and missing siding and the porch sagged dangerously. It was possibly that Grainger, having shot the delivery person, was now in the house waiting for us. Going into the house would be risking our lives.

"I'll go first," Jim said. He walked up to the door and tried the knob. It opened easily. So somebody was either using this house as a temporary flop, or was paying the taxes so it wouldn't be demolished.

Inside, the house was dark and smelled strongly of mildew, but to my surprise it was still furnished. Boxes lined the front hallway as though whoever had owned it, had planned to move but changed their mind or simply died. We walked into a living room and here the smell of decay was strong. Jim moved the flashlight around.

"Oh Jesus," he said. On the floor, at the foot of an armchair was the desiccated body of a cat, its mouth open in one final scream.

"This place gives me the creeps," I said.

"I'm hoping our perp left more information about his intentions," Jim said. He moved away from me, toward what I assumed was the kitchen. I heard a door open and close and then a yell.

I ran in the direction Jim had gone, but couldn't see him. "Jim," I called. "Where are you?"

There was a muffled voice from the wall beside me. It took me a minute to realize that there was a door in the wall, which, when I opened it, led to a cellar.

"Don't come down," Jim called. "The stairs have been cut. Let me get the flashlight." I waited for a few minutes and then a beam of light moved around showing where the stairs were broken in the middle. Jim was standing at the bottom in darkness. "Someone sawed through them so that anyone putting their weight on the step would break it in half."

This wasn't an abandoned house---it was a death trap.

"How can I help you?" I called.

"I don't think you can. I don't want you to get hurt trying to get down here. The best thing you can do is to call for help."

"Who do I call?"

"I don't know---the rescue squad, the police. Can you run to a neighbor?"

"I'm coming down," I said. "Together we might be able to figure a way to get out."

"Kiki, no," Jim said, but I was already inching my way down the stairs, holding onto the handrail and keeping my feet on the unbroken edges of the treads. When I got to the bottom, Jim was still standing there. "Why did you do that?" he asked.

"I didn't want to be alone up there." I moved to where he was standing and threw my arms around him. His physical presence felt reassuring. "And I didn't want to leave you alone down here." I moved away and studied him. "You're OK?"

"A little bruised, but I'm all right."

"Do you think we can get back up the way we came?"

"Possibly," Jim said. We were looking up at the open cellar door, illuminated by a small light from the upstairs. As we watched, the door swung closed and clicked shut.

"I think we've lost that option," Jim said.

"You're pretty optimistic for a man in a pickle."

"I've been in pickles before," he said. "Let's concentrate on getting out." He played the flashlight around the cellar. In one corner was a workbench with rusting tools and bits of sawdust. Another corner had tables and chairs piled up, clearly remnants from former occupants. But it was the third corner that made me draw in my breath. Piled from floor to ceiling were suitcases. Some of them were old, made of leather with snap closures and tags. Jim stepped toward the pile and touched a luggage tag that read E.M.

"Her name was Eleanor," he said. "But everyone called her Ellie."

"Losing her must have been awful," I said.

"It wasn't just losing the person I loved. It was living with my grandfather who hated me. I think I could have survived my mother's death, if I'd had someone who wanted me."

At that moment, I saw him as a child, trying to be brave in the face of unbearable losses. He had been wounded, and that wound was still there, even into his adulthood. I began to understand why he'd become an alcoholic after the death of his wife. Sometimes you can live through one horrific event, but the second one drives you to despair.

The second thing I realized in that moment was that I loved him. Sure, I had doubts. What couple doesn't? But I wanted to make his life happier and better than it had ever been before.I moved toward him and kissed him. "I'm glad I met you," I said.

He nodded, still overcome by the sadness of seeing his mother's case. "I love you," I said. It didn't matter if he said it back or not, I was saying what was in my heart.

He looked at me and then reached forward to kiss me. "I love you too," he said. "Now let's get out of here."

He began to play the flashlight slowly around the room. "We had a cellar like this in my grandparent's house," he said. "People rarely built them without some kind of window to the outside, because you can't always count on electricity, especially during a winter storm. In some of these houses, there was a door from the cellar to a storage room for winter vegetables or sometimes in older houses, the barn. The passageway saved the farmer from having to go out in the cold or rain. Let's look for something that looks like a door or a window."

It took us fifteen minutes of careful looking before we found an outline in the wall, partly obscured by a bookcase loaded with dusty jars of canned vegetables. I pulled the jars off the shelf and together we pushed the bookcase out of the way. Sure enough, the outline in the wall, had a door knob, almost invisible in the gloom. With a crowbar from the work bench, we pried the door open and then by the dying light of the flashlight we made our way through a root cellar to another door that led outside. By now it was full dark, and starting to rain. I walked past the van with the dead man to the edge of the wood.

"He's got to be somewhere close," Jim said. "Let's see if we can hear him."

"Hear him?"

"Shhhh."

We stood and listened. And then I heard it, the sound of an earth moving machine thunking into the ground.

"He's over there," Jim said. "Beyond the woods,"

I clutched my jacket closer. Jim had already headed toward the woods so I followed. The flashlight was dead, so we threaded our way past the trees guided only by the sound of the machine hitting the earth. And then we were at the edge of a stubbly field looking out at a small front-end loader, digging a hole in the ground.

"He's burying Mary Ellen and Jerry," I said. "Are they dead?"

"Don't know. If they aren't dead, he will bury them alive in that hole."

We hurried forward hidden by the dark. The front-end loader had a roof and headlights illuminating the digging. It was open on the side, and I could see Grainger sitting in the driver's seat. This was a small machine with the cab close to the ground. Nevertheless, the shovel was a formidable instrument that could knock a man sideways. Grainger was concentrating on his task and we were behind him, the noise of the machine hiding our approach.

"I'll take this side," Jim said.

"I'll take the other."

Simultaneously we stepped up on either side of Grainger.

"Get out," Jim said.

Grainger turned. It took him a minute to recognize Jim. Then he turned toward me.

"Where are Mary Ellen and Jerry?" Jim asked.

Grainger moved toward the open side, but I blocked him.

"Where are they?" I yelled.

He pushed himself away from the console. I lifted one leg and kicked him hard in the head, knocking him toward Jim.

"Jesus," he screamed.

He was outside in the dirt now, struggling to rise against the wet mud. Jim kicked him hard in the side. "That's for my mother," he yelled. He leaned in.

"Where are they?"

"They're dead," Grainger said. "If you're here to save them, you're too late."

"Stand up," Jim shouted and when Grainger didn't answer, Jim hauled him up and punched him square in the nose. It was still raining and both men were struggling to get purchase on the muddy ground. Jim punched and connected. Grainger moved backwards toward the hole, lost his balance at the edge and fell in. The hole was only four feet deep. Grainger could easily climb out, but as he started to clamber up the sides, Jim kicked him hard, knocking him back. I jumped up into the cab of the loader. I'd never run one of these things before, but I pulled back on the lever and the shovel rose on its stalk. I pushed the lever forward and the shovel descended.

"Wait," Grainger called, but I kept the shovel moving. My goal wasn't to kill him, just trap him in the hole.

"Where'd you put them?" Jim asked. He was leaning over the hole where Grainger was struggling, trying to avoid the heavy machinery which was going to pin him to the ground.

"Listen," Grainger said. "I'll pay you to let me go. How about twenty thousand." He was struggling to avoid the shovel, but I kept it moving, pushing him down.

"Where are they?" Jim called.

He didn't answer.

Jim motioned to me to lower the shovel. Grainger was now on his back in the hole.

"It wouldn't take much to crush you," Jim said. "Tell us where they are."

"In the barn," Grainger said. "In the car."

I had no idea where the barn was, but it had to be within walking distance.

I looked around. I could see a dark shape on the horizon. "It's there," Jim said.

"Should one of us stay and make sure he doesn't get away?" I asked.

Jim glanced back at the hole. It was impossible to see Grainger, trapped as he was by the shovel. "I think he's securely pinned," he said. "Come on, we might be able to save them."

Chapter Forty Two

We hustled across the rough scrub of the field. As we got close to the barn, we could see a light gleaming, and when we pulled open the door, the air was dense with exhaust. The car was running, and there was a hose snaking from the exhaust pipe into a window.

I yanked the door open. Mary Ellen was stretched across the front seat and Jerry was in the back seat.

"We need to get them outside," Jim said.

I looked at Mary Ellen. Was it already too late?

Jim had already taken her by the front shoulders and was pulling her toward the driver's side. I moved around to help him and together we got her outside. Then we got Jerry and did the same.

"Luckily, Grainger was in a hurry and didn't do a good job connecting the hose." Jim said. We were standing outside in the darkness, watching Mary Ellen and Jerry. I could still smell the car exhaust from inside the barn.

“What’s going on here?” someone said.

I turned around to see an old man. He was standing in the lighted doorway of the barn, a shotgun pointed at us. “Step away from them bodies,” he said.

Jim stayed where he was.

“I don’t see you with no gun,” the man said. “Seems to me I got the upper hand here.” He moved toward Jim, pushing the shotgun directly into his chest.

“No, don’t,” I yelled. “Please.”

He looked at me. “You some pussy he picked up? You two are gonna be just as dead as the folks lying on the ground.” He moved toward me and aimed the shotgun at my head. I waited, scarcely able to breathe.

“Don’t do this,” Jim said. “You’ll spend the rest of your life in jail.” We were standing in semi-darkness, the only light was from inside the barn spilling out onto the grass. Mary Ellen moaned and the man moved past me to aim the gun at her head.

At that moment, Jim moved behind him and kicked him hard in the back. The gun went off and flew through the air. Jim tackled him and they both went down.

“Get the gun,” Jim called.

I ran to where I’d seen the gun land and picked it up. “Hold it on him. I’m going to find something to tie him up with.”

When Jim came back with some duct tape, he said. “Hold the gun on him while I get this around him.”

“You think I’m gonna lie here and let you do this?” the old man said. He started thrashing around. I was holding the gun on him while Jim was wrapping.

“Keep still or I will shoot,” I said.

"Hah, you just a woman." He started to rise. Jim punched him in the face."

"Let's get him standing, so we can get his hands," Jim said

I reached down and grabbed the old man's hands, and at that moment he punched me hard in the face and I went down. Then he reached forward and grabbed the gun. He was surprisingly agile for an old guy. By the time, I'd scrambled to my feet, the old man was backing away the gun still pointed at us.

"This is the end, boy," he said to Jim. "We're saying goodbye right here." He hefted the gun to his shoulder, put his cheek against the stock. I could see his finger on the trigger.

"No," I shouted. "Don't do it." Slowly he turned toward me, his finger still on the trigger.

"You first then, lady?"

"Drop the gun. Drop it now or I will shoot."

The voice came from a figure in silhouette illuminated by the barn light.

The old man turned and the figure advanced. It was a woman in a uniform, holding a handgun. A cop.

"I said to drop the gun."

The old man dropped the shotgun.

"Step over here where I can see you," the cop said, motioning the old man toward the barn. She pointed at us. "You too."

When we were lined up in front of the barn, the cop said. "What's going on here?"

Jim pointed to Mary Ellen and Jerry lying on the ground. "They've been poisoned by carbon monoxide. They need to get to a hospital."

"He tried to kill us," I said, pointing to the old man.

The cop looked at all of us, trying to decide who to believe. She picked up the shotgun and handed it to me. "OK," she said. "I've got to call this in. Keep this on him." She motioned to Jim. "Come with me. You're going to tell me the whole story."

I was alone with the old man. We were both standing and I watched as he moved forward very slightly. My finger was on the trigger. "I will shoot you if you make another move," I said.

"You don't have the balls," he said. He moved toward me and I aimed the shotgun and fired it into his knee cap."

"Jesus Christ," he said, falling to the ground.

"Don't. You. Ever. Underestimate. A. Woman," I said.

Just at that moment, Jim and the cop came back across the field. Mary Ellen was moaning on the ground, and now I could hear Jerry.

"I've radioed for an ambulance," the cop said. She looked at the old man lying on the ground. "What happened here."

"He made a move and I shot him," I said.

She looked at me, but said nothing.

I moved to Mary Ellen who was moving around, struggling to talk. I sat down beside her and put my hand on her arm, feeling it's warmth. Maybe she would be all right. Jerry still had his eyes closed, but he was breathing.

"The man who tried to kill Mary Ellen and Jerry is pinned in a hole on the other side of the field," Jim said.

"This just gets more interesting by the minute," the cop said. In the light, I could see that she was young, about my age. "The department got a call about a man who delivered a machine to this address and never came home. His wife was frantic. That's why I'm out here. I never expected to find all this."

"The delivery person is inside his truck back at the house," Jim said. "He was shot in the head."

"Damn," the cop said. "We're going to need an ambulance, a detective, crime scene investigators, and a coroner. Almost the whole department." She moved away from us and I could hear her talking into her cell phone. We waited.

"Do you think we should check on Grainger?" I asked. "He's had some time to get himself free of that shovel."

"Where is he going?" Jim asked. "I don't think he has a car."

Knowing what I knew about Grainger, I wouldn't guarantee that he would stay in one place, but I didn't want to be the one to trudge back to find him when all the excitement was here.

The cop, whose name was Maria Gonzalez, had returned from making her call.

"Tell me what's going on here, from the beginning," she said.

Jim told her the story of losing his mother when he was nine. I told her about Grainger's trip to France, the one that never took place, and our joint decision to try and hunt down a serial killer.

"The cops do this much better than civilians," Maria said. "You should have talked to someone."

"I talked to the police when my mother disappeared," I said. "But I had no proof that he'd killed her, only that she'd never come back."

Maria nodded. "You were very brave," she said. "It could have ended otherwise. Clearly Granger, and him," she pointed to the old man lying on the ground, "were serious about what they did."

At that moment we heard the sirens, and two police cars pulled up, followed by an ambulance. Maria pointed the EMT's to Jerry and Mary Ellen on the ground. Mary Ellen had opened her eyes; Jerry's were closed but he was moaning.

"Those two are carbon monoxide poisoning," Maria said. "Take them in first." She pointed to the old man. "Gunshot wound to the knee. Leave him for the second trip."

Then Maria went to speak to the officers. I could see them nodding together and then one officer got in a car and drove off.

"He's gone to find your perp. You say his name is Grainger?"

I nodded. Maria turned to a tall, balding man, standing beside her. "This is detective Mark Pickens. He'd like to ask you a few questions."

"Want to sit inside the car?" he asked. "I brought hot coffee. Thought you folks could use it."

I was grateful for the coffee, and the detective was thorough with his questions. Later we went down to the police station and answered the same questions this time with our answers recorded.

When we'd finished answering questions, the detective asked if we would be willing to testify on the witness stand. We nodded.

"The man you call Grainger is in custody," detective Pickens said. "Apparently he's got a lot of bodies buried in the field out there."

"Have you been in the house? The suitcases owned by the women Grainger killed are in the basement."

Pickens nodded. "I got a call from the hospital. Your friends Mary Ellen and Jerry are awake. They will be in the hospital for a while, but we expect them to recover. He looked at me. "MacKensie Thomas, the man you shot in the knee, is in surgery. He owns the farm where Grainger buried the women."

"He may have shot the delivery person, too."

"In which case he will be charged with murder. I expect that both these men will be in jail for the rest of their lives."

I was starting to droop. It had been a long night, in fact it was almost daylight. Detective Pickens thanked us, shook our hands, told us that he would be in touch and that we were free to go. I wanted to say a word of thanks to Officer Maria Gonzalez but was told she had gone home.

In the end, we drove back to a motel and fell into bed.

Chapter Forty Three

I woke to sunlight streaming through the window and for a moment I forgot that I was lying in a bed in a cheap motel, with Jim beside me and that we had just, with a lot of effort, helped to capture a serial killer.

Jim was gone. I sat up, panicky. Had he decided to drive back to Florida without me having realized that since I'd done my part in helping him, I wasn't needed any more. Just then the door opened, and Jim, accompanied by the smell of coffee and hot muffins came in the door.

"Morning beautiful," he said.

"I thought you'd gone," I said.

"Where would I go?" He pulled the coffee and food out of the bag and laid it on the table.

"The police called," he said. "They want to see us this morning. At our convenience."

I sat up on the edge of the bed, trying to get my head in one place. Jim came over and kissed me. "It's over, Kiki. We caught them both. Mary Ellen and Jerry are recovering in the hospital. I want to go see them, and I have somewhere else I'd like to take you?"

"I'm not sure I can take any more surprises."

"This won't be anything dangerous."

"Give me ten minutes," I said, walking to the table and grabbing a coffee. Then I ducked into the bathroom, had a long, hot shower and put on some clothes. When I returned, Jim had turned the TV on and was watching the local news. A young woman was standing in front of the house where we'd been trapped. Police cars were parked on the grass, and a crowd of people had gathered. The caption under the picture said: Serial Killer Arrested in Oklahoma.

"Police last night apprehended a man named Gary Stark who appears to be the killer of multiple women. Stark was attempting to bury two people alive, but was thwarted in his attempt by the brave actions of local police and others."

"We're the others?" I asked.

"They're protecting our privacy," Jim said.

I guess that made sense, but I was still annoyed. We'd done a lot to catch Grainger. I wanted a least a bit of the credit."

"Also arrested last night was MacKensie Thomas, a local farmer, who is accused of the murder of Johnson Wright, an employee of Big Truck Rental."

The woman spoke for a few more minutes about the events of the night before, and then the police chief appeared, looking very official behind the bank of microphones. By then I had turned away. I'd had enough of Grainger. I wanted my life back.

Jim was still engrossed in the TV. When the show was over, he asked, "Where do you want to go first? The hospital? The police station?

"I want to see Mary Ellen and Jerry," I said.

"The hospital it is."

The hospital was small but well equipped and when we told them we were there to see Mary Ellen Barnes and her son the staff was guarded.

"Are you relatives?" a nurse asked.

"Her brother," Jim said. "And this is my wife."

No one asked for an ID, and fleetingly I thought about this soft security protecting people who'd narrowly avoided death. Our only admonition was not to visit for long.

They'd put them in the same room. Jerry was lying asleep, facing his mother. His cheeks were pink and he looked like he was recovering. Mary Ellen was watching television and crying.

"What's wrong?" I asked, pulling up a chair beside her bed.

"They've got him in handcuffs, and his face is all bruised. That's what police do. Beat people up."

"It wasn't the police," Jim said. "We put those bruises there."

"You did?"

"When we found him, he was digging a hole in the ground…your grave. He was going to put you and Jerry in it, whether you were alive or dead."

"He was a good man. At least to me."

"He was a killer, Mary Ellen. He murdered at least three women and I think many more. There's a stack of suitcases four feet high in the basement of a house we visited. They represent all the women he killed."

She was studying us, tears still in her eyes. "I tried not to drink the champagne," she said. "I spilled it on the floor and he got mad, and then he came back with another glass. I didn't sip much, but it was enough to put me to sleep."

"You're lucky you're alive."

At that moment, Jerry stirred in the adjacent bed, and opened his eyes.

"Mom?" he asked.

"I'm here, honey," she said, getting up from her bed and going to his, where she lay down beside him, holding him in her arms. "Thank you for coming after us," she said quietly.

Jim nodded. I went to the bed and hugged her awkwardly.

Our next stop was the police station where we asked for Detective Mark Perkins. In a few minutes he came out to the lobby. There were bags under his eyes, and his clothes were rumpled, as though he'd spent the previous night in the station.

"I appreciate your coming," he said, leading us back to his office.

When we were sitting in front of him, he said. "You folks are heroes, at least to the two people whose lives you saved."

"I'm not sure she feels that way," I said. "She still loves him."

"I expect lots of women did," Perkins said. He leaned forward. "I have a few more questions about the case."

We answered his questions. I gave him the phony driver's licenses and the credit cards, the advertising flyer from Rx by Mail and the postcard of St. Louis.

"You took a big chance," Perkins said. "It was lucky he didn't know you were following him."

"He had two people in the car he was anxious to bury."

"How did you know about the house?"

"We didn't. We knew Grainger was in Shawnee because of the zip code on the postcard and we took a guess about the house."

"MacKensie Thomas stopped paying taxes on the house years ago, but the county just ignored it."

"Did he live there?"

Perkins shook his head. "He had a little apartment in town."

"Why would he become a killer's accomplice?"

"Money. Normally, his part of the job was easy. He would make sure the house was open, rent a machine, provide Grainger with a place to sleep and a meal. He didn't usually get more involved than that. I have no idea why he shot Johnson Wright. That deed will get him the rest of his life in jail."

Perkins stood up and reached forward to shake our hands. "I appreciate what you've done folks. I may be talking to you again in the next few weeks, and we will ask you to testify at the trial. You are willing aren't you?"

"Sure," we said together.

We were shown out of the station. I got the feeling that all Perkins wanted to do was go home, have a shower and a meal and maybe a nap, but I think he would not do that.

"What next?" I asked. It was now almost mid-day.

"Two more stops," Jim said.

"You aren't going to tell me?" I asked when we were in the car.

"Nope." We drove away from Shawnee, out into the countryside. It was cold outside, but the skies were clear and the sun was out. I knew Jim had grown up here in Oklahoma. Was I looking out at the farm fields he had grown up with as a child?

We left the highway, and followed a small secondary road to a town called Antelope. The main street was dominated by a white steepled church, two restaurants, a dollar store, a feed and grain store and a lawyer's office. Not far away was an elementary school. The only places that seemed to be open were the restaurants.

"That was my grandfather's place," Jim said pointing to the feed and grain store. It was where I worked as a kid."

"And that," he said, pointing to a small white clapboard house, two houses from the store, "was my parent's house."

"Where did your grandfather live?"

"On a farm outside of town. I think it was torn down years ago."

I looked at the scene, trying to imagine Jim as a boy, walking in one direction to the school and in the other direction to his grandfather's store. But this wasn't *Lassie Come Home* or *Leave It to Beaver*. It was a story of a kid who had lost his parents and was living a nightmare of abuse. As much as the death of my mother had disrupted my life, Jim's disruption had been much worse.

"Ready?" Jim said.

"I feel like Scrooge in *A Christmas Carol*. Is this where I get to see my future self?"

"I'm showing you my past, Kiki, not yours. Yours is going to be whatever you want it to be."

We drove to the edge of town, to a newish brick building with smart plantings and a bright green lawn. The sign said Hockmeyer Home for the Aged.

I followed him into the lobby where I watched him talk to the lady behind the desk and then we followed him down the hallway to a small room. She opened the door and let us in.

"Mr. Martin," the woman said. "You have visitors."

The man was slender, ninety pounds tops, and his white hair looked like he'd styled it with a weed whacker. He was sitting, facing the window that looked out onto an empty field with nothing to look at—no cows, no birds, no industrial equipment.

"Mr. Martin," the woman said again.

The man turned and studied us.

"This is your grandson," the woman said. "Come to see you."

The old man was studying Jim; then suddenly he smiled. "Artie?" he asked.

"No," Jim said. "I'm…"

"You come to see me, Artie. I knew you would. Come here, my boy, let me see you."

"He thinks I'm my father, Arthur," Jim said.

"You brought that woman, but that's OK," the old man said. He looked at me. "Ellie, isn't it? And where's the boy. You still got the boy?"

"He's all grown up now," Jim said.

The old man bowed his head. I thought at first he was praying but when I saw his shoulders shaking I realized that he was weeping.

"I done wrong by you, son," he said. "I missed you and blamed them. I shouldn't a done that."

Jim nodded. I wasn't sure whether he was ready to accept the transformation in this old man who had been so cruel. But then he moved closer to his grandfather and was enfolded in a feeble hug. The old man was still weeping.

The door opened and the woman came in. “I’m sorry to see him so upset,” she said. “You are the first visitor he’s had in years. I was hoping you would cheer him up.”

Jim only nodded. I think it was difficult for him to talk.

We said good bye to the old man and walked out of the nursing home to the car. On the way, I took Jim’s hand and held it. I wanted to tell him that things would be all right, and that the world which had treated him so cruelly as a child was not a bad place. I wanted to tell him that I loved him, believed in him, wanted to live with him and have his children, but I knew that this was not the time. Those things would come. It was a bright, beautiful day and our future together stretched out with promise.

“Lunch?” Jim asked.

“Lunch.” I said.

The End

If you liked the book.

Think of writing a review as handing off this book to a friend, and saying "You should read this. You'll like it." You are not only helping the author, but you are helping other readers find a book they might like. Writing a review is easy. Click on my Amazon page "Marguerite Mooers *The Lies That He Told"* and under the name of the book is a line of stars. Click on the stars and it should take you to a box that says "Write A Review." Write what you honestly feel about the book. And thank you for being a reader and for helping me write the best books I can.

To My Readers

This is the place where the author thanks everyone who ever looked kindly on her writing, from her third grade teacher, Miss Honeyhips, who praised her early efforts, to the Wednesday night drinking and writing group who have been so lovely (albeit a little soused) in their praise.

Just kidding. I am really, deeply grateful to all of you who have bought (or borrowed, hopefully not stolen) my book. I am grateful to all of you who said it was a good book, loaned it to friends, e-mailed me (a word about that later), and generally made me feel good about myself. I owe you a huge debt. Writing is a lonely business, and words from friends keep me going.

Where do ideas come from? A question asked of me frequently. The idea for this book came from another book which had a main character who was a con man. This con man was selling drugs and used a young woman to shield himself from the police. Not a nice guy. But, I wondered if it were possible to create a character who, though he cheated people, was likable (and a romantic hero.) Enter Nate Marks.

I hope you liked Nate, as flawed as he is, and Kiki is no slouch as she struggles to overcome some formidable obstacles. I am also a sucker for happy endings. Hope you liked that too.

Which brings me to:

A word about e-mails.

A while back I neglected to respond to a reader's e-mail for which I got a few reviews reminding me that I had been bad. I am very very sorry. I never, ever want anyone who has taken the trouble to e-mail me to feel that I don't care. I do care. But things happen. In this case a secondary e-mail system that wasn't getting through, and by the time I realized what was happening the damage had been done. Can I say it again? I am very sorry that happened. I will do my very best in the future to see that if you e-mail me, I will respond promptly.

So, if you e-mail me, I will e-mail you back. I want to hear from you. I am interested in your honest thoughts about the book, even if they are not one hundred percent positive. You are my readers. You are the people I am writing for. I care what you think. My e-mail is funstories043@gmail.com

A Glossary of Terms

The English language is nimble and inventive and that inventiveness is never more apparent as in the specific words used by gamesmen and con men. In these cases, language provides a private club of meaning used to keep outsiders ignorant and knit the group together. The 'con' of 'con man' or 'Big con' probably had its origin in 'confidence man' a person who gained your trust before he set out to swindle you. The definitions below are courtesy of *Talk the Talk: The Slang of 65 American Subcultures* by Luc Reid.

Badger Game: A scam in which an attractive woman entices the victim to spend time with her in an intimate setting and then exploits the situation for money. For instance a hidden partner may take pictures and later blackmail the victim, or the woman may threaten to file rape or sexual harassment charges or a partner may burst in threatening to be a jealous husband.

The Big Con: Also called **The Long Con**. A large, complicated, high-stakes game which is very lucrative. The movie, *The Sting* is a good example of a 1930's Big Con, and much of the material for that movie came from a wonderful book, David W.

Maurer's *The Big Con*. Big Con's are not exclusive to the 1930's. Watch the movie *Side Effects* to see how a modern victim can be scammed in an elaborate setup. In addition to Long Cons there are Short Cons, confidence games which pay off immediately. At the beginning of the movie *The Sting*, you will see a short con in action when the grifters rob a numbers runner of his cash.

Three Card Monte: A confidence game in which the victim (the mark) bets on finding a specific card while the dealer moves the cards around. Three card Monte is a very old confidence game and is also called "The Broads" or "Follow the Lady" because the card being followed is usually the queen.

The Mark: the victim of a confidence game.

The Shill, The Booster, The Outside Man, The Roper: Confidence men don't work alone. They need confederates to bring in the marks, to convince the mark that the game is winnable, and to pay off local police so the game isn't interrupted.

Poker. Poker, like baseball, is a particularly American game. In his wonderful book *Poker: Bets, Bluffs and Bad Beats,* A. Alvarez says "...There was something about the combination of cards and money, cut-throat psychology and beady-eyed skill that suited the American frontier spirit just fine. As Walter Matthau once said 'The game exemplified the worst aspects of capitalism that have made our country great.' Poker, he meant, is a form of social Darwinism in which only the socially and economically fittest survive. Because winning at poker depends partly on how much you can bluff your fellow player, poker depends on making your own luck, rather than being lucky." And from poker comes the wonderful maxim that "you play the hand you are dealt."

All In: To bet all the chips you have left

Ante: a compulsory bet before the dealer puts down the cards

Bet the Pot: to bet the total value of money in the pot. Some games limit the amount you can bet to what is in the pot. Others are no limit.

Big Blind: In Omaha and Texas Hold em, the first player to the dealers left, **The Small Blind,** must put down a bet before he sees the cards. The second player to the dealer's left , **The Big Blind,** doubles that bet. The third player to the dealer's left, **Under the Gun,** must match his bet to the **The Big Blind**. Play moves around the table left to right to the **Cut Off** position, just to the right of the dealer, who plays last. Often groups who play for fun don't use the Big Blind or Small Blind positions.

Bluff: Raising your bet so it appears that you have a good hand, hoping that other players will fold.

The Button: The dealer is indicated by a white button which sits in front of him on the table. In professional play, the dealer does not play. In amateur play the dealer position moves around the table.

Call: to match a previous bet

Check: not to bet, reserving the right to call or raise if another player bets.

Flop: In Omaha and Hold 'em, the first three community cards which are laid down in the middle of the table, and with which players can ultimately make up a hand.

Flush: Hands in Poker from best to worst are: Royal Flush, Straight Flush, Four of a Kind, Full House, Flush, Straight, Three of a Kind, Two Pair, Pair and nothing.

Fold: to withdraw from the game

Hole Cards: the cards a player is dealt face down at the beginning of the game, a.k.a. Pocket cards.

Nuts: the best unbeatable hand "the stone-cold nuts."

Pot: the chips (or coins) in the middle of the table that represent the winnings

Raise: to call and increase the previous bet.

The River: In Omaha and Hold 'em the fifth communal card to be exposed.

The Turn: In Omaha and Hold 'em the fourth communal card to be exposed.

I could write a whole book about poker, but these are just some basic terms.

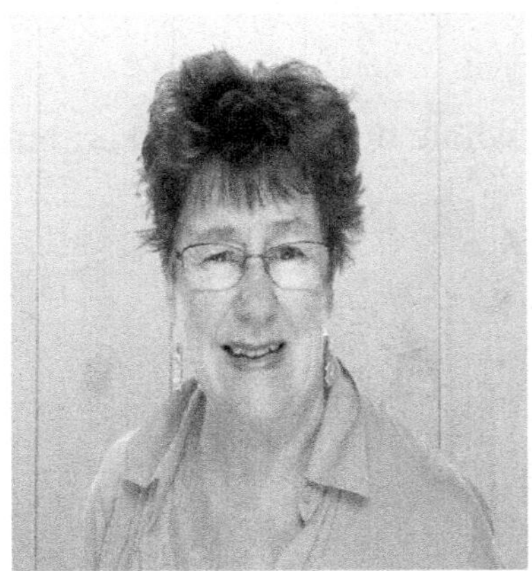

Before retiring, Marguerite Mooers taught inmates in a medium security prison in upstate New York, a job which gave her lots of material for crafting her murder mysteries. She is the author of numerous short stories and award-winning poetry, and in addition to being a writer is an enthusiastic watercolorist. Her previous novels are: *Take My Hand*, *The Shelter of Darkness*, *A Casualty of Hope, The Girl in The Woods* and *The Life That He Lived.* Find her on the web at margueritemooers.com.